Catherine Anderson

Morning Light

A SIGNET BOOK

SIGNET
Published by New American Library, a division of
Penguin Group (USA) Inc., 375 Hudson Street,
New York, New York 10014, USA
Penguin Group (Canada), 90 Eglinton Avenue East, Suite 700, Toronto,
Ontario M4P 2Y3, Canada (a division of Pearson Penguin Canada Inc.)
Penguin Books Ltd., 80 Strand, London WC2R 0RL, England
Penguin Ireland, 25 St. Stephen's Green, Dublin 2,
Ireland (a division of Penguin Books Ltd.)
Penguin Group (Australia), 250 Camberwell Road, Camberwell, Victoria 3124,
Australia (a division of Pearson Australia Group Pty. Ltd.)
Penguin Books India Pvt. Ltd., 11 Community Centre, Panchsheel Park,
New Delhi - 110 017, India
Penguin Group (NZ), 67 Apollo Drive, Rosedale, North Shore 0632,
New Zealand (a division of Pearson New Zealand Ltd.)
Penguin Books (South Africa) (Pty.) Ltd., 24 Sturdee Avenue,
Rosebank, Johannesburg 2196, South Africa

Penguin Books Ltd., Registered Offices:
80 Strand, London WC2R 0RL, England

First published by Signet, an imprint of New American Library,
a division of Penguin Group (USA) Inc.

First Printing, January 2008
10 9

Copyright © Adeline Catherine Anderson, 2008
All rights reserved

 REGISTERED TRADEMARK—MARCA REGISTRADA

Printed in the United States of America

continued . . .

"Another heartwarming chapter in the Coulter family saga is on tap in the always wonderful Anderson's newest release. . . . Anderson is at her best when it comes to telling stories that are deeply emotional and heartfelt." —*Romantic Times* (4½ stars)

Summer Breeze

"Anderson understands the inner workings of the human soul so deeply that she's able to put intense emotion within a stunning romance in such a way that you'll believe in miracles. Add to this her beautiful writing style, memorable characters, and a timeless story, and you have an unmatched reading adventure." —*Romantic Times BOOKclub* (4½ stars)

"The kind of book that will snare you so completely, you'll not want to put it down. It engages the intellect and emotions; it'll make you care. It will also make you smile . . . a lot. And that's a guarantee."
—Romance Reviews Today

My Sunshine

"Another winner from Anderson's compassionate pen." —*Library Journal*

"Sweet and sensual." —*Publishers Weekly*

"With the author's signature nurturing warmth and emotional depth, this beautifully written romance is a richly rewarding experience for any reader."—*Booklist*

Blue Skies

"Readers may need to wipe away tears . . . since few will be able to resist the power of this beautifully emotional, wonderfully romantic love story." —*Booklist*

"A keeper and a very strong contender for Best Contemporary Romance of the Year."

—Romance Reviews Today

Bright Eyes

"Offbeat family members and genuine familial love give a special lift to this marvelous story. An Anderson book is a guaranteed great read!"

—*Romantic Times* (4½ Stars, Top Pick)

Only by Your Touch

"Ben Longtree is a marvelous hero whose extraordinary gifts bring a unique and special magic to this warmhearted novel. No one can tug your heartstrings better than Catherine Anderson."

—*Romantic Times* (4½ Stars, Top Pick)

Always in My Heart

"Emotionally involving, family-centered, and relationship oriented, this story is a rewarding read."

—*Library Journal*

"[A] superbly written contemporary romance, which features just the kind of emotionally nourishing, comfortably compassionate type of love story this author is known for creating." —*Booklist*

Sweet Nothings

"Pure reading magic." —*Booklist*

Phantom Waltz

"Anderson departs from traditional romantic stereotypes in this poignant, contemporary tale of a love that transcends all boundaries ... romantic through and through." —*Publishers Weekly*

Coulter Family books by Catherine Anderson

Phantom Waltz
Sweet Nothings
Blue Skies
Bright Eyes
My Sunshine
Summer Breeze
Sun Kissed

Other Signet books by Catherine Anderson

Always in My Heart
Only by Your Touch

Francis Wayne Harrigan (1945–)
married
♥1969♥

Emily Sue Phillips (1946–1977)

Second Marriage (March 12, 2007)
Deanna (Dee Dee) Kirkpatrick (1948–)

Clinton Harrigan (1970–)♥
married
♥2007♥
→ ♥
Loni Kendra MacEwen (1976–)
→ ♥
Morning Light, 2008

Quincy Harrigan (1972–)
→ ♥
Story Yet to Come!

Parker Harrigan (1973–)
→ ♥
Story Yet to Come!

Zachary Harrigan (1975–)
→ ♥
Story Yet to Come!

Samantha Harrigan (1977–)♥
married
♥2007♥
→ ♥
Tucker Coulter (1970–)
→ ♥
Sun Kissed, 2007

Prologue

Loni Kendra MacEwen could barely contain her excitement. The two-bedroom house was small and dated, but she saw it with the eye of an interior decorator, and there were possibilities everywhere she looked. She moved slowly through the rooms, envisioning white priscilla curtains at the windows, a diamond-hard polyurethane wax on the worn hardwood floors, bright pillows and throws on the overstuffed sofa and chairs, and designer shades of paint on the walls. She could also imagine a cheerful blaze in the brick fireplace, with her huge yellow dog, Hannah, snoozing before the hearth.

Normally Loni never would have considered renting an old house, much less a furnished one, but something about this neglected bungalow appealed to her. Maybe it was the charming bay windows, the built-in bookcases at each side of the fireplace, or the old-fashioned archways trimmed in burnished oak, but she was more inclined to think it was the essence of the house itself; a warm, peaceful feeling had enveloped her the moment she stepped inside.

Smiling at her good fortune, she went to stand at the kitchen sink to gaze out the window at the large backyard enclosed by a sturdy, six-foot cedar fence. There was even an oversized dog door that opened into the attached garage. While Loni was at her shop, Hannah would have shelter from the weather, an important feature in the high-desert community of Crystal Falls, Oregon, where the winters could be long and harsh.

The sudden chirp of her cell phone made Loni jump. Expecting a call from her older sister, she hurried to the mahogany dining table and plucked the device from her purse. Bypassing hello, she answered with, "You'll never guess what."

Deirdre, a second grade teacher at Roosevelt Elementary a few blocks away, laughed and said, "You got the house!"

Sinking onto a ladder-backed chair, Loni pushed a curly tendril of dark brown hair from her eyes. "It was love at first sight. I just signed a one-year lease. I'm so happy I want to shout."

"Oh, Loni, what wonderful news! I was starting to think you'd never find a place that would take Hannah."

Having an eleven-month-old Fila Brasileiro mastiff that weighed nearly two hundred pounds did come with its own set of problems. Loni couldn't count the lease applications she'd filled out over the last two months that had been denied.

"I got lucky," she told her sister. "The man who owns the place lives in Portland, and he's had some bad experiences with property management companies."

"So he was motivated to lease the house without involving a third party?"

"Exactly. He never even blinked when I mentioned Hannah."

"What about when the place needs repairs? It's a long drive from Portland for him to fix a leaky faucet."

"If something goes wrong, he gave me permission to call a handyman, deduct the cost from my rent, and just send him the receipt."

"That works." Deirdre sighed. "I'm delighted for you, absolutely delighted."

Loni grinned. "Don't sound *too* enthusiastic, or I'll think you're glad to be rid of me."

"Ha. I've loved having you, and so has Michael. You know that. Can I come see the house? The boys have Kids' Club until four o'clock, and I was planning to go grocery shopping, but the heck with that. What's the address?"

Smiling happily, Loni grabbed the lease agreement and read off the information.

"Oak Street?" A note of alarm crept into Deirdre's voice. "Isn't that in an older section of town?"

Loni knew what was coming and ignored the question. "It's perfect for me and Hannah, Deirdre. Just wait until you see it. Very quaint, with darling bay windows, beautiful oak trim, and a fenced-in yard. There's even a dog door opening into the garage."

"Quaint?" Deirdre echoed. "Quaint as in old?"

"Yes, fairly old," Loni finally confessed. "I'm guessing it was built sometime in the forties."

"Oh, *Loni*, what on earth were you thinking? You'll

never be happy in an old house. You'll have psycho-metric divinations bombarding you left and right."

It never ceased to amaze Loni that her sister, the only nonclairvoyant female in the MacEwen family, knew so many paranormal buzzwords. "Psycho *what*?"

"Psychometric divination. That's the appropriate term for the phenomenon that sometimes occurs when you touch things."

"What's wrong with just calling it a nasty jolt?"

"Nothing except that it's boring."

"Boring suits me fine. I swear, if I had a deformed toe you'd call it a lower-digit deviation."

"Don't compare your gift to a deformity."

"Why not?" Loni's *gift*, as members of her family persisted in calling it, had adversely affected her entire life. As a child she'd had to be tutored at home. As a young adult, she'd been unable to hold down a job or attend college. Even now, when she was thirty-one, her social life was next to nonexistent. She rarely dated, she felt like a pariah at church, and as icing on the cake, she was forced to keep other decorators on the payroll so she could focus only on new construction. "It feels like a deformity."

With an ease born of long practice, Loni pushed away the negative thoughts and walked slowly to the living room, barely hearing her sister, who chattered in that shrill, nonstop way of hers when she got upset.

"Back to the house," Loni cut in, giving the small living room an appreciative look. It was going to be so lovely when she finished fixing it up. "I understand your concerns and know it would be best to rent a brand-new place. Unfortunately they don't grow on trees, and my applications for the few I found were turned down because of Hannah. Now I'm glad they were. I've done a complete walk-through here and touched practically everything—cupboards, door-knobs, windowsills, faucets, and even all the furniture. I've picked up nothing unpleasant. Not every surface affects me, you know. It mostly happens only when I touch a person or the possession of someone who's been through something terrible and needs help, or soon will go through something terrible and needs help."

"The house is *furnished*?"

"I sold practically everything before I left Washington, hoping to buy new. Now I can wait to worry about furniture later."

"Oh, Loni." Deirdre's voice went even shriller. "What'll you do if you start having problems and can't break the lease?"

"Live with you, I guess." Loni laughed. Trailing a hand over the back of the sofa, she said, "Would you stop, Deirdre? I'm a big girl. If I'd thought for a moment I might have problems here, I never would have rented the place."

"It still worries me."

"Well, stop worrying. It's a friendly little house. Have you ever walked through a door and felt instantly at home?"

"Yes," Deirdre replied, beginning to sound calmer. "When Michael and I were looking to buy, that's exactly how we felt when we finally found our house."

"Well, that's the feeling I got here. It's just right

somehow. I can't wait to start decorating. I'm thinking of sage green here in the living room, with a darker shade on the fireplace wall to accentuate the brick and oak. It's going to be a dollhouse when I'm finished with it."

"I'm sure it will be," Deirdre conceded. "You're a professional decorator, after all. And a one-year lease will be perfect, too. That'll give you time to get your shop on its feet and make sure you like living in Crystal Falls before you buy a place of your own."

Loni pirouetted slowly to take in the room again. "I know it's premature, but I'm no longer quite so worried about liking it here. All the snow was my biggest concern, but now that I've found this house I can cross that worry off my list. The driveway and front walk are pretty short. I'll be able to clear them in no time. I'm actually excited. Isn't that great?"

"It's fabulous." Deirdre released a taut breath. "I'm sorry for going on and on at you. I just want you to be happy, is all."

"I know that, and I honestly think I will be here. It's such a cute little place. Nice solid doors, too, inside and out. Once I get some dead bolts and a security system installed, I'll feel safe as a baby in its mother's arms."

"We need to celebrate somehow," Deirdre suggested, clearly trying to show the enthusiasm she had failed to at first. "How about a special dinner tonight?"

"That'd be nice." Loni glanced at her watch. "And since you worked all day, I'll do the cooking. How does beef bourguignonne with hot homemade biscuits sound? Gram's recipe only takes about three hours. I'll stop at a store on the way over to pick up everything I'll need. We can feed the boys hot dogs, get them into bed, and have a grown-up night."

"Beef bourguignonne? Yum. I haven't had that in ages. I'll call Michael and ask him to pick up a nice burgundy from the wine shop. Is there any kind you especially like?"

Loni was about to answer when a bright flash of light suddenly blinded her. The next instant she saw a jet-haired cowboy standing before the fireplace hearth, his booted feet planted wide apart, his work-roughened hands resting on his narrow hips. The shadow cast by the brim of his chocolate-colored Stetson did little to diminish the burning intensity in his dark brown eyes.

"Loni?" Deirdre's voice seemed to come from a great distance. "Loni, are you still there?"

Loni tried to speak, but her throat felt paralyzed. She finally managed a faint whisper. "Oh, God, Dee, it's him."

"Who?" Deirdre demanded.

Loni could barely hear her sister now. It was like being trapped in a snow globe. She was in the same small living room, but it was different now, exactly how she'd imagined it would look in a few weeks when she finished decorating. A designer shade of sage green covered the walls, and colorful rugs graced the gleaming hardwood floors. An awful dizziness set her head to spinning, and for a moment she thought she might faint.

Then her senses suddenly cleared, and the room came into sharper focus. The cowboy still stood before her. Under the blue shirt his shoulder muscles were bunched with tension. Loni could feel a cool breeze coming through an open window, and the scent of freshly cut grass wafted to her nostrils. Down the street somewhere, a dog was barking, and its owner yelled for it to be quiet.

She heard herself say, "That's an absolutely preposterous suggestion."

She started to turn away, but the cowboy clamped a hard hand over her arm.

"Look, lady," he said in a deep voice that curled around her like hot wisps of smoke. "I'm no happier about this mess than you are. All this hocus-pocus stuff gives me the willies. I'll also remind you that you're the one who sought me out, not the other way around."

Loni jerked her arm free of his grasp. "If I give you the willies, why are you even here?"

"That's a damned good question."

The vision evaporated as quickly as it came. An icy chill had raised goose bumps on Loni's skin, and she was shaking violently. The awful dizziness assailed her again, and she dropped onto the sofa, too stunned to remain standing.

"Loni!"

Deirdre's voice still sounded far away. Struggling to focus, Loni finally spotted the cell phone lying on the hardwood floor where she must have dropped it. With a trembling hand she scooped up the device and pressed it to her ear.

"I'm okay," she managed to croak, even though her head was still whirling.

"You scared me half to death. What happened? Did you fall or something? I heard a loud crash."

"I, um, dropped the phone." Loni swallowed to steady her voice. "It was him, Deirdre." Loni had been seeing the cowboy in her dreams practically all her life, but this was the first time she'd ever seen him in a waking vision. "My dream cowboy. It was my dream cowboy."

"*What?*" Deirdre asked incredulously. "Where did you see him? Does he live next door or something?"

"No, no." Another wave of nausea made Loni's stomach pitch. "I didn't actually *see* him. Not in the flesh, anyway." In the MacEwen family it went without saying what Loni meant by that. "He was standing in front of the fireplace—" Loni broke off and swallowed hard again. "He touched me, Dee. That's never happened before, not *ever*."

"You don't sound so good."

"I'm dizzy and sick to my stomach. He crossed over somehow."

"Crossed over? I'm not following."

"He was *real*." Loni heard the hysteria in her voice and struggled to calm down. "Not just a vision, but real. I actually *felt* his hand on my arm."

"I'll be right there," Deirdre said. "Sit down and don't move until I get there."

Loni had no trouble complying with her sister's orders. Still filmed with cold sweat, her body quivered with weakness, and every time she opened her eyes the room spun.

True to her word, Deirdre arrived in less than ten

minutes. She burst through the unlocked front door as if a full-scale avalanche were chasing at her heels, not a far stretch considering her attire, a powder pink parka over a sweater, and black slacks tucked tidily into fur-trimmed snow boots. Her cropped hair, spiked with styling gel, poked up every which way like swirls of rich, dark chocolate.

"Are you all right?"

"A bit better now, thank goodness."

Deirdre rushed over to the sofa, her bright blue eyes taking sharp measure of Loni's face. "Oh, honey, you're white as a sheet. Sit tight. I'll get you some water." She hurried to the kitchen, only to return just as quickly. "No drinking glasses. What was I thinking? The water probably isn't even turned on."

Throat still burning, Loni rasped, "That's fine. I don't need a drink." What she needed was to lie down in a dark room and regroup. "I'm just feeling a little sick." Propping her elbows on her knees, she buried her face in her hands. "I'm sorry about this. I don't normally feel so awful afterward. Only a little dizzy and disoriented for a few seconds."

"It's the house. I knew it would cause you problems." Deirdre sank onto the sofa and rubbed Loni's back. "Just look at you. Ice-cold and shaking like a leaf."

"It isn't the house. I've been seeing the cowboy all my life."

"Never when you were wide-awake and in the middle of a conversation. Trust me, it's the house. He's apparently been here at one time or another and stood by the fireplace. When you touched it you had a psycho-metric episode. That's all."

"No." Loni dropped her hands to meet her sister's gaze. "I didn't touch the fireplace. More to the point, this room was decorated just the way I hope to do it." Loni described the walls and other appointments. "I was seeing into the future, Dee, not the past."

"Precognition?" Deirdre frowned. "So he hasn't been here yet."

"No, not yet." Loni curled her arms around her waist. "I'm scared, Dee."

"Scared of what?"

"Of finally meeting him. That's what this means, you know, that he'll soon be standing right here in this room."

"And that's a bad thing? When we were girls it was all you talked about, meeting him someday."

Loni had long since abandoned the foolish, roman-tic notions of her youth. Men didn't take well to her psychic ability, and her dream cowboy would be no exception.

"I'm not a girl anymore." Loni groped for the words to explain how she felt. "My life is in a shambles. All I want is to pick up the pieces and move forward. The last thing I need is another complication."

"Meaning a man?"

Just the thought made Loni's stomach lurch again. "*Especially* a man."

"If it's the *right* man, it may be a lovely complica-tion. Why on earth does that possibility frighten you?"

Loni rubbed her sleeves, trying to rid herself of the chill that seemed to have settled in her bones. "I don't want to love someone who can't love me back or bails out because he can't handle my gift. I don't want to let myself need someone, only to lose him. And last but not least, I'm not thrilled with the thought of being laughed at because I'm still a virgin at thirty-one."

"Laughed at?" Deirdre rolled her eyes. "Trust me, Loni, the right man won't bail out, and he definitely won't laugh at you for being a virgin. He'll be delighted. At least, Michael was."

"You were a virgin when you met Michael?"

"What do you think, that I slept with every guy at university?" Deirdre fished inside her pocket as she pushed to her feet. Once at the fireplace, she had a cigarette clamped between her lips and a lighter in her hand. Tonguing the cigarette to one corner of her mouth, she added, "With Mom breathing down my neck all the time, when did I ever have a chance to be promiscuous? I couldn't even forget my coat and walk across campus without her calling me to scold."

Loni had suspected for some time that Deirdre was smoking again, but actually seeing her do it was a shock. "You shouldn't do that. It's bad for you."

Narrowing her eyes against the sting, Deirdre exhaled a puff of smoke. "It settles my nerves. Did you know that Mom called me last night right after Michael and I made love?"

"No. What did she want?"

"To inform me that my failure to urinate after sexual intercourse is probably why I have this bladder infection. Can you imagine how it feels to know she can tune in at will, even behind our closed bedroom door? It's an invasion of our privacy, and I can't help but wonder how much she saw. I love her to pieces. Don't get me wrong. But it totally pisses me off when I find out she's been spying on us. Even worse, I don't dare tell Michael why I get so cross with her sometimes. He'd die of embarrassment."

Loni had been on the receiving end of their mother's psychic ability, but she'd never really resented it. "Mom doesn't mean to invade your privacy, Deirdre. Something just cues her, and she tunes in for a few seconds. The house is brimming over with keepsakes from our childhoods. I'm sure she doesn't intentionally touch something of yours so she can be a bedroom voyeur."

"I know." Deirdre exhaled another lungful of smoke. "But even though I know it's unintentional, her dropping in like that totally freaks me out."

"It isn't easy for you, is it? Being the only normal female in the family, I mean."

"Correction. In our family I'm the *abnormal* one. Gram and Mom both have the gift, and so do you. One clairvoyant female in each generation, and my number didn't hit. It hardly seems fair, since I'm the oldest. Why did it pass over me and go to you?"

"You wish you were psychic?"

Loni couldn't imagine it. Yet, in many ways, that explained Deirdre's fascination with psychic phenomena and her penchant for memorizing all the scientific terms for them.

"I've always been the odd one out. I hear you and Mom and Gram talking, and it's like not knowing the alphabet at a spelling bee. I love all of you, and I enjoy being with you, but I feel like an outsider. I always have."

Loni could scarcely credit her ears. "Oh, Dee. I never realized you felt that way."

"I'm sorry for unloading on you right now. Bad timing. You have enough problems at the moment." She flicked ashes into the grate and sighed. "It's my guess that you're about to meet your cowboy, unless you can think of some way to alter the future."

Loni closed her eyes. "I can't alter the future. The Cheryl Blain incident proved that."

Deirdre snorted. "The Cheryl Blain *fiasco*, you mean. You did everything you possibly could, and it wasn't your fault she died. The police and news media are responsible for that."

Loni couldn't bear to think about it, especially not now. "I'm still not feeling well. Can you chauffeur me home and bring me back in the morning to get my car? I don't think I should try to drive right now."

"Sure," Deirdre said softly. She tossed the cigarette into the fireplace and stubbed it out with the toe of her boot. "I'm sorry seeing your cowboy has made you so sick."

Loni pushed weakly at the sofa cushion, struggling to gain her feet. Deirdre hurried over to grab her arm. As Loni came erect, the room seemed to tip off its axis.

"You okay to stand alone for a second?" Deirdre asked. "I'll go get your purse and coat."

Loni nodded even though she wasn't entirely sure she wouldn't fall. Deirdre vanished. Seconds later, she returned. With surprising deftness, she managed to push Loni's numb arms into the sleeves of her jacket.

"You're good at this," Loni murmured as Deirdre made fast work of fastening the buttons.

"It comes from dressing kids. You learn to get the job done quick."

Grateful for the thick folds of wool, Loni hugged the coat close. "Thank you. I was freezing." She glanced at the fireplace and then met her sister's worried gaze. "Any great ideas on how to avoid meeting a handsome cowboy?"

Deirdre smiled. "Only one. If you see a man in Wranglers and a Stetson, run like hell in the opposite direction."

Chapter One

Two months later

As Clint Harrigan crossed the parking lot to the automatic doors of the supermarket, the late-afternoon sunlight warmed his shoulders through the wash-worn cloth of his shirt. Normally the first summery days of June lifted his spirits, but they weren't doing the trick this year. Ever since his thirty-seventh birthday in March he'd been feeling depressed. It seemed like only yesterday that he'd been a snot-nosed college freshman with his entire adult life stretching ahead of him. Now, in what seemed like a blink, he was almost forty, had accomplished only a few of his goals, and felt as if time were running out.

Granted, his quarter-horse ranch was a highly successful enterprise. Financially, he was set, and not many men his age could say that. Only what about his personal life? He'd fully expected to have a wonderful wife and a passel of kids by now. Instead he was facing another lonely Friday evening, his plans revolving around a man-size frozen dinner, a six-pack of beer, his recliner, and the television remote control.

Unfortunately, as much as Clint dreaded spending another evening alone, he couldn't think of anything else he preferred to do. The honky-tonk scene no longer appealed to him. Neither did the dating ritual. He was tired of laughing at stupid jokes, dancing with women who tried to lead, and trying to fill tense silences with meaningless small talk. Oh, yeah, and he couldn't leave out the cell phones. It was damned disconcerting when a woman spent more time answering calls than she did talking to him.

The scent of oranges and flowers filled his nostrils when he entered the store. Hanging a right, he moved like a man on autopilot, his destination the beer coolers at the back of the building. Barely registering the blur of produce as he cut through the vegetable section, he wondered if his failure to marry wasn't mostly his own fault.

Maybe he was just too fussy about women. When he met an interesting gal, there were certain criteria she absolutely had to meet. Good sense of humor. Check. Strong faith in God. Check. Interesting conversationalist. Check. Respect for human life. Check. Appreciation of family. Check. Deep love of animals. Check. And, of course, he had to find her attractive. On that count he was fairly easy to please, his focus being more on a woman's inner beauty than her outward appearance.

Still, he'd be the first to admit that he'd ruled out a lot of women over one small quirk or another that drove him crazy. Why couldn't he focus on a lady's fine points instead of picking her apart? So what if the last gal he'd dated had bleated like a sheep when she laughed? She'd been nice enough, otherwise. And the gal before her—Janet somebody—might have been okay after some minor surgery to cure her postnasal drip. And he really should have given the coupon fanatic a little more time to grow on him. It wasn't a crime to be frugal, after all, and it hadn't been *that* bad dining out on buy-one-get-one-free coupons.

Like he was Mr. Perfect? Hell, no. He had as many faults as the next guy, the worst of the lot being that he was a control freak, according to his sister and brothers. He took their criticism with a grain of salt, though. *Someone* needed to take control and make the decisions. Otherwise everything was up for debate, and in the Harrigan family, debates quickly escalated into arguments.

Clint noticed an elderly lady at the far end of the produce department shaking a cantaloupe near her ear. What she was listening for, Clint didn't know.

"The best way to check for ripeness," he told her, "is to smell the stem end of the melon. The stronger the fruit scent, the riper the melon."

"I've been selecting melons longer than you've been alive, young man. I guess I know better than you how to tell if a cantaloupe is ripe."

"Sorry." Clint quickened his pace, his boot heels tapping sharply on the tile floor. "Just trying to help you out."

He was still muttering under his breath about grumpy old ladies when he reached the beer coolers. His mood promptly grew gloomier when he saw an empty spot where his favorite microbrew usually sat. That was *not* okay. Hailing a clerk, Clint asked, "Do you have any Crystal Pond Dark in the back?"

FRED was embroidered on the pocket of the man's blue smock. "If we do, it won't be chilled."

It wouldn't be the first time Clint had fast-chilled beer in the freezer. "Crystal Pond is worth the wait. I believe in supporting our local microbrewery." Clint also believed in pleasing his palate, and Crystal Pond Dark, rich and mildly sweet, was an awesome beer.

Fred shrugged and lumbered into the back room. Five minutes later he reappeared with a six-pack of longnecks. Clint had hoped to get a half-rack. Family poker night would be at his place tomorrow, and he'd need extra beer in the fridge. But he was in a hurry to get home and didn't want to stand there waiting any longer. He accepted the six-pack, said thank-you, and angled right to the freezer section, where he grabbed two man-size frozen dinners without bothering to check the fat content. His brother Quincy worried enough about cholesterol to keep the whole damned family healthy.

At register four, Clint took his place in line behind a slender, petite brunette in a silky cream white blouse and slacks the color of fresh-cut alfalfa. The male checker was taking forever to put in a new register tape. Clint tamped down his impatience. Why was it he always got in the slow line? He had an appointment with his recliner at five sharp to watch the evening news. Then he planned to vegetate for the remainder of the night. Absolutely no work. It was the weekend, after all. Even if he had nothing better to do, the stack of papers on his desk and all the data entries he needed to make on the computer could wait until Monday morning. His baby sister, Samantha, had been nagging him lately about becoming a workaholic. Well, hello? It wasn't as if he had a woman in his life to fill up his leisure hours.

His gaze cut back to the brunette, touching first on the trimness of her waist and then the gentle flare of her hips. *Nice.* Definite proof that dynamite sometimes came in small packages. He normally preferred feminine curves showcased in snug denim, but a world-class figure had to be appreciated no matter how it was wrapped.

The line moved forward, and the brunette set a blue shopping basket on the belt. Taking stock of her purchases, Clint saw that she'd selected a small package of gourmet cheese, a box of wheat crackers, and a bottle of merlot. He wondered if she would share the wine with a significant other, or if, like him, she would be spending the evening alone. Catching a glimpse of her delicate facial features and deep blue eyes, he decided she was either engaged or married. The truly beautiful ones usually were. No ring, though. That was interesting.

While the clerk rang up her purchases, the brunette lifted the flap of her shoulder bag to pluck out a folded red cloth and a credit card. When she reached to slide the card through the customer scanner, the rectangle of plastic slipped from her grasp and fell to the floor. Clint bent forward to pick it up just as she did, and they bumped heads so hard that his hat went flying.

"Whoa!" He grasped her by the arms to keep her from falling. "Sorry about that. Are you all right?"

The red cloth slipped from her fingers and fluttered to the floor. Then she weaved slightly, making him worry that she might pass out. He didn't think they'd hit that hard, but there was a blank, distant expression in her beautiful eyes.

"Ma'am?" he tried again. "Talk to me. Are you hurt?"

For a long moment that seemed like a small eternity to Clint, she continued to sway on her feet. Clint was about to ask the checker to call for help when she blinked back to awareness like someone waking from a deep sleep. Her blue eyes focused on him.

"Are you hurt?" he asked again.

Her oval face drained of color, and she jerked free of his grasp. Before he could guess what she meant to do, she ran from the market without picking up her credit card or paying for her purchases.

"I *hate* when people do that," the clerk said, still holding the bottle of wine in his hand. "Now I'll have to void the transaction and get someone to put all this stuff back on the shelves."

Clint collected his hat and settled it on his head. Then he crouched down to pick up the card and the wad of red material. The woman's name, Loni Kendra MacEwen, was stamped into the plastic.

Handing the card to the checker, Clint said, "She'll probably be back for this."

The man took the card and slipped it into the cash drawer. "If not, I'll give it to the manager and he'll take care of it. People forget their cards all the time."

Clint handed over the wad of cloth as well. "I'm not sure what this is."

"Shopping bag," the clerk said as his hand closed over the material. "Made out of parachute silk and has handles, just like our plastic shopping bags, only it holds more stuff, won't tear, and can be used again and again. Greenies buy them on the Net. They claim plastic bags are bad for the environment."

They were definitely bad for Clint's environment. He stored them in a kitchen drawer, and it seemed to him the damned things procreated in there.

"It was strange, the way she acted," Clint remarked, thinking of how the woman had swayed as if she might pass out. "I hope she wasn't seriously hurt."

"Moved too fast getting out of here to be seriously hurt," the checker replied as he punched in number codes to clear the register. "And trust me, I've seen stranger things than that. There are some really weird people wandering around out there."

"Hmm."

Shaking his head, Clint ran his credit card, signed for the charges, and left the building, carrying his unsacked purchases in the crook of one arm, his answer to the exploding population of plastic bags in his kitchen drawer.

Loni was shaking too badly to drive. Folding her arms over the steering wheel of her Chevy Suburban, she rested her forehead on the back of her wrists and closed her eyes. *Oh, God.* She'd finally met her dream cowboy, and his name was Clint Harrigan. So much for Deirdre's plan to avoid men wearing Stetsons. Loni hadn't even realized he was behind her in line.

How she knew his name, she wasn't sure. Normally she didn't pick up on people's names when they touched her, only images and thoughts and sensations.

But the punch from Clint Harrigan had been the strongest she'd ever felt, the images hitting her so hard and fast that she'd almost collapsed.

His little boy was in terrible danger. The instant Clint Harrigan had touched her, Loni had seen an orange raft capsizing in river rapids. Two adults, a man and a woman, had been thrown into the water along with the child and a Saint Bernard, but only the boy and the dog had resurfaced. *Cold, such a horrible cold.* The huge canine had seized the chest strap of the child's life preserver in its teeth and swum toward shore.

Still trembling, Loni sat back and stared through the windshield. *Trevor.* That was the little boy's name, and the faithful family dog was called Nana, after the lovable Saint Bernard in *Peter Pan. Oh, God, oh, God.* The adults hadn't survived. Though Loni hadn't been seeing through their eyes, she felt certain they hadn't resurfaced. Instead they had been sucked under by the powerful currents and carried downstream.

The knowledge made her feel sick. Two people had either just died or were about to die very soon. Yet when she gazed across the parking lot, shoppers went about their business, oblivious to the tragedy she'd just witnessed. A young mother was opening a box of animal crackers for her toddler before taking groceries from the cart and putting them into the back of her SUV. A middle-aged man was thrusting his arm through the partially open window of a Mazda to pet his miniature schnauzer before going inside the store. Loni felt so alone, so horribly alone.

She guessed the woman in her vision was the child's

mother. *Sandra.* That was the name that whispered in her mind. She wasn't sure who the man had been. The boy's stepfather, maybe? Loni only knew that Clint Harrigan, her dream cowboy, was Trevor's biological father. And though it made no sense, she also knew Clint Harrigan was the only person—the one and only person—who'd be able to save the child's life. *Crazy, so crazy.* But Loni had long since learned not to question her visions, only to believe in them.

She jumped with a start when Clint Harrigan emerged from the market and walked across the parking lot toward a blue Ford pickup. After she'd envisioned him in her dreams for most of her life, it felt eerie to be watching him now. He walked with unhurried ease, yet covered a lot of ground with his long, loose-jointed stride. He wore a light blue work shirt stained with dirt at one shoulder, the sleeves folded back over thick, sun-bronzed forearms. A hand-tooled leather belt rode his lean hips, its large silver buckle flashing in the sunlight with every step he took.

Loni studied him with detached fascination, taking in his faded jeans and the way his thighs bunched under the denim with each push of his booted feet. For some reason she'd always thought he'd be taller, possibly because she'd first dreamed of him when she was a child and all men had seemed huge to her. But instead of towering like a pine, he put her more in mind of the shorter juniper trees indigenous to the surrounding high desert terrain—rock hard to the very core and tough enough to withstand almost anything.

His jet-black hair needed a cut, lying in lazy waves over his forehead and caressing the collar of his shirt under the brim of his hat. His features, burnished to teak by exposure to the sun, might have been chiseled from granite, the blade-sharp bridge of his nose jutting out from between thick black eyebrows, high cheekbones underscoring his intense brown eyes. His square jawline, roped with muscle, angled to a deeply cleft chin.

What was it about cowboys that so many women found sexy? For the life of her, Loni couldn't figure it out. Born and raised in the greater Seattle area, she preferred men in dress shirts, khaki slacks, and slip-on loafers. But she had to admit, if only to herself, that no man in the city had ever made her feel the way she did now. Everything about Clint Harrigan screamed "masculine," and everything feminine within her responded.

His truck was as rugged-looking as he was, a big, high-clearance vehicle with huge knobby tires, a long wheelbase, and a grill guard and winch attached to the front bumper. Inside the four-door cab, a gun rack hung over the rear window, a lethal-looking rifle cradled in one set of brackets. What kind of man kept a weapon in his pickup? In Washington some private citizens had permits to carry concealed, but Loni couldn't recall a single instance when she'd actually seen a gun, unless it was holstered at the hip of a policeman or security guard.

Unaware that he was being watched, Harrigan opened the rear door on the driver's side of the truck, deposited his beer and frozen dinners on the seat, and then paused to slip a small, round can from the back pocket of his jeans. Loni stared in bewildered wonder as he cupped the can in the half circle of his thumb and forefinger, then sharply flicked his wrist to tap the lid. Chewing tobacco. Just the *thought* made her want to gag. He tucked a pinch inside his lower lip. *Nasty.* Didn't he know that stuff caused mouth cancer? He wouldn't be so handsome with half of his lower jaw surgically removed.

He glanced in her direction just then. *Oh, God.* Loni dropped lower on the seat, hoping he couldn't see her. Why, she didn't know. She had as much right to be in the parking lot as he did. She felt like a silly adolescent girl spying on a boy. His dark eyes swept past her Suburban and then swung back. He nudged up the brim of the Stetson and seemed to stare directly at her for a second. Then he frowned, tugged the hat back down, and swung up into the truck with the ease of a man who'd mounted a horse thousands of times.

Loni's heart was pounding like a kettledrum. She shrank even lower on the seat as his diesel truck rumbled by. Her dream cowboy. He was *real*. Though she'd always known that, deep down, it still came as a shock to actually see him in the flesh.

After he drove away Loni sat there for a long while, trying to regain her composure and right her senses. When she finally felt safe to drive, she headed straight home. Once locked inside the small house, she collapsed on the russet sofa, so exhausted she could barely move. Clint Harrigan. His image was still so vivid in her mind that she could see the crow's-feet that fanned out from the corners of his eyes and the deep creases that bracketed his mouth.

Two months ago, when she'd first envisioned him

here in this house, her only thought had been to avoid meeting him. Now she had a far more complicated problem: how to let him know his son was in mortal danger without jeopardizing the new life she was trying to create for herself in Crystal Falls. If she spoke to him on the phone, he might have caller ID. She could try the blocking code that the phone company had sent her, but what if it didn't work? Besides, how likely was he to believe a crazy psychic who telephoned him out of the blue? No. A face-to-face conversation would be better, only then he'd see her face. The consequences of that could be disastrous.

Worrying about it was giving Loni a headache, so she decided to let the problem ride for a few minutes. Sometimes she did her best thinking when she let go and thought about something else.

She pushed up from the sofa, kicked off her pumps, and walked barefoot to the kitchen. After putting the teapot on to boil, she let Hannah in from the backyard. Loose jowls wet with drool, the golden mastiff sniffed Loni's slacks like a jealous wife searching for the scent of strange perfume.

"No, I haven't been petting any other dogs," Loni said with a tremulous laugh that brought her perilously close to tears.

It wasn't easy to watch two people die. A part of Loni wanted to pretend it hadn't happened. Only what kind of person could witness a tragedy and then push it from her mind? Loni's mother and grandmother had tried to teach her how to distance herself from what she saw during visions, but so far Loni hadn't mastered the techniques. *Pretend it's something on television,* her mother, Annabel, lectured. *Hold part of yourself back*, her grandmother Aislinn advised. Only Loni couldn't do it. When she touched certain things the visions slammed into her mind with stunning force and without any warning. She never had time to brace herself or distance herself emotionally.

Part of the problem—in fact, *most* of the problem—was the extraordinary power of Loni's gift. The strawberry marks on her mother's and grandmother's napes were pale pink, while hers was a deep crimson. The mark suggested Loni's psychic abilities were multi-faceted and much stronger than theirs. During their visions they saw everything in black and white, and they couldn't often pick up on many details. Loni's visions were in living color, blindingly bright and brutally real. She didn't only *see*; she *felt* people's pain and terror.

Today in the grocery store, she'd felt the shock of the ice-cold water when little Trevor had plunged into the river, then his panic as he'd fought his way to the surface. Then she'd felt the awful numbness in his limbs as the frigid rapids pummeled him, driving the chill deep into his bones. How could she distance herself from that?

Even worse, how could she stop thinking about it?

Trevor's clothing would be wet now, and soon night would close in. If he was somewhere in central Oregon, and Loni felt certain he was, the temperatures would abruptly drop when the sun went down, possibly to below freezing before daylight tomorrow. How would the little guy survive?

Desperate to chase the frightening possibilities from

her mind, Loni crouched down to touch noses with Hannah. Everyone in the MacEwen family had argued against Loni's purchasing a Fila Brasileiro mastiff. The breed was renowned for being fiercely loyal, protective of their masters, and sometimes vicious. Hannah had proved everyone right on the first two counts; even at only thirteen months she was suspicious of strangers and diligently guarded Loni's safety. But vicious? Hannah had a sweet, loving nature and would never hurt anyone without good reason.

"You're a dear heart, aren't you?" Loni murmured as she ruffled the dog's floppy ears and folded her loose jowls up over her nose. "Just look how wonderful you are with Deirdre's little boys, and all the neighbor kids as well. You aren't mean. No, you aren't. You're Mama's precious girl. Yes, you are."

Loni sat back on her heels and grinned. In addition to the fact that Hannah made her feel safe when nightmares of Cheryl Blain brought her screaming awake, the mastiff had also become one of her best friends. Hannah never criticized or passed judgment. Her love was strong, steadfast, and without condition.

"We're a team," Loni whispered to her dog. "It's just you and me, baby."

As Loni looped her arms around the mastiff's thick neck, a brilliant white light flared before her eyes, and the next instant she was no longer in the kitchen but in rocky terrain peppered with pine trees. For a moment she felt confused and disoriented, but then her senses sharpened and she saw little Trevor huddled near a large boulder, the faithful Nana sitting beside him.

"You're my best friend," the child said to the dog. "We'll take care of each other. Huh, Nana?"

Loni felt the ache of cold in Trevor's feet, the icy stiffness of his soaked clothing. The smell of wet dog filled her nostrils. All around her, it was dark—oh, so very dark. Only the sliver of a waning quarter moon lit the landscape.

"I need Boo," Trevor whimpered.

Boo was the child's stuffed bear with tattered ears and a snub tail that he'd teethed on as a toddler. At home Trevor always needed his night-light on, with Boo and Nana cuddled close before he could go to sleep. Loni wasn't sure how she knew that. Her gift had always been strong, but never before had she seen and felt things quite this intensely.

Small body shuddering, the child whispered, "I'm cold, Nana. I'm so cold."

Still damp from the river, the Saint Bernard whined and licked the child's face.

"I want my mom and dad," Trevor cried as he hugged the huge dog's neck. "I had on my life jacket. How come you didn't save them instead of me?"

Loni's heart caught at the sound of the child's sobs. She wanted to catch him up in her arms and hold him tight, only she couldn't. Then the scene changed, and other images of the boy and dog flashed and swirled through her mind like the changing patterns of a kaleidoscope, all glazed with red. Loni knew what that meant. Blood. Soon it would come, lots and lots of blood.

The shrill whistle of the teapot jerked Loni back to the present. Running her hand along the wall to stay steady on her feet, she hurried to the stove to lift the pot from the burner. The unexpected lightness of the vessel startled her. The water had boiled nearly dry. How long had she been lost in another reality? Several minutes, at least, possibly as much as a quarter hour.

She became filled with alarm. In the past she'd zoned out long enough for people around her to notice, but never for several minutes on end. More important, she'd touched nothing to bring on the episode.

This wasn't right; it wasn't right at all.

Hannah whined up at her. Loni was shaking almost as violently as little Trevor had been. "I'm okay," she assured the dog. "It's okay."

Only it *wasn't* okay. She might have had a skillet of food on a burner and started a fire. Always before, her waking visions had come to her only when she'd made physical contact with a person or a possession imbued with an individual's essence.

Frightened by the implications, Loni called her mother. The moment Annabel heard Loni's story, she asked, "Is this the only time it's happened?"

"Yes. I, um . . ." Shoving a hand into her hair and making a hard fist, Loni tried to think. "No," she amended. "The day I rented the house I had a waking vision of Clint Harrigan in the living room. At the time I wasn't worried about not touching anything to bring it on. I was more concerned that the vision might mean I was about to meet him, and I didn't want that."

"This isn't right," her mom said, echoing Loni's thoughts. "I've never in my life had a vision without something to cue me. What if you'd been driving?"

That possibility had already occurred to Loni. "What am I going to do, Mom?"

Annabel fell quiet. Then she said, "Let me call Gram. She's much more knowledgeable about all this stuff than I am."

A few minutes after Loni ended the conversation, the phone rang. She picked up on the first ring, knowing it was her grandmother.

Aislinn MacDuff said, "Well, this is a fine kettle of fish. How many times have you had visions without touching anything to bring them on?"

"Once this evening, and once a couple of months ago. I'm worried, Gram. It's never happened like this before. Suddenly my gift is more out of control than usual. How can I protect myself if the visions start coming to me willy-nilly?"

"I'm worried, too. When I have a vision, this reality is eclipsed by what I'm seeing in my mind. I'm unaware of anything happening around me until it's over."

Loni nodded. "I normally zone out for only a few seconds. This time the teapot almost boiled dry. I'm guessing fifteen minutes, give or take, and the only thing I'd touched was Hannah."

"This is very serious, Loni. Until it stops, you shouldn't go out."

"I can't do that, Gram. They just finished remodeling my shop this week, and I'm right in the middle of moving in. I'd like to get open for business as fast as possible."

"You have the proceeds from the sale of your house

to cover you financially until you get the shop opened. A couple more weeks won't send you into bankruptcy."

"True, but needlessly squandering my capital doesn't make good business sense."

"It's dead you'll be if you're behind the wheel of a car when a *sicht veesion* blinds you!"

Aislinn MacDuff had lived in the States for most of her adult life and had lost nearly all her Scottish accent. She backslid only when she grew extremely upset or angry. The fact that she'd used the phrase *sicht vession*, a Scottish term for vision, suggested just how agitated she was.

Loni sank onto a chair. "Maybe I'm overreacting and it won't happen again."

"Nonsense. This man, Clint Harrison—"

"Harrigan," Loni corrected.

"Harrigan, then. He's clearly someone you were destined to meet."

"Gram, you need to calm down. Getting upset this way isn't good for your heart."

"My heart is perfectly fine." Even so, Aislinn took an audible breath and released it slowly. She sounded calmer when she continued speaking. "You've dreamed of this man for years. It only stands to reason that you're linked to him in some way we can't comprehend. I think that's why you're having visions without touching anything to bring them on—because the spiritual bond between you is so strong and a paranormal force of some kind is at work."

A paranormal force? Loni cupped a hand over her eyes and barely stifled a groan. Her grandmother was a wonderful person, but sometimes she got a little carried away.

"You're getting worked up again, Gram."

"I love you, child. When I think you're in danger, I can't help but get worked up."

"I know. But I won't be in danger. I'll be very careful."

"The way I see it, you have only one choice. And I'll tell you right now, you aren't going to like it."

"I'm listening."

"You have to go to this Harrigan fellow and tell him what you've seen. Chances are he won't believe you, and he may even toss you out on your ear. But at least you'll have done your best to save the child. Once you've done that, I'm guessing the visions will stop."

Loni's hand clenched on the phone. "I can't just knock on his door, Gram! He'd see my face. There has to be a way for me to contact him anonymously."

"He won't pay any heed unless you confront him in person."

"He probably won't pay any heed then, either."

"In that case, he isn't likely to tell many people, and you will have fulfilled your obligation to the child. Having the sight doesn't come without some measure of responsibility, you know."

"What about me, Gram? I know that sounds selfish, but what about me? What about my having a life?"

"I know you went through hell the last time you tried to intervene. I also know that your mother wants you to bury yourself down there in Crystal Falls and never acknowledge your gift to anyone again. But I disagree with her. You can't run from who and what you are, sweetness. This situation is proof of that."

"So you think I should track Clint Harrigan down, tell him my story whether he wants to hear it or not, and let the chips fall where they may?"

"That's my advice. You'll never have any peace otherwise. The little boy is in grave danger. When your visions are glazed with red, it always means blood. You know that as well as I do. If you do nothing and Trevor dies, how will you live with it?"

Tears rushed to Loni's eyes. "If I *do* intervene and Trevor dies, how will I live with it? I failed last time, and I still wake up in a cold sweat from nightmares about poor Cheryl. Even if I go to Clint Harrigan and he believes me, no one will be able to find the child tonight. He's in a wilderness area somewhere. In my last vision he was wet and shuddering with cold, his only source of warmth a wet dog. If he's in central Oregon, and I think he is, it may drop below freezing. How will he survive until morning?"

"Leave that to God," Aislinn replied. "You have only to believe in the gift that He's given you and follow through, doing all that you can." Aislinn lent emphasis to her statement with a brief silence. "God doesn't make mistakes, sweetheart. You were born with an extraordinary ability. Don't you think He wants you to do good works with it?"

"A lot of people believe a gift like mine is from Satan, that I'm innately evil."

"Balderdash. You're a child of God. I baptized you myself right after you were born, and then you were formally baptized later. A sweeter, dearer person never breathed, except for the Virgin Mother, of course, and she's an impossible act to follow."

"The catechism of the Catholic Church clearly states that fortune-tellers, psychics, clairvoyants, and all paranormal activities are strictly forbidden."

"You're not a fortune-teller, and the word *psychic* is a very broad term that covers everything from charlatans with tarot cards who charge by the hour to true clairvoyants who were simply born with second sight. Have you ever once used your gift for financial gain? Have you ever once participated in a séance, trying to communicate with spirits? Do you own a crystal ball or wear crystals on your person? Do you draw hexagons on the floor and mix potions in a cauldron, or make voodoo dolls and put curses on your neighbors?"

Loni couldn't help but laugh. "It's a pentagram, not a hexagon, and no to all of the above. Of course I don't."

"Precisely. You're simply different, sweetie. You were fashioned from a very special bolt of cloth by God's own hands, and He had his reasons for giving you this gift. It's your responsibility to put it to good use."

Loni mulled over her options, but in the end she had to accept that her grandmother was right. If little Trevor died, she would regret her failure to intervene for as long as she lived.

"Okay," she said, straightening her shoulders. "I'll find Clint Harrigan, and I'll tell him what I've seen. Just know this, Gram: If it all blows up in my face again, you have to move with me to Idaho. I'm not going someplace new with no family anywhere near me.

When I left Lynwood, where you and Mom are, that's why I came to Crystal Falls, because Deirdre is here."

"Idaho? Why Idaho?"

"It's as good a place as any. Do you prefer California?"

Aislinn laughed. "I'll take Idaho. It's closer to your mother." Aislinn had lived only a few blocks from her daughter for as long as Loni could remember. "No hick towns, though. With Lynwood being so close to Seattle I've grown accustomed to all the great shopping, and couldn't give that up."

"Boise is a good-size community. I'm sure you could shop there to your heart's content."

"Let's just hope it doesn't come to your having to move again," Aislinn replied. "Do what you must, and if it all goes sour, we'll deal with it then. Just be sure to call your sister, Loni. It isn't safe for you to drive yourself anywhere right now. In the meanwhile, my rosary beads will be clacking."

As she broke the connection, Loni was smiling. She always felt better after talking to Gram.

Thirty minutes later Deirdre arrived at Loni's house. She breezed in without knocking, her short, dark hair tousled from the wind, her blue eyes snapping. Loni glanced up from where she sat at the kitchen table.

"I can't believe Gram talked you into this."

Loni had briefed Deirdre on the situation over the phone. "She didn't talk me into anything. She only reiterated what I already know. I can't run from this. I can't deny who and what I am. This is something I have to do."

"Does Mom know?"

Loni had just found Clint Harrigan's address and number in the Crystal Falls phone book. She jotted down the information and tucked the folded paper into her purse. "Of course Mom knows. She has the eye, remember? There's not much that gets past her."

"Has she telephoned?"

"No."

"Then she doesn't know. She's probably busy cooking supper. Later tonight, just about the time Daddy starts snoring in the recliner, she'll touch something of yours, tune in, and have a fit of hysterics. You *know* how she's going to react."

"You're right," Loni acknowledged wearily. "I do know, and that's precisely why I'm not calling her. We'll only argue, and I can't handle that right now."

Deirdre held up her hands. "You need to talk to her before you go through with this. Once it's done there'll be no turning back. You have a *right* to a life, Loni. Think of yourself for once."

"It's my decision to make, and I've made it," Loni replied. "Nothing Mom says will change my mind. There's a little boy out there who's going to die if I don't talk to his father. How would you feel if it were Kirk or Kinnon? Would you want me to turn my back on one of them?"

"That's not fair."

"If I think only of myself, will that be fair to Trevor?"

"Lonikins, I love you for your kind heart, and I know how you feel. I'd want to help Trevor, too. But at what cost? Do you want reporters and desperate parents breathing down your neck again? Try to look at it from my perspective. You're my little sister, and I love you." Deirdre flopped down on a chair, her lightweight jacket parting at the front to reveal her trim figure. "I can't bear to watch you go through that again. I want you to meet some nice guy, get married, and have a family, not live on the run, trying to piece your life back together again and again."

Loni circled the table to hug her sister. "Marriage isn't for me. You know that."

"It could be." Deirdre returned Loni's embrace, her body taut with the intensity of her emotions. "Just ignore these visions, Loni. Pretend you didn't have them. Please, won't you just try? If you won't do it for yourself, do it for me."

"I can't pretend I didn't have the visions. Two people died, and a little boy may yet. Try to understand."

Deirdre drew back, tears swimming in her eyes. "Being your sister totally sucks. You know it? Watching what you go through has broken my heart a thousand times."

"That's why your name is Deirdre Lavena, meaning sorrowful joy," Loni replied. "And why mine is Loni Kendra, meaning lonely clairvoyant. We all have our purpose in life. Mine's to be psychic. Yours is to feel glad and sad, both at once, because you love me."

"See there? That's a perfect example of how crazy our family is, all of us cursing our kids with names that have a special meaning. Who started that tradition, anyway? I think it's stupid."

"If you think it's stupid, why'd you do it yourself when Kirk and Kinnon were born?" Loni pushed at her hair, the mussed curls springing back under her fingers with a will of their own. "And I have no idea who started it. Someone in Gram's family, I suppose, probably generations ago."

"You're hell-bent on doing this, aren't you?"

Loni nodded. "I have no choice. A little boy needs my help. Whether I can do anything for him or not remains to be seen. But I have to try."

Sprawled on his recliner, Clint was channel surfing and enjoying his third beer of the evening when his doorbell rang. Living on a ranch, he had very few callers come to his front door. A Girl Scout selling cookies, most likely. Every year he was hit up at least twice and always got suckered in for packages of sweets he never ate.

None too pleased at the interruption, he muted the television, kicked down the footrest with the heel of one boot, and went to answer the summons. Only a little after eight, it wasn't fully dark yet, and he was startled to see the brunette from the supermarket standing on his welcome mat. She was just as lovely as he remembered, with delicate features, striking blue eyes, and a cloud of dark curls that fell to her shoulders.

"Well, hello," was all he could think to say.

"Hi."

Over the alfalfa green slacks, she wore a knee-length red wool coat to ward off the evening chill. Looking down at her, Clint was reminded of the Christmas season, his favorite time of year.

"I don't have your credit card, if that's why you're here," he was quick to inform her. "I gave it to the grocery clerk."

"No, no, that isn't it. I, um—" She broke off and laughed nervously. "I'm not really sure how to start. By introducing myself, I guess." She thrust out a slender, fine-boned hand, then appeared to brace herself, as if she might receive an electric shock from the contact. "My name is Loni MacEwen."

"Clint Harrigan." Clint shook hands with her, acutely aware of how cold and fragile her fingers felt. Then he stepped back so she could come inside, where it was warm. "How did you . . . ?" The question died on his lips. He had never seen the woman before this afternoon and hadn't given her his name. But it seemed rude to ask how she'd tracked him down. "What can I do for you?" he asked instead as he closed the door behind her.

She stood in his large foyer, her face pale above the collar of her coat. "Actually, Mr. Harrigan, it isn't what you can do for me, but what I can do for you."

"I see," he said, only he didn't see at all. Faintly amused, he asked, "And what is it that you can do for me?"

Her pale lips thinned. He saw her throat work to swallow. Then she looked up, her eyes so big and blue that he almost forgot what his question had been.

"I, um . . . I'm a clairvoyant," she said unsteadily. "I have the second sight." She held up a hand. "I know. That sounds really far-out, and maybe even a little crazy, but it's true. When people touch me like you did today, sometimes I . . . *see* things."

A clairvoyant? Clint didn't put any stock in all that paranormal baloney. "That's interesting," he said politely, "but I don't believe in clairvoyants. It's against my religion."

"Even so, you need to hear me out. Please. I've risked a lot by coming here."

Clint crossed his arms over his chest, thinking how pretty she was. Too bad her elevator didn't go clear to the top floor. "Fine, I'm listening."

She moistened her lips with the tip of her tongue. "Today when you grabbed my arms, I had a vision."

This was more entertaining than anything on television, Clint decided. "Go on."

"I saw some people shooting the rapids. I'm not sure which river, but the raft—one of those big orange ones—capsized. The man and woman weren't wearing life jackets, but the boy, a dark-haired little fellow who looked to be about seven or eight, was wearing protective gear, and he bobbed back up to the surface. The family dog, a big Saint Bernard named Nana, swam with the child to shore."

It was all Clint could do not to hoot with laughter. Who in his right mind would take a Saint Bernard anywhere on a river raft? But she was really getting into the tale, and he didn't want to stop her while she was on a roll. "You know the dog's name? That's . . . incredible."

"I know the child's name, too. It's Trevor." She searched his face for a reaction. "Does that mean anything to you?"

Clint shook his head. "Should it?"

"Yes," she said, her voice so faint he barely caught the word. "He's your son."

Clint cocked his head. "My what?"

"Your *son*. What's more, his life is in grave danger. He's going to be badly injured, and you'll be the only person who can save him."

Clint had heard enough. Grasping her elbow, he gently but firmly turned her toward the door. "As I said, Ms. MacEwen, this is all terribly interesting, but I don't have a son. I've never even been married."

She braced against the pull of his hand. "You *do* have a son, Mr. Harrigan. We both know children can be conceived outside of wedlock, and sometimes the biological father is never notified. I think the mother's name was Sandra. That's what came to me, anyway. Did you ever date a woman named Sandra?"

That was none of her damned business. Tightening his hold on her elbow, Clint drew open the door and gave her a firm push. Once outside on the porch, she swung back around, thrusting a business card at him.

"Please, at least take this so you can contact me later if you change your mind."

"No, thanks."

"You have to believe me," she cried. "You *do* have a son, and he's going to die if you don't help him. Doesn't that matter to you?"

If Clint had had a son, it would have mattered a great deal, but he was a childless bachelor. "Good night, Ms. MacEwen. Go home and take a Valium. If you're still delusional in the morning, I advise you to call a doctor. You need help."

Resisting the urge to slam the door in her face, Clint settled for firmly shutting it. The lady was crazier than a loon. Visions? He had to give her high marks for imagination. That was quite some story she'd fabricated. The checker at the supermarket had it right: There were a lot of weird people wandering around out there.

Still shaking his head, Clint turned out the lights and headed upstairs to bed. Four o'clock would come early. Even though it was the weekend, his horses still had to be fed and watered each morning, and the stalls still had to be cleaned. An orange raft? A Saint Bernard named Nana? A dark-haired little boy named Trevor? After stripping down to his boxers, Clint flopped onto his king-size bed and stared thoughtfully at the ceiling. He felt absolutely certain that Loni MacEwen was a nutcase. But one small detail bothered him.

How the hell had she tracked him down? The question was still circling in his mind as he said his prayers and drifted off to sleep.

Loni slumped onto the passenger seat across from her sister, slammed the car door, and puffed air at her bangs. "What a lowbrow *jerk*."

"Well," Deirdre mused aloud, "I can see that went well."

Loni took a deep breath and settled back, trying to shake off her anger. "Believing in psychics is against his religion. He also says I'm delusional, that I should go home and take a Valium."

Deirdre turned the headlights on bright to navigate the country road back to town. "I hate driving at dusk."

Loni squeezed her eyes closed. It was so like Deirdre to change the subject, trying to give her a chance to calm down.

"It's too dark to make out the deer," she went on,

"but not dark enough for their eyes to shine when the light strikes them. I'm always afraid to go very fast for fear I'll hit one."

Loni said nothing.

"You've done your best," Deirdre reminded her gently. "That was the plan all along. Right? You've fulfilled your obligation to little Trevor, whether his father believed you or not."

"He didn't. Not even close. I think he almost laughed at one point."

"Try not to be too rough on him. Out of the blue, you knocked on his door and told him a crazy story. He has no idea who you are. Not everyone is lucky like me and personally knows three psychics. As a result, a lot of people think it's all a bunch of hogwash."

"You're defending him."

"Yeah, sort of, I suppose. Was he *that* nasty?"

"Not nasty, exactly. *Mocking* would be a better word."

Deirdre mulled that over. "At least he heard you out before showing you the door. It could have been worse."

"He listened, but he didn't *hear*." Loni swallowed hard. A burning sensation washed over her eyes. "Why did God give me this gift if no one but me believes in it? What purpose does it serve?"

"I believe in it," Deirdre reminded her. "Don't take it so hard. You knew before you went to see him that he probably wouldn't listen."

"I just wanted . . . " Loni braced an elbow against her door to cup a hand over her eyes. "Trevor's out there, and he needs help. Clint Harrigan is the only person who can save him. God. I can't do this. It hurts too much."

"Don't let it hurt. You've done your part. The rest is up to your dream cowboy."

"Don't call him that. Not ever again. Just take me home, Deirdre. I'm exhausted."

As the car bumped along the road, Loni tried to console herself. It wasn't her fault that Trevor's father was a blockhead. She'd done everything she could, and that was all that God could expect of her.

After navigating the darkening streets of Crystal Falls, Deirdre turned onto Oak and parked in front of Loni's rental. "Want me to come in? Michael's with the boys. I'm in no hurry. We can open a bottle of wine and drink our woes away."

Loni shook her head. "Another time, maybe. Right now I just need to sleep."

Except when Loni went inside and crawled into bed, sleep refused to come. She curled her arm over Hannah, who always slept beside her. But nothing, not even the rhythmic sound of the dog's snores, soothed Loni. *Trevor*. He was out there, shuddering with cold. When Loni closed her eyes she saw him sharing a chocolate bar with Nana, who lay curled around the boy to keep him warm. It was a sweet vision, but also a terrifying one. Trevor was in a wilderness area and all alone except for his faithful dog. The child might survive for a few days, but in the end he would meet with tragedy.

Loni had seen his blood.

Chapter Two

Clint hit the floor before dawn the next morning. After a fast shower while still half-asleep, he dressed hurriedly and went downstairs to grab a cup of wake-me-up, already brewed and waiting in the carafe of the automatic coffeemaker. Thirty minutes later he was in the stables feeding his horses, surrounded by all the smells he loved: leather, alfalfa hay, grain, and even manure. This was his world, the place where he felt most balanced and at ease. The whickering of the animals soothed him like a lullaby did a baby.

At the other side of the arena Clint's ranch foreman, Hooter McElroy, worked in tandem with him. Routine. Clint could have done the drill with his eyes closed. Instead his senses were heightened with pleasure, making him acutely aware of everything around him.

When he and Hooter met at the far end of the cavernous arena, Clint asked, "You believe in psychics, Hooter?"

Hooter, a short, stocky man of fifty-six, soon to be fifty-seven, tweaked his graying handlebar mustache as he considered the question. A twinkle of laughter danced in his green eyes. "You mean like them people on Court TV who help the cops solve crimes?"

"Yeah." Clint patted Melchisedek's shoulder. The animal was a beautiful seven-year-old sorrel gelding that Clint had raised from birth. "What's your take on them?"

Hooter, who'd once been employed by Clint's father and then had come to work for Clint as a foreman, adviser, and friend, was like a member of the Harrigan family. He scratched under his hat, a battered, tan Stetson that he'd been wearing for as long as Clint could remember. "Well, now, I don't rightly know. I like watchin' the programs, but I ain't real sure people can do such things. I seen where one guy could look at a map while he was holdin' somethin' belongin' to a missin' person, and then he could pinpoint right where that person was."

"Did you believe it?"

Hooter spat tobacco juice. "I like to think it's possible. Sure would come in handy when I lose my keys."

Clint chuckled. He could always count on Hooter to make him laugh. "I watch those programs, tongue in cheek."

"That a polite way of sayin' you think it's a bunch of horseshit?"

"I reckon so," Clint replied.

Only one thing still bothered Clint about Loni MacEwen's strange visit last night: How the hell had she known where to find him? Maybe she'd waited out in the supermarket parking lot yesterday afternoon to get his license plate number. People could cross-reference information like that on the Internet if they had the right software. He'd seen a dark-haired woman sitting in a Suburban parked near his vehicle. A glare of sunlight on the windshield had kept him from seeing her clearly enough to be positive it was Loni MacEwen, but there was a strong possibility that she'd been watching him.

It was the only reasonable explanation Clint could come up with.

After finishing with the horses he worked at other chores until eight, then returned to the house for breakfast. Fresh coffee, eggs, bacon, and hash browns were on the menu. While he cooked, he turned on the kitchen television to keep him company. The ranch was too far from town to get cable, so he had a satellite dish, which gave him a large selection of viewing choices but didn't offer local news. As a result he had to watch a Portland station, which kept him informed of what was happening across the state but only occasionally featured stories about Crystal Falls or the surrounding area.

So he was surprised to hear the anchorwoman mention the Shoshone River and the Shoshone Wilderness Area, both in central Oregon. Interest piqued, he stopped cracking eggs into the skillet to look at the television. A male reporter dressed in casual clothing came on the screen. Behind him lofty ponderosa pines, a frothy stream, and rocky terrain created a gorgeous backdrop.

"This is Scott Holmes, reporting to you live from the Shoshone Wilderness Area. Behind me you see the Shoshone River. Early yesterday afternoon Senator

Robert Stiles, his wife, and their young son embarked on a rafting trip at Trevlow Landing, many miles east of here." The camera panned the river, lingering on some white water upstream. "You're seeing class-two rapids, which the Shoshone River is famous for, attracting rafters from all over the state because they can normally be navigated without much difficulty. But apparently the Stiles family encountered some sort of trouble as they made their way downstream." The camera swung away from the white water to zoom in on a large orange raft that had been pulled up onto the rocky bank. "Authorities believe that the raft holding Senator Stiles; his wife, Sandra; their eight-year-old son, Trevor; and Nana, the family's Saint Bernard, capsized. Search parties are combing the banks of the Shoshone for miles up- and downstream, hoping to find evidence that the family made it out of the water, but so far their efforts have been fruitless."

The camera lens retracted to give a broader view, revealing a uniformed forest ranger standing beside the reporter. Scott Holmes turned the microphone toward the other man. "Roger, as I understand it, the searchers have found no evidence that the Stiles family may have survived the accident?"

The ranger shook his head. "Not at this time, no, but we're still searching. Countless volunteers have joined forces with experienced team leaders. They covered both sides of the stream last night with flashlights and made another pass again this morning. But in rugged terrain like this, it's possible to miss something. We haven't given up hope."

"And if further efforts turn up nothing?"

The ranger's expression grew grim. "For now that kind of speculation is premature. We have every reason to hope that Robert Stiles managed to get his family to safety."

Scott Holmes came back on the screen. "I understand that Senator Stiles is an experienced white-water rafter and woodsman who often brings his family into this area."

Roger's face reappeared on the camera. "Very experienced, according to his parents." He smiled slightly. "He grew up at the north end of the state and has always loved outdoor recreation."

"Yet the search parties have discovered two adult-size life jackets. Doesn't that suggest that the senator and his wife may have ignored water safety guidelines?"

"Not at all," the ranger replied. "It's true that two adult life jackets have been recovered, but we have no way of knowing how many flotation devices were aboard the raft. People sometimes carry extra gear."

"Is it true that helicopters equipped with heat sensors have flown over the terrain on both sides of the river for many miles up- and downstream?" the reporter asked.

"Yes, but again, in this kind of terrain it's possible to miss something."

The camera zoomed back in on Scott Holmes's face. "There you have it, folks. Though there is still every reason to hope that the Stiles family will be found safe and sound, the searchers have turned up nothing. Stay tuned to KTVY for further updates."

Clint forgot about his hunger, his full attention now

riveted on the television. A picture of Senator Stiles flashed on the screen, followed by a bust shot of his wife. Staring incredulously at the woman's face, Clint clenched his hand over an egg, shattering its fragile shell.

"Damn!"

Barely able to jerk his gaze from the television, he grabbed for a towel to wipe the slime from his fingers. Nine years ago Sandra Stiles's last name had been Michaels, and Clint had dated her. Honey brown hair, green eyes. Oh, yes, he remembered her well. They'd been an item for over six months, and at one point he'd almost asked her to marry him. Later they'd decided they weren't right for each other after all, and they had ended the relationship on good terms. Shortly thereafter Sandra had moved back to Sweet Home, a small town at the north end of the state where she'd been raised.

Clint had kept in contact with her by phone for a few months after she left the area. It had been the only responsible thing to do. During one ill-fated sexual encounter, the condom had torn, putting Sandra at risk of becoming pregnant. During all those phone conversations following their breakup, she'd never once hinted to Clint that she was carrying his child.

But, oh, God, what if . . . ?

Cold sweat broke out on Clint's body. He turned off the stove burners and sank onto a kitchen chair to stare in dazed disbelief at a photograph of little Trevor Stiles, a jet-haired, brown-eyed eight-year-old. Could Trevor be his son? The picture faded from the screen, but the kid's face remained clear in his mind. Black hair, big brown eyes, a dimple on the chin that could one day become a cleft, and a nose that might bear the Harrigan stamp when the boy matured to manhood.

Feeling strangely numb, Clint went back over all that Loni MacEwen had told him. An orange raft, a little boy named Trevor, and a Saint Bernard called Nana. *Did you ever date a woman named Sandra?* When she'd asked that question last night Clint had been too outraged by her audacity to think of Sandra Michaels, who'd long since been consigned to that curtained part of his brain where old memories grew dimmer with each passing year.

Clint propped his elbows on the table and rubbed his eyes. The Sandra Michaels he'd known had been a straightforward, honest woman with unshakable integrity. If she'd been pregnant with his baby she would have told him. Clint felt certain of that. But how could he discount Loni MacEwen's story when she'd described the rafting accident in such detail?

There had to be a rational explanation. Maybe MacEwen was one of those women who became obsessed with strange men. He'd already determined that she might have cross-referenced his license plate number to learn his name. It followed that she might also have seen or heard a news flash yesterday afternoon about the Stileses' rafting accident.

That was it, he decided. That had to be it. He had no idea how she might have discovered that he'd once dated Sandra. Maybe she was a friend of Sandra's and had come by the knowledge that way. Clint only knew he didn't believe in psychic phenomena, never had and never would.

Determined to banish all doubt from his mind, Clint called an old high school buddy who worked at the local television station. When a female receptionist answered the phone, Clint asked to speak with Darrel Armstrong.

Seconds later Darrel came on the line. "Hey, Clint, how's it goin'?"

It was good to hear Darrel's voice. Clint hadn't bumped into him for almost a year. "I can't complain too much. How about you?"

"Busy, man. I've moved up the ladder to full-time newshound. They're running me ragged." Papers rustled, and Clint heard the faint clack of a keyboard. "So what's up?" Darrel asked.

"I'm curious about a news bulletin I just saw on a Portland channel, the disappearance yesterday of Senator Robert Stiles and his family during a rafting trip."

"Tragic, isn't it? Why things like that happen to decent people, I'll never understand. Half the population of Oregon will be in mourning over Robert Stiles's death."

"No bodies have been found yet," Clint reminded him.

"I know, I know," Darrel replied. "The ranger was making happy talk about there still being hope, but— unofficially, of course—I think the family most likely drowned. The Shoshone River's white water isn't too bad, but its undertows are treacherous. Someone drowns in that damned river almost every year."

The thought that Sandra might be dead sent a chill up Clint's spine.

"If he's dead, it'll be a huge loss for our state,"

Darrel went on. "Robert Stiles was honest and sincere. Don't see that very often in a politician."

Clint didn't follow politics closely, but if Sandra Michaels had married the man, he took it as a high recommendation. "Sandra, his wife . . . I used to date her. She's a fine person."

"Hey, buddy, I'm sorry to hear that. I guess this hits pretty close to home for you, then."

Clint passed a hand over his eyes. "Yeah, it does. She was a good friend. But that isn't why I called. I'm wondering if you might be able to tell me when word of the rafting accident first went public?"

"This morning," Darrel replied without hesitation. "They only found the raft a couple of hours ago. The way I understand it, the Stiles family was following friends down the river, but the senator put in to shore for a bathroom break, and the other raft got way ahead of them. They'd all agreed to meet at Boulder Bend, a popular camping spot for rafters. I'm not clear on whether they planned to spend the night there or continue downstream after stopping to rest. I only know the Stiles family never showed up at the designated meeting place.

"After waiting a couple of hours, the friends grew concerned and called the ranger station by cell phone, but it got dark before any search parties could be brought in by helicopter. Volunteers did their best with flashlights, but they didn't have much luck."

"Senator Stiles is an important man," Clint pointed out. "Surely there were preliminary news bulletins notifying the public that he and his family were missing?"

"At first nobody really thought they were missing.

The rapids they went through aren't that big a deal. The authorities believed Stiles had probably put in to shore because something had gone wrong. Sometimes a rock will poke a hole in the rubber and the raft will take on water. Even after finding the gear they still thought the family could be stranded somewhere, waiting for help. Unfortunately the helicopter sweeps along the river turned up nothing but the capsized raft, which may have drifted countless miles before it caught on the rocks. If Stiles and his family had made it to shore, they would have stayed by the river so they could be easily spotted from the air."

Adults would have stayed by the river, but an eight-year-old boy might wander away from the stream and get lost. Clint felt cold, as if the temperature in the kitchen had plunged several degrees. "So you're absolutely positive the public wasn't informed of the incident yesterday?"

"Certain sure, man. Why are you asking?"

"You wouldn't believe me if I told you," Clint replied.

After ending the call, Clint just stood there, staring at the phone. When he'd collected his thoughts, he grabbed his Stetson and left the house to go see his dad, whose ranch bordered Clint's to the south. Rather than saddle a horse for so short a jaunt, Clint chose to ride his ATV, a battered red Kawasaki. As he cut across his own pastures to reach his father's, opening and closing gates as he went, he tried to slow his racing thoughts by focusing on the land he loved so much.

Originally a twelve-hundred-acre parcel, it had been divided into six equal portions seventeen years ago by

Frank Harrigan, the family patriarch. Frank had kept one section for himself, and deeded over the others to each of his five children when they turned twenty-one. Clint, being the oldest, had been the first to get his chunk of land and a hefty amount of working capital to start his own business.

To date, sixteen years of his life had been invested in that business. Every fence post, every board, and every blade of grass were the result of countless hours of his hard work. For the first five years, he'd slaved from before dawn until after dark to make a go of his horse ranch, which he'd named the Circle H, after his dad's ranch, the Bar H. Clint's three brothers had followed suit, Parker dubbing his spread the Rocking H, Quincy calling his the Lazy H, and Zach's pulling in the cow's tail as the Crooked H. Only Samantha, the youngest and the only girl, had departed from the Harrigan tradition, naming her spread the Sage Creek Ranch, after a stream that meandered over the twelve hundred acres.

When Clint finally reached his father's land, he turned on the seat of the ATV to look back, his gaze caressing the lush green fields, then lingering on his two-story post-and-timber home, the red-roofed arena, the outdoor stable, and a clutch of other outbuildings. The sight centered him, untangling his thoughts so he could focus on the question that tormented him. *Is Loni MacEwen for real?*

Frank Harrigan was helping his new wife fix breakfast when Clint rapped on the back screen door and entered the kitchen. "Mornin'!" Frank said. "You're just in time to eat and do the dishes."

Dee Dee, a plump woman with warm blue eyes and bottle-enhanced red hair, playfully slapped her husband's shoulder. "Don't pay him any mind, Clint. I enjoy cleaning up. Want some coffee?"

Clint had known and loved Dee Dee most of his life. Shortly after his mother had died giving birth to Samantha, his dad had hired Dee Dee as a housekeeper, and she'd quickly wormed her way into all their hearts, becoming a surrogate mother to Clint and all his siblings. This spring, only a few months after Samantha married Tucker Coulter, Frank had finally made the redhead an official member of the family.

"No coffee, thanks," Clint said. "I'm nervy enough without any more caffeine."

Dee Dee's gaze sharpened on his face. "What's wrong, dear? You look like you just lost your best friend."

"An old friend," Clint amended as he hooked his hat over the finial of a chair back and sat down. "Sandra Michaels, a lady I once dated. I just heard on the news that she may have drowned yesterday afternoon in a rafting accident."

"The senator's wife? Yes, we saw the news story." Dee Dee crossed the kitchen to lay a hand on Clint's shoulder. "I'm so sorry. Were you terribly fond of her?"

"At one time I almost asked her to marry me."

Slowly, haltingly, Clint related the details of his relationship with Sandra Stiles, and then told them Loni MacEwen's outlandish story. Dee Dee's eyes went wide as she sank onto a chair across from Clint. Frank turned the burners off and came to sit beside her.

"So this woman claims Trevor Stiles is your child," Frank reiterated.

"Crazy, isn't it?" Clint forced a laugh. "It's possible, I guess. Only I can't believe Sandra would have kept it from me. We kept in contact for a few months, and she was as honest as the day is long. I point-blank asked her a couple of times if she was pregnant, and she said no."

"Sometimes women lie about things like that," Dee Dee said. "They fear a custody battle—or they don't want to be bothered with driving back and forth to give the father visitation—and other times they're in a new relationship and don't want the past to complicate the future."

"Sandra wasn't like that," Clint insisted. "She never would have kept my child from me. I'd bet my life on that. She was a great person, very fair-minded and forthright. She also knew I'd never dream of suing for custody."

Frank rubbed his jaw, then rocked back on his chair. "At this point the boy's parentage isn't the primary concern. This MacEwen woman says the child's in danger, and only you can save him. If it was me, that's what I'd be thinkin' about."

"You don't seriously believe she's on the level?" Clint searched his father's dark eyes. "We're Catholic. It's against the tenets of our faith to believe in stuff like that."

"I'm quite familiar with the guidelines of the Roman Catholic Church," Frank reminded his son. "And if you were talkin' about a woman in a Gypsy caftan, using smoke, veils, and a crystal ball, or someone chanting over tea leaves, I'd completely agree that she was far-out, probably a fake, or worse, calling upon dark forces to foretell the future. The Church asks us to avoid things like that, and rightly so. It keeps us out of trouble. But I'm not sure we're comparin' apples to apples. It sounds to me as if Loni MacEwen may be a genuine clairvoyant who only wants to help a little boy. There's certainly nothin' evil in her intent, as far as I can see. Has she tried to milk you for money?"

"No. I didn't get that impression. I just find it difficult to believe her story."

Frank shook his head. "What of all the great saints who had visions? And what of the men who wrote the Bible? The Book of Revelation was revealed to John in a dream. That isn't to mention all the other ancient prophets and prophetesses we read about in scripture. Do you think all of that's a bunch of tripe?"

"No, of course not." Clint pushed at the country-blue pepper shaker. "But those people were inspired by God and had a divine message to deliver."

"If people like that existed in biblical times, why not now?" Frank countered. "That isn't to say I believe Ms. MacEwen is a prophetess, but I can't rule out the possibility that her ability may be a God-given gift."

Dee Dee rested a loving hand on her husband's arm. "I have to side with your dad, Clint. I'm from a devout Catholic family, but my grandmother was a clairvoyant."

Clint arched an eyebrow. "You're kidding."

"I wouldn't joke at a time like this. It's a very grave situation. Grandma Stevenson was a very religious woman. She read the Bible, attended daily Mass, and prayed the rosary every day of her adult life. There was certainly nothing evil about her, but she did have second sight. Not to the degree that Loni MacEwen claims to have, but she still amazed us sometimes. Once while visiting my mother, she jumped up and said she had to go, that Grandpa had just cut his leg with the chain saw. By the time we got to their house, Grandpa had a tourniquet on his thigh to slow the bleeding, and all we could do was rush him to the hospital." Dee Dee lifted her hands. "Sometimes people have extraordinary gifts that the rest of us can't understand or explain. What of that saint who was able to be in two different places at once? That was actually documented. Don't you suppose there are people of other faiths who wonder if he wasn't a charlatan—or colluding with dark forces to enable him to do that?"

Clint had known Dee Dee too many years to suspect her of lying. He could only shake his head in amazement. "So both of you think Loni MacEwen may have been telling me the God's honest truth?"

"I wouldn't rule out the possibility," Frank said. "If she isn't a psychic, how in hell did she know so many details about the raftin' accident before it became public knowledge? Pretty impressive, if you ask me. And as far as I can see, she has no ulterior motive. Why not take her at face value until she does or says somethin' that exposes her as a fraud?"

Even as Clint nodded, his mind balked at the possibility that Loni MacEwen was a genuine clairvoyant. "Well, thanks for talking to me. You've given me a lot to think about."

"Just don't think on it too long," his father warned.

"If that boy is out there, every second counts. It's rugged, harsh terrain, and crawlin' with predators."

Clint went directly home and tried to find Loni MacEwen in the phone book. There were several MacEwens, but when Clint dialed the numbers and asked for Loni, people either hung up or told him no one by that name lived there. Mentally kicking himself for refusing to take the woman's business card, Clint tried calling Information next. The operator was no help. Loni MacEwen's number was unlisted, and the operator wasn't allowed to give it out.

Frustrated beyond bearing, Clint finally resorted to calling his uncle Hugh, a state trooper who usually worked the evening shift. After explaining his dilemma, Clint asked, "Is there any way you can feed her name into your computer network and get me her address?"

"I'm a patrolman, Clint. I don't normally use the computers, and even if I did, we're not supposed to give out that kind of information to the general public."

"I see." Clint sighed. "Well, it was worth a shot."

"A psychic, you say?"

"I know it sounds far-fetched, Uncle Hugh, but on the off chance that she's for real, she may be able to help me find the Stiles boy."

Hugh sighed. "If she has an Oregon driver's license, maybe I can get her address. Bess, one of our dispatchers, is a nice lady and a whiz on the computer. If she's at the station I'm pretty sure she'll do a search for me on the sly."

"I really appreciate this, Uncle Hugh."

"Haven't done anything yet. Just keep your fingers crossed that Bess is working today. The other dispatchers are so gung ho and by-the-book, they spit-shine their name badges."

Five minutes later Hugh called Clint back. "Bad news. Bess is working swing. Won't be at the station until four. Can you wait that long?"

Clint couldn't see that he had a choice. "Yeah, sure. Let me give you my cell phone number, just in case I'm not at the house."

While Clint waited for his uncle to get back to him, he worked with the horses— bathing, grooming, lunging, riding, and cleaning stalls. At five he still hadn't gotten a call from his uncle, and hunger from not eating all day sent him back to the house. After making a sandwich he settled on the recliner to watch the evening news. A chunk of meat lodged in his throat when a special news bulletin interrupted the usual programming.

Scott Holmes, reporting live from Shale Gorge, announced that the bodies of Senator Stiles and his wife, Sandra, had just been recovered. The camera zoomed in on two body bags being carried away from the river on stretchers to a waiting helicopter. Then Scott Holmes returned to the screen.

"Rescue teams are still in search of the child's remains," he said solemnly, "but so far the boy and dog haven't been found. A helicopter equipped with heat sensors has also covered the surrounding areas and turned up nothing."

The regular evening news team, a man and woman, took it from there, debating Trevor Stiles's chances of survival, if by some miracle he was still alive.

"The Shoshone Wilderness Area has a large cougar population. Doesn't it, Peter?" the blond anchorwoman asked her colleague.

"I'm afraid so, Grace. There are also a lot of black bears in that area. They don't normally feed on humans, but they can be very dangerous all the same."

The newswoman shook her head. "At that elevation the June temperatures are still dropping to below freezing at night. I also understand that the Stiles family was on a day trip, making it unlikely they took very much food."

Peter agreed. "Even if they went prepared for every eventuality, which rafters sometimes do, the supplies are probably at the bottom of the river. If little Trevor Stiles is alive, it's unlikely that he'll remain that way for long."

Clint had heard enough and shut off the television. No longer hungry, he got up to pace. Though he refused to believe Trevor Stiles was his son, there was no denying that the boy might still be alive. And if he was, every wasted minute took him one step closer to death. Why the hell hadn't Uncle Hugh gotten back to him yet?

While he waited, Clint began planning. *You'll be the only person who can save him.* Those had been Loni MacEwen's exact words. At the time they'd made no sense to Clint, but now he realized he might be able to play a key role in the child's rescue. He had a stable full of riding horses, ten of them trail ready because he and his brothers had been planning to go on a three-day ride sometime next week. Over the last few days, Clint had been slowly changing the animals over to weed-free alfalfa cubes, required by Oregon law to protect some wilderness areas from toxic weed infestation.

Searchers on foot in a wilderness area would fan out from a base camp, going only so far before being forced to turn back. With pack animals Clint could carry camping gear and enough food to last several days, enabling him to cover more ground and press ever deeper into the wilderness at a faster clip.

The phone rang just then. Clint grabbed the portable that he kept by the recliner. "Clint here."

"Hi, son. It's Uncle Hugh. Sorry it took me so long, but there was a traffic pileup on Highway Ninety-seven. Bess needed four hands and two sets of ears there for a bit. She just now got back to me."

"Did she get the address?"

"Sure did. And it's a lucky thing, too. Loni MacEwen only recently moved to Oregon. A lot of people ignore the thirty-day law and don't get a new driver's license for months after moving into the state. Do you have paper and pen handy?"

When Clint finally knocked on Loni MacEwen's door, it was after seven, and less than two hours of daylight were left. Little Trevor Stiles was in for another long night—if he was still alive. All Clint could do was pack as quickly as possible, load up his horses, and reach the south trailhead in time to ride in at dawn.

From inside the house, he heard a deep, rumbling growl, followed by the soft tap of footsteps. Then came the rasp of three locks being disengaged. After opening the door, Loni MacEwen just stared at him, her hand clenched over the doorknob. Clint couldn't decide who looked less pleased to see him, the lady or her huge yellow dog. The beast was the largest canine he'd ever seen, with a massive head, droopy jowls, and folds of loose skin around its neck. If she wanted a horse, why didn't she just buy one?

"Hi." It was all Clint could think to say.

Dark circles of exhaustion underscored her pretty blue eyes. She wasted no time on pleasantries. "How did you find me?"

"Let's just say I'm resourceful."

"What do you want?"

Clint hadn't completely worked that out for himself yet. "I saw the news story about Senator Stiles and his family drowning. Seems to me it's a little too much to be a coincidence, so I dropped by to talk to you."

"I just took a couple of Valium, Mr. Harrigan. I'm delusional, remember?"

This wasn't going well. Clint cut a hard glance at the dog, which still hadn't stopped growling. "Will he attack?"

"He is a she, and she only attacks disagreeable cowboys."

Clint guessed he had that coming. He studied the dog for a moment, concluded that the ungainly creature was all growl and no bite, and then returned his gaze to Loni MacEwen. "You're not going to make this easy for me, are you?"

"Should I?"

Clint rarely apologized to anyone. The words *I'm sorry* always caught at the back of his throat. But when he knew he was in the wrong, he at least tried to make amends. "I was a little rude to you last night."

"A little?"

"Okay, a lot rude. It's not every day a psychic knocks on my door and tells me an outlandish story about a son I don't have and how he'll die if I don't save him. But I'm here now, and I'm ready to listen."

Loni wanted to close the door in his face, just as he'd done to her last night. Only she couldn't. He was Trevor Stiles's only hope. All day long she'd been pelted by visions of the child. He was still alive and trying to find his way out of the wilderness. Every step he took led him farther away from the river and rescue.

Snapping her fingers at Hannah, Loni drew the door open more widely, silently inviting Clint Harrigan in. He stepped across the threshold, cutting the mastiff a wide berth as he strode to the fireplace. *Flashback.* Just as he had in her vision two months ago, he turned to face her, his booted feet set wide apart, his work-hardened hands resting on his hips. Though he wasn't an exceedingly tall man or brawny by gymnasium standards, he dwarfed the small living room, filling it up in a way that made her feel claustrophobic. As she pushed the door closed, she shot a grateful glance at the open window, which at least let in some fresh air.

Apparently disturbed by Clint Harrigan's angry stance, Hannah growled and moved toward him. Loni dashed forward to grab the dog's collar. Harrigan ignored the mastiff, keeping his dark gaze riveted on Loni. After making Hannah sit, Loni straightened to stare back at him. As had happened in her vision, she felt the cool breeze coming in through the open window, and the scent of freshly cut grass wafted to her nostrils. Down the street somewhere, a dog started barking, and its owner yelled for it to be quiet.

Without preamble, Harrigan said, "I'm going into the Shoshone Wilderness Area to find the boy. I need you to come with me."

"That's an absolutely preposterous suggestion."

She started to turn away, but he clamped a hard hand over her arm.

"Look, lady," he said in that deep, smoky voice she remembered so well. "I'm no happier about this mess than you are. All this hocus-pocus stuff gives me the willies. I'll also remind you that you're the one who sought me out, not the other way around."

Hannah growled low in her throat, prompting Loni to jerk her arm free of Clint's grasp before her dog grew more agitated. "If I give you the willies, why are you even here?"

"That's a damned good question. I'm a doubting Thomas. I'll tell you that up front. I've never put much stock in clairvoyants."

Loni folded her arms. "Which prompts me to ask again, why are you here?"

"Because my gut's telling me I should be—and also because I'm taking what you might call a calculated leap of faith."

"Calculated?"

"There's no way you could have heard about the rafting accident yesterday afternoon. The story didn't go public until this morning. I called and checked to be sure." He tugged on his ear, his posture and expression both indicating that the discovery troubled him. "So I can only conclude that maybe you are a psychic. Either that or you have an inside source of information."

At least he was honest. "I do have an inside source of information." Loni tapped her temple. "It's right up here, Mr. Harrigan. And just for the record, I'm no happier about that than you are."

He gave her a long study. "Meaning?"

"I never asked to be psychic. I was born this way. Trust me when I say it isn't always fun."

He nodded as if that made a strange sort of sense to him. "No," he agreed, "I don't suppose it is, especially not if everyone reacts to you the way I did."

"People's reactions are only part of the problem. The other part is knowing about things others don't and being unable to do anything. Your little boy, for instance. He is absolutely terrified, and he's in grave danger. In the visions he seems so close I can almost touch him, only, of course, that's impossible. He can't hear me. He can't see me. There's nothing I can do to help him."

He bent his head, effectively blocking her view of his face with the brim of his hat. "I can't handle that. You saying he's my boy, I mean." He looked back up at her. "You've been right about everything else, including the fact that I once dated his mother, but I think you're getting your signals crossed about me being his dad. Sandra was one of the most honest people I've ever known. She wouldn't have kept my child from me. I know that absolutely, without a trace of doubt."

Loni considered that revelation. It told her two things about him: that he was stubborn and that he was fiercely loyal, even to an old flame. Given that she was

Scottish and just a little mule-headed herself, she couldn't hold a stubborn streak against him, and she admired loyalty in anyone. It was also gratifying to discover that he had come to accept, however reluctantly, that she was actually receiving signals, no matter how inaccurate he deemed them to be.

"All right," she conceded. "Maybe I am getting my signals crossed." Loni knew that wasn't the case, but he'd come three-quarters of the way, and for the moment Trevor's parentage didn't really matter. Bottom line, he was a little boy in desperate need of this man's help. "I'll try to refrain from referring to him as your son again."

He inclined his head, a brief dip that barely passed for a nod. His body relaxed, and something resembling a smile fleetingly touched his molded lips. "Don't misunderstand. I'd love to have a kid. I just can't bring myself to believe Sandra was capable of that kind of deceit. It didn't work out for us, but that was no more her fault than mine. She was a fantastic person."

Loni saw grief in his eyes, and she mentally added another check mark to the good. He'd loved Trevor's mother, at least as a very dear friend, and he was shaken by her death.

"I'm sorry," she said softly. "That she died, I mean. I know it must be hard for you."

"Yes. Not hard like it would be if I lost a family member, but sad all the same. I can't believe she's gone."

A taut silence settled over the room. Then he said, "So what else have you seen?" He bent to scratch behind Hannah's ears. The mastiff moved closer to his leg, her brown eyes going blank and dreamy. "About the boy, I mean. Do you have any idea which side of the river he's on?"

Loni searched her memory. "No, I'm sorry. I only know he's using a compass, maybe trying to find his way to a road."

"Holy Mother," he rasped. "If he's going in the wrong direction he'll find no road." When he stopped petting Hannah, the dog leaned happily against his leg. "He could walk for fifty miles."

Though Loni knew nothing about the area Trevor was in, she'd already reached the same conclusion. "Looking on the bright side, Nana kept him from freezing to death last night. He also has two packs with him. I assume they must have washed up on the riverbank after the raft capsized. Fortunately the food inside one of them—candy bars, nuts, crackers, and the like—is in water-resistant packaging."

"He'll go through that in only a few days, even if he rations himself."

"Yes. Especially since he's sharing with Nana, who's as ravenous as he is. On another positive note, the dog caught—or will catch—a rabbit, so I'm praying she'll do that more than once so Trevor won't starve."

"What do you mean, 'caught or will catch'?"

"My visions don't come with the time and date blinking in one corner, Mr. Harrigan. I'm seldom sure if I'm seeing something that's already happened, or if it's happening right then, or if it will happen in the future. I also see things out of sequence sometimes."

A deep frown pleated his forehead. "That has to be confusing."

Loni wasn't certain whether he was being sincere or condescending. She decided it didn't matter. He was there, and he was listening. "It's like being born with eleven toes. You get used to it."

He nudged the hat farther back on his head. "You actually see pictures of all this stuff inside your head?"

Loni's visions were more like film trailers, projected onto a 3-D screen, but she saw no point in correcting him. "Yes. When Nana brings the rabbit, Trevor finds a small ax and butane lighter in one of the packs, and he's able to build a fire. Evidently someone has taught him at least a few survival skills. He manages to skin the rabbit and cook it, anyway. He and the dog share the meat." She remembered something more. "Last night in one of my visions, wolves were howling. Trevor was terrified. He and Nana were inside a cave of some kind. I'm not sure how deep it went. I couldn't see the sky, only a faint glimmer of moonlight at the opening. That may be why the helicopter with the heat sensor has picked up nothing yet, because when they combed the area Trevor was in, he was shielded by thick stone."

"The heat sensors are a fabulous search tool, but they aren't always a help. Just last fall a boy got lost on a hiking trip, and so far as I know, he was never found." He rubbed his jaw. "As for hearing wolves, you must be getting your wires crossed again. Coyotes, possibly."

Loni shook her head. "No, I'm certain it was wolves. They sound different from coyotes. I've watched enough wildlife documentaries to know that."

"To my knowledge there are no wolves in this

section of the Cascades. Wolves were reintroduced to Idaho back in 1995, and a fledgling population has been reported in Washington's northern Cascades, but I've heard nothing of wolf sightings in Oregon."

"I heard wolves," Loni insisted. "I don't know how many, but I'm certain there was more than one."

"You have that much faith in what you see and hear during these visions you say you have?"

"Do you question what you see and hear?" she countered.

He drew his cell phone from his belt and punched some buttons. A second later he said, "Parker, it's Clint. You keep up on the wildlife in this country more than I do. Have you heard anything about wolves in the Shoshone Wilderness Area?" He listened for a moment. "An acquaintance of mine says she heard wolves in that area recently. Do you think that's possible?"

Loni's shoulders stiffened. Clint's gaze locked with hers.

"So essentially you're saying it's not likely." His brow furrowed in a thoughtful frown. "Really? You never mentioned that." Another silence. "Interesting. But you couldn't be sure?" He nodded. "Yeah, true enough. So what's your conclusion?" He finally nodded and said, "Thanks, bro. I'll catch you later."

He snapped the phone closed and clipped it back on his belt. "My brother. He can't say if you actually heard wolves or not. He did relate some interesting facts, though. While on a trail ride in that area last fall, he saw tracks he thought might be wolf, but they could just as easily have been those of a large dog. It's hard to tell the difference unless you're a trained tracker, which he's not, and hikers do take dogs with them along the trails.

"That said, a dead wolf—roadkill, evidently—was found along the highway outside Burns a couple of years ago. Another radio-collared wolf, a black female, crossed the Snake River into the northeastern part of the state. The authorities transported her back to Idaho, and she was found dead sometime after that. He can't remember if the carcass was recovered in Oregon or across the state line. I guess a couple of other wolves have also crossed over and met with untimely ends, one illegally shot."

Loni raised her chin. "If you're going to doubt every word I say, Mr. Harrigan, I can't be of much help to you."

"I'm a doubting Thomas. I told you that. You say you heard wolves. To my knowledge there are none in Oregon. Naturally I'm going to check it out."

"And now that you have . . . ?"

"I can't rule out the possibility that you heard wolves."

Loni arched an eyebrow. "So what do you plan to do about it?"

"It's not what *I'm* going to do, Ms. MacEwen, but what *we* are going to do."

"We?" she echoed. "As I said earlier, my going with you is a crazy idea."

"Not so crazy, if you think about it. The kid's on the move. You said so yourself. I'll never find him without your help."

"That isn't how it works. I've told you all I know. The rest is up to you."

He shook his head. "Do you have any idea how large that area is—or how far a child might walk in one day? You have to go along to help me pinpoint his location."

"You don't understand." Loni tried to think of a way to explain. "I can't summon the visions. They just happen. If I went with you, there's no guarantee I'd see anything more."

"I'll take my chances. You've been seeing the kid and his dog today. Right?"

"Yes, but . . . I've never even been in a wilderness area."

"I have. No worries on that count."

"And just like that, I'm supposed to go with you? I know next to nothing about you, Mr. Harrigan. Smart women don't take off alone into the wilderness with strangers."

"Look in your crystal ball and get to know me real fast then."

"I don't have a crystal ball, and I resent your implying that I might."

"Look into the future then; see if I'm going to murder you the first time you turn your back on me."

"I can't look into the future at will, either." Loni clenched her teeth. She pried them apart to add, "I really don't appreciate the sarcasm. Do you think that will convince me you're trustworthy?"

"That child's life is on the line. I'll also point out that I'm prepared to trust *you*. And that's not an easy thing for me. I've been a skeptic all my life, and now I'm trying to rearrange my whole way of thinking."

"I've never even gone camping," Loni confessed.

An expression of sheer amazement flickered over his face. "Never?"

"I was raised in the Seattle area. My dad's a banker. My mom's a horticulturist. He loves tennis, and she's into long-distance bicycling. As a family we only ever did city stuff—going on bike rides, playing tennis, visiting museums, shopping along the waterfront. The closest we came to camping was one summer when my folks rented a cabin at the lake for a couple of weeks."

"We'll work it out. I can't promise you the Hilton, but if we take enough pack animals in with us, I can at least make sure you're reasonably comfortable."

"Pack animals?" she echoed.

"Horses."

"*Horses*? You expect me to ride a horse?"

"Yes, unless you prefer to walk. With horses we can take enough supplies to last us at least a week. Searchers on foot can venture only so far from base camp before turning back. We'll be able to push deeper because we'll have our food and camping gear with us."

"*Horses?*" Loni echoed again. She'd never been within arm's reach of an equine. "I'm sorry, Mr. Harrigan. I don't ride."

He gave her a measuring look. "It appears to me you have all the necessary equipment. I'll teach you the rest." When Loni hesitated, he added, "Do you want to save this child or not?"

"Of course I want to save him."

Loni thought of Trevor's tear-streaked face, his lips blue from the cold. If there was a chance, however slim, that she might help Clint Harrigan find the boy, how could she say no? As Gram had pointed out last night,

Loni had the proceeds from the sale of her Washington home to keep her afloat financially until she got her shop open for business. A delay of a few days wouldn't send her into bankruptcy.

Reaching a snap decision, she said, "All right, I'll go with you. Just understand from the start that I may be more trouble than I'm worth."

She hurried into the kitchen to phone her sister, who would have to look after Hannah during her absence. Fortunately Deirdre had a key to the house and could pick up the dog after Loni had left.

"You're going to *what*?" Deirdre cried.

"I'm going with Mr. Harrigan into the Shoshone Wilderness Area. He hopes I can help pinpoint Trevor's location."

"On *horseback*? You'll get bucked off and break your neck. Have you lost your mind?"

Loni had already asked herself the same question. "Maybe, but it's something I have to do."

After ending the call, Loni hurried to the bathroom to collect her toiletries and cosmetics, then ran to her bedroom to start packing her clothes. She nearly jumped out of her skin when Clint Harrigan spoke from directly behind her.

"Forget the suitcase. Just toss everything in a pillowcase. We'll be putting all of it into packs, anyway." He picked up a pair of her slacks. "Don't you have any jeans?"

"Of course." Loni held them up as evidence.

He eyed the flowers embroidered over one pocket. "And that's it, only one pair?"

"I wear jeans on the weekends sometimes. One pair is all I need."

He grabbed one of her running shoes. "Where are your boots?"

Loni's only boots were calf-high with three-inch heels. She didn't think they were what he had in mind. "I don't have any boots. Not the right kind, anyway. I don't hike or ride horses, so all I have are fancy ones to wear with dresses or skirts."

He stripped the case off one of her pillows and began sorting through her clothing, stuffing some of it inside, throwing other things onto a discard pile. "No worries. My sister, Samantha, is about your size. I'm sure she'll be happy to lend you some riding boots and all the clothes you'll need."

"That's my warmest sweater," she protested as he flung it aside.

"If it gets wet and we try to dry it near a fire, it'll melt. You need fleece, and lots of it. It's light, very warm, blocks against the wind, and air-dries fairly fast." One of her favorite sweatshirts went on the discard pile. "That'll soak up water like a sponge. You could dry it by the fire, but it'd take two days."

To Loni's relief he didn't linger over her lacy underwear. He just put it in the pillowcase uncontested. Her Pooh Bear nightshirt didn't pass muster, though, and when he grabbed her toiletry bag, Loni reached to rescue it.

"I'll need all of that."

"You won't need this," he said, holding up a tube of mascara. "Or this," he added, plucking out a lipstick.

"Bare essentials, and that's it. I can't burden my horses with anything unnecessary."

In the end all that remained in Loni's cosmetic bag were her hairbrush, a tin of medicated lip balm, tampons, sunscreen, and her toothpaste and toothbrush. He even discarded her travel mirror.

His high-handed manner started to make Loni angry. But then she thought of the horses, which would be carrying everything on their backs, including her, and she felt ashamed for getting miffed at him. He was only looking out for his animals, and she couldn't fault him for that.

So instead of blistering his ears with a critique of his behavior, she said, "I appreciate the help. Like I said earlier, I'm a total dunce when it comes to this kind of thing."

He angled her a sharp look; then his eyes warmed. He didn't exactly smile, but his mouth twitched at one corner. "I'm a dunce at some things myself. Riding bikes in the city, for instance. I'd probably get myself killed."

The taut feeling in Loni's throat that always came with anger vanished almost as quickly as it came, and she laughed. "Even experienced bicyclists can get themselves killed in the Seattle area."

"Same goes for wilderness rides." He went back to sorting through her clothing. "If I seem pushy and overbearing, it's only because there's no time to waste. We have to reach the south trailhead tonight, grab a few hours' sleep, and start in at dawn. And trust me, packing for a wilderness trek on horses isn't anything like loading a bike. It'll take me a few hours to get our gear ready. I not only have to pack for us, but also for my animals."

"I'll help if you'll tell me what to do."

This time the twitch of his lips eased into a crooked grin. "Offer accepted."

Chapter Three

Leaving Clint Harrigan to finish with the packing, Loni made her rounds of the house, pulling blinds and cutting the power to all the small appliances she used on a regular basis. All the other household gadgets were routinely left unplugged except when she needed them.

She was bent over and twisted awkwardly at the waist with her head behind the television when he startled her once again by speaking from directly behind her.

"You worried about fire while you're gone or something?"

Loni finished jerking the cord from the receptacle and turned to face him. He held the top of her embroidered pillowcase bunched in one fist. Not for the first time she felt a jolt of amazement to actually be standing face-to-face with him. He looked exactly as he had in her dreams, dark and ruggedly handsome, but in the flesh he had a much greater impact on her nerves, giving her a strange and purely feminine case of jitters.

She had to make a concentrated effort to collect her thoughts and recall his question.

"Most appliances are energy vampires, especially this one." She could only hope he didn't notice that her hand was shaking as she patted the television console. "This monster sucks power even when it's turned off because it's always on standby for a click of the remote control."

She expected him to snort with disdain, the way most people did. Instead he said, "I never thought of that. How much electricity does a television use when it's turned off but still plugged in?"

"I'm not sure, but every little bit adds up." Loni could have recited dozens of statistics, but her views on the average American's wasteful consumption of energy and natural resources didn't seem all that important compared to the peril little Trevor was in. She pushed a curly lock of hair from her eyes. "And you really shouldn't get me started. I can go on and on."

"Sounds like a good topic of conversation for while we're on the trail. Maybe I'll learn something."

"Or you'll be bored to distraction. Not everyone shares my interest in environmental issues." She grabbed her blue parka from the narrow coat closet, collected her purse, then bent to give Hannah farewell pats and hugs before turning out all but one lamp so Deirdre would be able to see when she came in. "Okay, I'm ready."

He followed her out onto the porch. As she fumbled to lock the door she was acutely aware of him standing behind her. She could have sworn she felt his warm breath stirring her hair.

As they walked toward his vehicle, his boot heels tapped the cement behind her, his pace slowing to accommodate hers. The illumination from the streetlights enabled Loni to see that the rifle was still in his truck. As he drew abreast of her near the front bumper, he hooked a thumb toward her Suburban, parked in front of the garage.

"What's a greenie doing with a gas hog like that?"

"Greenie!" she said with a laugh. "I'm not a greenie or a spotted-owl lover simply because I try to cut down on my power consumption and worry about carbon dioxide emissions. That's half the problem in this country. People are afraid to dwell too much on environmental concerns for fear of being labeled a fanatic."

He opened the rear door on the driver's side of the Ford and tossed the pillowcase on the backseat. "I can relate to that. People call me names, too—cowboy, buckaroo, goat roper, or shit-kicker. They also assume I have no secondary education, can't understand long words, never read books, and can only dance if I'm wearing a Stetson and holding on to my belt."

Given the fact that Loni had thought of him as her dream cowboy practically all her life, she felt a pang of guilt. "You don't like being called a cowboy?"

The brim of his Stetson shadowed his face, obscuring his expression so she couldn't tell whether he was smiling or scowling. "No better than you like being called a greenie. I'm a horseman. I suppose you could call me a buckaroo and be halfway on target."

Loni lifted her shoulders in a bewildered shrug. "What exactly is a buckaroo?"

"I'll explain on the way. And my question still stands—why the gas hog?"

"I'm an interior decorator. I couldn't find an economical van large enough to haul all the things I need for my work." She eyed his pickup. "And just for the record, my Suburban sips fuel compared to Big Gulp, here." She patted the truck fender as she circled around to the passenger side. "Fair is fair. Why do you drive a tank and carry a weapon everywhere you go?"

"I discovered the hard way that I can't pull an eight-horse trailer with an economy truck. The rifle is for emergencies I pray will never happen."

"On your ranch?"

"That's right. When I was teenager one of my father's stallions tried to jump a fence to reach a mare and impaled itself on a post."

Loni winced. "Oh, my, how horrible."

"It was horrible, all right, and only made worse when my dad had to run all the way back to the house for a rifle to put the poor critter out of its misery. I've made sure I have a weapon handy ever since."

The picture that formed in Loni's mind made her stomach clench. "The poor stallion," was all she could think to say.

He opened his door just as she opened hers. She watched him swing up onto the seat by catching hold of a ceiling grip, but she was too short to reach the one on her side. *Problem.* There was no running board for her to step up on, and the vehicle was jacked up off the ground higher than her hip. To complicate matters, in the dim light she could see junk piled ankle-deep on the floorboard.

He closed his door and glanced over at her. "Something wrong?"

"I forgot my stilts."

He extended a hand to her. Loni clasped his hard fingers and hiked up one leg to brace her foot on the door runner. The next instant she catapulted into the cab and almost landed on the center console.

"Oops," he said as she caught her balance and plopped on the passenger seat. "Sorry about that. You're a lot lighter than you look."

Lighter than she looked? *What a charmer.* Loni wondered if the five pounds she'd gained while redecorating the house and renovating her shop had all settled on her hips. Too much fast food, no time to work out. She was one of those unfortunate people who constantly struggled to stay trim.

She bent forward over her parted knees to scoop up items from her purse, which had somehow slipped from her shoulder and spilled onto the floorboard while she was airborne. Her searching fingers met with countless items not belonging to her: greasy wrenches, ropes, oily rags, strips of leather, pieces of straw, and oddly shaped metal things she couldn't identify in the shadows. While her head was still pressed against the glove box, the truck rumbled to life, the roar of the diesel engine almost deafening, the vibration of the dash rattling her teeth.

When she sat back to fasten her seat belt, she couldn't help but smile. Her dream cowboy? She'd obviously misinterpreted the meaning of her dreams. Clint Harrigan was her exact opposite. She was a fanatic about keeping her vehicle tidy; his was a total wreck. She was passionate about energy conservation and protecting the environment; he'd never even thought about it much. She liked him well enough so far, but she honestly couldn't imagine the two of them ever being anything more than friends.

In no time at all they would drive each other crazy.

Three hours later Clint was ready to head out. He'd decided to take eight horses, two to carry riders and light packs, another pair to carry his and Loni's gear and supplies, and four more to pack in enough feed to last a week. The equines would be working hard, and if there was little grass available along the trail for grazing, each horse would require fifteen to twenty pounds of cubed alfalfa a day.

Even by taking along four pack animals to carry only the feed, Clint would be exceeding the recommended weight load per horse by twenty pounds the first day. Fortunately the alfalfa would dwindle rapidly, until the four extra horses would be carrying almost nothing toward the end of the trip.

That would be good. Clint expected to be traveling over rugged terrain much of the time, possibly well away from the beaten path. The four lightly worked horses could be used to spell those carrying heavier loads, affording all the animals intermittent rest periods along the way.

Mentally going over his checklist to be sure he had forgotten nothing, Clint angled across the stable yard toward his truck, which he'd left running with the heater on high to keep his psychic search partner warm while he took care of last-minute details. As he passed the horse trailer he noticed a tire that looked low. *Great.* If it wasn't one thing it was another.

He lowered the tailgate of the Ford, vaulted up into the bed, and pawed through the maze of paraphernalia and gear until he found the portable air compressor and a tire gauge. After plugging the compressor into a special outlet he'd had installed behind the left wheel well, he jumped back to the ground and crouched to inflate the tire. Only, no sooner had he let loose with a blast of air than the truck engine died.

Now what? Like he needed vehicle trouble to cap off an already exhausting night? Muttering curses, he strode the length of the truck, jerked open the driver's door, and leaned in to restart the engine. To his surprise he found the ignition key turned off. He angled a puzzled look at Loni.

"Did you just cut the engine?"

In the glow of the yard light her big blue eyes glistened. "Yes. If you're going to leave a vehicle for more than thirty seconds, you waste less fuel if you turn off the engine and restart it when you return."

Clint bit down hard on his back teeth. He was tired, both mentally and physically. It was no easy task to prepare for a wilderness ride, and he hated doing it in a rush. If he forgot something important, it could result in disaster—not only for him and Loni, but also for his horses.

"I *need* the truck to be running right now," he said slowly, making a concentrated effort not to raise his voice.

"Oh." She lifted her shoulders in a shrug. "Sorry. I didn't realize."

Over the course of the evening Clint had come to understand that there was a host of things this lady didn't realize. She seemed to be frightened of the horses, yet she took stupid risks, stepping too close behind them and compounding the offense by speaking without first letting the horse know she was there. That was a very good way to get kicked. He was going to have his hands full making sure she didn't get hurt. Fortunately the eight horses he'd chosen for the journey were used every year for trail riding and were pretty much bulletproof.

"I'm trying to air up a trailer tire." He'd long since lost track of how many things he'd had to explain to her. She understood none of the terms that came second nature to him. "The compressor runs off DC power. The engine needs to be running in order for it to work."

A few minutes later, when Clint got in the truck, Loni was huddled against her door and didn't look over at him. He wondered what she was pissed about but decided not to ask. The silence was a relief, allowing him to think without interruption.

As he drove out to the main road, he mentally went back over his packing list. Had he remembered the Banamine, in case a horse got colic? Check. Penicillin for possible infections? Check. Pack saw? Check. Small ax? Check. Space blankets? Check. Gel pads for Loni's saddle? Check. Hooter's miracle salve, in case she got saddle sores anyway? Check. Cowbells? Check. A first-aid kit for the horses? Check. A first-aid kit for humans? Check. The portable cell phone charger, adaptors, and double-A batteries? Check.

"The wolves are back."

Clint lost his thought and scowled at her. "What?"

"The wolves," she said thinly. "They're back, and they sound closer tonight. Nana didn't growl the last time, but she's growling now."

A prickle of unease crawled up the back of Clint's neck. She stared straight ahead, a distant look in her eyes. It was eerie.

"Are you there with them right now?" Clint could almost hear the theme song for *Twilight Zone* playing in his head.

"No. I wouldn't be talking to you if I were."

"I see."

"I was with them while you were airing up the tire, though."

Now he understood her silent withdrawal when he'd climbed into the cab. "You okay?" It was all he could think to say.

"Yes," she said softly. "But Trevor is afraid to close his eyes."

Clint thought he saw tears in hers, and an odd tightness moved into his throat. She was totally serious. A part of him still wanted to believe it was all a sham, that he'd catch her in a lie sooner or later. He wasn't sure why it was so difficult for him to simply buy her story, but it was.

She fixed him with a frightened gaze. "Will they hurt him, do you think?"

"The wolves?" The tightness in his throat grew more pronounced. "I don't think you should worry about that. We're not even sure there are wolves out there."

"I'm sure," she countered with unshakable conviction. "Is there a possibility that they'll hurt him?"

"I'm no expert on wolves, never having lived in an area where they're common. But if they're like most predators, they'll only attack a human if they're starving. It being early June, I think that's unlikely. There should be plenty of wild game in that area to keep their bellies full."

Clint didn't often lie by omission or tell half-truths, but in this instance he felt justified. Until they found Trevor, there was nothing Loni could do to help the child. So why add to her worries? Besides, what he'd told her was essentially true: Most predators hesitated to attack adult humans. He'd simply failed to mention that Trevor, being a little guy, was an easier mark. If there were indeed wolves in the wilderness area, the boy's only hope might be Nana, the faithful Saint Bernard, who was probably large enough to make a wolf think twice before taking her on.

In the greenish glow of the dash lights, he saw Loni's body relax. Dressed in his sister Samantha's clothing, she at least *looked* ready for a trail ride. Snug Wrangler jeans showcased her hips and shapely thighs, an oversize fleece jacket enveloping her upper body. The John Deere baseball cap that Sam had lent her sat on the dash, as yet unused, but not for long. Come tomorrow the bill of the cap would come in handy for shading her eyes.

"I wish I could reach out and hug him," she said softly. "No child should ever be alone like he is right now."

"He has Nana," Clint reminded her. "Judging by all

you told me, that Saint Bernard will fight to the death to protect him."

"Yes," she agreed. "I believe she will."

"So stop worrying," he advised. "Saint Bernards are huge dogs. Even if one or two wolves get in too close, they'll have a hell of a time taking her down."

It was around midnight when they reached the south trailhead. While Clint unloaded the horses from the trailer, Loni decided to make herself useful by gathering firewood. After finding a flashlight in the truck, she set off into the nearby trees to collect fallen branches and sticks. The crook of her left arm was piled high with fuel when it suddenly dawned on her that she'd wandered farther from the truck than she intended.

Time to turn back. Picking her way with the flashlight, she retraced her steps. Only she walked and walked without reaching the clearing. Not good. Loni's pulse rate quickened. *I'm not lost*, she assured herself. She couldn't be. She'd gone only a little way. The truck was probably a few feet from her, and she simply couldn't see it.

"Hello?" she called. "Mr. Harrigan?"

No answer. Loni strained her ears, but all she heard was the night wind whispering in the trees.

"Hello?"

With a shaky sigh she shone the flashlight around, trying to spot something familiar. *Problem*. All the ponderosa pines and slick-leaf bushes looked alike. She couldn't be sure whether she'd come this way earlier or not.

Determined to stay calm, she decided the smart thing would be to walk in ever-larger circles until she stumbled upon the clearing. So off she went, making the first circle, the wood still clutched in one arm. Every few steps she hollered for Clint, hoping she'd hear him shout back.

It took Clint the better part of an hour to get the horses settled in for what remained of the night. He had to string a high line between two trees, no easy feat in the dark. Then he had to tie the horses off, spacing them far enough apart to prevent any kicking or entanglement in the lead ropes. Once he got them fed and double-checked all the ropes, he set himself to the task of building a fire pit and pitching the tent.

He was searching for the pack that held the tent when he suddenly noticed the silence. A prickle of alarm raised the hair on his arms.

"Ms. MacEwen?"

Thinking she might be in the truck, Clint opened the driver's door to check. The cab was empty. He closed the door and turned to gaze at the surrounding woodlands. Why hadn't he paid closer attention to what she was doing? He'd no sooner asked himself that question than the answer came to him: He was accustomed to trail riding with mostly experienced people, and it was never necessary to watch after them or keep tabs on their whereabouts.

"Ms. MacEwen?"

When she didn't answer Clint cursed under his breath. *No way. She wouldn't have wandered off.* The last time he'd seen her, she'd been zigzagging through the trees with a flashlight, collecting firewood.

Clint found another flashlight under the seat of his truck and set off in that direction. Some clairvoyant he had on his hands. If she was so damned perceptive, how in the hell could she possibly get turned around only a hundred yards from camp?

Relief eased some of the tension from his shoulders when he found her tracks. After following them for a while, he realized she was moving in widening circles, an excellent strategy if only she'd been moving closer to the clearing. Instead her tracks became ever more erratic, the circles becoming long ovals, figure eights, and then aimless meandering. She was clearly confused and had lost all sense of direction. Even worse, she was moving east, ever farther from the clearing.

A cougar screamed, its cry cutting eerily through the cold night air. *Shit, shit, shit.* His camp partner was out there somewhere, alone and unarmed. Clint stopped to check the magazine of his sidearm for cartridges, then, just to be on the safe side, injected one into the chamber. He didn't want Loni or himself to become an oversize feline's midnight snack.

"Loni!"

He kept shouting her name until he was almost hoarse, but he heard no answering call.

The flashlight batteries were going dead. Loni whacked the casing with the heel of her hand, hoping to brighten the fading beam. That didn't help. *Oh, God.* She was growing truly frightened now. She'd been walking for what seemed like forever, yelling Clint's name every few steps. There was no question about it: She was lost. And soon she would have no light.

She'd long since tossed away the wood she'd found. Now she truly understood how frightened Trevor must be. She could hear things in the woods around her, could feel eyes on her. Only wild animals, she assured herself. But what kind of animals? Deer were harmless enough, but what of coyotes, wolves, cougars, and bears?

Right then a piercing scream rent the night. It sounded close and startled Loni so badly that she almost wet her pants. Urgently hitting the flashlight again, she gulped down panic. *Stay calm; think.* Just because she'd never been in a wilderness area didn't mean she was a total idiot. She'd watched tons of survival movies. If two dogs and a spoiled cat could travel hundreds of miles to find their way home, she could surely make her way back to the clearing.

What she needed to do was get her bearings, only she hadn't taken any to start with. *Stupid, so stupid.* She'd been within sight of the clearing when she first started walking, and she honestly hadn't thought there was any risk of her getting turned around. Now the flashlight beam had grown so weak it barely illuminated the ground in front of her. She began tripping over branches and stumbling into holes. It was time to stop walking, she decided. The last thing she wanted was to fall and get hurt.

The feeble flashlight beam blinked out just then, plunging her into total blackness. Loni froze in her tracks, her eyes aching as she struggled to see. Overhead only slivers of faint moonlight shone through the thick canopy of trees. She remembered reading some-where that when a person got lost in the woods, the smartest thing to do was stay in one place and wait to be found. She was a little late in deciding on that course of action, but better now than never.

Waving one hand in front of her and tapping the ground with her feet, she moved cautiously forward. When her palm finally met with rough bark, she turned her back to it and slid down the tree trunk to sit on the ground. *This is better.* She felt safer, anyway. She set the useless flashlight beside her, not wanting to lose it in case Mr. Harrigan had extra batteries.

Huddling there in the blackness, listening to the pines creak and groan in the wind, Loni thought once again of poor little Trevor. With the thought came the bright flash of light that always preceded one of her vi-sions. The next instant, she felt cold rocks all around her. The dank, musty smell of damp earth and rotting pine needles filled her nostrils. Nana lay curled around Trevor, her huge, furry body insulating him from the cold.

Just as he had been earlier, Trevor was still in a small cave. Only where was it located? Loni listened for the river, but the only sounds she detected were the soft, rhythmic snores of the boy and dog, and the whishing of the pines swaying in the wind.

Finally the vision winked out, much as the flashlight had, and despite all her efforts Loni could see nothing more. Tears flooded her eyes because a helpless little boy was lost—and now so was she.

A branch snapped about twenty feet from her, the sound cracking in the darkness like a rifle shot. Loni almost parted company with her skin. She gulped and strained to hear. A bear, maybe? All she had to defend herself with was the flashlight. Why hadn't she thought to find a long stick?

"So there you are."

"Mr. Harrigan?" She sprang to her feet and peered through the inkiness, trying to locate him in the shadows. "Thank God you found me. I've been scared half to death."

She heard more twigs snapping. Then he suddenly emerged from the blackness, his pale blue shirt all she could make out at first. As he drew closer she was able to discern his outline, and then finally his face. His eyes glinted like flint striking steel.

"Did your flashlight go dead, too?" she asked.

"No." His voice sounded strained. "I've been turning it on every few seconds to find your trail, then turning it off to save the batteries. What the *hell* were you thinking to wander off in the dark? And damn it, don't you know to stop the minute you realize you're lost? I've been tracking you for almost an hour. There are critters in these woods with *very* big teeth. Did you hear that cougar scream?"

"No . . . yes. I guess maybe so. I heard a scream, anyway." She just hadn't known it was a large cat. "Is that how cougars sound?"

"It's how female cougars sound."

Loni couldn't blame him for being angry. She'd given him a bad scare. She started to apologize, but he cut her off.

"That cat is close, and she probably has kittens to feed. Do you know that a cougar can leap from a crouch as far as thirty feet, hitting its prey with such force that the spine snaps? It's early June. Predators that survived the winter may be *very* hungry right now. One unarmed clairvoyant would make a tasty meal for that cat and her babies."

Loni forgot all about offering him an apology. "I thought you said there was plenty of wild game for predators to feed on at this time of year."

"Maybe there is; maybe there isn't. It all depends on how hard a winter it was."

"How hard a winter was it? Didn't Oregon get a lot of snow this year?"

"These mountains always get a lot. You'll be seeing it tomorrow. This early in the year it hasn't all melted off."

"So you lied to me."

"I didn't lie." He picked up her flashlight and tucked it under his belt. "I just didn't tell you the whole truth. You were upset about Trevor. I saw no point in worrying you even more by listing all the dangers he might encounter out here. For all I know, maybe there *is* plenty of game."

"Where I come from, failing to divulge the whole truth is the same as lying, Mr. Harrigan."

He gave her a hard look. "Call it however you see it, Ms. MacEwen. All I did was try to ease your mind."

He set off without glancing back to make sure she was following.

"*Wait!*" she cried. "I don't want to lose you."

"Then pick up your pace. It's late, I'm tired, and it's a long way back to camp."

Loni scrambled after him, but the darkness and the

deadfall at her feet slowed her down, and soon she couldn't see him.

"Clint? Don't leave me. I can't find the way back by myself!"

He reappeared so suddenly that she gave a startled squeak. His breath wafted over her face, warm, steamy, and smelling of wintergreen. After seeing him dip snuff, she couldn't delude herself into thinking that he'd been sucking on breath mints.

"What seems to be the major malfunction here?" he asked.

"I can barely see my hand in front of my face. It's *dark*, in case you haven't noticed, and *you* have the flashlight."

"It isn't *that* dark. Are you night-blind or something?"

"I guess maybe so. I can't see where I'm putting my feet."

"A night-blind psychic? Can you explain that to me?"

A flare of temper turned Loni's cheeks hot. "What's to explain?"

"It makes no sense. How can a person with second sight be night-blind?"

"I don't know. That's just how it is."

He huffed under his breath. "If I find out this is all a hoax and you've dragged me out here on a wild-goose chase, I'm not going to be a happy camper. Do I make myself perfectly clear?"

"Pretty clear. Now let me clarify something. This is *not* a hoax. What do you think, that I'm *crazy*? I'm cold, exhausted, and hungry. I've been walking for what seems like forever in someone else's boots, which don't fit me right, and now I have blisters on both heels. My butt is wet from sitting on the ground. I have bark and sticks in my hair, and slivers in my fingers. A *hoax*? If I wanted to lead you on a wild-goose chase, Mr. Harrigan, I'd do it at Macy's with a latte from Starbucks in my hand!"

"*Macy's*?" he echoed in bewilderment.

"Furthermore, I'm the unhappy camper. I didn't want to come out here in the first place. It was *you* who insisted on it."

"A decision I'm already coming to regret. How can you help me find that child when you can't walk a hundred yards from the truck without getting lost yourself?"

"I never said I could help you find him!" Loni had grown so angry she was shaking. "I tried to tell you this isn't how it works, that I can't summon the visions at will. They just come—or they don't. I have no control over them."

She pushed past him, stepped into a hole, and almost fell. After regaining her balance, she struck off again.

"Where the hell do you think you're going?"

"Back to the truck. Once there I'm calling my sister and going home. This was a bad idea from the start."

"You're heading the wrong way."

Loni stopped, knotted her hands into fists, and turned to peer at him through the gloom. "It's the way you were going a minute ago."

"No, it's not." Was that *laughter* she heard in his voice? Flashlight now on, the beam pooling at his feet, he stood in the reflective glow, a thumb hooked over his belt, one hip cocked, one knee bent. With a swing of his head, he said, "I was going that way."

Correcting her course, Loni set off again.

"Tree dead ahead!"

She patted the air in front of her. "There isn't a tree."

"Take three more steps and you'll find it. Probably with your nose."

She clenched her teeth and carefully inched forward.

"Watch out for that log, too. I have enough to worry about without you falling and breaking your fool neck."

Loni drew to a stop. "Are all cowboys so charming?"

"Are all greenies so entertaining? I could sell tickets." He sauntered toward her. Coming to a halt less than an arm's reach away, he turned off the light and said, "Listen to us, calling each other names like a couple of kids. I don't know about you, but I'm thinking we need to back up and start over. You with me on that?"

Loni wanted to smack him before she let go of her anger. How dared he suggest that this was all a hoax? "Certainly. You go first."

"With what?"

"An apology."

He rubbed his jaw, then kicked at something she couldn't see. "I was a little cranky."

"A *little*?"

"Okay, a lot. I'm tired, worried about the trip, and you scared the ever-loving *shit* out of me. It's not easy to track someone in the dark. I was afraid I might not find you." He rubbed beside his nose this time. "And, quite frankly, I got pissed when you called me a liar."

"I didn't call you a liar, precisely. I only said you lied to me about one thing."

"There's a difference?"

"Oh, I see. So it's okay for you to call me a liar, but it's not okay for me to return the favor?"

"I never called you a liar."

"Did so."

"Did not."

"Did so."

"I did *not!*"

"What was all that about this being a hoax and a wild-goose chase then?"

"Oh, that."

"Yes, *that.*"

He swept his hat from his head to whack it against his leg. His curly black hair glistened like polished jet in the faint moonlight. "I shouldn't have said all that. It's just hard for me, you know? I never had any call to believe in psychics until today, and I'm still struggling with it. You're an oxymoron personified. Who ever heard of a night-blind clairvoyant? How is it you can see things I can't, yet be as blind as a bat in the dark?"

Loni folded her arms. "Is this how you always apologize?"

"I'm not doing it to suit you?"

"You might try saying, 'I'm sorry I acted like a jerk.'"

He settled his hat back on his head. "Okay, fine. I acted like a jerk. Does that satisfy you?"

Loni bit back a smile. "I'm getting it. You can't say you're sorry, can you?"

"Sure I can."

"Then say it."

He gazed off for a moment.

"It's really easy. Repeat after me. 'I'm sorry.' "

He sighed and kicked something again. "Okay, fine. If that's all that'll satisfy you, I apologize."

She couldn't help herself and laughed. "You *still* didn't say it. Come on, a big, rugged fellow like you should be able to spit out two little words."

She heard the hollow *plunk* of his throat as he swallowed. "Fine. I'm sorry." The words sounded clipped and forced. "I was out of line to accuse you of leading me on a wild-goose chase. And I shouldn't have chewed you out for getting lost."

It was Loni's turn to sigh, and with the release of breath, all her anger left her as well. "I'm sorry, too. It was kind of you to try to ease my mind about Trevor, and I shouldn't have gotten mad about it. There's nothing I can do for him, after all." It was her turn to nudge invisible things around on the ground with the toe of her boot. "And now I'm worried. Really worried. I'm fairly certain he's no longer near the river."

"He's not?"

"No, he's still in a cave—a really small one compared to the one last night, so maybe it's only a narrow fissure in the rocks. I think it goes in pretty far, though. I couldn't see anything, not even a bit of starlight."

"Why am I not surprised?"

She decided to let that pass. "Anyway, when I listened I couldn't hear the river."

"Shit. If he'd follow the river, it would eventually lead him to the highway."

"Would it? Hmm. The next time I get lost I'll remember that."

He chuckled. Then he sobered. "I really am sorry I accused you of being a fake. A night-blind psychic. It blew my mind away."

"And I'm sorry I wandered off. One minute the truck was right there, and the next it was gone. I thought I knew the way back, only I didn't."

"How bad are the blisters?"

"Pretty bad."

He stepped in close and took hold of her arm. "Let's go to camp. I've got some goop that'll fix you right up, and tomorrow, thank God, you'll be riding, not walking."

"I never thought I'd say it, but riding sounds really, *really* good all of a sudden."

They set out and had been walking quite some time when Loni felt compelled to bring up their argument again.

"I need to clarify some things," she said. "My second sight isn't a physical ability. I'm not even sure it's a mental ability. It's more like having a receiver inside my head, something over which I have no control. I can't summon a vision. In fact, they mostly take me by surprise. And I honestly think I could be stone blind and still *see*. Does that make any sense?"

"No," he replied. Then, as if to take the sting out of his answer, he smiled at her. "Very little of this makes sense to me."

That was fair, Loni decided, and also honest. Instead of feeling offended, she appreciated his candor. At least she knew exactly where she stood with him.

"What's it like?" he asked suddenly. "Having a vision, I mean."

"Sort of like watching a movie, only not. More like virtual reality, actually. I'm *in* the vision. I can feel, taste, smell, and hear things. I'm *there*, only not."

"That must be spooky as hell."

"Sometimes."

"Tree." He drew her sharply to the left. "How long have you been clairvoyant?"

"All my life." With her free hand she rubbed the nape of her neck, where her scarlet birthmark was hidden beneath her hair. "In my grandmother's family, one female child is born with the gift in every generation. It skipped my older sister, Deirdre, and I got it instead."

"You don't sound too happy about it." He pulled her sharply to the right. "Fallen log. Don't trip."

Though Loni's eyes burned with the attempt, she couldn't see the obstacle. "I'm not happy about it," she confessed. "As I told you earlier tonight, it isn't always fun."

"If it happens in every generation, there must be others in your family."

"My mother and grandmother," she replied. "Only their abilities aren't as strong as mine."

"How's that?"

Loni stepped into a hole and would have fallen if not for his steely grip on her arm. "Ouch!"

"What? Did you twist your ankle?"

"No, I bit the tip of my tongue." She pressed the throbbing end against her teeth to ease the sting. "Where were we?"

"You were going to explain how your gift is stronger than your mother's and grandmother's."

"Oh. Every few generations one of us is born with several abilities instead of just one."

"Several? I'm not following."

As much as Loni detested the use of psychic terms, there were times when they came in handy. "The word *psychic* is a blanket term to describe an individual with some form of ESP. There are clairvoyants, clairaudients, telepaths, those with telekinetic abilities, psychometrists, mediums, channelers, and diviners. But only a rare few have multiple abilities."

"And you're one of them?"

"Yes."

"Hmm. What abilities do you have?"

"It's simpler to list what abilities I don't have. I can't move objects with my mind, and I don't communicate with the spirit world in any way. I'm also a total loss at map divination."

"Map *what*?"

"Some psychics can locate missing persons by studying a map, commonly referred to as map witching."

"But you can read minds?"

Loni tensed, for this was when most men ran in the other direction. "Yes, to a degree. In visions I'm often able to pick up on someone's thoughts, but mostly I'm just empathic, picking up on physical sensations and emotions."

He pushed his hat back to give her a long look. "If you tried, could you read my mind?"

Loni shook her head. "It only happens in visions—which sometimes occur when someone touches me, like yesterday at the supermarket when we bumped heads. And then I only saw the rafting accident, my focus mainly on Trevor."

"Mainly?"

"I somehow picked up on your name," she revealed. "That's never happened before that I can remember." A wave of sadness washed over her as she recalled another time when she might have saved a young woman's life if only she'd received that kind of information. "Trevor's name came to me as well—along with the dog's and Sandra's. Only I didn't get their surname like I did with you."

"So that's how you found me last night, because you learned my name when I touched you?"

Loni nodded. Then, glancing up at him, she said, "You think I'm totally crazy, don't you?"

Clint wasn't sure what he thought. He knew only that believing in her story came hard for him. "No, I don't think you're crazy." *Inventive* seemed a better word, but for the sake of their mission to find Trevor Stiles, he decided to keep that opinion to himself. "I'm just sorting my way through as best I can."

"And trying to believe me?" she offered.

"Tree," he muttered.

She stumbled against him as he changed course, her smaller and much softer body bumping full-length against his. Upon impact he heard her breath rush from her lungs.

"You okay?"

"Fine," she assured him.

Clint had been so interested in her story that he'd forgotten to watch where he was going. He drew to a sudden stop.

"What?" she asked tautly. "Did you hear something?"

He released her arm and drew his flashlight from under his belt. "Shit," he said under his breath.

She pressed closer to him. "Is there something out there?"

There was a multitude of things out there. Clint just couldn't say for sure that his truck was one of them. "It's fine. No worries. I'm just trying to get my bearings."

Sammy, Clint's baby sister, had a strict rule against vile language, especially in mixed company, but that didn't stop him from thinking, *Fuck*, with a big F. He'd lost his bearings. A horrible urge to laugh came over him, only frustration quickly burned it away.

He turned in a full circle, trying to get a fix on the stars. *Yeah, right.* The tree canopy overhead was so thick that he could see only patches of sky.

"Oh, God. We aren't lost, are we?"

"I have never been lost in my entire life," Clint assured her. "I know exactly where I'm at. I just don't know precisely where our camp is from here."

She made a faint squeaky noise. "Oh, *God.* We *are* lost."

"We are *not* lost. Just be patient and let me get a fix on which direction we need to go."

Only that was impossible. It was too damned dark to see the surrounding terrain. Despite his disavowals, he was, quite simply, lost. Somehow he didn't think that news should be shared with a city slicker whose eyes were already wide with fright.

So instead Clint seized hold of her again and began

doing precisely what he'd railed at her for doing: He wandered around in the woods. Keeping a tight grip on her arm, he finally stumbled into a small clearing where he could see the sky and get his bearings.

"The truck is due west of us," he informed her.

Pulling her close to his side, he set off again, helping her over logs, grabbing her closer when she almost fell, and hating the necessity because it felt really good when her slender body pressed softly against him.

Loni MacEwen was one fine armful of woman.

Chapter Four

When they got back to camp, Loni resumed her search for firewood, keeping the truck and trailer in sight this time. While she worked, Clint pitched the tent and attached space blankets to the interior walls with Velcro tabs to insulate against the cold. Then he took the coffeepot down to the river, filled it with water put through a compact hiker's filter, and returned to camp to lay a fire for morning.

Loni stood near the tent, shivering and rubbing her arms. "Please tell me you don't expect me to sleep in this thing."

Clint crouched down to arrange the firewood she'd collected. "The tent is all we've got for shelter."

"You want me to sleep on the ground under that swatch of flimsy nylon in a wilderness area full of wolves, bears, and cougars?"

Clint wished now that he hadn't dwelled quite so much on the predatory prowess of mountain lions. "Trust me, you'll be perfectly safe."

"Famous last words. Bears attack people in tents. I've heard about it on the news."

"Those were grizzlies. Around here all we have are black bears. As a general rule the only time they bother campers is if food is left out."

"I'd still rather sleep in the truck."

He watched as she collected her sleeping bag from inside the tent and hurried to the vehicle.

"You won't be very comfortable in there," he called after her. "Or warm, either."

"I'll be fine."

Watching her ungainly ascent into the vehicle, Clint had to swallow back a chuckle. Up with first one foot and then the other, she twisted, grabbed for purchase, tried standing on her tiptoes to get one buttock up on the door runner, and finally resorted to crawling in. This tactic involved some interesting maneuvers that stretched the borrowed jeans taut across her rump, lending a whole new definition to the term *skintight* and making him appreciate as never before the fact that he had excellent night vision.

As she bedded down on the backseat, Clint wondered how she would manage in the middle of the night if nature called. He went to the truck, swung up over the tailgate, and searched for a feed bucket, which would at least provide her with something to step up on to enter the vehicle more easily.

Moments later, when he tapped on the rear door window, she came up on her knees, the pale oval of her face inches from his on the opposite side of the glass. He stepped back as the portal swung outward and the interior dome light came on.

"Yes?"

She sounded disgruntled and a little breathless—a

result, he felt sure, of her recent and difficult ascent into the vehicle. "I found you a bucket. It'll simplify matters if you need to"—he broke off right before he said, "take a leak," and quickly came up with—"use the restroom during the night."

Even with the light behind her and her face in shadow, he saw the scowl that pleated her delicately arched eyebrows. "I'm sorry?"

In Clint's social circle, when someone said, "I'm sorry," with a questioning inflection, it equated to, "Pardon me?" or "Could you repeat that?" So he raised the pail a little higher and tried again. "For in the middle of the night, just in case nature calls. It should make things a lot easier for you."

Her eyebrows arched higher. "You expect me to—" She broke off, stared at the bucket for a long moment, and then shook her head. "No, thank you. That's very thoughtful, but I'd rather just . . . you know."

Clint *didn't* know, so he lowered his arm, studied her for a long moment, and then upended the bucket on the dirt. "Suit yourself. But I'll leave it here, just in case you change your mind. I apologize for the long step up. This is my ranch vehicle, and when the fields go soft, the jacked-up undercarriage is all that keeps it from high-centering in the mud."

She fixed him with those large eyes. How, he wondered, could anyone's eyes look so damned beautiful in the semidark? It was as if they absorbed every flicker of moonlight and turned to molten silver. Made a man want to take a deep breath and dive in.

Pressing a slender hand to the base of her throat, she

said, "Oh! It's a *step*? I thought you meant for me to go in it."

Clint glanced down. It was a five-gallon feed bucket and wide across the brim. He rubbed beside his nose, a habit of his when he couldn't think what to say. Experience should have taught him by now that two rubs always served him better than one.

"Sweetheart, if you try sitting on that bucket you're liable to fall in. You're not that broad across the beam."

Silence. And then she laughed. It was a nice sound, he decided, light and almost musical, definitely a huge improvement over the gal who'd bleated like a sheep.

"Thank you. I *think*."

He went back over what he'd said and wanted to kick himself. Nothing like telling a woman he'd been taking measure of her backside. The brief lull in conversation gave him time to determine that he'd only dig himself a deeper hole if he said anything more. He circled the vehicle to open the front passenger door.

Still sitting up, Loni flashed him a questioning look. He popped open the glove compartment and fished through the contents to find the spare magazine for his nine-millimeter pistol.

When she saw the ammunition case, she asked, "What do you need that for?"

"I probably won't need it," he replied. "It's just a safety precaution."

"A precaution against what, chipmunks?"

Clint couldn't help but laugh. She had a good sense of humor. He was coming to enjoy her wit. "I was thinking more of the cougar."

"Aha! And you wanted me to sleep in that tent?"

"It's highly unlikely that the cougar will come near our camp. They're timid animals, and they usually try to avoid humans." He pushed on the uppermost cartridge to make sure the magazine was full. "That said, a female mountain lion might be desperate with hunger at this time of year, especially if she's nursing kittens. When I'm in a wilderness area I always err on the side of caution."

"You'd actually shoot her?" Concern laced her tone. "What about her babies?"

"I'd fire warning shots first. The sound normally frightens animals away. If that failed, and it came down to your life or the cougar's, I'd have no choice to make." He winked at her. "Just for the record, I've done a lot of riding in wilderness areas and was forced to kill an animal only once."

She twisted around to sit more erect, fully visible to him now through the console space between the two front seats. The sleeping bag sagged in thick folds around her waist. Even with her dark hair in a tangled mass of curls around her shoulders, she managed to look pretty. "What forced you to kill an animal?"

"I was a teenager at the time, and my father was still a novice at trail riding. We hobbled all our horses and put them out to graze. When we weren't watching the lead horse wandered off, and all the others followed. We were left stranded out in the middle of nowhere and had to walk back to base camp carrying as much of our gear and supplies as we could, saddles included. We were in for a long trek and ran out of food."

She looped her slender arms around her knees. "What kind of animal did you kill?"

"A rabbit. That was only an appetizer for the six of us. Fortunately my dad was more skilled at hunting and kept us from starving. After that we went on short trips until we became more experienced at wilderness riding."

"Did you ever find the horses?"

"Oh, yeah. They were at the trailhead waiting for us."

Her cheek dimpled in a teasing grin. "I'll bet you never hobbled the horses again."

"Sure, we did." He slipped the magazine into his shirt pocket. "We just made sure they were *effective* hobbles and put cowbells on the horses so we could tell where they were without watching them constantly."

"So *that's* why you packed those cowbells. I thought they were for scaring away bears."

Clint chuckled. "Black bears really aren't that much of a problem. If you get between a sow and her cubs, you may have some trouble on your hands, but for the most part they avoid humans. If you make enough noise along the trail, they'll usually clear out of the area."

"I still think I'll pass on sleeping in the tent, if it's all the same to you."

"Just so long as you understand that you'll have nothing but the tent to sleep in once we hit the trail."

She muttered something indiscernible.

"Now would be a good time to do what we can for those blisters."

He closed the door, strode to the back of the truck, and rummaged through the packs for the first-aid satchel. Moments later, when he circled around to the

rear passenger door again, Loni was sitting on the edge
of the backseat with her bare feet dangling in the cold
night air. The dome light behind her ignited her dark
hair, creating a golden nimbus around her head and
shoulders. Clint set the opened kit on the floorboard.
Bracing one foot on the bucket, he curled a hand over
her slender ankle, lifted her foot onto his knee, and
shifted in the illumination to get a close look at her
heel. The blister was an angry red.

"No broken skin yet," he noted. "That's a good
thing."

Her foot was small, with a high arch and dainty toes.
Clint had never had a foot fetish, but as he painted her
blisters with a clear liquid-bandage product, he finally
understood why some men did. *Red alert*. She was a
very pretty lady, but they were out here on a serious
mission, and complicating things with physical attraction wasn't a good plan.

She shivered when he grasped her other ankle. He
glanced up. "Cold?"

"No, I'm fine."

If she wasn't cold, why was she shivering? He also
noted that her voice sounded strained. Was it possible
that she found him as attractive as he did her? Most
likely not, he decided. She was probably just cold and
didn't want to complain.

When the first layer of liquid bandage had been applied, Clint leaned a shoulder against the door frame to
wait for it to dry. "One word of caution: If you do get
up during the night, don't wander too far from the
truck. All right? I'd hate for you to get lost again."

"Don't worry. I learned my lesson on that count."

He checked to see if the medication on her heels had dried and then applied another layer. "That should help protect the blisters come morning. Just make sure you wear the wool socks Sammy lent you, two pairs if the boots are a little too big."

"That's a good idea. I didn't think of it."

Clint closed the first-aid kit. "I don't know about you, but I'm worn out. I'm thinking it's time to turn in."

"Me, too." She shifted on the seat and extended an arm to close the truck door. "Good night, sleep tight."

The portal slammed shut before Clint could reply. He watched her through the window until the dome light blinked out. Then he fetched his saddle and sleeping bag, found a flat area at the opposite side of the fire pit, and prepared his bed. Before pulling off his boots, he went down on one knee, crossed himself, and whispered his nightly prayers, a habit drilled into him since childhood. Back then he'd always begun with, "Now I lay me down to sleep." Over the years he'd altered the words, but the essence remained the same. The day was done, and he needed someone up there to keep an eye peeled while he grabbed a little shut-eye.

He lay down, pillowing his head on the saddle. A glance at his luminous watch revealed that it was almost three in the morning. At this time of year in the Oregon Cascades, the sun rose just a few minutes shy of five thirty. *Damn.* In a little over two hours he'd have to be up and ready to go.

With a weary sigh he zipped up his sleeping bag, settled his hat over his eyes, and tried his damnedest to fall asleep. Unfortunately thoughts of Loni circled in his mind, holding drowsiness at bay. A multitalented psychic? He'd heard of clairvoyants, but clairaudients were new to him. Where he hailed from, folks who heard voices got hauled away to the loony bin. And what the hell was a psychometrist?

A grin settled on his mouth as he recalled their heated exchange in the woods. He admired that she'd given back as good as she got. *Macy's*? She was definitely a city girl through and through, but despite her lack of wilderness know-how, she seemed game to stick with this for however long it took.

Still sitting up with her feet outside the sleeping bag to let her heels dry, Loni watched Clint Harrigan prepare for bed, cowboy style. She couldn't believe he meant to use a saddle for a pillow, just like she'd seen in the movies. When he suddenly went down on one knee and crossed himself, she experienced a strange, tight sensation at the base of her throat. There was something formidably sensual about a strong, rugged man genuflecting in a wilderness area and bowing his head to pray.

Loni couldn't drag her gaze from him, and the longer she stared, the more pronounced the tightness in her throat became. A purely knee-jerk reaction, she assured herself. It was like coming upon a priceless work of art and being entranced by the sheer beauty of it. A man limned in silver by the moonlight, hat in hand, broad shoulders hunched, his posture blatantly masculine and yet supplicant, both at once.

All around him ponderosa pines loomed like giant sentinels. Yet when Loni broadened her scope, the trees seemed minuscule compared to the mountains, and the mountains, in turn, were dwarfed by the immenseness of the sky. They were all just tiny specks of humanity, she thought bleakly. How frightened Trevor must be right now, a little boy lost in all this vastness.

The thought made her heart hurt as she shimmied into the sleeping bag and drew the downy folds close for warmth. With the darkness pressing in on her like a thick blanket, she, too, crossed herself and prayed.

It seemed to Clint that only seconds passed before someone was shaking him awake. He tipped his hat back, cracked open his eyes, and saw Loni kneeling beside him. In the faint light of predawn she looked more like an angel than a flesh-and-blood woman, her oval face and delicate features as flawless as fine ivory. In his sleepy state he momentarily entertained the notion that she wanted to join him in his sleeping bag, a possibility that he didn't find distasteful.

No such luck. Instead of moving closer she sat back on her heels. "We're on the wrong side of the river."

"*What?*"

"Trevor is on the other side of the river," she repeated.

Coming slowly awake, Clint sat up and smoothed a hand over his hair. "How did you suddenly determine that?"

"The compass. When I was trying to go to sleep something about the compass kept nagging at me, but I couldn't think what it was. It finally came to me in a dream."

"A dream?" Clint had dreams as often as anyone. In his experience they were mostly a lot of bunk.

"I do my best thinking when I'm not trying to think," she explained. "When my brain was finally at rest, the answer came to me. In all my visions of Trevor using the compass, the needle was pointing north."

"So?"

"The river was behind him."

Clint rubbed his eyes and blinked to clear his vision. "Holy shit," he muttered, more to himself than to her. When he thought of all the treacherous terrain that lay to the north between the river and the first paved highway, he cringed. "Are you certain he's on that side?"

"I'm positive. Portland is to the north. Right? I think Trevor and Nana are trying to go home." She rubbed her hands over the denim stretched tight over her bent knees. "I know it'll be a big pain in the neck to load the horses back up and move to the other side. I wish it had dawned on me sooner, but it didn't."

Clint unzipped the sleeping bag, bracing against the cold as he reached for his boots. "It's not your fault." Tugging his socks up, he added, "And it won't be that much trouble to load the horses. They're all accustomed to it."

She pushed to her feet. Just then a helicopter flew over. They watched it level out, heading east.

Clint sighed and shook his head. "If they're only searching the terrain along the river, they'll never find that boy, no matter how much fancy equipment they have. He and that dog could be ten miles from the water by now."

"You believe me."

The incredulity in her voice brought Clint's head around. He nudged his hat back and gave her a disgruntled look. "I'm getting there."

Hugging herself against the chill, she frowned at him. "I don't get it. What changed your mind?"

Clint pulled on his boots while trying to formulate an answer. "Didn't say I'd changed my mind. I said I'm getting there." He shifted onto his knees to roll up the sleeping bag. As he worked he glanced up at her. "Mainly it's you, I guess. You seem like an honest person, and I can't ignore the fact that you're here, willing to do whatever has to be done to find the boy, even if it means riding a horse, sleeping in a tent, and putting your life in the hands of a man you barely know. That makes it really hard for me to believe you're lying—unless, of course, you're crazy, and I don't think that's the case, either."

She laughed softly. He really did enjoy that sound. "I'm not so sure. Agreeing to come with you isn't the sanest decision I've ever made."

"Or the easiest decision you've ever made, either, I'm thinking. But you're here, willing to put your bacon on the plate. I can only conclude that you sincerely believe every word you've told me—that Trevor Stiles is out there somewhere, and only we can save him." When the ties on the sleeping bag were secured, he tossed the bedding to her, pushed erect, and swung his saddle up onto his shoulder. "I can continue to doubt you at every turn, which will do nothing but slow us down, or I can try to set my reservations aside and just go for it."

"And you've decided to do the latter?"

"Let's just say I mean to give it my best shot."

*   *   *

A few minutes later, when Clint walked down to the water to wash up, he saw searchers in bright orange vests preparing to drag the river at first light. The authorities were obviously convinced that the child and dog had drowned. Clint imagined that similar operations were taking place both up- and downstream.

When he returned to camp he informed Loni of what he'd seen. His voice edgy with frustration, he finished with, "It doesn't appear to me that they're expanding the search, or intend to anytime soon."

Crouched by the small fire, she glanced up from pouring some coffee. Holding a blue enamel mug out to him, she said, "Both adults drowned. Naturally they're convinced that the child must have, too."

Clint accepted the cup and took a careful sip of the scalding-hot brew. "We should talk to the search coordinator. They're wasting their time down there. They should be combing the forests a lot farther north of here."

She stared gloomily into the licking flames.

"What's wrong?" he asked.

"Nothing." She closed her eyes, then her lashes fluttered up. "If we go to the person in charge and tell him what we know, we'll have to give some sort of explanation, won't we? Otherwise he won't listen to us."

Clint studied her thoughtfully. "That's true. Do you have a problem with that?"

When she looked up at him, her eyes had gone dark with shadows. "Telling him I'm a psychic, you mean?" Her soft lips thinned over her teeth. "He isn't going to believe me. You know it, and I know it. So why even bother?"

Clint crouched down across the fire from her. "Whether the search coordinator buys your story or not, at least you'll have planted the thought in his mind that Trevor may still be alive and farther north than they think. When they find nothing in the river, they may decide to widen their focus. Not to say we can't find him in time by ourselves. Don't get me wrong. But it'd sure as hell be nice if we had some help."

As though to shield her thoughts, she looked off into the trees. Clint was starting to get a very bad feeling.

"We at least need to talk to him."

Face pale, features drawn, she nodded but didn't speak.

"Something's eating at you," he ventured. "From this point forward we're partners. Right? If you have a problem talking to the authorities, you'd better tell me now. I don't like surprises."

She shifted her gaze back to him. Her eyes were the most incredible shade of blue he'd ever seen, rivaling the dusky, rose-streaked morning sky behind her. "I have no criminal record, if that's your worry."

"What then?"

She set her cup on one of the rocks that Clint had placed around the pit last night. "About a year ago I got sucked into a big mess."

"What kind of mess?"

"A young woman named Cheryl Blain had been missing for about six months. Her parents and the authorities believed she was dead." Her throat worked as she struggled to swallow. "I'd just received the Decorator of the Year award, and the Blains read about me in the paper. They visited my shop and asked me to redo their home. It was where they'd raised their daughter, and everywhere they looked they were reminded of her."

Clint wondered where this was heading—and how it had anything to do with the search for Trevor. "Go on."

She drew up her shoulders, the burgundy fleece jacket bunching in folds at either side of her slender neck. "Normally I don't work with the general public. I prefer to do only new construction, model homes mostly." She narrowed her eyes against a waft of smoke. "Older homes can be a problem for me." Her mouth thinned again and quivered at the corners. "Sometimes I'm okay, but other times I pick up bad vibes."

"How do you pick up bad vibes?"

"By touching things. My sister calls it psychometric divination, the ability of some individuals to divine information by touching a person or an object."

"Ah." Now Clint knew what a psychometrist was. "And that happens to you in old houses?"

"In some, not all." She drew in a shaky breath and exhaled in a huff. "The Blains liked my bold decorating style and would settle for no one but me to redo their home. I felt sorry for them, I guess. They were grieving and heartbroken, and I couldn't tell them no."

Clint glanced at the sky. The sun would be completely up soon, and he still wasn't sure where this story was going. "So you redecorated their place?"

"We never got that far." A distant, wistful look

entered her eyes. "I went to their home to give them a bid. When I entered Cheryl's bedroom, which was just as she'd left it, I had a vision, a violent, terrifying vision." Her gaze sharpened on Clint's. Pale before, her face had now gone chalky white. "Cheryl wasn't dead," she said tautly. "She'd been abducted and was being held captive somewhere."

"For six months?"

She nodded. "I heard her pleading for help."

"*Heard* her?" Clint struggled to wrap his mind around that. All of this was so foreign to him, and this story sounded like something straight out of a Hannibal Lecter film. Six months was a hell of a long time for a woman to be held captive. "What did you hear her saying?"

"It was more what I heard her thinking," she corrected. "She was gagged and couldn't speak. In her mind she was pleading for help. She knew he was going to kill her if someone didn't find her soon."

Clint turned his cup between his hands, feeling chilled despite the warmth of the fire. "So you *can* read minds."

"Sort of." She flapped a hand. "Only not in the way you mean. It was more like her thoughts became mine, like she was whispering inside my head. Does that make any sense?"

None of this made sense. But Clint had reached a point where it made even less sense to think she was lying. "Sort of. So when you heard her thoughts, what did you do?"

"I staggered from the bedroom and collapsed in the hall. My entire body throbbed with pain—*her* pain."

"Her pain?" he repeated stupidly.

"I'm empathic. I mentioned that last night."

She'd told him a lot of stuff last night. He'd grasped only about half of it.

"During a vision I often experience the person's physical sensations. When Trevor fell into the river I felt the shock. Not as acutely as if I'd fallen into the water myself, of course, but I felt it, nonetheless.

"Anyway, I knew Cheryl was in grave danger, and if someone didn't help her quickly, she was going to die." The tendons along each side of her throat corded with tension. "I'd long since sworn off telling anyone about my gift. Most people react the same way you did. But I had to tell Cheryl's parents. How could I not?"

"How did they respond?"

"They didn't believe me at first. Their daughter had gone missing six months before. Traces of her blood had been found in her car. She'd been a wonderful daughter, very responsible and thoughtful. The Blains were convinced Cheryl would have found some way to call home if she were still alive."

"Only she couldn't call."

"She was bound hand and foot." She passed a trembling hand over her eyes. "She was so real in my mind—as real as her parents, who were standing right in front of me. It took some fast talking, but I finally convinced them I was telling the truth."

"So they called the police?"

"Not immediately. We needed more information." She touched her cup as if to pick it up, but then left it on the rock. "Mrs. Blain brought me one of Cheryl's most cherished possessions, a baby doll she'd had since early childhood. I held the doll, closed my eyes, and for the first time in my life successfully summoned a vision. I needed to get a clear picture of where Cheryl was."

Clint no longer cared how this pertained to the present situation. He was too caught up in the story. "Did you see anything?"

"Yes, a small metal building near an irrigation canal with heavy equipment parked in a nearby lot. I also heard single-engine planes flying overhead. There were pipes and what looked like oversize wrenches inside the shed. I also saw Cheryl's captor. He was thirtyish, with blond hair, and blue eyes that looked"—she broke off and stared blankly into the flames—"insane. It's the only way I can think to describe his eyes. There was an expression of indescribable evil on his face when he leaned over her."

"You actually *saw* him?"

With a start Clint realized that he'd gone from dubious to completely sold between one heartbeat and the next. How could he not believe this woman? The pain and lingering horror that he saw on her face would have convinced anyone. Now he understood why she had so many dead bolts on her doors and a dog the size of a horse. After living through something like that, any halfway intelligent person would beef up home security.

She finally lifted the cup but didn't drink. Instead she gazed into the murky contents as if searching for answers to questions he couldn't even fathom. "Yes, I saw him." She tossed away the liquid. "Saw him, heard him, and *felt* what he did to her. My picture of him was so clear I later worked with a sketch artist, enabling the authorities to apprehend him."

The coffee Clint had just swallowed tried to push back up his throat. "Sweet Jesus."

"Anyway, Mr. Blain felt we had enough then to call the police. Sadly for Cheryl, the officers who answered the call didn't believe my story. They took notes and were polite, but it was obvious to me as well as to the Blains that they were struggling not to laugh. John Blain was furious. His daughter was in danger of being killed, and the police thought it was a joke.

"He made some more phone calls. I was horrified when I realized he was speaking to members of the media. I pleaded with him not to give out my name, but in that moment all he cared about was Cheryl and causing such a stink that the police would have to do something. He wanted the story plastered on the front page of every newspaper in the greater Seattle area, and he wanted television stations to broadcast it as well. He wasn't going to let his daughter die without one hell of a fight."

"No, of course not." Clint tried to imagine what it must have been like for Loni, but he simply couldn't. "So the story went public, and your name was in the newspapers and on all the newscasts. That must have made your life difficult for a while."

"Worse than difficult—it was pure hell. To make a long story short, the police came under fire for not following up on the leads, and they finally started visiting all the small airports in the area, looking for the canal and shed I described. Sadly, all the media hype spooked Cheryl's captor. Three days after the story went public, her body was found in an irrigation canal near a small airport. She'd been missing for over six months, but she'd been dead for only twelve hours."

Nausea burned in the pit of Clint's stomach.

"The instant her body was found, the media noted how similar the location was to the one I'd described, and overnight I became the hottest news story the area had seen since the manhunt for the Green River Killer."

Clint was finally beginning to understand her reluctance to seek out the search coordinator. "Is that why you ended up in Crystal Falls—to escape all the publicity?"

"The media are like vultures picking at a carcass. They wouldn't leave me alone. I had frantic parents calling and coming to my shop, begging me to help find their missing children. I would have if I could, but that isn't how it works. The visions come or they don't, no matter what I touch. They'd shove things into my hands, and I tried, I really *tried*, but nothing would happen. But they refused to believe that. They offered me money. They grew angry. One father even got physical, convinced I wouldn't help because he had only ten thousand dollars."

"Oh, Loni."

"It's never been about financial gain. If I could, I'd sell everything I own and spend every dollar I have to be *rid* of this. Most of the time it doesn't feel like a gift. It feels like a curse. And it was especially bad after Cheryl's death. I'd think the worst was over, and then another child or teenager would go missing, kindling interest in me all over again."

And now she was about to step forward and let the vultures have another go at her. Clint tossed out the cold dregs of his coffee. The liquid hissed when it hit the rocks. "And now you're afraid the same thing could happen all over again."

A silence fell over them, the only sounds a whisper of breeze and birds twittering to greet the day. "Gram says I can't run from this. I'd rather not speak to the coordinator, but if I can convince him I'm telling the truth, it may save Trevor's life. Like you said, we may be able to find him on our own, but having some help sure wouldn't hurt."

"Maybe we can get around telling him your name."

She shook her head and pushed to her feet. "Trevor is all alone out there. I've *seen* him, heard wolves. I know how frightened he is. He'll be found much faster if I can make that search coordinator believe me, and the only way I know to do that is to tell him about Cheryl. By making a few phone calls, he can verify the story. Maybe this time because of Cheryl, it will be different. Maybe this time my gift will actually save someone." She lifted her hands. "I've got to try. No matter how it turns out, I've got to try. Trevor needs me to do this for him."

Clint couldn't argue with her reasoning. He only wished he could think of some way to protect her.

Chapter Five

Ten minutes later Loni and Clint were down at the water. About a dozen people worked exhaustively to drag for Trevor's remains. Even well below the rapids in what appeared to be calmer water, the swiftness of the current made the job difficult. People on both banks manned anchor ropes, trying to keep an aluminum riverboat, equipped with an outboard motor, from drifting downstream. Iron grapnels and gaffs were being tossed overboard, then hauled back up again. Loni felt particularly sorry for the two divers. Even with wet suits to protect them from the icy water, they had to be chilled to the bone.

The search coordinator, a Crystal Falls policeman named Richard Conklin, had joined the local search-and-rescue team years ago and was now a knowledge-able veteran. He seemed to be a decent man. Despite his obvious disbelief when he heard Loni's story, he maintained a courteous, professional manner.

Directing a look at Loni, he asked, "What did you say your name was again? I didn't quite catch it."

"Her name is Loni MacEwen." Clint thrust out his hand. "I'm Clint Harrigan, a local rancher."

"Harrigan?" Conklin frowned slightly. "You related to Samantha Harrigan, the gal whose quarter horses were poisoned last year?"

"My sister."

"So you're Hugh Harrigan's nephew?"

"I am. You know him?"

"Back when I was a state boy, we used to patrol the same stretch of highway occasionally." Conklin grinned. "I know him rather well, in fact. We've shared many a thermos of coffee. You raise horses, too?"

"It's what you might call a family enterprise," Clint replied. "That's why I'm here, actually, because I have a stable of horses. When Ms. MacEwen told me her story, I offered to take her in on horseback to look for the boy."

Loni met Conklin's gaze straight-on when he turned to look at her again. "I've never had the honor of meeting a real psychic."

As the policeman spoke he smiled politely, a little too politely, in Loni's estimation. She'd seen that expression on the faces of two other law enforcement officers in the not-so-distant past. "I know it's a lot to take in and that you may have your doubts, but the validity of my story can be verified." She gave him a brief account of the Cheryl Blain case. "Call anyone in law enforcement in the greater Seattle area, and they should vouch for me."

Conklin nodded. "I may radio in and have someone do that."

"Trevor needs help *now*."

Conklin rubbed his jaw. "This is a huge rescue attempt, with a lot of law enforcement officers involved. I'm only in charge of this search team. Convincing my superiors to stop dragging the river to hare off into the mountains on a psychic's say-so isn't likely to happen. We've found no evidence that Trevor Stiles or the dog ever made it out of the water."

"But he did make it out," Loni insisted. "I've had several visions of him. He and the dog are traveling north."

Conklin removed his knitted cap and stuffed it into the pocket of his parka. "I'm not questioning your sincerity, Ms. MacEwen. I'm only saying we've combed each side of this river in both directions."

"How far upstream?" Clint hooked a thumb at the raft, which had been pulled up onto the riverbank the previous day. "That thing could have drifted for miles before it caught here on the rocks."

"Trust me, starting from where the Stiles family was last seen by their rafting buddies to a point several miles downstream from here, we've walked every inch of shoreline. No one has seen any footprints to indicate that the boy survived. A child and a dog that size would surely have left tracks or disturbed earth somewhere if they'd made it out of the water."

"Maybe it was rocky where they climbed out," Clint suggested. "You also have to remember that the soil in this area is comprised mostly of volcanic ash. It blows in the wind like talcum powder. Isn't it possible the boy's footprints were faint by the time your searchers came upon them, possibly so faint that they weren't noticed? They were searching with flashlights, weren't they?"

"We covered the same ground again yesterday morning in broad daylight."

"*After* God knows how many people walked through, obliterating any evidence."

Conklin squinted against the brightening sunlight. "Most of my volunteers are very experienced."

"Most, but not all?" Clint countered. "What if a less experienced person covered the stretch of ground where the Stiles boy left the stream? Isn't it possible that something could have been overlooked?"

"Possible, but not probable," the coordinator replied. Smiling at Loni again, he added, "I'll tell you what. If we find nothing in all the hot spots where bodies traditionally hang up, I'll consider your suggestion that we should concentrate north of here. I'll also call the King County police to verify your story. Does that ease your mind any?"

Loni felt Clint move away from her. She was too upset to glance after him. "Trevor is running out of time. If nothing else, can you at least have a helicopter equipped with a heat sensor comb the northern woodlands?"

"Do you have any idea how much one of those helicopters costs per hour?" He shook his head. "I'm sorry, Ms. MacEwen, but I need some physical evidence that the child left the stream to justify a request for more aerial searches. We've combed the terrain on either side of the river, both on foot and from the air. We've found zip."

Clint returned to Loni's side just then. She clutched

his shirtsleeve, signaling that she was ready to go. They thanked Conklin for his time and trudged up the slope back to their camp.

En route Loni said, "He isn't going to search north of the river. He didn't believe a word I told him."

"No, I don't think he did either. Pisses me off how narrow-minded people can be sometimes."

As recently as last night Clint had been as reluctant to believe her as Conklin was. Grateful for his support, she said, "Thank you for backing me up down there."

He flashed her a sheepish grin. "I can be slow to make up my mind, but once I do, I don't waffle."

Each of them smiled as they covered the remaining distance to camp. Once there Loni was surprised to see what looked like sweat streaming down Clint's darkly tanned face. With the mountain chill still riding the morning air, she couldn't help but be concerned.

"Are you all right?"

He plucked off his Stetson. "Right as rain. Only a little wet." Reaching into the bowl of the hat, he plucked out a small brown blob that dripped water through his fingers. Proffering it to her, he said, "I saw this in the raft. No one was paying any attention, so I swiped it. You reckon it might be Trevor's?"

Loni's heart caught. The object he held was a small, waterlogged stuffed animal. "I can't believe you took that. You could get into serious trouble."

"Trevor's already in serious trouble, and I'm pretty sure they aren't going use it. I didn't see any tracking dogs, anyway. I know there's no guarantee you'll see anything if you touch it, but I thought it'd be worth a shot."

Loni stared hard at the toy. "Oh, Clint, I think it's Boo."

"Who?"

"Boo." Loni took the wet blob from his hands. "Trevor's stuffed bear."

When Loni's face went suddenly still and her eyes became unfocused, Clint knew what was happening even before she swayed on her feet. His first instinct was to grab her by the shoulders to keep her from falling, but he stopped himself. She was obviously picking up on something by touching the bear, and he didn't want to jerk her back to reality by making physical contact.

Each second that passed seemed to last a small eternity. Loni didn't appear to see him now—or even be aware of him. It was the eeriest experience he'd ever had. Watching her made his skin pebble with goose bumps.

Finally she pressed the soaked teddy bear between her breasts, and her eyes refocused on him, however blearily. She weaved on her feet like a drunk. "He's still okay," she whispered, smiling tremulously. "He and Nana were sharing a bag of corn chips."

Unable to stop himself now that she was mentally with him again, Clint caught her by the arms. "Are you okay?"

"Just a little dizzy and disoriented." Her eyes fell closed. "It'll pass in a moment."

Clint could understand why it might make her feel disoriented. In a very real way she'd just had an out-of-body experience.

Her lashes fluttered up again. "Better now," she said with a smile that dimpled her cheek. "He's okay. That's the important thing. He's still okay."

It took over a half hour to load all the horses and gear back into the truck and trailer before moving to the north side of the river. Then Clint spent another hour putting Decker packsaddles and half-breeds on six of the animals, which he followed with boards and manties that had all been carefully weighed the previous night at his ranch.

Loni sat on a rock, nibbling on a piece of jerky while she watched Clint work. He moved with an unconscious grace, bending, crouching, and then pushing to his feet with seeming ease. The muscles across his back created a tantalizing play of movement beneath his shirt, stretching the blue cloth tight whenever he strained to lift something. She also liked his hands, broad and square at the base, his fingers long and thick with calluses. For just an instant she recalled the sturdy grasp of those fingers over her ankle when he'd treated her heel last night—how their warmth had penetrated her skin, how firm and heavy his leathery palm had felt.

Dismayed by the train of her thoughts, she asked, "Is there anything I can do to help?" Trevor was out there somewhere, and she was anxious to get going. "Four hands can accomplish more than two, and I'm a quick learner."

"I know it probably seems like I'm taking forever, but careful attention now may save us a heap of time later."

It all looked unnecessarily complicated to Loni. "I saw you weighing and tagging everything that went into the packs last night. Why is that?"

"It's important to keep the loads on a packsaddle the same weight on both sides," he explained. "It's all deadweight, and if it gets off balance it's unnecessarily hard on the horse." He patted the contraption on one horse's back. "These packsaddles and boards allow me to balance the weight to some degree, but as we consume our supplies, we'll be lightening the loads. It's easier to repack the manties if everything in them is already weighed and tagged."

"You'll have to repack along the trail? The process took hours last night."

"It'll be much faster now."

Loni could only hope he was right. "So when will we check in at a ranger station?"

He gave her an odd look. "Why would we do that?"

"Isn't there a law requiring it?"

"No law that I'm aware of. Inexperienced hikers sometimes check in as a safety precaution, and smart mountain climbers do as well, but I'm an experienced trail rider. We also have no idea of our precise destination or how long we'll be gone."

"So we'll just ride in there, and no one will know where we are?"

"I'll know where we are," he told her with a grin.

"What about our search for Trevor? Do we need permission or anything?"

"I don't think so. The more people looking for him, the better, and in an unofficial way we did notify that search coordinator of our intentions."

A few moments later he drew the horses into a single-file line, tying them together with lead ropes lengthened with pieces of cord that looked like heavy twine.

"What are the strings for? They don't look strong enough to hold."

"Good observation. They're called breakaways. If anything goes wrong with one horse, they snap, keeping the other horses safe." He flashed her a slow grin. "Breakaway strings have saved my ass more than once."

"Don't the horses figure out that the strings won't hold?"

"These horses are all trained for the trail. They know the breakaways won't hold if they throw a fuss, but they rarely do. Hagar, a sorrel mare back at the ranch, is never taken on trail rides because she's a string jerker. I was never able to break her of it."

Hagar struck Loni as being a strange name for a horse. "Wasn't Hagar the handmaid of Sarah, Abraham's wife?"

"Know your Bible, do you?"

"I can't quote chapter and verse, but, yes, I've read it a few times. Evidently so have you."

"I'm Catholic. We read scripture at every Mass. I've also done a lot of reading on my own."

He said *Catholic* as if it were a private club he belonged to. Loni was tempted to burst his bubble by telling him that she, a clairvoyant, practiced the same faith. But she decided to err on the side of caution. He was only just now coming around, and she saw no point in needlessly complicating matters.

As he continued to ready the horses, Loni came to learn their names. Uriah, a nine-year-old gelding, was a reddish brown horse with a black mane, tail, and lower legs. Clint said Uriah was a bay, which made no sense to Loni at all. Bay leaves were green. Then there was the gelding, Dagan, a flaxen chestnut, reddish brown of body with a blond mane and tail. The horse looked more like a palomino to Loni, but what did she know?

"Do you give all your horses biblical names?" she asked. "Dagan, god of the Canaanites. Correct?"

"That's right," Clint replied. "You *are* up on your Bible."

"Why the biblical theme?"

"My sister, Samantha, claims every horse breeder should have a theme. Her horses are all named after spices, barbecue sauce, or whatever else she can find in her kitchen. I aimed for something a little more dignified."

"So what are the other horses' names?"

There was Ezekiel, a six-year-old dun gelding; Malachi, another flaxen chestnut; Bathsheba, an eleven-year-old buckskin; Delilah, a fourteen-year-old sorrel; Jemima, a seven-year-old roan; and Sapphira, a blue roan, thrown by Samantha's deceased mare Cilantro.

"Who was Sapphira?" Loni asked. "I can't remember reading about her in the Bible."

"Sapphira was a woman executed by God for lying." He winked at her. "What do you want to bet she had gorgeous blue eyes just like yours?"

Loni decided to let that pass, and a few minutes later Clint pronounced them ready to go. Loni was assigned

Uriah as her mount. She was surprised and touched to see that her saddle was cushioned with gel pads. That was where all sentimentality ended, however. Her heart leaped into her throat when Clint interlaced his fingers to give her a leg up.

"I can't," she squeaked.

"What?"

"I'm afraid of heights. I can't." To Loni the horse suddenly seemed as tall as a skyscraper. "I just can't."

"Uriah is a big old love, Loni. I handpicked him just for you. He's so calm and trustworthy I could lay a baby at his feet."

Loni fixed him with a horrified look. "A baby? Are you out of your *mind*?"

He chuckled. "I wouldn't actually do it. That's just an expression among horsemen." He unlaced his hands and curled an arm under the gelding's neck to pet him. "You can't walk. You've already got blisters starting on your heels. By the end of the day they'll be raw sores. Trust me. This horse won't hurt you."

Loni wasn't so sure. But Trevor was out there, and she was wasting precious time. "All right," she said thinly. "All right."

Clint created a stirrup with his hands again. Loni placed her left foot on his interlaced fingers, then reached high to grab the saddle horn. The next instant she was on the horse.

"Oh, God." Uriah sidestepped, making her grab his mane. "Oh, *God*. Why is he looking at me like that?"

Clint was adjusting her left stirrup. "Because he can smell your fear, and he's alarmed. In his opinion you can't possibly be afraid of him, so there must be some other danger."

"He can *smell* my fear?"

"Yes, so stop worrying the poor fellow and calm down."

Loni gulped and stared into the horse's soft brown eyes. "Are you sure he won't buck me off?"

"I'm almost certain of it."

"Almost?"

Clint grinned up at her as he adjusted the other stirrup. "If a wasp flies up his nose, he'll buck. If he comes upon a rattlesnake, he'll rear. No horse on earth is absolutely guaranteed never to throw his rider."

Hands still clenched in the horse's mane, Loni asked, "Are there very many bees and snakes out here?"

Less than two hours into the ride Loni felt as if she'd slipped on ice and done the splits, injuring every muscle and tendon from her ankles to her groin. The baseball cap Samantha had lent her was making her scalp sweat, but Loni was afraid to turn loose of the saddle horn to scratch where she itched. To make matters worse, she and Uriah were last in line, eating the dust raised by twenty-eight hooves clomping the dirt ahead of them. Even if she'd wanted to voice a complaint, Clint was riding at the front and too far away to hear unless she shouted at the top of her lungs.

To distract herself from the myriad discomforts, Loni tried to admire the scenery. Until they reached the area where Conklin believed the raft had capsized, they were following the river upstream at a steady pace. The incessant roar of the white-water rapids soon gave way to a peaceful woodland silence, allowing her to hear the songbirds and the breeze whispering softly in the ponderosa pines. At one point she saw another search party, hard at work dragging the river. Then the searchers were blocked from view, and she looked ahead again.

Occasionally, as they rounded a sharp bend in the river, she was able to see distant snowcapped peaks that jutted up through fluffy, white clouds to touch a powder blue sky, making her marvel that the first settlers had found passes through them to reach the fertile coastal valleys beyond. It was like being in a postcard wonderland, everything she saw almost too beautiful to be real.

Farther along, the trail grew frighteningly narrow and rocky, plunging sharply at some points, and then turning steep, often pitting both horses and riders against the rugged terrain. Following Clint's lead, Loni lay forward over Uriah's neck during the climbs and leaned back in the saddle during the descents. At times she so pitied her mount that she was tempted to get off and walk. Only Clint's warning about her blisters becoming raw sores forestalled her from trying.

Every once in a while he turned on the saddle to glance back and ask how she was doing. Determined not to whine, Loni's stock answer was, "I'm fine." Only she wasn't. Even with the gel pads to protect her rump and inner thighs, she felt as if she'd been bouncing her butt repeatedly on a rock.

"Try to bear your weight with your legs!" he called back to her several times.

Loni tried, she truly did, but her thigh muscles weren't strong enough to support her weight very long without going into cramps. Soon she was bouncing on the saddle again.

Despite her constant concern for Trevor, she was inexpressibly grateful when Clint stopped around noon in a grassy clearing to rest the horses. As he dismounted, he called, "Sit tight for a second and I'll come help you dismount."

Loni was too eager to get off the horse to wait. Pulling her right foot from the stirrup, she pushed up on her left leg, swung out of the saddle, and promptly found herself sitting butt-first in the dirt. Her legs had folded beneath her as if her bones were made of hot wax. Oddly, she felt no discomfort from the fall.

Clint came running. "I told you I'd help."

"I didn't think I needed help." She glanced up. "But my legs are asleep." She wiggled one foot. "Correction. Even my butt's asleep."

Uriah snorted and wandered away to eat grass. Clint hunkered down in front of her, his dark eyes twinkling.

"This is *not* funny."

"I'm not laughing." He extended a broad palm to her. "Come on. I'll help you over to a grassy spot."

Too exhausted to argue, Loni placed her hand in his. As he pushed erect he drew her up with him, seeming not to notice her weight at all. Clamping a hard arm around her waist, he half carried her to a shady place under a pine. With every step Loni winced. It felt as if a thousand needles were pricking the soles of her feet.

She sighed with relief when he lowered her to the

ground. She lay back, arms flung outward from her body, and groaned, far too battered to care what he thought.

"You okay, sweetheart?"

Loni tucked in her chin to stare up at him. *Sweetheart?* As she recalled, they were barely on a first-name basis. "I'm not sure," she answered honestly.

"The first time in the saddle can be rough." He crouched beside her. "I was hoping the gel pads would help."

"It was very thoughtful of you to bring them. I can't imagine what shape I'd be in without them."

He sat back on his heels, his muscular arms draped loosely over his bent knees. "Once I've tended to the horses I'll bring you some water and a protein bar. Maybe that'll perk you up."

Loni doubted anything short of a long soak in a hot Jacuzzi would perk her up, but she didn't want to worry him by saying so. The moment he left she sighed and let her eyes fall closed, wishing with all her heart that they could camp there for the night. Not possible. They'd been riding for only about four hours. In order to catch up with Trevor they needed to keep going until dark. The thought made her groan.

Once Clint had watered the horses, he left them to graze while he went to check on Loni. She lay under the tree like a discarded rag doll, her head lolling to one side, the green bill of the John Deere cap shading her closed eyes. Depositing the canteen and protein bar on the grass, Clint hunkered beside her. Fast asleep. A sad smile touched his lips. Though she hadn't complained a single time, he knew the morning's ride had been hard on her. By tonight she'd be in a world of hurt.

Before waking her he allowed himself a moment to admire the delicate lines of her heart-shaped face—the arch of finely drawn brows, the feather of long, dark lashes against her cheeks, the fullness of her rose pink mouth. He especially liked her small, straight nose. She was a beauty, no question about it.

With the back of his hand, he nudged her shoulder. She jerked awake, her lashes fluttering as a yawn stretched her mouth wide. "I'm sorry." She moaned softly as she struggled to sit up. "I didn't mean to drift off."

"Take these." He caught her hand, cupped her palm, and dropped in two ibuprofen. "They'll take the edge off."

She popped the pills into her mouth, chasing them with water from the canteen. "Thank you." She wiped her lips with the back of her hand. "The water is wonderful."

"Help yourself. I have a filter. We won't run short."

She tipped the canteen to her mouth again, her larynx bobbing in her slender throat as she gulped. When she'd drunk her fill, Clint found himself staring at her lips. The shine of moisture made them look far too kissable for his peace of mind. They'd only just begun their sojourn into the wilderness, and already he was thinking about things he shouldn't. Not good. They had a mission to accomplish, and he needed to keep his mind strictly on business.

He sat beside her to rest while she nibbled on the protein bar. She took small bites, flicking the pink tip of her tongue over her bottom lip to catch the crumbles of chocolate. He couldn't recall ever having seen anything so sensual, and wondered if she was doing it on purpose to drive him crazy. The suspicion no sooner crossed his mind than she stuck half the bar into her mouth and slowly withdrew it, skimming her teeth the length of it. Watching her made his stomach clench.

He'd been too long without a woman, he decided. Normally he kept busy at the ranch and put in long, hard days. At night he was usually too spent to think much about sex. But he wasn't tired now—at least, not tired enough to be around a beautiful woman without wanting her. He pinched the bridge of his nose and closed his eyes, determined to ignore the ache that was forming low in his belly.

"Headache? You should try some of the ibuprofen."

It would take a hell of a lot more than a couple of pills to cure what ailed him. Clint sprang to his feet. "Time's wasting. You about ready to mount back up?"

She finished the bar in two big bites, brushed her fingers clean on her jeans, and tucked the wrapper in her pocket. "As ready as I'll ever be, I guess."

For the remainder of the day, except for brief rest stops, Clint pushed the horses and pack animals ever deeper into the wilderness. In some places the manzanita grew so thick on the hillsides it looked almost impenetrable. In the ravines snow lay in blue-white patches at the bases of the trees, giving testimony to the fact that winter temperatures still held the mountains in their frigid grip at night. Even so, spring grass shot up in yellow-green bunches, and hardy wildflowers lent splashes of pink, blue, and yellow to an otherwise green-and-brown landscape.

As they rode, Clint pointed out Western tanagers, chipping sparrows, yellow warblers, red-breasted sapsuckers, robins, a pair of harlequin ducks with a half dozen ducklings, and, at one point, even a gorgeous bald eagle soaring above them.

In all Loni's life she'd never seen such an abundance of wildlife. Lodgepole chipmunks and golden-mantled squirrels scrambled over the rocks, chattering angrily at the invasion of horses and mankind into their territory. Mule deer, startled away from the river by their approach, bounded into thickets and disappeared. A mother raccoon, leading a queue of waddling babies, cut across the trail in front of them. Late in the afternoon Loni even glimpsed a mountain lion in the distance. The sighting left her feeling chilled and more than a little uneasy about the coming night.

Clint seemed constantly on guard, sometimes stopping to search a hillside, other times cocking his head to listen. The rifle from his truck now rode in a leather boot just behind his saddle, and as the sun began to set Loni saw him unfasten the strap of the gun holster at his hip. With mounting dread she realized there were dangers all around them that she couldn't fathom. As exhausted as she was, she had no idea how she would sleep with only the thin nylon walls of the tent as a barrier against nocturnal predators.

Just before dark, when the sun finally dipped below the mountains behind them, Clint brought his horse to a halt, pushed up in the stirrups, and hollered back,

"This spot looks about as good as any to make camp for the night. What do you think?"

Loni craned her neck to see around him. Just ahead, a bend in the river provided a shallow pool. Off to the left, a small, flat area was carpeted with grass and encircled by trees. "You're the expert."

This time Loni knew as she dismounted to keep a death grip on the saddle horn until she was sure her legs would support her. Even then, her knees wobbled with every step. Biting her lip at the pain, she led Uriah to the clearing. After watching Clint for a moment, she spoke softly to the gelding as she removed the saddlebags and then loosened the girth strap around his belly. She staggered and almost fell when she pulled the saddle from his back.

"Whoa! I'll get that." Clint hurried over to relieve her of the burden. "I don't want you to hurt yourself."

"I'm sure your sister lifts saddles off of horses all the time."

"True, but she's been doing it for years. There's a trick to it. We call it the swing-and-drop maneuver." He flashed her a crooked grin. "Try muscling that much weight at head height and you'll hurt your back."

Loni already ached in every joint of her body. The last thing she wanted was a strained back, too. So instead of wrestling with saddles, she only helped loosen them and then allowed Clint to do the lifting.

When all the horses were relieved of their burdens, they rubbed them down and took them to the river to drink. Oddly, Loni enjoyed that part most. Uriah truly was a sweetie. He reminded her a little of Hannah, snuffling her clothing and giving her affectionate nudges. Bathsheba was precious, too, if you overlooked the fact that she was a tiny bit spoiled. In a way Loni could sympathize. This trip was rather hard on a pampered lady. Maybe, she decided, that was why she enjoyed petting the horses. She could stand in one place and not wiggle her butt muscles very much.

They'd hobbled the equines in the clearing and she was feeding them handfuls of grass, enjoying the tickle of their lips on her palm, when Clint hollered for her help. He was trying to string what he called a high line between two trees, and he needed her to hold the rope.

She was so exhausted she wanted to weep by the time they got all the animals fed and settled in for the night. But the work was still far from finished. Rocks had to be found to encircle a fire pit Clint quickly created with a short-handled spade. Wood had to be collected. The tent had to be put up. By the time Clint got a fire going she was ready to drop in her tracks. Her inner thighs burned like fire. Her butt felt as if it were black and blue. Her legs threatened to buckle every time she took a step.

"Here, have a seat," Clint said.

Loni glanced behind her at the folded sleeping bag he'd laid on the ground. It looked wonderfully soft and tempting. But she hurt too much all over to bend her knees and sit. As if sensing her dilemma, Clint took her hands.

"Lean your weight against me. I'll lower you down."

Loni felt ridiculous, but she honestly couldn't get down there by herself. He deposited her, rump-first, on the cushiony folds, making her landing as gentle as possible.

Loni was about to thank him when he said, "Drop your pants."

Certain her ears were deceiving her, she said, "I beg your pardon?"

"You heard me. Drop your pants."

Chapter Six

Loni couldn't think what to say. He wanted her to drop her jeans? Hands at his hips, booted feet set wide apart, he stood before her, as unbending as a tree, his dark eyes holding hers in a relentless grip.

"You're saddle sore," he said.

As if she needed him to tell her that? She had a very bad feeling her abused posterior had somehow been added to his evening chore list, right up there with lifting the horse's hooves to check their frogs for stones.

"Has anyone ever mentioned that you need to work on your lead-ins?"

He gave her a bewildered look. "My what?"

"Your lead-ins. You shouldn't just walk up to a woman and tell her to drop her pants."

"I shouldn't?"

Loni glimpsed a twinkle of amusement in his coffee brown eyes. "No, you *shouldn't*. It would be far nicer if you *eased* your way into it, saying something like, 'You seem to be in a lot of discomfort. Maybe I'd better have a look.'"

He nodded. "All right. You seem to be in a lot of

discomfort. Maybe I'd better have a look." He nudged his hat back to smile at her. "Is that better?"

"Not really."

He chuckled. "No matter how I say it, you're not going to like it."

"You're right. I'm not in the habit of dropping my pants in front of men."

"I never thought otherwise, which is precisely why I thought the direct, no-bullshit approach was my best option. To put it simply, you're in serious trouble. If I don't rub you down with Hooter's special salve, you may not be able to walk tomorrow, let alone ride."

"Surely it won't be *that* bad."

"I've seen people so stiff and sore, they couldn't get out of bed the next morning."

"Really?"

"Would I lie to you?" He held up a staying hand. "Forget I asked that."

Loni had to struggle not to laugh, and if that wasn't crazy, she didn't know what was. "What kind of special salve is it?"

"Basically, a miracle cure for the pain you're in right now."

"If you'll bring it to me, I'll apply it myself."

As he strode over to a pack that lay nearby, he said, "This is no time for modesty, Ms. MacEwen. I know my way around saddle sores, and you don't."

"The saddle sores happen to be on *my* posterior, Mr. Harrigan."

"I have no designs on your posterior. I'm more worried about your legs."

Loni had to admit that her legs were horribly sore.

Muttering under her breath, she attempted to remove her borrowed footwear, no easy task when it hurt to bend her knees. Tossing the tube of salve onto the sleeping bag, he crouched in front of her and grabbed a boot by its heel.

"Let me, sweetheart. At the best of times riding boots are a bitch to get off. I've got a bootjack in almost every room of the house."

"What on earth is a bootjack?"

"A V-shaped gadget that sits on the floor. You stand on one end, stick the heel of your other boot in the V, and after a little cussing and tugging, the boot comes off."

"Maybe you should wear lace-ups."

He looked appalled. "Lace-ups? When you're wading through horse puckey all day, you have to take your boots off every time you go to the house. Laces are too much trouble."

With an expertise born of long practice, he tugged the first boot off and tossed it aside. The second one soon followed. Then he reached to unfasten the waistband of her jeans. Loni grasped his wide wrists and gave him a startled look.

"You seem to be in a lot of discomfort," he said with a teasing grin. "Maybe I'd better have a look."

She laughed in spite of herself, and the next thing she knew, the denim was being peeled down her thighs. To his credit he kept his gaze on her legs, and his manner was so businesslike that it helped to calm her jangled nerves.

When he saw the purple marks on her inner thighs,

he swore under his breath, twisted the cap off the tube, and squirted some clear ointment onto his palm.

"This is going to set you on fire," he warned. "But as soon as the burning stops you'll feel better."

Loni jumped when his hard hand slipped between her legs. "I really don't think—"

That was all she had time to say. The next instant she was hissing air through her teeth, trying her best not to cry out.

"I know it hurts." His voice had gone deep and gravelly. "But it has to be done."

Loni locked her jaws. But just as he'd promised, the sting soon began to abate. Kneeling between her parted thighs, he massaged her flesh, his hard fingers kneading deep to reach the tortured muscles.

"Try not to feel embarrassed," he told her. "I've seen women at the supermarket wearing less than you are right now."

Practically speaking, he was right. During the summer Loni sometimes made grocery runs wearing shorts and a blouse, and she never felt indecently exposed. But somehow this was different. It was also next to impossible for her to relax with a man's hands touching her in such intimate places.

Only, *oh*, it did feel good. He knew precisely where the soreness was, and the gentle but firm strokes of his fingers soon chased the stiffness from her muscles. To distance herself from the humiliation, she tipped her face up to the darkening sky, wishing the butterfly puzzle at her gynecologist's office were pinned up there for her to study. Finding individual butterflies in the swirls of color always distracted her until the most mortifying part of an exam was over.

When he'd finished with her thighs he said, "Roll over on your stomach."

Her gynecologist could give him some lessons in bedside manner, Loni thought. But in a weird way, his no-nonsense, "let's get this over with" tone eased her self-consciousness. To her surprise she was actually able to move without whimpering.

He spent the next few minutes working on the backs of her legs. Then he handed her the salve. "I'll let you handle the rest."

Loni decided he was referring to the places under her panties. She was grateful when he turned his back to put more wood on the fire, allowing her some privacy. After applying the medication she tried to mimic his massage techniques, pushing in deep with her fingers to reach all the throbbing spots. Sadly, her attempts fell far short of his, but she did the best she could, then shimmied into her jeans and tugged the boots back on.

"I'm decent."

He glanced back over his shoulder. "Feel better?"

Loni was surprised to realize that she did. "Much better. What is this stuff, anyway?"

"You don't want to know."

"Yes, I do. It's fabulous."

"It's horse salve."

"*What?*"

He chuckled. "You see? Now you're appalled. It won't hurt you, I promise, and come morning you'll be able to ride again."

"Horse salve." Loni squinted to read the label in the waning light. "Oh, my gosh, it *is* horse salve."

"A jockey back East came up with the concoction to treat racehorses with pulled tendons or sprains. Then he patented the recipe and began marketing it. That's probably why it burns so bad when you first apply it, because he created it to radiate heat through a horse's coat, and we apply it to bare skin. My ranch foreman, Hooter, discovered that it works even better on humans than it does on equines, and we've been using it on the trail ever since. Even veteran riders who don't get on a horse all winter can get saddle sore during the first spring ride."

Loni could still feel the heat radiating deep into her tortured flesh. It wasn't quite as wonderful as sitting in a hot Jacuzzi, but it came close. "I'm glad you thought to bring it."

He grinned and winked at her. "I brought it along especially for you."

"Which must mean you weren't worried about getting sore yourself. Do you ride frequently, then, even in the winter?"

"Oh, yeah. That's why I built that huge arena, so my horses and I can stay in shape even when the snow's ass-deep to a tall Texan."

Loni had never sat by a campfire after dark. On the one hand the blackness of the woods around them was unnerving. The light of the flames seemed to compound her night blindness. But when she wasn't thinking about long-toothed predators sneaking up behind her, she found herself mesmerized by the dancing tongues of fire and the orange embers that occasionally snapped and shot up sparks. She also enjoyed the wonderful smell of the wood smoke. It was far better than any campfire scene she'd ever watched in a movie. You missed the true ambience when you were sitting on a sofa, munching popcorn.

Popcorn. Mmm. That sounded so good.

She wasn't expecting much by way of an evening meal, but Clint surprised her with delicious smelling beef stew heated right in the cans. He used a folded piece of leather to protect his hand as he turned the containers and occasionally stirred the contents with a camp spoon.

Watching, Loni found it easy to imagine him in an Old West setting. Whether he liked the term or not, he was the very epitome of a cowboy, from the crown of his brown Stetson to the toes of his dusty riding boots. His blue chambray shirt, soft with wear, skimmed his torso, showcasing his lean, muscular upper body. He seemed as comfortable in a crouch as most people were sitting on a stool, giving the impression that he could hold the position for hours without his leg muscles tiring. With the pines silhouetted in feathery black against a navy blue sky behind him, and the campfire limning him in amber, he looked like a man from another era.

"That smells divine," she said, inclining her head at the stew. "I didn't realize I was hungry until now." *Liar, liar, pants on fire.* Where was the Orville Redenbacher Kettle Korn when she needed it?

A horse chuffed and whinnied. Pushing easily to his feet, Clint went to check on the animals. In the darkness his deep voice carried to her on the crisp night air, his affectionate rumblings making her smile. His horses weren't mere possessions to him, but friends that he cherished.

She admired his gentle way with them, and also his limitless patience. In only a day Loni had come to realize that each horse had a different personality and its own little quirks. She suspected that many horsemen would view any headstrong behavior in an animal as unacceptable, but Clint humored his horses as much as possible, allowing each of them to be individuals. Bathsheba, for instance, had to have her treats, her favorite being tender baby carrots. If Clint forgot to reward her periodically throughout the day, she started whinnying, much like a spoiled child that grew whiny. Then there was Malachi, Clint's mount, a gorgeous thirteen-year-old flaxen chestnut gelding who *insisted* on always being in the lead. If Clint fell back in line for too long, Malachi would take the bit in his teeth and trot back up to the front. When the horse reached what he clearly believed to be his rightful place in line, he made sounds that Clint laughingly called "Malachi's happy grunts."

Oddly, Clint's leniency with his horses never resulted in obstinate behavior. He respected the equines, and in turn they seemed to respect him. It was heartwarming to watch man and animals interact. Clint was firm and demanding when necessary, but after watching him all day, Loni had determined that he preferred using a reward system to encourage obedience rather than force a horse into compliance.

After checking each of the animals, he headed back

toward Loni, stopping off en route to rummage through a pack. When he returned to the fire, he held a plastic bottle of whiskey in one hand. With a quick turn of his wrist, he uncapped the container, tipped it to his lips, and then wiped the mouth clean with the tail of his shirt before passing it down to her.

"Not much by way of a before-dinner cocktail, but it'll have to do."

"Oh, I—"

"Have some. It's part of the Harrigan saddle-sore cure, not to mention that it'll help you sleep."

She smiled and took the bottle. "Cheers." She took a swig, shuddering at the burn. "Oh, *nasty*."

He reclaimed the whiskey, took another swallow, and then replaced the cap. "It always tastes better the second time around."

A few moments later Loni could attest to the truth of that. The next swallow did taste better. She was feeling relaxed and languorous by the time supper was ready. Clint sat beside her on the sleeping bag as they partook of the stew and a sleeve of saltine crackers. Both of them were so hungry that they barely came up for breath between bites. The taste of the stew, the scrape of their spoons against the cans, the smoky scent—*ah*, it was wonderful, as close to an orgasm as Loni had ever come. As her appetite for food waned, she thought about the injustice of that. Other women had sex and babies, thinking nothing of it, while she satisfied her cravings with kettle corn produced by Orville Reden- bacher, a man who'd been dead for at least ten years.

Loni couldn't finish her portion, so Clint happily consumed what was left. When the meal was over he tossed the cans on the fire and went to wash their spoons in the river. She watched with some interest when he returned, toed the cans from the flames, and stomped them flat before putting them in one of the packs.

"There's hope for you, after all," she teased when he came to sit beside her again. "I'm impressed, Mr. Harrigan."

"Clint," he corrected. "And why are you impressed?"

"You burned the cans clean and now you're going to pack them out."

"Of course. I may not use silk shopping bags or unplug my television when I'm gone, but I do respect the environment. I want this beautiful wilderness area to be here for the next generation."

"When I get home I'm going to plant a tree. It's a thing I started doing a few years ago, planting a tree after every vacation. I figure it helps to make up for my consumption of fuel. Trees are wonderful environment healers."

"You need a piece of land, honey. Didn't look to me like you have that much yard."

That was true. "I'll find room. At my last house I planted a tree in memory of Cheryl. It made me feel better somehow."

They sat in silence for a while. An owl hooted somewhere in the darkness. The sound made Loni shiver. "I wonder how Trevor's doing."

Clint gazed off into the night. "Hopefully he's doing fine. He's got Nana riding shotgun. No more visions of him today, I take it?"

"None." She waited a beat. "That worries me. Yesterday I had a half dozen. Now, nothing."

"Maybe that's because we're both out here now, determined to find him, and God doesn't feel you need any more clues as to his whereabouts until we've moved in closer."

Loni stiffened and glanced surreptitiously at his face. He was staring into the fire now, making it difficult for her to read the expression in his eyes. "God?" she echoed softly.

His gaze shifted to meet hers. "Of course, God. Where else would visions like yours come from?"

A lump lodged at the base of Loni's throat, and a burning sensation washed over her eyes. "A lot of strangers don't share that sentiment. In fact, in the not-so-distant past, neither did you, as I recall."

"I'm not exactly a stranger anymore."

Loni recalled the embarrassing thigh massage he'd given her earlier and smiled. "No, I guess you aren't. But you've come around rather quickly. Most people remain wary of me for much longer."

"Sounds to me like there's a story in there somewhere."

Loni went back to studying the flames. "We all have a story or two, I suppose. That doesn't mean we feel comfortable sharing them."

He chuckled. "True. I've got a couple of stories I don't feel comfortable sharing, myself. I'd sure like to hear yours, though." He angled her a questioning look. "I can't begin to imagine what your life has been like."

"In many ways it's been incredibly boring."

"Boring?" This time his chuckle became a deep, rich

laugh that warmed her insides much like the whiskey had earlier. "You have a satellite dish in your head with no control over the programming. How can that possibly be boring?"

It was Loni's turn to laugh. "A *satellite* dish?" Then, "Now that I come to think of it, you're right. It is sort of like that, especially the lack-of-control part. I ended up having to be homeschooled because of it."

"Homeschooled? Why was that?"

Loni tipped her head back to regard the sky as memories of her childhood came to the forefront of her mind. "For one thing it was extremely difficult for me to concentrate in a contaminated environment."

"Contaminated?"

She tried to think of a way to explain. "Touching used books. Sitting in an old desk that had been occupied by other kids day in and day out, year after year. Physically connecting with the teaching staff and other children. My brain came under constant fire with visions, and that distracted me from learning. At six I also tended to be a bit too forthcoming with the information that came to me in visions, which proved to be rather unsettling for some individuals."

"I definitely hear a story in that statement," he said with a smile. "Stirred the shit a little, did you?"

"That's a unique way of putting it, but I suppose it's apt. My first-grade teacher, Mrs. Stone, was not amused when I warned her to stop drinking in the evening before she went to the grocery store, and the principal wasn't exactly thrilled when I told him it wasn't very nice to hit his wife, that my daddy said we should only pick on people our own size."

Clint barked with laughter. "No wonder you had to be homeschooled. You were exposing everyone's dirty little secrets."

Loni couldn't share in his amusement. "Yes, well, a six-year-old isn't well versed in the art of prudence, and I hadn't yet come to understand just how different I was. I thought lots of people had visions, and I saw nothing wrong with trying to warn people that something bad might happen." She leaned forward to toss a pinecone onto the fire. "Unfortunately, no one listened any better then than they do now, and it was easy for them to hush me up. Mrs. Stone continued to drink and drive until she ran over a small boy one evening en route to the market. He died instantly. She served a jail sentence, lost her job, and her life was pretty much destroyed—a fitting punishment. The little boy's parents were devastated and never got over losing him."

"Oh, God. What a tragedy." His amusement effaced, he grew quiet for a while. Then he said, "I'm almost afraid to ask what happened with the principal, but my curiosity is killing me."

"He continued to hit his wife and one night he went too far. She fell, hit her head on the hearth, and broke her neck. I can't remember now how long he spent in prison, only that his own kids testified against him in court. He had a very long history of abusive behavior."

"Now I understand why you couldn't concentrate at school. Did you know ahead of time that those people would die?"

"Oh, yes. I just wasn't given a chance to tell my teacher or the principal the *rest* of the story. It was . . .

difficult for me. I couldn't comprehend why people refused to listen."

"A child that age should know nothing about things like that."

"Knowing about such things was hard, but the worst part was being helpless to stop it. That's still a problem for me."

"It's too bad you can't learn how to filter the signals," he mused. "Or get to a point where you can receive signals only when you know you can help."

"Then I might miss something important. Trevor, for instance."

"You would have heard about it on the news in plenty of time."

Loni supposed that was true.

"So how was homeschooling? Did your parents teach you, or did they hire a tutor?"

"My mom had a garden nursery. I went with her to work in the mornings, and she took afternoons off to tutor me. I mostly enjoyed not having to go to school, the only drawback being that I had few friends. My sister, Deirdre, was a godsend. At least I had a playmate when she got home in the afternoon."

"So when you got older were you able to attend high school?"

Loni shook her head. "I couldn't cut it in college, either. I don't do well in public situations. Way too much stimulation. I tried the university thing for a while. I'd learned a lot about how to shield myself by then, and I think I might have managed if I hadn't needed a job to help pay my way. With no experience under my belt and needing to work odd hours so I could attend class, waiting tables was my only employment option. Dealing with a constant flow of customers didn't work for me. My bosses weren't thrilled to find me zoned out in the register area, sometimes with the cash drawer open. I kept one waitress job for almost a week. My all-time *worst* work experience lasted for only forty-three minutes."

"You got canned in less than an hour?"

"I'm talented. What can I say?"

He regarded her with somber contemplation. "So you never went to college."

"Oh, yes. I did telemarketing for a few years, and then I was able to get my degree online. A lot of universities offer correspondence courses nowadays, and it's less costly than attending classes on campus. I'm so grateful that option became available to me. If I'd been born a decade sooner it wouldn't have been. Now I decorate model homes and make a fairly good living. At least, I *did*. I'm only just now getting my business started in Crystal Falls. I'll hopefully do well here, but that remains to be seen."

"You aren't able to see your own future and know how your business will do?"

Loni chuckled. Before she could answer the question, he cut in with, "I know, I know. That isn't the way it works."

"If it were, I'd be a millionaire. Just imagine how well I could do at the races!"

He dug a trench in the dirt with the heel of his boot, and then smoothed it away. "Do you enjoy interior decorating?"

"I *love* it. The textures, the colors. It's very much an

art, and challenges me creatively. I've even won some awards. Mostly, though, I love it because I can work alone in sterile environments, yet still earn a good income and be independent."

He arched a dark eyebrow at her. "You still haven't touched on the God element of your story."

Loni searched for the first glimmers of starlight in the charcoal sky. "Many people take certain passages in the Bible quite literally, so to their way of thinking, all clairvoyants are evil. Over the years I guess you might say I've encountered a lot of unpleasantness. Being a clairvoyant has adversely affected my entire life—academically, socially, spiritually, and even romantically."

He picked up a pine needle and tossed it onto the embers. They watched it ignite and then become a shriveled thread of bright orange before winking out. "Had a few men run scared, have you?"

Loni puffed air into her cheeks. "That's a good way of putting it." She angled him an amused glance. "Some men thought I was lying about my gift, others thought I was crazy, and a memorable few were terrified that I might be able to read their minds."

He laughed again. "Maybe they were thinking things they didn't want you knowing about."

"Possibly, only I can't imagine what."

His dark eyes, already sparkling with amber from the fire, warmed with a mischievous twinkle. "Being a healthy American male with a normal libido, I have a fair idea what may have been on their minds. You're a beautiful woman."

Loni couldn't think what to say. A hot flush moved up her neck.

"Now I've embarrassed you." He leaned forward to toss another needle into the fire. With the firelight playing over his face and delineating the well-muscled slope of his shoulders, Loni thought he was far more beautiful than she was. "It's the truth, though. The first time I saw you, I thought, 'Wow.'"

Loni had always considered herself to be average in the looks department. "You're very kind."

"Kind, hell. Standing behind you in line, I definitely enjoyed the view. You were wearing alfalfa green slacks and a silk blouse the color of cream."

"Ecru."

"Is that what it's called? Ecru, then."

"And the slacks are patina."

He flashed a dazzling grin, his teeth gleaming in the flickering light. "I have a theory about women and compliments. The conceited ones who think they're God's gift to mankind always gush and bat their eyelashes when you tell them they're pretty. The ones who aren't self-confident say dumb things like, 'You're very kind,' and then they pretend the compliment was never paid. To me, they're the most beautiful of all, because they honestly don't realize how drop-dead gorgeous they are."

Loni rolled her eyes, trying her best not to blush any more than she already was. "Patina is the green color of copper after it oxidizes."

"I know what patina is. I also know a beautiful woman when I see one."

"You're very—"

She broke off. His dark face had moved closer to hers—perilously closer. His breath, laced richly with whiskey, wafted across her cheek. "Your eyes are the prettiest blue, and they change color all the time," he whispered. "Right now they remind me of moonlight reflecting on lake water on a hot August night." He dropped his gaze to her mouth. "I may regret this later, but damned if I can stop myself."

Loni had no such problem. She planted a hand at the center of his chest. "If you're thinking about kissing me, forget it."

"Why?"

"You chew tobacco. I'm sorry, but *yuck.*"

He chuckled. "Only on Fridays. It's my beer-and-tobacco day. The rest of the time I drink water or coffee and suck wintergreen breath mints."

"Oh."

"Any other concerns?"

"Yes. I, um, don't think it's wise for us to —"

"Hold the thought."

The deep timbre of his voice seemed to enfold her in warmth. He curled a big hand over her shoulder. Through the jacket, the gentle grip of his fingers radiated heat, making Loni wonder how it might feel if no fleece shielded her skin. Madness. Their gazes locked. For just an instant it seemed to her that the world fell away. She glanced at his firm lips, how they shimmered in the firelight, and suddenly, instead of feeling alarmed, she wanted him to kiss her more than she'd ever wanted anything.

As if he sensed that, his burnished face drew closer, his dark eyes holding hers until her vision was eclipsed by a coffee brown blur. As lightly as a butterfly wing his lips touched hers. She expected him to deepen the kiss. That was how it had always happened before, anyway, not that she'd ever particularly enjoyed the wet press of a man's lips on hers or the scrape of teeth that often followed. But Clint kept the contact almost nonexistent, a tantalizing caress that made her breath hitch with expectancy while her heart began to slog, each beat knocking hard against her ribs. She pressed closer. He murmured something, groaned, and slipped a hard arm around her waist. Loni made tight fists on the front of his shirt.

She *wanted*. He tasted faintly of the whiskey, too, slightly sweet and completely intoxicating. His lips felt like sun-warmed silk as they grazed hers. She leaned in, needing, yearning. It was the first time in her life she'd ever felt true desire, and it was a heady experience. Her limbs felt weak and tingly. An electrical sensation moved through her torso, everything within her quivering at the zing.

Catching her chin in one hand, he pressed gently on her jaw to part her teeth. Then he angled his head to deepen the kiss, the tip of his tongue tracing her lips and then plunging deep to taste the recesses of her mouth. As the urgency between them mounted, every rational thought in Loni's head evaporated. Abandoning her hold on his shirt, she hugged his strong neck. He moaned again, the sound thrumming through her. Then he tipped her back over his arm and gently lowered her to the sleeping bag. Through her fleece jacket, his chest abraded her breasts, making her body arch and tremble.

Then she felt his palm on the bare skin of her midriff. *Yes.* She wanted his hands all over her.

To her great disappointment he suddenly lifted his head. She blinked dizzily, trying to bring his dark face back into focus. He kissed the end of her nose, then trailed his lips lightly up the bridge to kiss her forehead.

"Wow," he whispered huskily.

Shivering with yearning, Loni closed her eyes and smiled. *Wow* was right. Some things in life were so wonderful it was hard to let them end. He was right to stop, though. Practically speaking, they'd known each other for a very short time. It didn't matter that it felt like much longer. There were also her moral convictions to be considered. Though a part of her resented still being inexperienced at thirty-one, a much larger part of her believed that sexual intimacy outside of marriage was wrong. She wasn't willing to lose her virginity to just anyone, especially not a cowboy with whom she had almost nothing in common. When this was over they'd undoubtedly go their separate ways and probably never see each other again.

He sat up, offered her a hand, and drew her up beside him. Then he reached behind her to reclaim his hat, which she must have sent rolling when she hugged his neck. After settling the Stetson just so on his head, he treated her to a long, questioning study, his mouth curved in a slight smile. He reached to straighten her cap and brush a curl from her cheek, the graze of his knuckles making her skin tingle.

"I'm thinking we need to call it a night. We'll have to be awake and at it well before dawn."

Loni's legs protested as she got up. Hooter's salve had worked wonders, but she was still sore. Clint rose and collected the sleeping bag in his arms. Inclining his head for her to lead the way, he fell in behind her as she walked to the tent. She was grateful for the illumination of firelight so she could see.

"No worries, okay?" He lifted the tent flap and shook out her sleeping bag. "I'll be sacked out by the fire only a few yards away. If you need me, just holler. I'm a light sleeper."

Loni nodded, already dreading his departure. It was so dark away from the fire, and the nylon tent offered scant protection. Nevertheless she bent at the waist, entered, and called good night as she tied the little nylon strings that held the flap closed, no easy task in the dark. Then she patted the ground to find the sleeping bag, sat to remove her cap and boots, and hugged her knees to say her prayers. In the middle of a Hail Mary, she imagined Clint kneeling by his sleeping bag to pray, just as she was, and she lost her concentration.

As her eyes adjusted to the darkness, she realized it wasn't really so dark after all. Light from the fire washed over the walls of the tent, illuminating the interior slightly. She finished her prayers, saying the last one for Trevor, and then crawled into bed, zipped the bag, and ordered herself to go instantly to sleep.

Fat chance. Her heart hurt, and this time not over Trevor. She felt sad for herself. Why did the only man she'd ever met who could make her blood run hot have to be a cowboy who waded around in horse manure all day? As much as she liked him and enjoyed his company, she couldn't picture herself in a lasting relationship with him. Their backgrounds and life experiences were too different. She could never be happy living on a horse ranch, and he'd be miserable in town. Her idea of entertainment was a movie and dinner out, or going to a play in the city. His was to go horseback riding in the wilderness.

How could two people who were so fundamentally different ever build a life together that fulfilled both of them?

Chapter Seven

Sleep eluded Clint. Head pillowed on his saddle, he tried counting stars instead of sheep, but thoughts of Loni kept circling in his mind. That kiss . . . It had been amazing. He'd kissed his share of lady frogs and a few princesses as well, but never in his memory had one simple kiss aroused him so completely or touched him so deeply. He kept remembering the wide, wary look in her eyes, and then the awkward first contact, her soft lips pursed, her teeth clamped closed. Years ago, when he and his brothers had still been young enough to occasionally come across an inexperienced female, they'd called it the "virgin pucker."

Maybe he was misreading her. That had to be it. He guessed her to be in her late twenties, maybe even early thirties. Beautiful women, even clairvoyants who'd never been in a lasting relationship, didn't make it to that age without garnering a good deal of sexual know-how along the way. Maybe she hadn't believed him about the chewing tobacco. That would explain the pursed lips and locked jaw. Even for Clint, who greatly enjoyed a few pinches of Kodiak on Friday nights, the thought of kissing a woman with that crap in her mouth wasn't a pleasant thought.

Counting stars wasn't working, he finally decided. Giving up, he settled his hat over his eyes. That had to be it, he concluded wearily. She'd been afraid he had something nasty in his mouth. He sighed and stared into the absolute blackness provided by the crown of his Stetson. He had probably just imagined that hesitant sweetness when she'd finally parted her lips and surrendered to the kiss, and it must have been a figment of his imagination that she hadn't been sure where to put her hands at first. But he was positive about one thing: The shiver that had run the length of her slender body when he touched her bare midriff had been caused by desire—or his name wasn't Clint Harrigan.

Enough. What the hell was wrong with him, anyway? He didn't normally obsess about women. It was the long time since he'd been with someone, he supposed. His body was clamoring for release. *Too bad, so sad.* He'd made a promise to himself about never again having sex with anyone outside the bonds of holy matrimony, and he meant to keep it.

It seemed to Clint that he'd only just fallen asleep when something woke him. He nudged his hat up and saw Loni huddled near him by the fire, her sleeping bag drawn like a lumpy, oversize cape around her narrow shoulders. As the haze of sleep parted, he noticed that her face looked chalk white.

Pushing up on one arm, he asked, "You sick?"

She shook her head and reached to pull the sleeping

bag closer around her body. It was then that Clint noticed how badly she was shaking. He unzipped his bag to sit up.

"What's wrong?"

"Bad dream."

A bad dream had caused this? Clint had been treated to some doozies over his lifetime, and to his shame he'd jerked awake, trembling with fright, even as a grown man. But it passed quickly. He always just opened his eyes, determined where he was, and reasoned the fear away.

"When I have bad dreams," he offered, "I just remind myself they aren't real, and then I'm okay."

"Th-this dream is."

"Is what?"

"R-real. It h-happened."

Clint's heart skittered and missed a beat. "Did you dream about Trevor?"

She shook her head. At the movement, a sheen of perspiration became visible on her face in the firelight. "Ch-Cheryl Blain."

It took Clint a second to remember who that was.

Loni finally met his gaze. Her lovely eyes were now a dark, stormy blue. Clint mentally circled what she'd just told him. *Bad dream, Cheryl Blain.* The Blain girl had been tortured before she died.

"Ah, honey." It was all he could think to say.

"I miss Hannah, I guess. She sleeps with me. After a dream she always makes me f-feel better."

Clint could understand that. Just the dog's warmth and the sound of her breathing probably helped Loni to ground herself in reality again. Not allowing himself to think beyond the moment, he pushed up on his knees, caught Loni in his arms, and then sat back on his bed, depositing her and the tangle of sleeping bag in the V of his bent legs.

"No, no, I'm f-fine," she protested. "I don't n-need—"

"The hell you don't." Clint tightened one arm around her and tucked her head under his chin, determined to hold her until the night terrors abated. "I may not be Hannah, but I'll do my best to fill in for her."

He felt her relent, her body going soft against him. "Hannah s-snores and farts."

Even now she had a sense of humor. "If I fall asleep, I'll definitely deliver on the snoring part. You may have to wait until tomorrow night to hear my version of a flatulent symphony, though."

"Why t-tomorrow night?"

"Chili with beans for supper."

She chuffed with laughter and snuggled closer. Clint thought she was shaking less now, but it was hard to tell for sure through all the bedding. Turning his wrist, he noted the time: a quarter after two in the morning. He'd hold her for fifteen minutes, he decided. Give her plenty of time to escape the clutches of the nightmare, and then he'd get her tucked back into bed.

"I miss all my dead bolts and the security system, too," she whispered. "After a Cheryl dream I wake up so frightened it feels like my skin is being turned inside out."

"I can't provide any dead bolts," he murmured against her hair, "but out here I'm a damned good security system. I have a sixth sense of my own when it comes to camp perimeters. I wake up if anything comes around."

"You didn't wake up when I came to the fire. If I'd been a serial killer, you'd be dead."

"You belong here at camp. I don't wake up when the horses move around, either. My sensor only goes off when something or someone comes in from the surrounding woods. Even chipmunks have been known to startle me awake. You're safe, I promise, serial killers notwithstanding." He waited a beat. "Need to talk about it? The dream, I mean. Sometimes it helps."

"Heavens, no. There aren't words." She stirred slightly. "Besides, we always talk about me. I'd rather hear about you for a change."

"What would you like to know?"

She took a second to reply. "Why is it so hard for you to say you're sorry?"

His heart panged. "That's a story I've never told anyone."

"Maybe so, but I'd really like to hear it."

Clint heard an echo in those words and smiled against her hair. He'd said almost exactly the same thing to her earlier that evening. And she had a point, he supposed. He'd told her very little about himself. He just wished she'd asked a different question.

"It's a long story, dating way back to my childhood."

"I don't care. It'll take my mind off the dream."

Clint gathered his courage. In all these years he'd never talked with anyone about it, not even his brothers.

"It was five days after my seventh birthday," he began huskily, and as he said the words, he was taken back through the years to a cold March day, when the anemic winter sunlight had barely thawed the crust of ice on the ground from the previous night. "My mom was pregnant with my sister, Samantha. At the time I didn't pay much attention, but looking back on it now, I think she must have been in the latter part of her eighth month and due to drop anytime."

"Drop?"

"Buckaroo lingo. Due to go into labor, I mean. I was out in front of the house, playing with my new puppy, a birthday present from my folks. His name was Tug, and he'd crawled in under the porch. I thought he was stuck."

"That's a cute name. Did he like to play tug-of-war?"

"Oh, yeah. Anyway, my mother opened the front door." In his mind he could still see her clearly, only now through the eyes of a man. "She was pale, very pale, only I didn't register it then. I was too busy worrying about that silly dog. I was also lying on the ground, with the porch deck blocking my view of her from the hips down. She said, 'Clinton James, I need you to run and get your daddy. Tell him I need him at the house straightaway.' I said, 'Okay, Mama,' and went back to calling Tug the instant she closed the door. I probably dawdled for five minutes, maybe less, maybe more, until Tug finally came out from under the step. Then I ran to find my father, just like Mama told me to.

"Anyway, she was hemorrhaging. While I scooted around on my belly on the frozen ground, my mother was inside bleeding to death." Clint swallowed hard, not sure he could finish. A lump had lodged in his throat, making it difficult for him to talk. "When Dad and I got to the house there was blood all over the kitchen. Mama was sitting on a chair, too weak to stay standing, I guess. I'll never forget the pool of red all around the chair. She looked up at Dad, her face so white she looked dead, her eyelashes fluttering as if she could barely keep her eyes open. 'What took you so long?' she asked my father. 'I told Clinton James to get you straightaway.'"

"Oh, *Clint*."

He blinked, glad now that her head was tucked under his chin because she couldn't see his tears.

"I realized then that I should have raced to get my father immediately. As he scooped Mama up out of the chair to carry her to the car, I started crying and saying, 'I'm sorry, Mama. I'm sorry, Mama. I didn't know you were bleeding. I didn't know.' My father couldn't walk for me getting in his way, and he yelled, 'Sorry never fixed nuthin', boy. Stop your blubberin' and open the damned door for me!' So I ran ahead, doing as he told me, so scared . . . well, let's just say I've never been that scared in all the years since. And I had every reason to be. Once Dad got her to the hospital, they tried to transfuse her and go in to fix whatever was causing the hemorrhage, but she died on the table. They performed an emergency C-section to save Samantha." He swallowed again. "So there you have it. That's my story. 'Sorry never fixed nothin'.' And my dad was right. Saying I was sorry sure as hell didn't fix my mother. To this day I still have trouble saying those words."

She said nothing for what seemed to him a very long time. "Guilt is a terrible thing. You still blame yourself for her death. Don't you?"

How could he not? The five minutes he'd wasted trying to coax Tug from under the porch might have made the difference between life and death for his mother. A week later he'd given Tug away, a self-inflicted punishment, and he'd never owned another dog since.

"Yeah, I blame myself," he admitted.

"You need to talk with your dad. You haven't ever, have you?"

"No. There never seemed to be a good moment. When I was small I was afraid to bring it up. He loved my mother more than life itself, and he grieved for her for years. Later . . . well, it just never felt right, some-how."

"He needs to say those words to you, Clint."

"What words?"

"The words that never fix anything." She rubbed her cheek against his shirt, leading him to suspect he wasn't the only one with tears in his eyes. "He never should have said that to you. You were just a little guy. It wasn't your fault she started hemorrhaging."

"No, I understand that now. But knowing some-thing and feeling it, deep down inside, are two differ-ent things. As for my dad, he was in a panic. He probably doesn't even remember what he said to me. He's a good man, my dad, and a wonderful father. It's the only time in my whole life that he ever said any-thing cruel to me, and I don't think he meant to then."

"Let him tell you that. Talking with him may not make it easier to say you're sorry, but the feelings you have about your mother's death aren't healthy. You need to talk to him."

Clint knew his feelings weren't healthy. His brothers treasured their memories of their mother, while he tried never to think of her. "I'll consider it."

"Please do. You're a good man. You don't deserve to feel guilty over something that was never your fault in the first place."

He released a shaky breath. "I just wish she'd told me. You know? Instead she acted as if nothing really bad was wrong."

"Of course. You were just a little guy. She probably didn't want to frighten you."

"She didn't, and she died for the mistake."

"But it was *her* mistake. She should have at least made you understand how important it was that you find your father immediately. Because she didn't, you dawdled for a couple of minutes, a very typical thing for a child to do. Have you ever stopped to think that she might have died anyway, Clint? Your ranch is quite a drive from town. Chances are, your dad couldn't have gotten her to the hospital in time no matter what."

Clint had never thought of that, but he realized Loni might be right. It was a very long drive to town—such a distance, in fact, that they'd recently had a family conference to decide the best course of action if an emergency with Frank occurred. Though Clint's dad was in excellent shape for a man his age, he was still at risk now for stroke or cardiac arrest, and the emergency response time to his home would be slow. Frank had eased his children's minds by saying he'd rather die of a heart attack than leave the land he loved so much. Quality of life mattered more to him than quantity, and he didn't want his kids worrying needlessly

over the inevitable. One of these days he would have a
health crisis, and if he died en route to the hospital, no
one would be to blame. It was his choice to make, and
that was the way he wanted it.

Clint realized he felt as if a thousand pounds had
been lifted from his shoulders. He tightened his arms
around Loni, glad of the sleeping bag, which kept the
embrace asexual. "Thanks for talking to me. I actually
feel better about it than I have since she died."

"I'm glad," she said softly.

He thought about it for a moment. "I'm surprised
you had to ask me about it. It's more your style to have
seen it in a vision."

She didn't respond for several seconds. "I didn't say
I hadn't."

Clint tipped his head around to meet her gaze. Her
eyes still shimmered with tears. "You already knew?"
He didn't know whether to laugh or wring her neck.
"Why'd you make me tell you the story then?"

"Because you needed to tell it."

He couldn't help but smile. She was right. He had
needed to tell it. Instead of wringing her neck, he settled for placing a soft kiss on the crown of her head.
Then, turning his cheek against her hair, he let his eyes
fall closed. He'd hold her for just a few more minutes,
he thought. Then he'd walk her back to the tent.

Her bed was vibrating. Loni frowned in her sleep,
then came slowly awake, wondering how that could
be. She didn't own a vibrating bed. She lifted her lashes
to stare stupidly at a sea of blue. Not her blue sheets.
And the blankets lying on top of her felt way too heavy.

"Oh!"

She jackknifed to a sitting position, horrified to discover that her vibrating bed was Clint Harrigan's chest, the expanse of blue the front of his chambray shirt. He lay sprawled on his back, legs spread wide to accommodate hers. She stared at the front of his jeans, where moments before her pelvis had been nestled. Was it only her imagination, or was the fly of his Wranglers protruding more than usual? Her gaze shot to his face. His sleep-rumpled black hair lay in lazy waves over his high forehead, and his jet-black eyelashes were fluttering as he stirred awake.

"How did I . . . ?" She pushed a hand into her tangled hair, wincing when her fingers encountered knots. "When did we . . . ?"

He blinked slowly awake. When he finally focused on her, his brown eyes looked confused for a moment; then they cleared. "Sorry. I only meant to sit there a few minutes more and then hustle you off to bed. I must've nodded off." He pushed up on one elbow, noted the early morning sunlight that pooled around them, and said, "Well, *shit*. We've slept half the day away!" He reached for his boots. A moment later he swore again, this time even more vehemently. "My *hat*. Would you just look at my hat?"

He held it up for her to see. The crown was smashed flat on one side. Loni wasn't sure how much a Stetson cost, but she had a hunch they were expensive. "Oh, Clint, I'm sorry."

"Not your fault." He pushed his fist into the bowl and the crown sprang back into shape—sort of. When he settled the Stetson on his head, he looked a little lop-sided. "I'm the one who flattened it."

That was the last time they spoke for nearly an hour. There followed a frenzied rush to break camp, get the horses saddled, and be on their way, their sense of urgency so acute that they skipped morning coffee, settling for water instead, and ate granola bars for breakfast after they hit the trail.

Loni couldn't say getting back in the saddle was a pleasant experience. Her muscles screamed in protest, and her tender backside panged with Uriah's first step. But after about fifteen minutes she began to feel somewhat better, able, at least, to face another long day of riding without whimpering at the thought.

The terrain began to change by midmorning. They'd passed through the gorge and come to an area where the river widened out and flowed lazily along, its green depths seeming to barely move. Instead of rising like walls only a short distance away at each side of the stream, the mountains were set farther back now, creating swaths of flatland along the riverbanks.

Clint waved to Loni, inviting her to come forward and ride abreast of him. Malachi snorted and threw his head, clearly affronted to have Uriah usurping his position as lead horse.

"Calm down," Clint scolded, running his hand along the gelding's neck. "You don't always have to be in front."

Loni reined Uriah back just a bit so Malachi could stay a neck ahead. That seemed to smooth the older gelding's ruffled feathers. Clint flashed her an appreciative grin. "Thanks. He's a wonderful animal, just a little arrogant around the edges sometimes."

"Has he always been that way?"

Clint reached over to tug the bill of her cap down. "You don't watch it, you'll end up with a nose to rival Rudolph's. Best to keep your face shaded. Here in the mountains the sun doesn't feel that warm, but it'll blister you all the same. As for Malachi, he came along when I was first getting my horse-breeding business well established. He thinks he's the founding father of the stable. He isn't, of course. Methuselah has that honor, but he's a good-natured old stallion who allows Malachi his delusions." He leaned sideways to get his canteen. After taking a drink, he passed her the canvas-encased vessel. "I miss my coffee. How 'bout you?"

Loni normally drank tea, but she did miss her morning caffeine. Her cell phone rang just then. Startled, she handed back the canteen, fished in her jacket pocket, glanced at the caller ID, and opened the communication device.

"Hi, Mom."

Annabel MacEwen wasted no time on greetings. "What in heaven's *name* do you think you're doing? And why haven't you been answering your phone? You hare off into the wilderness with a total stranger without even showing me the courtesy of *discussing* it with me first?"

Loni had forgotten to readjust the phone volume, which she'd set on high while she worked at the shop, where workmen were making noise. She poked futilely at buttons, trying to turn it down.

"What's that beeping noise?" Annabel cried. "Are you trying to hang up on me?"

Loni stopped pushing buttons. "Of course not. Can you just calm down?"

"Calm down? I have been worried absolutely sick. Do you think I don't know what's happening out there? You're not the only one with second sight, you know. I can't believe you slept with him. He's a total stranger, young lady. At least have a care for your safety—if not for your own sake, then for mine. How will I live with it if something happens to you? What if he's a homicidal maniac? You have no way of knowing, not for sure."

Loni held the phone away from her ear. Her gaze locked with Clint's. His firm mouth quirked at one corner, his eyes dancing with laughter.

"Even if he doesn't murder you in your sleep, what about the new life you're trying to make for yourself? When I told you to talk with your grandmother, I thought you'd have the good sense not to take *all* her advice! I saw you speaking to a policeman this morning. Oh, Loni, what *are* you thinking?"

Loni pressed the phone back to her ear. "Mom. Mom? *Mom!*"

"What?" Annabel asked crossly.

"You're shrieking. Clint can hear every word you're saying."

"Good." Annabel took an audible breath to refuel. "That's my daughter you're playing fast and loose with, young man. Isn't it bad enough that you've dragged her out into that wilderness area, and on *horseback*, no less? She's never ridden a horse in her life!

What if she falls? What if it bucks her off? And then you compound it by seducing her the second night out? You'll have my husband to deal with when this trip is over; mark my words. From this point forward, I highly recommend that you comport yourself like a gentleman."

Loni drew the phone from her ear again. Clint arched an eyebrow, studying the silver apparatus as if it were a strange object that had just dropped into her hand from outer space.

"Noo-noo-noo-noo, noo-noo-noo-noo," he sang softly.

Loni recognized the sound track of her favorite old TV show, *The Twilight Zone*. She nearly choked trying to stifle a startled giggle, and she wasn't successful enough by far.

"Are you *laughing*?" Annabel's voice had gone from shrill to piercing. "Can you share the joke? I fail to see what you find so amusing."

"I'm sorry, Mom. It's just . . . Never mind. If you'd let me get a word in edgewise, I'll—"

"A word from you would have been much appreciated *before* you made the decision to seek out Mr. Harrigan. A word from you would have been even more appreciated *before* you took off into the wilderness with a complete stranger."

Loni sighed. "I'm sorry I didn't discuss it with you first, Mom. I just took it for granted you knew what was going on without my calling you."

"Ha! Deirdre blistered my ears so bad a couple of months ago for innocently dropping in on her and Michael that I swore off touching things to look in on either one of you. And how am I repaid for trying to be a courteous mother? My daughters cut me totally out of the loop."

Now that Loni came to think of it, her mother hadn't called to scold her about not taking her vitamins in over a month. "Oh, Mom, I'm *sorry*. I didn't know you'd sworn off."

"Yes, well, I've seen the error of my ways, and I'll never do it again. If I'd been checking on you as I should, I could have stopped you from pulling such a crazy stunt."

"No, you're wrong about that. This is something I had to do. And that's the main reason I didn't call you, because I already knew exactly what you'd say."

"That you'd lost your mind, perhaps? That's exactly what I would have said!"

"But I haven't. I can't run from this, Mom. A little boy's life is on the line."

"So was Cheryl Blain's, and you nearly destroyed yourself trying to save her. Now you're about to do the same thing again. You could end up having to leave Crystal Falls. Where will you go next? And what of the thousands of dollars you've spent remodeling that shop? You don't have the money to start over again somewhere else."

Loni sobered, for she shared all the same concerns. "I don't have any answers. I only know this is something I have to do. If it blows up in my face I'll have to trust in God to bail me out somehow."

That took the wind out of Annabel's sails. "Sometimes God can't bail us out, Loni. We mess up so badly His hands are tied."

"I'll face that when it happens. For now all I can do is go where He leads me."

Annabel sighed. Loni knew by the sound that her mother's rant had finally ended.

"He's very good-looking," she continued, but in a calmer tone. "When you used to describe him I couldn't get a clear picture in my mind. In my opinion he's a little *too* handsome, though, the kind who's undoubtedly broken a lot of female hearts. Have a care, Loni. Don't end up being another notch on his belt."

Clint arched an eyebrow again.

"Mom, he can still hear you."

"Oh." Annabel lowered her voice. "Be careful. That's all. I don't want to see you get hurt, physically or emotionally. I'm sorry for carrying on so, but I truly have been frantic."

"I should have called, so I'm the one to apologize. I just . . . well, I wanted to avoid a quarrel, I guess. As for not answering the phone, it hasn't rung." Loni thought of the mountains that had hemmed them in on all sides until a few minutes ago. "No reception, I suppose. We're in a more open place now."

"Please be safe, sweetheart. I love you so much."

"I love you, too. And try not to worry. Not everything you saw was exactly how it seemed."

"Meaning you didn't sleep with him?"

For the first time in her life Loni finally understood why Deirdre sometimes grew so upset with their mother. It was unsettling to be spied upon during one's most private moments. "Not in the biblical sense, no." Loni frowned slightly. "Which of my possessions have you been holding to zoom in on me, anyway?"

"Your blankie."

"My what?"

"Your blanket. Remember? You couldn't be without it when you were small."

"Do me a favor and put it away," Loni said firmly. "I'm thirty-one years old, Mom. I'm entitled to some privacy. Put it back in the cedar chest and communicate with me the normal way, like other mothers do."

"And how might that be?"

"By phone."

"Ha. You just said it yourself, no reception. I'm hugging this blanket until you're safely out of there."

After ending the conversation, Loni rode beside Clint in silence for several minutes. She couldn't be certain how much he'd overheard, only that he'd gleaned enough to probably be full of questions. She wasn't really surprised when he finally spoke.

"What did she mean when she talked about how you used to describe me? I didn't get the impression she was referring to the recent past."

Loni briefly considered lying to him. It wasn't something she did often, though, and she feared lack of practice would have her mucking it up. "I, um . . . had dreams about you."

"Dreams about me," he mused aloud. "What kind of dreams?"

"Uneventful ones, mostly. I just dreamed of you is all."

"When?"

Loni shifted in the saddle to give herself a moment to formulate an answer. "Now and then."

"Now and then *when*?"

She wasn't very well practiced at evasion, either. "All my life."

Silence, a very long silence. He angled her a questioning look. "You've dreamed of me all your *life*?"

"Mostly. Not when I was really tiny, I don't think, but then, maybe I just can't remember back that far. Since I was about five, for sure. I called you my dream cowboy. That was part of the shock for me when we met at the grocery store. I'd dreamed of you all my life, and suddenly there you were, a real, live man."

"*That* is weird. I mean . . . that is *really* weird. Did I always look like I do now, or did we grow up together without me knowing about it?"

Loni gnawed her bottom lip, trying to imagine herself in his shoes. Correction, in his boots. After he'd heard her mother's tirade she thought he was handling all of it pretty well. "You looked just as you do now. I've always known, way deep down, that I was destined to meet you someday. I just never thought it would be under these circumstances."

"Trying to rescue a child, you mean."

She nodded.

"So what circumstances were you expecting?"

Heat pooled in her cheeks. She tugged the bill of the John Deere cap lower to conceal the blush. No such luck. He saw it anyway.

"*Romantic* circumstances?"

Loni really, *really* wished he would let it drop. But she supposed that was too much to ask. "I outgrew the notion long before I met you. I'm a woman now. I realize how silly it was for me to think . . ."

"Think what?"

Loni shot him a resentful look. "Must we discuss this? It's a little embarrassing. You know?"

"No, I *don't* know, and yes, we must discuss this. If I've been the leading man in your dreams all your life, I think I have a right to know what kind of dreams they were."

"It wasn't like that. Nothing ever happened in the dreams. I just *saw* you; that's all. As a teenager I fantasized about you a bit, thinking . . . oh, I don't know, the silly things all young girls think about, I guess."

"That we were going to fall in love?"

In truth, Loni had always believed in her younger years that Clint Harrigan would be the one great love of her life. She couldn't bring herself to admit that to him, though. "I'm older now, and a whole lot wiser. I understand that nothing like that is remotely possible between us."

Another long silence. Then he did the nose-rubbing thing, which she was quickly coming to realize was a nervous habit, his way of stalling when he couldn't think what to say. "Did I miss something?"

Loni frowned at him in bewilderment. "What do you mean?"

He gestured with one hand. "Did I imagine that kiss we shared last night? What do you mean, 'nothing like that is remotely possible'? Was it *that* bad?"

He looked so offended she had to laugh. "No, of course it wasn't bad. It's just . . . well, think about it. We're nothing alike. The inside of your truck looks like a junkyard."

"All that *junk* is important. Tools of my trade, so to speak."

"Maybe so, but there's a total lack of organization. How on earth do you find anything?"

"I manage. And I fail to see how the condition of my truck factors in. Haven't you heard? Opposites attract."

She shot him another look, this time a searching one. "Are you saying you're attracted to me?"

"I don't find you unattractive. As I recall, I told you that last night." He thumped himself on the forehead. "Oh, that's right. You thought I was just being nice. News flash: I don't swap slobber with a woman I find unattractive."

Loni wrinkled her nose. "Yuck."

"You've never heard of swapping slobber?" A twinkle of devilment entered his eyes. "I don't kiss a woman I find to be unattractive, then. Does that suit you better?"

"Much, thank you."

"Back to the dream-cowboy thing. Why isn't anything like that remotely possible for us? Do you dislike me?"

"No. I like you a lot. It's just that I don't think we suit. I was raised in the greater Seattle area, and my lifestyle is so different from yours. I know next to nothing about ranching, even less about horses, and can't picture myself being happy, over the long term, in a rural setting. By the same token I can't imagine you being happy in the city. There's also my clairvoyance to consider. Everything about me is against your religion. Remember? Your words, not mine."

"I've changed my mind about that, and you know it as well as I do."

"You have, and I appreciate it very much. But the

fact remains that you find it unsettling." She hummed the sound track of *The Twilight Zone* as a reminder. "My mother is home hugging my childhood security blanket. For all I know she's spying on us right now. Tell me the thought of that doesn't bother you."

That shut him up, but only for a moment. Then he lifted a hand as if to wave and said, "Hi, Mrs. MacEwen. She hasn't become a notch on my belt yet, but the day's still young."

Loni giggled. What was it about him that made her want to laugh all the time? Especially when their reason for being here was both serious and urgent. "You are incorrigible. She's very worried about that, you know. If she's tuned in she'll have fits and drive Daddy crazy all day."

"Good. She'll be too busy bending his ear to spy on us." He rode in silence for a few feet. "I'm confused. I distinctly remember you saying that your abilities are much stronger than your mother's. Yet it seems to me she has a much better handle on her gift than you do."

"How is that?"

"She has no trouble touching your blanket and tuning in to see what you're doing. But now you aren't able to summon visions by touching Trevor's bear. They just come to you or they don't."

"True, but there's a special link between my mom and me. She has also practiced, making her ability stronger when it comes to Deirdre and me. We are her daughters. She couldn't do the same with a stranger."

"Hmm."

Frowning thoughtfully, Clint said nothing more. Loni was greatly relieved. She'd been half-afraid he might return to the subject of her dreams about him. The last thing she wanted was to get backed into a corner and confess that she'd fantasized about falling wildly in love with him for most of her life.

Several hours later Loni realized she hadn't had a vision of Trevor in over twenty-four hours, and she couldn't stop worrying about him. Frightened for his safety, she fished Boo from her saddlebag. But when she held the still-damp bear in her hands, nothing came to her.

Still riding abreast of her, Clint watched as she stuffed the bear back into the bag. "Nothing, huh?"

"No. It really worries me."

He gave her a pointed look. "Maybe you should try harder. Your mother has mastered the art of tuning in on you at will. If she's learned to focus her concentration that well, why can't you?"

"I've always shied away from trying to strengthen my power."

"Why?"

She struggled to put her feelings into words. "As it is, I leave it up to God. If I strengthen my gift and circumvent Him, how will I know for certain that what I see is sent by Him?" She gave him an appealing look. "It's extremely important to me that I not use my gift in any way displeasing to Him."

"Damn, you're starting to sound like a Catholic."

Loni was so tempted to pluck her rosary out of her jacket pocket and wave it under his nose. It was all she could do to stop herself. "What if I were a Catholic? Would that be so difficult for you to conceive? And for your information, it isn't only Catholics who want to comply with God's will."

"Of course it isn't only Catholics who—" He broke off and sighed audibly. Then he slanted her a crooked grin. "Are we having our first fight?"

Loni refused to smile, absolutely refused. "You didn't answer my question. What if I were a Catholic?"

"You'd probably be so riddled with Catholic guilt over being a clairvoyant that you'd be hiding in a closet, afraid to come out. It would be very difficult for someone like you, so innately and powerfully gifted as a clairvoyant, to find peace with her gift and be a practicing Catholic. You'd be so worried about misusing your abilities that you'd—" He stopped his horse and gave her a study so intense that her cheeks burned. Then he said, "I'll be damned!"

His outburst was so loud and vehement that Loni flinched and Uriah snorted.

"Why the hell didn't you tell me?" he demanded.

She drew Uriah to a halt. "There was never a good moment."

"You're a *Catholic*?" He phrased it as a question, but it was more a statement. Then he jerked off his hat, wiped his forehead with his sleeve, and stared off into the trees. "Suddenly all the pieces fit. A clairvoyant who's afraid to use her gift. It was staring me right in the face, and I didn't see it."

"I'm not *afraid* to use my gift," she corrected, stung by the accusation. "I simply refrain from trying to control it. It's not like athletic ability or being artistic, you know."

"Why isn't it?" He nudged Malachi back into a walk

and whistled to the packhorses to fall in behind him. "Forget everything you were ever taught in religious education about clairvoyants, Loni. Your gift doesn't fall into that category. If you were ever told different, put it straight out of your mind. It's an ability given to you by God, and He surely wants you to *use* it. Otherwise why would He have given it to you? Take this thing with Trevor, for instance. Why do you think God has sent you visions about the boy?"

"So I can possibly save his life."

"Exactly. Saving a life isn't evil. *Taking* a life is. Do you think God wanted Michelangelo never to hone his talents as an artist? What a loss to the world that would have been. Do you think Joan of Arc covered her head with a blanket, trying not to have her visions? No. Instead she prayed and meditated, opening herself to God so He could communicate His will to her. Do you think Saint John felt *evil* when he had visions that inspired him to write the Book of Revelation?"

"No, of course not. But I'm not a saint, and I don't receive profound messages."

"The hell you don't. It's pretty damned profound when you see things that could help you save a life."

"Yes, but—"

"No buts. Every life is precious. You can't save every kid in the world, and you can't save every Cheryl Blain. What you can do, though, is hone your skills to the utmost of your ability so you can save a lot of people in your small corner of the world. Prayerfully, of course, and with God's help. It's my opinion that you can't go wrong if you strengthen your gift through prayer and never use it in any fashion contrary to God's teachings."

"I can't believe that *you* are lecturing *me*. On Friday night you explicitly told me that believing in clairvoyants was against your religion."

"Yeah, well, I was wrong. Look at me. I'm a goat roper. What the hell do I know? When I talked with my dad, he set me straight. There are clairvoyants of the bad sort and clairvoyants of the good sort. You have to be a *thinking* Christian to realize the difference, and I never bothered to think about it because I didn't believe people like you really existed.

"Now I *know* people like you exist and I *have* thought about it. You don't use your gift for financial gain. You don't use it to your advantage at all. In fact, it appears to me that it has adversely affected your entire life. I was flippant that night, and I was rude to you as well. I'm *sorry.* All right? I never meant to hurt you. I thought you were a fruitcake who'd find someone else to bother once I got rid of you."

"You just said it."

"I just said what?"

"The words that never fix anything."

He scowled at her. Then he plopped the hat back on his head. "It's a good thing nothing between us is remotely possible, because I swear, you'd drive me to drink. I'm apologizing to you from the bottom of my heart, and you throw the words back in my face."

"I didn't mean it that way at all."

"How did you mean it, then?"

"They worked. The words, I mean. They just fixed my hurt feelings."

He gave her a wary look. "Are you having me on?"

Loni smiled. She couldn't help herself. "No. I feel better. It *did* hurt my feelings when you said people like me are against your religion. It bothered me even more when I realized your religion is *my* religion. It's something of a sore spot."

His mouth quirked at the edges, a telltale sign he was trying not to grin. "I imagine it is. But we'll take care of that."

"How?"

"We'll sit down with Father Mike. He'll set you straight."

Loni shuddered. "No, thanks. I've come to a place where I feel good about who and what I am, but I don't discuss it with priests—or nuns, for that matter. It's one of those things I've decided is a matter of conscience."

"Well, from where I'm standing you haven't worked your way through it enough to take charge of your life." At her resentful glare, he held up a hand. "Hear me out. Instead of controlling your gift, you're allowing it to control you. Do you think God meant for you to be miserable your entire life? Tell me I'm wrong. Are you or are you not miserable a lot of the time?"

"You have no idea what this is like for me."

"No, probably not. But judging by the little I've seen, you're definitely miserable. There has to be a way to block some of the stuff that comes to you. You're picking up things from the past, things from the future, and things from right now. Do you think God meant for it to be a big muddle? Do you think He meant for you to be pelted with visions and be unable to help anyone with the information He sends you? Hell, no. He gave you a powerful gift, something most people can't even imagine. You're a walking miracle of creation, *His* creation. How can you think He doesn't want you to make the most of it *and* have a wonderful life in the process?"

Loni rubbed her temple. "Can we drop it for now? I'm getting a headache."

"Sure. Just think about it. Okay?"

Loni fell back to the end of the line and did little else *but* think about it. It was true that she'd never tried to control her visions. In a way Clint was right. She'd always been afraid to do so because her gift was so powerful and multifaceted. What if she attempted to focus, really focus, and gained control of it? Wouldn't she be running a terrible risk of only *thinking* she was in control? There were dark, evil forces in the world. She'd looked into the eyes of a serial killer and seen true evil. People who didn't believe in the dark side were living in a bubble. She was terrified of opening up a channel of communication and receiving signals from the wrong sources.

But was that having true trust in God? If her gift was heaven-sent, which she knew it was, and if she attempted to control it only through heartfelt prayer and meditation, why should she be afraid? God wouldn't answer her prayers if she'd be opening herself up to evil forces. He'd just say no.

Hands shaking, Loni drew Boo back out of the saddlebag. Clutching the stuffed bear to her breast, directly over her heart, she prayed for the first time in her life to gain control over her visions. *Please, God. Not just for my sake, but also for Trevor's, help me, please help me.*

Holy Mother, in all your goodness, please pray for me and also for Trevor.

Clint had just checked the time and decided they had approximately three good hours of daylight left when he heard Loni shout his name. Pulling Malachi to a halt, he shifted on the saddle to look back. She had urged Uriah into a trot to reach the front of the line, and she bounced on the saddle with the horse's every step. Just watching her made Clint wince. He'd be rubbing her down again tonight with Hooter's miracle cure. That was a given.

"Right here!" she said breathlessly as she brought the horse to a sudden halt, sending up a cloud of dust. "This is where they left the water."

Clint glanced around. There was some white water a way upstream, and the current was swift, but he'd seen a dozen likelier places over the course of the day where two adults might have drowned.

"Did you just have a vision or something?"

Her eyes glowed with inner light. "No, not a vision. I just know. This is where Trevor and Nana left the water." She flung her arm to indicate a rocky draw between two tree-studded hills. "They went that way, right up through there."

Clint had been keeping an eye peeled for tracks. All he'd seen were footprints left by searchers. But he'd been around Loni long enough to know she wouldn't be telling him this without good reason.

"All right." He loosened the packhorse line from his saddle and looped it over her saddle horn. "Stick tight with the horses. I'll ride up and have a look. If I can pick up their tracks, we'll start in here."

To avoid missing anything, Clint headed up the draw in a zigzag pattern, leaning forward over Malachi's neck to scan the ground ahead of them. At first he saw nothing. He was about halfway up and starting to think Loni had to be mistaken when there, right in front of him, shielded from the wind by a boulder, was one large paw print. Only one, but it was enough to set Clint's heart racing. A few feet farther up he saw a small shoe print. He drew Malachi to a halt, dismounted, and covered the next fifty yards on foot, leading the horse behind him. Though wind had obliterated most of the tracks, he saw enough to convince him.

"Damn, she's good."

Shoving his hat back, he took the measure of the terrain he'd have to take the horses through. It was rocky, but passable. He smiled grimly. There wasn't a chance in hell that they'd find Trevor before dark. The rafting accident had occurred last Friday, and it was now late Monday afternoon, putting the kid three full days ahead of them. But if they busted ass, pushing the horses and not stopping to rest as long as there was enough light for the equines to see by, they might close the distance within two days. Maybe less if Trevor's strength was flagging and making him stop more often.

Eager to share the news with Loni, Clint mounted up and turned Malachi back toward the river.

Chapter Eight

An hour later they had crested the ridge. Eager to begin the descent down the opposite side of the mountain while there was still enough sunlight for safe travel, Clint was mildly irritated when Loni hollered from the back of the line for him to wait. He turned in the saddle to watch her ride toward him.

"What's up?" he asked when she drew her mount to a stop near him.

"That's the wrong way." Flinging out an arm, she pointed toward the setting sun. "He's in that direction."

Over the course of the last two days Clint had come to trust in Loni's instincts as he'd never believed possible, but the footprints, not yet obliterated by the wind, didn't lie. "Honey, I've seen a few of Trevor and Nana's tracks, and they aren't heading west."

She frowned in bewilderment. "I don't know how that can be. I feel it here, Clint." She pressed a fist to her sternum. "He's over there." She pointed again. "I'm certain of it."

Problem: Clint's experience in tracking told him to

follow the boy's trail. If they went haring off in another direction, he might play hell finding the kid's tracks again.

"Will you bear with me on this?" He indicated the faint tracks he was following. "All my experience tells me to stay on his trail, honey. Maybe your signals are crossed. You can't deny the evidence of your own eyes. Right?"

"I have two pairs," she reminded him. "And my second set never steers me wrong." She studied the ground again. "I can't understand it. But okay. Maybe I'm misinterpreting my signals."

"Did you have a vision?"

She shook her head. "I can't explain. Maybe it's because I've been praying. I just *know*."

Clint didn't want to make light of her feelings. "Has it ever happened like this before?"

"No. It's new. I've only ever seen things in visions until now."

He thought it over. "Since it's new, I think we need to stick with the tried-and-true methods. If you have a vision of him, and your feelings prove to be correct, we can always alter our course."

She nodded in agreement, but her crestfallen expression told him she wasn't happy about it. When she'd resumed her position at the back of the line, Clint dropped off the ridge, grateful that the steep terrain seemed to be a lot less rocky on the north slope. Protection from the south wind had also preserved Trevor's and Nana's tracks, leaving him a trail that was easier to follow.

The late-afternoon sunlight was starting to wane

when Clint noticed the tracks had suddenly veered northwest. A few minutes later he was cursing under his breath. The boy and dog clearly had altered their course and were now headed due west, precisely where Loni had tried to direct Clint in the first place. It wasn't long before he heard the sound of rushing water. Soon he came upon a creek.

After dismounting, he waited for Loni to ride the length of the line to join him at the stream's edge. Offering her a shamefaced grin, he said, "I should have listened to you. I wasted a good hour following his trail."

She swung off the horse. He was surprised to note that her legs didn't appear to wobble, though she did walk stiffly. Most people took three or four days to break in to the saddle. "So I was right?" She looked around and beamed a smile. "At least he found water. That's great. Isn't it?"

Clint was relieved that she seemed to bear him no animosity for making such a bad judgment call. A lot of people would have been unable to resist rubbing it in. "It's definitely a good sign. If he follows the creek as long as he can, he won't get dehydrated."

"How long do you think it'll take us to catch up with him?"

"He headed in on Friday, so he's got a full three-day jump on us. It all depends on how fast we can cover ground." Clint moved around the horses to see the lay of the land along the downhill course of the stream. The descent was peppered with huge ponderosa pines and a good deal of deadfall. "If he stops to rest a lot, maybe a day and a half. Two if he's traveling at a steady pace."

"I kind of doubt he'll travel very fast," she replied. "My nephews, Kirk and Kinnon, always fall behind when Deirdre and I go walking in her neighborhood."

"They do?" Clint hadn't been around youngsters very much. Judging from what he'd seen, the ones under ten were like farts in a hot skillet, darting every which way at high speed. "I guess I'll have to take your word for it. Kids aren't my specialty."

She smiled. "For all their seemingly boundless energy, they get sidetracked easily and tire more quickly than we do."

"Let's hope."

"Can we ride a little longer today?" she asked. "I'm anxious to catch up to him."

"Me, too, but it's turning dusk. If you're up to it we can take a break and ride a little farther after it's fully dark, using a flashlight to check for tracks. But my horses are sight-impaired right now. In uneven, steep terrain like this, that's dangerous."

She looked around, frowning in confusion. "I can still see fine."

"An equine's eyes are different. They have more rod cells than cone cells in their retinas. At night, when it's fully dark, they have excellent eyesight, better than ours by far, but at this gray time of evening they can't see very well at all, their version of night blindness. I don't want one of my horses to break a leg."

"How interesting." She rubbed Malachi's nose. "Poor baby. It's awful trying to walk through stuff like this when you can't see, isn't it?"

The gelding chuffed and whickered, nudging her with his nose. Loni smiled and gave him another scratch. Watching her, Clint recalled his dating checklist and gave her high marks for loving animals. There were a lot of areas where she'd earned high marks, he realized.

With a sigh she zipped up her fleece jacket against the evening chill. "We may as well make camp here then. In full darkness, using a flashlight, wouldn't we run a risk of losing Trevor's trail?"

"The tracks haven't been disturbed by the wind as much on this side of the ridge, but there is that possibility if he stops following the creek. The water will take the easiest downhill course, which may not always be due north. If the boy's using a compass, he might get worried and follow the needle instead of the water. In that case we could lose him."

"God forbid. I've been praying and trying to strengthen my abilities, which I'm almost certain gave me that gut feeling earlier, but there's no guarantee until I've practiced more that I'll get any gut feelings tomorrow."

"So you're taking my advice about trying to gain control?" He made no attempt to conceal his pleasure at the news. "That's great, Loni."

He glimpsed that glow in her eyes again.

"I was a little scared at first," she confessed. "But then, after thinking about it, I realized that was dumb. God won't help me strengthen my abilities and then leave me to my own devices."

"No, that isn't how He works. Just always remember to keep Him close, and you'll do fine."

Clint began tending to his horses. The animals had put in a hard day and deserved some pampering. He was pleased to have Loni assist him. She still had a tendency to move in too close behind an animal, despite his constant warnings, but she'd learned a lot otherwise. When it came time to rub the horses down, he heard her talking to them as if they were human, and she seemed to enjoy handling them now that her fear was abating.

"How come Uriah always raises his head to look down his nose at me when I'm talking to him?"

"He's using his binocular vision."

"His what?"

"Horses have both monocular and binocular vision. In monocular mode, excluding their blind spots, they have a radius of vision that ranges from three hundred and twenty to three hundred and fifty degrees." Clint pushed against Bathsheba's flank to turn her slightly as he rubbed her down. "When you're riding Uriah he will mostly be in monocular mode, his eyes working separately. Picture a clock lying flat on the ground, and yourself in the saddle, sitting at twelve o'clock and facing forward with the clock numbers all behind you. In monocular mode Uriah can see from the left side of his nose to an angle of about eight o'clock behind your left shoulder and from the right side of his nose to an angle of about four o'clock behind your right shoulder."

She rubbed the horse's velvety muzzle. "That's amazing. Talk about having eyes in the back of your head."

Clint chuckled. "It really is amazing when you think about it. The problem is, in monocular mode Uriah has a blind spot the width of his nose directly in front of him. When you stand in that blind spot to pet him, like you are right now, he has to raise his head and focus binocularly down his nose to see you."

She combed her fingers through Uriah's black forelock. "I'll be darned. When I first met him it frightened me when he threw his head up and rolled his eyes at me like this."

"It scares most greenhorns. They think the horse is spooked. Not so. He's only focusing. You ever tried to look through a set of binoculars at something close up?"

"No."

"Try it sometime. Damned near impossible. You have to back off a little to see."

"It must be horribly confusing to see monocularly with two eyes."

"For us it would be. The horse sees the left side of the trail separately from the right, two entirely different pictures. Fortunately he possesses interocular transfer, so he recognizes what he's seen with his left eye when he sees it with his right, and the monocular vision gives him a much broader view than ours, protecting him from predators. One of these times you may be riding happily along, and Uriah will suddenly spin around and throw up his head. You'll think something spooked him. But the truth is, he's just seen movement monocularly. He's spinning and throwing up his head to focus binocularly so he can tell what moved and how far away it is."

"So the monocular vision isn't very clear."

"No, and because the horse evolved as a prey

animal, he uses monocular vision most of the time to keep an eye out for danger." Clint grabbed the curry-comb to remove the tangles from Bathsheba's tail. "Their perfect vision is twenty/thirty-three on the human scale, so it's not nearly as clear as ours. Their depth perception in monocular mode isn't very good either, thus the spinning and focusing when they see movement." He looked over Bathsheba's withers to make eye contact with Loni. "That's why your habit of approaching a horse from behind is so very *dumb*. He can't see you until you step into his monocular range. Always talk to the horse so he knows it's you approaching. Otherwise he's liable to spook and kick you clear into next week."

"Have you ever been kicked?"

Clint chuckled. "Does a bear shit in the woods? Yes, ma'am. Had a horse break my femur once. Trust me when I say you don't want it happening to you."

When the animals had cooled down enough to drink, Clint and Loni led them in pairs to a flat spot along the stream to consume their fill of water. Then they strung the high line and fed all the equines a ration of alfalfa cubes, working together yet again. Loni had once told Clint that she was a fast learner, and she hadn't lied. Once he showed her how to do something, she remembered every step the next time. Definitely a lady who had potential as a horseman's wife.

The thought gave Clint pause. But then he wondered why. On so many levels he and Loni just seemed to click. He'd gone with his gut on all the other big decisions of his life. Why not on this one?

*   *   *

After setting up camp Loni went searching for firewood. It still wasn't fully dark, so she enjoyed the opportunity to stretch her stiff legs, confident that she wouldn't get lost because she could still see the horses and the tent. She had almost a full armload of nice-size branches when she came across footprints. Trevor's. When she looked more closely, she also spotted Nana's tracks, following behind the boy's.

Setting the wood down, Loni followed their trail for a way. She wasn't entirely certain why. It was just a feeling she had. Moments later she understood. Up ahead was an outcropping of rock, and as she drew closer, she saw an opening. It was the cave where Trevor and Nana had slept the first night. She felt certain of it.

Picking up her pace she covered the remaining distance in only seconds. At the cave opening, the ceiling of which hit her about chin-high, she leaned over and went in. Silence. Light from outside illuminated the interior, creating a shadowy gloom. Loni spied a candy wrapper lying on the ground. When she picked it up, an image of the child and dog sharing a chocolate bar flashed through her mind. Smiling sadly, she sat there for a while, trailing her fingertips over the disturbed earth where Trevor and Nana had lain.

"You had me worried."

Loni glanced up to see Clint leaning down to peer in at her. "Sorry. This is where he slept the first night. When I saw it I had to come in."

Clint moved forward, shoulders hunched to keep from hitting his head. "Nice digs. He's a smart kid. Sleeping in here protected him from the wind and probably from the cold as well, to a certain degree." He sat beside her. "Picking up anything?"

"Only memories." She patted the dirt beside her. "This is where they cuddled together that first night when I heard the wolves."

"Maybe we'll hear them tonight."

Loni shivered and rubbed her arms. "Oh, I hope not."

He chuckled. "No worries. You have me to protect you."

"I'd hate for you to have to shoot a wolf."

"Me, too."

She sent him a wondering look. "You like wolves?"

"Never been around them, but I've seen photographs, and I think they're the most gorgeous creatures on earth. Aside from horses, of course. There's a huge political battle being waged right now over their growing populations in Montana and Idaho. Ranchers are up in arms because their livestock is threatened, and activists are up in arms because the reintroduced wolves were once indigenous to those areas. They want the ecological balance to be restored."

"Which side are you on?" Loni asked, almost afraid to hear his answer.

"I lean real hard toward protecting the wolves. Dumb answer for a rancher, I know, and I might change my mind real fast if they moved into the Crystal Falls area and started killing my horses." He gave her a sheepish look. "I know it's not masculine to admit it, but my horses are my babies. I'd take on a chain saw bare-handed to save one of them. I'm sure there are ranchers who raise cattle and have prize bulls or cows who feel the same way. Same for sheep ranchers, I reckon. You build your line year by year, improving on it with your breeding choices, and money can't replace one of those animals if it's senselessly killed.

"That said, my heart breaks at the thought of decimating the wolf population. Yes, they're predators, but so are humans. We've only prettied it up by raising and harvesting our meat. I hope they find a way to protect the livestock *and* the wolves. If we can send a rocket to the moon, it seems to me we should be able to set up electronic perimeters of some kind around pastureland to protect livestock."

"I never thought of that. An electronic field, you mean?"

"They've proven that deer avoid high-frequency beepers installed on automobiles. Use of the device has reduced roadkill. I can't remember by how much, but it's substantial. Most states haven't passed a beeper law because there's a concern that the natural migration paths of the deer might be interrupted, and also that some deer might be afraid to cross a highway to reach water. But what if something like that could be installed on fence lines that repels wolves but doesn't bother the deer, cows, and sheep?"

Loni had to bite back a smile. He was in dead earnest, making her realize how badly she'd misjudged him that first night at her house. Clint gave a great deal of thought to some environmental issues, and in her book, they were all important. "Let's hope someone's thought of that and they're working to invent something."

*   *   *

Once back at camp Clint unearthed a portable cell phone charger, connected his phone to it, and then dug a fire pit while Loni gathered rocks to encircle the depression.

"I've never seen one of these," she said of the portable charger as she took a seat beside it on her folded sleeping bag. "It runs on batteries so you can charge your phone anywhere?"

"Sure does." Using a lighter, Clint ignited the dry pine needles he'd piled under the wood as tinder. "It comes with a wide selection of adaptors. I'll recharge your phone, too, as soon as mine's done."

"My mom hasn't called back. I'm thinking we must be out of signal range." Loni dug her phone from her pocket. "Sure enough. It says, 'No service.'"

"Tomorrow we'll find a high spot to call out. I should check in with my dad, too, just so he won't worry, and you can ring your mom to fight with her some more."

Loni laughed. "We don't normally quarrel like that. The Cheryl Blain thing has been almost as hard on her as it's been on me. She's protective of me now in a way she wasn't two years ago, so afraid something like that will happen again."

"When you talk about it, I get the feeling that the Blain situation happened long ago. It's only been two years?"

"A very long two years. It seems like a century. Some things are so devastating that they eclipse everything else until you begin to heal."

"My dad told me that once when he was talking about my mother's death. He said that for a very long time, everything before and after seemed surreal, like in a fuzzy dream, and his only reality was the pain of losing her."

She nodded. "That's exactly it. I didn't know Cheryl, and I didn't love her, but I was *there*, and I felt what she felt. For me it was up close and personal. I couldn't sleep well for months, and even now I still have the nightmares."

"I can't blame your mom for never wanting that to happen to you again."

Her eyes misted. "Thank you for that. Mom can be a little overwhelming at times, but her heart is in the right place. We're close, she and I. She's always been my support system, the only person, aside from Gram, who really understands me. Her meddling in my personal life is mostly my fault."

"How's that?"

"I've leaned on her, always stayed in the Seattle area until now. I bought a house in Lynwood, just across town from them, to keep the familiar around me. I even started my business there. It sounds weak, I know." She shrugged and glanced away. "If I'd set up shop in Seattle, my clientele probably would have tripled, but even though the city isn't that far away, the traffic makes for a long commute. I wanted to be closer to my parents, closer to my childhood home, and closer to Gram and her homemade chocolate-chip cookies. She lives only a few blocks away. In a very real sense I never left the nest."

"That isn't being fair to yourself," Clint countered. "It's not as if you lived with your folks. I count on my family, too. All of us kids live right there on the land where we grew up, within shouting distance of Dad. We socialize. When something goes wrong we circle the wagons. What the hell's wrong with that?"

"Nothing, I guess. I did live with my folks for a while, though. After I sold my house, but still had my business on the market, I couldn't find a rental that would take Hannah."

"So? That's how it should be. You needed them. They were there for you."

"Yes, but in the process of being there for me, my mother changed. She saw firsthand how insane my life was, with people phoning or coming to the door at all hours, both day and night. She watched me lose weight, get circles under my eyes, and jump at my own shadow. Now she's like a tigress protecting her kitten, frantic to keep me safe. We weren't really fighting when we talked. It's more like we're trying to reestablish a healthy playing field."

Clint bent low to blow on the feeble flames. "I know you weren't really quarreling. I was just giving you a hard time." He glanced up. "I wish my mother were around to fuss over us. Losing her was hard on us all, especially Samantha, the only girl."

"I think it was probably hardest on you," Loni pointed out. "Samantha didn't have to contend with feelings of guilt."

"Oh, yeah, she did. Still does, I think. In her mind our mom died to give her life."

"I hadn't thought of that."

Clint sat back on his boot heels. "She and I have always been thick. When she was tiny and Dad had to work, it was my job to watch out for her. My feelings for her are more paternal than brotherly, I think, and in return, I think she feels more dependent upon me than my brothers. In some ways I'm like a second dad to her."

"It must be great to have a large family. I have only Deirdre. We're very close, but I've often wished I had more siblings, and so has she."

"Family is important." He watched the fire catch, his expression solemn. "Now that the subject has come up, something's been troubling me."

"What's that?"

"At first you were so convinced that Trevor was my son. Have you changed your mind about that?"

"You asked me not to talk about it."

"I'm rescinding the request. It's uncanny how accurate your visions seem to be. You were so certain at the beginning. Can you explain why?"

Loni looped her arms around her knees. "No, I can't. Some things just come to me in the visions, and I simply know, if that makes any sense. It came to me that Trevor is your child, and in answer to your question, no, I haven't changed my mind about it."

During the tension-laden silence that followed, Loni recalled the translucent crimson that had tinted some of her visions. She wondered if she ought to mention it to Clint. Since he had broached the subject, she decided she should. "In the very first vision of Trevor, it came to me that his life would be in danger and only you would be able to save him. Do you recall my telling you that?"

"I do, yes." His firm lips twitched in a suppressed smile that deepened the slashes bracketing his mouth.

"I thought you were crazier than a loon at the time." He met her gaze, his own alight with self-derisive laughter. "I've come a long way, baby."

Loni smiled back at him. "Yes, you have." She thought carefully before she continued. "How open are you to the possibility that Trevor *is* your son? I don't want to upset you."

"Now that I've come to know you, I'm open to almost anything. It's still extremely difficult for me to believe Sandra would have kept my child from me, though. On the other hand, I've come to trust in you and your insights far more than I ever trusted her. I mean no slight to Sandra. She was a fabulous person. But you, Loni MacEwen, are fabulouser."

"Fabulouser?"

"A deliberate error, and there you go again, unable to accept a compliment. Repeat after me: 'Thank you, Clint.'"

She grinned. "Thank you. Is that better?"

"You're getting there."

"If it won't bother you to talk about it, there is something I haven't mentioned. In the early visions I had of Trevor, sometimes everything was bathed in red. For many clairvoyants a crimson overlay signifies blood, and judging by how much I saw of it, I believe Trevor will be gravely injured, and somehow you—and only you—will be able to save his life."

A thoughtful frown pleated Clint's brow. Then his gaze sharpened on hers. "Of *course!*" he cried. "It's all finally making sense. I have type O-negative and CMV-negative blood. I'm what they call a baby donor. If I don't go in to donate every fifty-six days, the phone starts ringing. Blood like mine is in huge demand. That's why you got signals that only I can save Trevor. If he were badly injured and needed an emergency transfusion, my blood type is universal."

"Universal? What's that mean?"

"It means almost anyone, regardless of blood type, can receive my blood. Type O-negative blood is quite rare, constituting only about seven percent of the population. When you toss in CMV-negative, my type becomes *extremely* rare."

"What does CMV-negative mean?"

"It means my blood isn't contaminated with the cytomegalovirus." He shrugged and laughed. "It's a fairly common herpes virus, but in newborns or immunosuppressed individuals, it can cause severe systemic damage. If Trevor gets hurt and needs an emergency transfusion, I'm your man. At least, I think I would be. They normally prefer to do cross-matching before giving a transfusion to be certain there will be no alloimmunity or antigen issues. A mismatch can be really dangerous, if not fatal. But in a life-or-death emergency when they don't know a patient's blood type, a transfusion of O-negative blood would be the safest bet. If the child will certainly die without it, I'd think a doctor would take his chances."

"Possibly."

"Maybe that's why you sensed a link between Trevor and me—not necessarily because I'm his dad, but because I may be the only person around to give him blood. Even major hospitals often run short of type O-negative. I remember reading about a shortage somewhere down in California recently. What if Trevor ends up at a jerkwater clinic somewhere that has no matching blood products? My blood would work in a pinch, no matter what blood type the boy is."

"What if Trevor is type O-negative?" she asked.

"In that case, the only blood type he can receive is type O-negative. We're universal donors, but we're not universal recipients. A different blood type will kill us."

Loni wondered if he realized what he'd just told her. If Trevor had type O-negative blood, only seven people out of every hundred around the world could give him blood. "Do children inherit their blood types from their parents?"

"Sometimes. It's mostly a genotype crapshoot, though. Parents often can't give blood to their own children."

His reasoning made sense. But Loni couldn't turn loose of the belief that Trevor was Clint's child. Instead of forcing that assumption on him before he was ready to accept it, she settled for saying, "Let's just hope his injury isn't so bad that he needs a transfusion."

Chapter Nine

Supper that night was a little more elaborate than the prior evening. Clint's belly button felt as if it were fastened to his backbone, so in addition to chili with beans, he got out the mixings for corn bread and started a pot of coffee. Loni's rapt attention to the bread-making process amused him

"Thinking about trying this someday, are you?"

Crouched at his elbow, she nodded and smiled. "Maybe tomorrow night. I'd like to help as much as I can. This camping-out business is kind of fun, actually." She eyed the skillet he'd set aside. "Are you going to try baking the bread in that?"

"I'm not going to try. I'm going to do it." After removing an egg from a plastic backpacker's carton, he cracked it into the dry mixture. "You slap on a lid, keep it at the edge of the fire, and constantly move the skillet to maintain a fairly even heat. Pretty soon it's done to a turn."

"Are the eggs safe to eat after being out of the refrigerator for so long?"

"I carry a small collapsible cooler filled with ice gel

packs. I don't take a lot of perishables, but if we get up early enough tomorrow I'll make you some bacon and eggs."

"Yum. That sounds so good, my mouth is watering."

When the corn bread was ready for the fire, Loni offered to man the skillet. She looked so cute crouched by the rocks, her expression ever so serious. Clint paused while opening chili cans simply to study her. In the deepening darkness, with the firelight bathing her in gold, she was so damned pretty. Plus he was coming to like almost everything about her. He had a bone-deep feeling that she was the lady he'd been waiting all his life to meet. The thought was oddly frightening, mainly because he had no idea if she was beginning to feel the same way about him.

After getting the chili cans settled in the embers to heat, Clint made each of them an Irish coffee, using packets of sugar and creamer, followed by generous dollops of whiskey. When he handed Loni her mug, she took a sip and treated him to a look of blissful appreciation.

"This is too good for *words*," she said, taking another taste. "Thank you!"

By the time supper was over and they'd washed and repacked all the cooking utensils, it was time for bed. Clint settled beside the fire, his rifle leaning against a rock within easy reach, his nine-millimeter Glock in the holster at his hip. He planned to sleep with an eye open all night, just in case his psychic sidekick actually had heard wolves in this area. Better safe than sorry.

From inside the tent Loni called good night to him. As he called back, he was reminded of one of his favorite childhood television series, *The Waltons*. He was smiling as he tipped his hat down over his eyes, thinking of himself and Loni as parents, with a passel of kids calling good night from every bedroom in the house. It was a nice thought to fall asleep on.

Three minutes after midnight Clint jerked awake with every hair on his body standing straight up. The forlorn howl of a wolf trailed off in the darkness, quickly followed by another off to his right. *Shit.* They sounded close.

Clint grabbed his Remington, pushed to his feet, and strode quickly away from the fire so he could see without being blinded by the light. He was about twenty feet past the horses when his eyes adjusted to the darkness. Turning a full circle, he caught movement off to his left, a wraithlike blur of grayish white darting between the trees. Malachi threw his head up, whinnied plaintively, and pulled against the ropes.

"Easy, boy, easy." Clint returned to calm the horses. All of them were becoming spooked, not that he blamed them. Though the equines had never heard a wolf, they instinctively knew they were in danger. "No worries, Bathsheba. I'm here." Moving down the line, he stopped to reassure each horse, standing with Delilah and Jemima a bit longer than the others because they seemed to be more upset. "It's okay. Just big dogs." With lethal teeth and hunger gnawing at their ribs, unless he missed his guess. It was the only reason he could determine that wolves would come in so close to humans.

"Clint?"

He turned to see Loni standing near the fire, arms locked around her waist, face pale with fright. "Over here," he called.

She started toward him.

"Tree!" he called.

She stopped dead. Clint moved out to meet her.

"I heard it," she said. "Was that or was that not a wolf?"

"More than one," he replied. "I'm sorry I ever doubted you. Don't know how the hell they got into this area, but I'm sure Oregon Fish and Game will be interested in the news when we get back to town."

"Will they try to hurt the horses?"

Clint was no expert on wolves, but these struck him as being pretty bold. That told him the wild game, their only source of food, was probably scarce. The normal behavior of any species went out the window when starvation set in. For all he knew, if the wolves got desperate enough they might even attack him and Loni.

"They might go for the horses," he finally replied. "Can you help me move them closer to the fire?"

"Sure, but I'll need a flashlight."

Thirty minutes later, when the horses were positioned where Clint could watch them more closely, Loni came to the fire, lugging her saddle. "I'm sleeping with you," she announced. "No way am I returning to that tent!"

Clint didn't argue with her. He just helped her make a bed between him and the flames, where he felt she'd be safest. While they worked, the wolves moved closer. He could tell by the sound of their cries. At one point the hair on the back of his neck prickled. He could have sworn he heard one of them whine only a few yards away.

"You're gonna think I've lost my mind," he told Loni, "but what do you think would happen if I fed them?"

She fixed him with startled blue eyes. "Is that wise?"

"No, not by half. Every wilderness how-to book I've ever read says never to feed wild animals. It teaches them bad habits and may encourage aggressive behavior in future encounters with humans."

"We probably shouldn't, then."

A wolf whined again, and this time Clint had no doubt that the animal was just beyond the firelight. "I think it's a couple," he whispered.

"A what?" she whispered back.

"A male and female. They mate for life, as I recall. Maybe they've got youngsters. That might explain why they didn't follow Trevor and Nana out of here. Only the male can leave the pups for any period of time. The female is probably nursing them. If he hunts too far afield, returning with enough meat to keep her nourished would be one hell of a chore."

"I think they regurgitate. I remember reading that somewhere. He'd bring back meat for her and also up-chuck all he had in his stomach. Then he'd return to the kill to feed himself. But you're right. Traveling back and forth over too great a distance would be difficult."

"Not to mention that he might return to find the meat devoured by another hungry predator. I think they're starving, honey."

"Oh, how sad. Why doesn't he catch squirrels and rabbits and take them back to the nest?"

"Den," Clint corrected, but beyond that he had no answers. He only knew this pair of wolves was apparently hungry enough to enter the fire ring. If that happened, Clint might have time to get off only one clean shot. "I haven't seen any rabbits. Have you?"

"Only in that one vision when Nana caught one for Trevor."

"Which probably means they're scarce through here," he mused aloud. "Squirrels are just as hard to catch, and there's not much meat on them. As for deer, fawns are the easiest prey, but they won't start dropping until early summer, probably a couple of weeks from now. There are elk herds in these mountains, and the cows calve in early spring, but they're a larger species, and elk bunch up to protect their young, making the calves harder to take." He thought about it for a moment. "You remember that bacon-and-egg breakfast I promised you?"

"Will they eat bacon and eggs?"

"Darlin', I think they're ready to eat *us*."

She shivered and rubbed her arms.

"I've got some steaks and sandwich meat, too," he told her. "We can make do with canned goods and jerky for the rest of the trip."

She gazed off into the darkness, the expression in her huge eyes a mixture of fear and compassion. "Let's feed them, then."

Keeping his rifle close, Clint got all the perishables out of the pack. He hacked the raw steaks and sandwich meat into chunks; then he and Loni mixed the meat with eggs, two cans of stew, and a little cornmeal for filler. After dividing the concoction into two camp pots, they walked out into the darkness, Clint carrying his rifle and one portion of the food, Loni carrying a flashlight and the other portion. It was the scariest walk of Clint's life. To guard their backs he kept turning in circles, ready to fire the Remington from his hip if a gray blur leaped out at them from the trees.

After depositing the food offerings, he pivoted on his heel every few steps all the way back to the fire. The horses whinnied and chuffed, relieved to see them again. Clint moved down the line, petting each equine before rejoining Loni. Taking the flashlight from her hand, he flipped it on and directed the beam into the woods.

"Look," he said to her.

Loni pressed close to his elbow. A smile lit up her whole face when she saw the two wolves devouring the food. "I sure hope it doesn't taste like more," she whispered. "They might have us for dessert."

Clint burst out laughing and bent to kiss her forehead. "You and me both. We're fresh out of meat."

Fortunately the wolves left after finishing their meals. A few minutes later, from what sounded like the top of the ridge, two distinct howls rang out simultaneously through the night. Afterward there was nothing more.

"Do you think they were saying thank-you?" Loni asked.

Clint checked to make sure he had a cartridge in the Remington's chamber, a purely nervous gesture, because he'd jacked one in when he first woke up. "I prefer to think they were saying good-bye."

*   *   *

A few minutes later Clint and Loni were settling down by the fire. Clint had no intention of sleeping, but he saw no point in alarming Loni by telling her that.

"You don't have to use your saddle as a pillow, you know."

Loni sat forward to zip up her sleeping bag, and then leaned back. "I've seen cowboys doing this in movies for years. I may never have another chance to try it." She wiggled her butt around to get comfortable. Then she sighed. "This isn't half-bad. Almost like a recliner."

Clint huffed with laughter. "I've never saddle-slept with a woman—unless I count Samantha."

"You won't be saddle-sleeping with a woman tonight, either. We just served dinner to a pair of wolves, thank you very much. I won't sleep a wink all night."

"You need to rest. I can keep watch."

"No way. I'll stay awake with you." She studied the stars above them. "Who do you think came up with the idea to use a saddle for a pillow? It really is quite comfortable."

"In the days of the Wild West, men on the trail slept with their saddles to prevent them from being stolen. In many cases a saddle and weapons were a drifter's only assets, except, of course, for his horse, his boots, and his hat."

She sighed. "I think I need a Stetson to put over my face to get the full effect."

He picked up his hat from where it rested on his boot beside him and tipped it over her eyes.

"It smells." She lifted the brim to grin up at him.

"How long have you worn this thing without getting it dry cleaned?"

"Dry cleaned? My *hat*? I clean it every once in a while with a pad from the hat store, and I set it on its crown to air out every few days, but I'd never risk putting it through a dry-cleaning process." He grabbed the Stetson and took a sniff. "Smells okay to me. City girls. Fussy, fussy, fussy. It's only about ten years old."

"*Ten?* And it's never been dry cleaned? I rest my case." Her cheek dimpled in a smile. "You look so affronted. Hat fetishes must be a cowboy thing. Right?"

Clint hooked the hat over the top of his boot again. "A *horseman* thing. I don't raise cows, don't milk cows, don't pasture cows. Therefore I am not a *cow*boy. I'm also well past my majority, so the term *boy* doesn't fit me, either. As for my hats, I own three, two for switching back and forth, and one for dress—a black one, just in case I'm required to wear a tuxedo."

She chortled with amusement. "You're having me on. Right? Surely you don't wear a Stetson with a tuxedo."

"What do you think, that I'm suddenly going to change who I am for a fancy dinner or wedding? It's a dress Stetson, very fancy, with genuine eagle feathers tucked into a silk band."

"No way."

Clint chuckled. "You're right. No feathers. And my tux is Western-cut, so the hat and suit go good together. I don't look strange or anything."

"In your opinion?"

He narrowed an eye at her. "You going to have a

problem with me wearing my dress duds when I finally convince you to marry me?"

Her cheek dimpled again. "I'm far more worried about the boot pullers in every room of your house."

"Now you're picking on my bootjacks? I swear, lady, what's it gonna be next, the horseshit on my Wranglers? I suppose you'll be one of those wives who makes a man shower and change clothes before he gets any supper at night."

Her expression went suddenly serious. Clint felt his throat tighten. Here it came, the rejection he'd been dreading. He wasn't sure how he would handle that. In a very short time he'd come to care very deeply for her. It was almost as if they'd been destined for each other—and perhaps they had, judging by her lifelong dreams of him. He only knew he'd never met any other woman who'd made him feel like this. She'd actually helped him feed wolves a few minutes ago. And she *liked* his horses. How could a man fail to fall in love with a woman like that?

"I have a hunch you already shower every night, and in the overall scheme of things, that's a small wrinkle compared to some others that concern me."

"So you've been thinking about it, too? About us, I mean." He took that as a very good sign. "Tell me about the wrinkles. Maybe I can iron them out for you."

"I decided a long time ago that marriage—to anyone—isn't for me. My being a clairvoyant makes everything too complicated. The Cheryl Blain thing, for instance. I've had to uproot myself, give up my entire life and try to start over from scratch. I could never ask my husband to do that if something bad happens again."

"Can we try not to worry about things that haven't happened and may never happen?" he countered.

"I'd love not to worry about it, but isn't that impractical?" She gestured helplessly with one hand. "Of course I want to find love, get married, and have a family. And maybe, just maybe, I'm thinking I may have realized the first part of that dream, now that I've met you. But it's still a dream, Clint. A normal life will probably never be possible for me."

"Bullshit. Everything's possible. What other wrinkles are you worried about?"

"Our backgrounds. We're so different." She swung her hand. "I've actually come to see how fun it could be to go on wilderness rides—the wolves excluded, of course. Under any other circumstances I think I would have a great time—*if* occasional baths could be worked into the daily routine. I'm beginning to feel more than a little grungy after living and sleeping in the same clothes since we started out."

Clint nodded. "Agreed. Normally we have a good scrub every day. In fact, these mountains are peppered with hot springs, so sometimes you can do it in style. It's just that we're racing to make time on this trip."

"I know." She drew up her knees, fussing with the sleeping bag to keep her lower body shielded from the night air. "It's more the everyday aspects of life that I feel might be a problem. You're a rancher. I'm from the city. I'm inclined to be very neat. *Meticulous* might be a better word. I love to decorate my house, too, and you might hate all the frills and folderol. I also love a little culture in my life, things unavailable in a town like Crystal Falls and especially on a ranch." She gave him a sad look. "You like country-western music, and I'm into classical. I also love to see plays and an occasional ballet. Someday, when I can afford it, I'd like to travel a little, too. I want to tour Europe, and I absolutely must see Scotland someday. My family comes from there. My idea of a happy, contented life is far different from yours."

A contented glow warmed Clint's chest. "So I'm not alone in thinking there could be—or maybe already *is*—something really special happening between us?"

She gnawed on her lower lip. "No, you're not alone. At first I just liked you." She turned a troubled gaze on him. "Now I . . ." She shook her head. "We barely know each other. Thinking this way is crazy."

"If we were any other two people in the world, maybe so." He reached to smooth a dark tendril of hair from her cheek. "But I'm your dream cowboy, remember? I think we were destined to meet. That's why I've never found anyone else I want to be with. God wanted me to wait for you."

"Really?" A shimmer of tears made her eyes sparkle in the firelight. "You've never wanted to be with anyone else?"

"Never. Not for the long haul, anyway. As for culture, I buy season tickets to the Portland Broadway plays and drive up there every few months. You ever see *Hairspray*?"

Her expression brightened. "*You've* seen it?"

"And loved it. Took in *Peter Pan* last summer, too. Samantha used to go with me. We always had a blast together, doing the big-city thing. Of course, Portland isn't quite as large as Seattle, but you can still go to museums, enjoy fine dining, and have a little culture in your life. It's only about three hours away."

"You actually drive to Portland to see plays?"

"Yes, and now my traveling buddy just went and got married. You want to apply for the position?" He studied her sweet face, and in that moment he knew he was a goner. If he looked for a hundred years, he'd never again find anyone quite like Loni. "On the way up we can take turns listening to our music of choice. I'm not much for classical, but I don't reckon my ears will rot and fall off from listening to it, just so long as John Michael Montgomery and George Strait get equal time with Leonardo da Vinci."

Her eyes rounded with horror. "Leonardo da Vinci was the famous Renaissance artist, not a composer."

Clint strove to keep his expression carefully blank. "He *was*?"

She puffed air at her wildly curly bangs. "You are *impossible*. I thought for a moment—"

"I *am* college educated, you know. I was just trying to make you laugh. You're way too serious about all this. You haven't mentioned anything yet that two mature adults who care about each other can't work out."

"What about the ballet?"

He shrugged. "I've never gone to a ballet, but I don't guess watching a pretty lady prance around in a tutu would be so bad."

She elbowed him in the ribs. He grabbed his stomach. "What the *hell* was that for?"

"*My* husband will *not* drool over ballerinas in tutus.

So if you'd like to apply for the position, Mr. Harrigan, get that idea straight out of your head."

"I was only joking. I don't really have a thing for tutus. French bikinis, maybe."

She nailed him in the ribs again, which made him laugh. "Maybe instead of watching the ballerinas, I'll just tip my hat down over my eyes and take a nap. It might be safer that way."

She grinned and snuggled back on the saddle. "What about my love of decor? I constantly change things—repainting, buying new stuff, decorating for the seasons, moving the furniture. I'm afraid that would drive you nuts."

"Moving the furniture might pose a problem when I come home drunk, but I only do that every week or so."

This time she didn't take the bait. "Would you please be serious?"

"The truth?" Clint gave her a sidelong look. "I never really notice how rooms look. It might bother me if you painted every wall in the house bright purple, I guess. But mostly I don't pay much attention. My idea of decorating is to hang up a new calendar the first of January."

"My point exactly. My idea of how a home should look may make you feel emasculated."

"It'd take a hell of a lot more than gewgaws and lace curtains to make me feel feminine, darlin'. Just so long as you leave my recliner and remote control alone, I won't give a damn."

"And how about those boot pullers?"

"Those have to stay."

"Are they ugly?"

"Probably, but horseshit on the area rug is uglier. If we can negotiate a deal, here's what I'll do. There's an ironsmith in town who's handy with fine work. You pick out whatever you want to be on my bootjacks, and I'll have him fancy them up for you. You can even have bows and roses on the damned things. I don't care, just so long as they're functional."

She giggled. "You romantic devil, you."

Clint had to struggle not to laugh with her. "What're you wantin' from me, diamonds?"

"Well, not that we'll ever get that far, mind you, but if we did, I would want an engagement ring, and since I've waited so long to get one, I'd want something phenomenal."

He pretended to consider the request. "I guess I could spring for a ring. That shouldn't make too big a dent in the four million that I've got invested for retirement. I'm kind of worried about all the traveling, though, and keeping you in classical CDs. Might be I'll have to put you on a budget."

She lay very still for a long moment. "Did you say four *million*?"

"Did I stutter or something? My daddy is loaded. Maybe I forgot to mention that."

"You most assuredly *did*. Not that I care one way or another. I used to make a very nice income of my own and hope to again. But after telling you practically everything about myself, I would think you might have at least *mentioned* the fact that you're rich."

"I'm not rich. I have a lot of expenses—the animals, the ranch buildings, payroll, maintaining the land.

Nowadays four million barely earns enough interest for a generous monthly income after retirement. Not that I'll ever totally retire. Ranching isn't just a job to me; it's a way of life, and I won't be giving it up just because I get old. Can you handle that?"

"Just so long as you can handle my still working as an interior decorator. That's more than just a job to me, too." She sent him another serious look. "Are we crazy to be talking like this?"

"I don't think we're crazy. Seems to me we're being smart. Checking out the lay of the land before we venture across it, so to speak. It's good to know what you're getting into before you take the leap."

She frowned slightly. "I don't know that I'll ever have the courage to take that leap, but it's fun to think about."

"It doesn't take courage to leap, darlin'. You just close your eyes, let go, and jump. It's landing that can be a bitch. That's why we're being smart to talk about it before we reach the edge of the cliff."

She smiled. "That's true, I suppose. If you never plan to retire, how will I ever visit Scotland?"

"I've got a ranch crew. There'll be nothing to stop me from taking vacations whenever I want. That's one reason I've worked so hard to squirrel retirement money away. I'd like to travel, too, only I'm hankering to visit Ireland, where all my people hail from."

"Aha! No wonder I suspected a few times that you'd been kissing the Blarney Stone."

"Innocent of the charge. I've never visited my grandparents' homeland. I'm just gifted with Irish charm."

"And Irish stubbornness."

"Takes a Celt to know a Celt, I reckon. You're a little stubborn yourself." He grinned at her. "Not that I'm finding fault. I just have one question. I didn't think the Roman Catholic Church had much of a foothold in Scotland."

"Yes, well, you think Leonardo da Vinci was a composer, so what can I expect?"

"Seriously. How'd you come to be Catholic?"

"I don't actually know. Both sides of my family have been for generations. You're actually correct in thinking that Catholics are a minority in Scotland. I think they comprised only about sixteen percent of the general population when the last census was taken."

"But wasn't Catholicism outlawed there at some point in history?"

"Yes," she said with a twinkling grin. "That occurred after the Scottish Reformation, I think. But we Scots are stubborn. Some of us remained Catholic and worshiped in secret, and over the centuries, the political situation evolved to accept Catholicism again."

"I'm glad. I gave up on ever marrying a Catholic a long time ago. All I cared about was finding someone with a deep faith in God. But finding someone who shares my religion is a really nice plus."

"I agree. I won't have to explain why I can't eat meat on Friday during Lent and why I fast sometimes."

Clint nodded. Then, after taking a deep breath for courage, he said, "Speaking of which, there's something I need to talk with you about."

"Well, I'm not planning to sleep tonight, so shoot."

"It's not that big a thing, really. Just another small wrinkle to iron out."

"We've done pretty well ironing them out so far. What is it?"

Clint got that weird, tight feeling in his chest again. But sooner or later she was going to start wondering why he hadn't kissed her a second time, so he had no choice but to tell her.

"I can't have sex."

Chapter Ten

L oni was certain she hadn't heard Clint right. She'd felt his arousal last night when he kissed her, and she'd seen evidence of the same yesterday morning when they first awakened. How could he possibly be impotent?

"I'm sorry?" She turned a questioning gaze on him. "Could you repeat that, please?"

His normally burnished face had taken on a ruddier hue. "I can't have sex," he informed her huskily. "I gave it up."

She searched his dark eyes, which were usually alight with mischief. Not now. He appeared to be dead serious. "Lent ended on Easter."

"No, no, not for Lent. I mean I gave it up permanently."

"*Permanently?*" Loni had been waiting all her adult life to finally experience the joys of womanhood, and now the man of her dreams was telling her he'd given up sex? This couldn't be happening. "Why on *earth* would you do that?"

"Not permanently. Bad choice of words. Outside of

wedlock, I mean. I promised myself I'd never again have sex unless I was married."

"Oh, I see." Only she didn't see at all. If he had indulged in sex previously, what had possessed him to turn over a new leaf right before he met *her*? She was thirty-one years old. She'd followed the rules her entire life. Was it so wrong for her to wish she could do something really, *really* bad for once? Something deliciously bad, of course—like making love under the stars with the man of her dreams. Literally, the man of her dreams. "What led you to reach that decision?"

He rubbed a hand over his face and then blinked as if to bring the world back into proper focus. "I know it doesn't sound very macho, but I reached a point where I didn't like myself anymore, and I realized I had to straighten up my act. There were a lot of women over the years. Not dozens or anything." He flashed her a meaningful look. "I don't want you to think I was one of those guys who picked up a different woman every Friday night. But over the years, starting when I was a freshman in college, I'd occasionally meet someone I liked well enough to date for a while. I never set out to have sex with anyone. It always sort of . . . Well, you know how it goes. You're only friends, and you don't expect the relationship to go there, but somehow it does, and then you feel bad about it."

Loni *didn't* know how that went, and she found the situation very frustrating, despite all of her moral convictions.

"Anyway, that was the pattern. I'd meet someone, screw up, go to confession, and have every intention of never doing it again. Only I eventually would. Six months later, maybe a year. I wasn't a monk, after all. I wasn't married. Like any young person, I needed to go out and have fun, and when you hang out at honky-tonks, people tend to pair off toward the end of the evening, even if they don't arrive there with a date."

"What's a honky-tonk?"

"A bar with a dance floor, most times with a live country-western band. Anyway, a little over a year ago I met this gal. She was fun, and I enjoyed her company. Following my usual pattern I dated her for a while, content to have someone to go out with and not expecting anything more. She was divorced, had two teenage kids. She seemed okay with just being friends. She didn't dress seductively or press me for anything more than a quick kiss good night. I honestly thought . . . Well, looking back on it, I should have known it would happen sooner or later. I'm a man. I have needs. Sometimes certain parts of my anatomy take over, and my common sense flies out the window."

"So you had sex with her."

"Yeah. She'd never seen a foal born, and I had two mares that were ready to drop. I invited her out to the ranch for supper, and then we went to the arena to attend a birth. I rarely bring women home, as in almost never, because my dad lives close, but with the foal coming, I made an exception."

"You can actually predict the time of a birth that closely?"

"Not to the hour, no. But we can tell when a mare's in labor. Anyway, it was a great evening. We had fun. And when we went back to the house to get her things so I could drive her home, she was suddenly all over me. Before I knew quite how it happened, it was over. She apologized; I apologized." He raked a hand through his hair. "It's a nasty feeling when you do something like that with someone and both of you regret it afterward. The sex was good. I mean—" He broke off and waved a hand. "When a man goes as long as I do between times, it's *always* fairly good."

Loni drew her sleeping bag up around her chin. She really, *really* didn't want to hear about his sexual exploits. It had been *good*? How was that supposed to make her feel? Jealous was how it made her feel. She wanted to poke him with her elbow again, only this time not in fun.

"Anyway," he went on, "I really thought we'd both agreed that a serious relationship wasn't for us, that we'd return to the way things had been, just being friends. Only I soon realized that wasn't her plan at all. All of a sudden she started buying me gifts. Expensive stuff. One time a belt buckle trimmed in real gold with my initials engraved on it, and then a money clip that must have cost the earth. I knew she couldn't afford that kind of money with two kids to support. I also realized she was getting serious. I started getting nervous, really nervous, so I took her out to dinner one evening and told her we needed to end it, that I liked her a lot as a friend, but that I didn't love her and would never love her."

"Oh, Clint."

"She seemed okay. I took her home. About three o'clock in the morning I got a call from her sixteen-year-old son. His mother had just been rushed to the hospital. She'd OD'd on sleeping pills."

"Oh, dear *God*."

"She didn't die. What shook me to the core was that my callous treatment of another human being had made her want to take her own life. She had *kids*, for God's sake. They *needed* her. I almost destroyed their world."

"She can't have been emotionally stable, Clint."

"No. Come to find out she had a history of emotional problems—" Clint broke off and met Loni's gaze. "But there I go again, making excuses. The bottom line is, you can never look into someone's heart and know, really know, what she's all about. In her mind she'd created a fantasy romance between us, and to her that was the reality, not my saying I counted her only as a friend. I should never have had sex with her. She was okay until then. It was only *after* that she started with the romantic cards and presents, only *after* that she developed the big emotional attachment.

"They put her in the psych ward. She received the counseling she needed. And I went to Father Mike for the counseling I needed. You can't live your life the way I was living mine. Looking back, how many other women have I hurt? Maybe they didn't take sleeping pills, but they may have suffered in other ways. We have the Ten Commandments for a reason, and they are rules even an atheist should follow. If we don't, we hurt people. There's no way to get around it. Sexual intercourse is the most intimate act two people can engage in. Bonds are formed. You can lie to yourself and pretend differently because *you* feel okay, but you're not around the next morning to see how *she* feels. Do you understand what I'm saying?"

Loni did understand. "Is she okay now?"

"She called once to tell me she was sorry. *She* was sorry. Damn, I felt like such a jerk. Come to find out her dad walked out when she was a teenager. She felt rejected and looked for affirmation with boys. Later with men. Her marriage was a repeat performance of her childhood. Her husband came home one evening and told her he didn't love her anymore. She had been hurt over and over again, and my decision to stop seeing her pushed her over the edge. When she called, she assured me she was feeling better, still in counseling, and back on the right track. Asked if I'd like to do lunch. I could tell she still wasn't over me, that she hoped there might still be a chance for us."

Loni turned on her side to watch his expressions. "So you decided never to risk hurting anyone again."

"Yeah, essentially. But more than that, I promised myself I'd never have sex outside of marriage again. Until I met you I had pretty much given up on ever getting married, so for me it was a lifetime commitment. If you can't do something right, don't do it at all. My dad's told me that all my life. It just took me thirty-six years to figure out that the rule should also apply to sex. It's not for sport. It's not a game. The stakes are very high for some people."

He rubbed a hand over his face again. "I hope you'll bear with me on this. I want to kiss you again, I swear to God, but I'm afraid I'll lose control if I do. And I can't do that. Especially not with you. When it happens between us, it has to be right, not just in our eyes, but also in God's. I want to build a life with you—love you, raise a family, grow old together. Why risk starting out on the wrong foot when it requires only a little willpower to wait and do it right?"

Loni sighed. He looked over at her, clearly eager for her answer. For a moment she couldn't think what to say. Finally it came to her.

"How do you feel about very short engagements?"

He laughed. "It can't be too short. Father Mike will insist on our taking marriage preparation classes."

"How do you feel about getting married in Reno and *then* taking marriage preparation classes?"

His amusement faded. "We can't do that, honey. We're both Catholic."

She sighed again. "You've had your turn at confession. Now it's mine. I haven't ever."

"You haven't ever what?"

A hot, itchy feeling crawled up her neck. "Had sex."

He shot her an incredulous look. "Come again?"

"I've never had sex."

A deathly quiet settled between them. When an ember popped behind her Loni almost jumped out of her skin. Clint just stared at her with a blank look on his face. When he finally spoke his voice sounded strained.

"Well, *hell*."

Though they didn't talk any more, they were both still awake at dawn and up in time for Loni to wash at the creek, a thoroughly chilling experience, which she tried to tell herself was invigorating. *Yeah, right.* She used a rag to freshen up, scrubbing her armpits without removing her shirt. Then she rinsed the rag to use again later and knelt on a rock to wash her hair. The water was so icy it made her teeth ache. Once in the tent she freshened her nether regions and put on a set of clean clothes. She felt halfway human by the time she joined Clint at the fire for morning coffee.

"Wish we still had the eggs and bacon," he informed her. "We can't head out until full light because the horses can't see that well. There's plenty of time to cook."

"I think the wolves needed the food more than either of us does."

They settled for sharing a heated can of corned beef hash and the leftover corn bread. Even that tasted pretty darned good. Loni decided the mountain air and the smell of wood smoke increased her appetite somehow. Normally corned-beef hash ranked low on her list of favorites.

Over their second mug of coffee, Clint asked about her romantic relationships to date.

"I never had one, obviously."

He gave her that stunned, incredulous look again. "There must have been men, Loni. You're beautiful."

"I was asked out. But it never went anywhere. I'm not exactly normal, you know. I felt it was only fair to be up-front with people, so on the second date I always told the men the truth about myself. When I did, I watched for their reactions, which covered a broad range. Most of them never called for a third date. Those who did . . . well, I could see no point in taking it any further because I knew they wouldn't be able to handle my clairvoyance over the long haul."

"So you turned them down."

She nodded. "And, like you, I finally came to think I'd *never* meet someone. When I was twenty-seven, maybe twenty-eight, I even started to dread meeting you."

"Me? *Why*?"

"Because I . . ." She couldn't think how to explain. "When you're young, being a virgin is okay. In this day and age, with a large percentage of girls becoming sexually active in their teens, it isn't *normal*, but at least it's not too weird. In your early twenties you start to feel sort of funny about it. 'What's wrong with me? Why can't I find someone?' That sort of thing. Then your late twenties roll around, and you're embarrassed to even tell a girlfriend. I just couldn't imagine finally meeting you and having to confess that I was still a virgin. It makes you feel like something icky hanging on a clothing rack that nobody ever wanted."

"Ah, honey. You're a gorgeous lady. Any guy in his right mind would want you."

Loni felt tears burning at the backs of her eyes. How she felt was her problem. She didn't want to share her emotions and make him feel pressured to break his promise to himself. But deep down she didn't believe he wanted her—at least not in the way she *needed* him to want her.

"We should probably start getting the horses ready to roll out," she said, tossing the remainder of her coffee onto the fire. "Do you want me to smother the flames, or would you prefer to do it yourself?"

"I'll do it."

She hurried away to tidy her clothing bag and stuff her soiled garments into a plastic sack. As she worked, the morning breeze dried the wetness on her cheeks. She took a deep, cleansing breath. Madness. The most

awful part was that she concurred completely with
Clint on his reasons for not wanting to have sex outside
of marriage. It was wrong. She'd been taught that all
her life, and in her heart she believed it to be so. It was
just . . . Oh, she didn't know. A female fantasy, she supposed. When you fell in love with a man, he was supposed to want you beyond all reason. She wanted him
to grab her, kiss her, and then mindlessly start tearing
her clothes off. She wanted to be *devoured*. She wanted
the sweaty, hot, primal sex that she saw in movies.

Was that so much to ask?

The third day on the trail was a blur of sameness for
Loni. Once again she was at the back of the line, staring
at Ezekiel's golden rump and brown tail as they followed Trevor's trail downstream. Without any sleep to
fortify her she slumped her shoulders, barely noticed
the birds and squirrels, and found herself occasionally
nodding off in the saddle. Not a good situation. If she
fell asleep she might fall off the horse.

In an attempt to stay awake, she took Boo from her
saddlebag and prayed for help in learning how to summon a vision. At first she found it difficult to concentrate. But then she came upon the trick of picturing
Trevor's sweet little face. *Focus, focus*. And suddenly,
with surprising ease, she got the flash of light, and
there Trevor was, lying beneath a tree with Nana curled
around him. The child looked pale, but otherwise fine.
He had a smear of chocolate at the corner of his mouth
that Loni very badly wanted to touch. Only of course
she couldn't. He was such a sweet little fellow—and,

oh, how very much he looked like his father. The resemblance was so striking, it was almost—

Kerwhump! Loni blinked and grabbed for oxygen. The world spun in a dizzying circle around her, the trees leaning crazily at unnatural angles. And, oh, God, she couldn't *breathe*.

"Are you all right?"

It was Clint's voice, but he seemed to be calling to her through a tunnel. She blinked, her mouth working like that of a gaffed fish. Then Clint's hands were on her shoulders. He sat her up and began whacking her on the back. Finally, *finally* she was able to drag in a lungful of air.

"What happened? Did you pass out? Are you sick? One minute everything was fine, and the next, Uriah started raising hell. When I looked back you were sprawled on the ground, staring at the sky."

Loni couldn't immediately talk. When she found her voice she squeaked, "I had a vision."

"A vision?" Clint saw Boo. Grabbing the stuffed bear, he shook it in front of her nose. "Damn it, Loni. How smart was that? You can't let yourself have visions while you're on a horse. What're you trying to do, kill yourself?"

She could breathe easier now. "I didn't think it would work. I was just practicing."

"Practicing?" He grabbed her in a fierce hug. "You scared the daylights out of me. Don't *ever* do that again. Do you hear me?"

Loni could see his point and also why he might be upset, but when he released her from his embrace, she couldn't help but smile. "I *did* it, Clint. Don't you see? I concentrated on Trevor's face, and I actually *did* it."

He sat back on his heels, his dark eyes still filled with concern. "That's great, sweetheart. But have a care with your safety from now on. Try to have visions only when you're sitting on solid ground. All right?"

Loni nodded. But despite the slight glitch in her timing, she felt absolutely glorious. "Trevor's fine. Perfectly fine, Clint. He and Nana are sleeping under a tree, and I know he's eaten recently because he had chocolate on his mouth. And you know what else?"

He smiled slightly and shook his head. "No, what?"

"I know that's where they are right this second. Always before I've never been sure if something I saw had already happened or might soon happen. Not this time. I *know* it was a right-now vision."

"That's great, honey. And you've only been trying for a short time. With more prayer and practice you'll soon be controlling your gift instead of allowing it to control you. Just don't do any more practicing on a horse."

Loni dutifully returned Boo to her saddlebag before she mounted back up. But as soon as they stopped, she promised herself, she would try to see Trevor again.

Clint felt like the world's worst jerk. Here he was, falling Stetson over boot heels in love with a woman, it was her very first time, and he was half-afraid to touch her for fear he'd lose control. If that wasn't a fine how-do-you-do, he didn't know what was. Loni deserved a proper courtship—walks in the moonlight, holding hands, kissing and whispering sweet nothings, dates, candlelight dinners, dancing to romantic waltzes, and more kisses, all on her doorstep, of course, because he didn't dare go in for a nightcap. And phone calls, of course—the kind where two lovers were happy just to hear each other breathe when they ran out of things to say.

Spurred by sudden inspiration, Clint checked his cell phone reception status. To his surprise he had three solid bars, enough to get out. Only he didn't want to call out and talk to his dad. That could come later. He turned on the saddle to shout to Loni, motioning for her to come to the head of the line. With six horses spaced a body length apart between them, it was impossible to converse otherwise. They were on a narrow trail in an area crisscrossed with deadfall, so it took her a few minutes to guide Uriah through the maze. When she reached Clint, she gave him a questioning look.

"What's your cell phone number?" he asked.

As she gave him the number, he punched the digits into the phone's memory. Then he grinned. "That's all I needed, just your number."

"It couldn't wait until lunch?"

"Nope."

She rode Uriah back through the deadfall. The moment she'd resumed her place in line behind Ezekiel, Clint dialed her number. She gave him a startled look, then grinned and fished her cell phone out of her pocket. With a tinkling laugh, she said, "How may I help you, sir?"

Clint nudged Malachi back into a walk. "You can talk to me. I'm lonesome up here all by myself."

She laughed again. "What do you want to talk about?"

"Anything, just so I can hear your voice."

"Okay. What's for supper?"

"I haven't thought about it. We've got canned roast beef, chicken, tuna, some cream of mushroom soup, and rice, some instant mashed potatoes, cornmeal but no eggs—I guess we could make hardtack. I honestly don't know. We'll have to get creative."

"Maybe we could do a camper's version of chicken-and-rice casserole."

"Sounds great to me, just so long as I get a kiss for dessert."

Long silence. "We'll see what can be arranged."

They went on to discuss her first crush on a boy, which happened during her prematurely aborted first term at university. She'd been hugely attracted to a boy named Russ, with bright red hair and blue eyes, who never noticed she was alive. Clint told her about his first love—a girl named Melinda who wore her hair in braids, had braces, and hadn't known he was alive, either. Next they talked about their favorite movies of all time, his *Dances with Wolves*, hers *Casablanca*. Then they went on to describe their favorite scenes. Clint discovered that his beautiful clairvoyant was a hopeless romantic. She discovered that he was an incurable animal lover because he was still upset over Two Socks, the wolf in his movie, being so heartlessly killed.

During lunch Clint recharged his cell phone and then replaced the charger batteries, giving the unit to Loni so she would be able to use it as a power backup and talk with him most of the afternoon. Maybe he couldn't provide her with all the dating rituals just yet, but at least they could have romantic, get-acquainted conversations over the phone. First, however, they both needed to call their parents.

"Dad wishes us all the best of luck," he told Loni when they'd both finished checking in.

"My mother says for you to keep your pants zipped."

Clint barked with laughter. "I think I'm going to like your mother. We're going to have to break her of spying on us, though."

"As soon as there's a need, I'll speak to her about it."

Clint felt pretty sure he detected a dispirited note in her voice. "I know you will."

They spent the next two hours discussing their most embarrassing moments—his being when he'd mistaken a steer for a bull at a rodeo event, something his brothers had yet to let him live down, hers being when she'd left a ladies' restroom with a string of toilet paper trailing from the waistband of her slacks. Then they moved on to the topic of literature. His favorite book of all time was *Where the Red Fern Grows*, followed at a close second by *The Yearling*. She'd loved *Gone with the Wind* and *Jane Eyre*.

When his cell phone battery began to run low, he said good-bye and thought for the remainder of the day's ride. There had to be other ways, besides talking on the phone, to give Loni the romantic courtship she deserved. He only had to put his mind to it.

Along toward dusk Clint began watching for a likely camp spot. Fortunately Trevor's trail had continued to follow the downhill course of the stream.

Having water nearby made caring for the horses a lot easier. It also made cooking less of a hassle, especially when it came time for cleanup.

After setting up camp, a process that excluded erecting the tent because Loni was still worried about wolves, and didn't care to sleep alone, Clint got the horses settled in for the night and then went down to the creek to shave. As he was washing up and dipping his razor into the water, he kept thinking that something wasn't right. Finally, like a bullet between the eyes, it occurred to him what it was: The water felt oddly warm.

Back at camp Loni was sitting on the sleeping bag with Boo clutched to her chest. Judging by her beatific smile, she'd just succeeded in summoning another vision. "This is *so* wonderful, Clint. Thank you for encouraging me to do it."

"Saw him again, did you?"

Her smile broadened. "I did. He and Nana have a fire, too, and they're cooking a rabbit and a squirrel for supper. That is the *sweetest* dog. She brought Trevor the game without eating any of it first. It's share and share alike."

"Sounds to me like the boy has taught her that. He shares everything with her, doesn't he?"

"He does. You're going to be so proud of him once you get to know him. He's such a neat kid. Honestly, he is." Her smile froze. Then she gulped. "I'm sorry. I forgot for a moment that you still don't believe he's yours."

Clint rubbed his freshly shaved jaw. "I'd love it if he were. Truly, I would. I've always wanted kids." He tidied his damp hair, then stuck the comb back into his hip pocket. "That's something we've never really talked about—whether or not you want kids."

"Of *course* I want kids. I'd just given up hope of ever having any." A troubled frown pleated her brow. "Um, there is one thing, Clint. Remember my telling you that in my family a clairvoyant female is born in every generation?"

"I remember that, yes."

"Well, there's only my sister, Deirdre, and me, and she's got two boys. She's very unlikely to have any more children. She had a tubular pregnancy and lost one fallopian duct. The other one is partially blocked."

"What are you saying, that it'll be up to you to have a clairvoyant daughter?"

She nodded. When he didn't immediately speak, she asked, "Will that bother you?"

Clint crouched by the fire to study her lovely face. It was damned near a perfect oval. "Not so long as she looks exactly like you and is half as sweet."

Her cheeks turned a pretty pink. "She may look like you. Yours is the more dominant complexion."

"Just so long as she gets your nose, we can keep her."

She laughed and rolled her eyes. "It won't bother you, having a clairvoyant daughter? Chances are she won't have as strong a gift as mine. Possibly, I suppose, but normally it happens only every few generations."

"Sweetheart, I'll love her if she's got a third eye in the middle of her forehead. Stop worrying. All right?"

She nodded. "So what shall we fix for supper?"

"The rice dish sounds great to me. But before we

start cooking I'd like to meander up the hill for a way. Will you be all right here alone for a few minutes? I'll leave you my rifle."

"I don't know how to use a rifle."

Clint showed her how to release the safety. "Just point it and pull the trigger. All I ask is that you don't shoot one of my horses."

She leaned the rifle against a rock near the fire. "I'll be sure to point well away from them."

Clint crossed the creek by jumping from one rock to another. Once on the other bank, he found a way up through the sheer crags of rock to crest the rise, and then he followed the sound of bubbling water. He'd walked only a few feet before he found what he was looking for. Loni was in for an after-dinner treat tonight, he thought with a grin. Talk about a romantic setting—this was it.

His only worry was how on earth he was going to resist making love to her when he brought her up here.

Chapter Eleven

Supper was divine. Loni created their rice dish, sipping Irish coffee as she cooked. Clint reclined beside the fire, talking with her while she worked. He was, Loni decided, the handsomest man she'd ever seen. His skin was the color of caramel toffee, her favorite treat. His thick, wavy hair shone in the fading light like polished jet. His features were purely masculine, reminding her of chiseled granite. She loved his sharp nose, his firm yet mobile mouth, and the deep cleft in his square chin. Freshly shaven and wearing a clean blue chambray shirt, he looked almost good enough to eat, and when he flashed her one of those glamorous grins, she was tempted to have a taste.

She settled for feasting on the rice-and-chicken concoction, which was amazingly good. After they were both replete, they enjoyed another Irish coffee and then went to the creek to wash the cooking utensils. Loni felt just a little tipsy, which made her laugh a lot. At one point Clint grabbed her arm, afraid she might topple into the water.

"Remind me to mix your coffees a little lighter to-morrow night. I think you're just a wee bit drunk."

She laughed as if that were the funniest joke she'd ever heard, realized it wasn't really that humorous, and quickly sobered. "Hmm, I guess maybe so."

When the gear was all repacked for the next morn-ing's ride, Clint stoked the fire, then fished some tow-els from a pack and slung them over his shoulder. "I haven't seen hide nor hair of those wolves since last night. I watched for tracks today, too. I think it's safe for us to leave the horses for a while. We'll still be within hearing distance."

Loni watched him tuck a bar of bath soap into his shirt pocket. "Where are we going?"

He winked at her. "Go grab a full change of clothes. I found a hot spring."

"Are you *serious*?"

"I'm dead serious. You're about to enjoy sitting in one of God's Jacuzzis."

When Loni returned with her clothing and a dispos-able razor that Clint had either overlooked or deliber-ately left in her cosmetic bag, he was waiting with his rifle cradled in the crook of his arm. "For just-in-case. The pool isn't far from the top of that rock." He indi-cated the spot with an inclination of his dark head. "If there's trouble, I'll hear the horses acting up and be able to get a clear shot from up there to protect them."

"Do you think the wolves will come back?"

"I doubt it. We gave them enough food to hold them for a while. But when it comes to the safety of my horses, I leave nothing to chance. You want to grab the flashlight? It'll be full dark by the time we return."

Loni almost tumbled into the creek trying to get across. Clint, following behind, caught her arm to help steady her. "You're definitely a little drunk, Loni mine. Don't fall in the drink, and whatever you do, don't drop the flashlight."

She was laughing helplessly by the time she made it to the other side. When Clint joined her, he bent his dark head and stole a quick kiss. Then he straightened, his gaze solemn and searching. "You are so beautiful. I keep thinking I must be dreaming."

"I hope not. If you are I must be, too, and if that's the case I don't want to wake up."

When Loni saw the pool, she was mildly disappointed. Russet-colored deposits discolored the rocks, a sulfuric smell rose with the steam, and the water looked murky. "I think it needs a good chemical shock."

"No way," Clint said with mock horror as he placed his change of clothes and the rifle on a nearby boulder. "It's supposed to look that way. And when you get out your skin will feel like you just spent a week at a ritzy spa. The minerals are fabulous."

Setting the clothes she'd brought beside his, Loni went to the edge of the pool and bent to test the temperature. "Oh, my *stars*, it *is* like a Jacuzzi. There are even rocks to sit on. How lovely!"

"Are you gonna admire it all night or get in?"

It suddenly occurred to her that bathing in the pool would require that she remove her clothing. While she had enjoyed fantasizing about having wild, passionate sex with Clint, when it came down to reality, she'd never been naked in front of a man.

"How are we going to do this?" she asked.

"I'll keep my boxers on, and you can wear your panties and T-shirt. We can hang everything by the fire tonight so it'll be dry by morning."

Clint turned his back to her, she followed his lead, and they began to undress. Loni heard one of his boots plop on the rocks. One of hers soon made a similar sound. Before she knew it, she was down to her panties, her bra, and the T-shirt. Getting her bra off without removing her top proved to be tricky, but she managed by tugging the straps down each arm, and then pulling her hands through the loops.

"You decent?" he asked.

"Sort of."

They turned to face each other again. Loni took one look at him and almost swallowed her tongue. She'd expected his torso to be white from lack of exposure, but his chest and arms were nearly as brown as his face. A mat of black hair covered his bulging pectorals, then tapered to a dark line that disappeared beneath the waistband of his shorts.

"You have an all-over tan."

"I work without my shirt sometimes."

"But your legs are brown, too."

He glanced down. "Sort of, I guess. That's just the color of my regular skin."

His regular skin was *gorgeous*. He had sculpted thighs furred with silky black hair. Loni even thought his feet were attractive. His anklebones were far sturdier than hers, big and sort of squared. He had nice toes, too. She wished she could slip him a Mickey and study every inch of him without his knowing. Unfortunately he was very much awake—and staring back, which made her skin feel itchy all over. Did he think her thighs were too big, her knees too knobby? And, oh, how she hoped her boobs didn't look droopy without a bra. The T-shirt was old, limp, and did little to hide her imperfections.

"I feel like a dumpling."

His dark gaze traveled slowly over her. "You're the most gorgeous dumpling I've ever seen."

"And white. I'm *so* white. I'd die for skin like yours."

"I love your skin," he protested. "Opposites attract, remember. If you were brown like me, I might not think you were so damned pretty."

He climbed into the pool first, gimping on the rocks because the soles of his feet were tender. Watching him, Loni concluded that she'd never seen so many muscles. Every inch of his body was toned, and as far as she could tell, there wasn't an ounce of fat on him.

"Do you work out?" She tried to pass it off as a casual question, but her voice had an odd, twanging sound.

"Every day." His dark eyes twinkled mischievously up at her. "I work out in the open stalls. I work out in the paddocks. I work out in the stable. I work out in the hay shed. I work out—"

"Enough!" she cried with a laugh. "I get the picture."

He held a hand up to her. "Come on in. The water's great." As she started to step in, he added, "Ah, honey, the insides of your legs are still bruised."

In midstep Loni tried to splay a hand over the apex of her thighs to hide the crotch of her panties, lost her balance, and fell in on top of him. To Clint's credit he did manage to catch her, but the full impact of her weight, hitting him squarely on the chest, propelled him backward. The next instant Loni was in hot water over her head. She came to the surface sputtering and coughing with hanks of hair plastered over her eyes.

"Are you all right? Damn, girl, what're you trying to do, drown me?"

Loni batted the water with her palms, unable to see. "Yuck. It tastes *awful*."

He caught her to him with an arm that felt as hot and hard against her back as molten steel. She sucked in a quick breath. Using his free hand, he pushed the hair from her face. Loni blinked up at him, her eyes burning from the water. His black eyelashes were spiked with wetness, the tips shiny with droplets.

"You are so sweet," he said huskily. "I've never in my life felt like this about anyone. Have you?"

"No, not ever." Her feet didn't touch the bottom. She clung to his thick shoulders, loving the feel of his bare skin under her hands. "For the last several years I convinced myself that my teenage romantic fantasies about you were foolish. Now I'm wondering if I wasn't a lot smarter as a kid than as an adult."

He turned in the water with her, his hard legs grazing hers, the coarse hair on his thighs tickling her sensitive skin. "You never got around to telling me about those dreams."

Loni trailed a fingertip along his jaw. Her throat felt suddenly tight. "I'd just see you," she whispered. "Before I ever actually met you, I knew exactly how your mouth would tip into a smile, how your eyes would twinkle with laughter, how you'd scowl when you were thinking. And way deep in my heart I always knew, *always*, that I would love you. It was only when I got older that the possibility began to frighten me."

He caught her fingertip between his lips, the hot, wet sweep of his tongue over her flesh making her heart leap. Releasing her, he asked, "How could the possibility of feeling like this frighten you?"

"I was afraid of caring—of needing. I didn't want to make myself vulnerable like that, only to have you walk away. Not many men would take me on, Clint. Even if I learn to control my gift to some degree, my life will never be normal, and if you stay with me yours won't be either."

"Honey, I'm not going to walk away. *Ever*. And what's normal? If I could change you—if I could take your gift away from you—I wouldn't. It's part of who you are, and whether you believe it or not, it's all the little things, plus the big ones, that make each of us so special. I wouldn't change a single thing about you."

Her throat went tight. "You're sure?"

"I've never been so certain of anything. I love your sense of humor. I love the way you laugh. I've been searching for you—for *this*—all my life. Every time I met someone new, I'd think, 'Maybe this time,' but it never happened."

Loni relaxed slightly. "Maybe God was saving you for me."

"No maybe to it. He meant for us to be together. Don't you feel that?"

She did, but the tightness in her throat wouldn't allow her to speak. So she nodded instead.

He smiled, his eyes shimmering yet aching with emotion—and when she searched his gaze, she felt *loved*. It was the most incredible feeling, a certainty within her that he would always be there for her, that his affection for her would be as strong and unbendable as he was himself.

His mouth was only inches from hers, and her gaze dropped. She felt his breath hitch in his chest. His eyes went from coffee brown to almost black.

"We can't do this," he said thickly.

Swallowing hard to regain her voice, she said, "You're right. It's not as if we're a couple of irresponsible teenagers with no thought for anything but our raging hormones."

"We need to stay focused on what really matters— our future."

"Absolutely. We need to go sit on the rocks."

"You at one end of the pool, me at the other."

She nodded. "We're adults. We've agreed that it's best to wait until we're married. We just have to be strong and stick to our guns."

He moved through the water, every push of his hard thighs against hers a sensual torture, until her feet touched the rocks. Then he released her. Unable to break eye contact with him, she backed away, her feet finding purchase on the ledge of stone behind her. As she rose from the water the T-shirt streamed water, the drenched cotton sticking to her skin. She tugged at the knit, but the moment she turned loose it sucked close again.

Clint's gaze dropped. His jaw muscle ticked. And

then, with lightning-quick speed, he seized hold of her wrist, jerked her back into the water, and said, "*Damn!*"

That was all he said, just that one word, and the next instant he was kissing her. It was everything Loni had ever dreamed it might be. His mouth was hungry and demanding, his hard hands urgent yet gentle. She gave herself up to the kiss, letting her body melt against his. The deepening dusk and steam enveloped them, creating a moist, sultry cocoon that separated them from the world around them.

With that first contact of lips and tongues Loni forgot everything but the feelings exploding within her. He was twilight and mist, shadows and heat, shivers of delight and mindless desire, a man who made love as he did all else, with practiced exactitude and elemental strength, and with a blatant directness that might have embarrassed her had she been with anyone else.

Clasped so closely to his chest, she found no room for shame to come between them—no room for second thoughts. She surrendered to him as a blade of new grass does to the wind, bending under his strength, vulnerable to his every caress. Dimly, she felt him tugging the T-shirt off over her head, and then his mouth was at her breast, surrounding one nipple with heat, a moist, drawing heat. With one stroke of his tongue he laid bare every nerve ending in the rigid bud of flesh that crested her nipple. Then his teeth came into play, lightly grazing, gently pulling. Loni made fists in his black hair, let her head fall back, and cried out at the shocks of sensation.

"You are so sweet, so wonderfully, impossibly sweet," he whispered.

When he drew her legs around his hips, she locked her ankles at his lower back, riding high above the water now, her breasts his for the taking. He took until she thought she would certainly go mad with the longing that was building to a crescendo within her.

In a dizzying blur of movement, she found herself perched at the edge of the pool with him trailing soft kisses over the bruises on her inner thighs. She didn't know where her panties had gone, only that she was no longer wearing them. When she realized where he meant to kiss her next, she was appalled. *This* didn't happen in the movies, not that she'd ever seen, anyway. She planted a staying hand at the top of his head.

"I don't think—"

"Don't think," he whispered against her skin, the caress of his lips sending jolts of delight streaming through her. "Trust me, sweetheart. Just trust me."

She trusted him. She *did*. She'd followed him into the wilderness, trusting him with her very life. It was just— "Oh, *my*. I don't think . . . Clint? What're you . . . I just . . ." And suddenly there were no words. A shriek bubbled up at the base of her throat, her body tensed, and sensation exploded through every cell of her body.

Her muscles were jerking as if she'd just had a seizure when he joined her on the rocks. She splayed a hand on his chest to measure every hard beat of his heart.

"I can't," he whispered roughly, burying his face against the slope of her neck. "Not here, sweetheart. Not on the damned rocks."

She heard the tortured strain in his voice, felt it in his shuddering torso. Vaguely she registered that he was afraid of hurting her. Hot tears stung her eyes. His willingness to deny himself in order to protect her touched her deeply. But she wasn't made of fragile glass. The timeworn stone beneath her was smooth and warm. Catching his dark head in her hands, she angled her face to kiss him, conveying to him in a language as old as womankind that she wanted him, right there, right *now*.

He groaned, murmuring against her lips, the words disjointed, his thoughts tumbling forth in a confused rush. "You're a virgin . . . Not on the rocks . . . Too sweet, too precious to me. I can't."

Loni deepened the kiss, invading his mouth with thrusts of her tongue just as she yearned for his throbbing manhood to invade her body. She felt no fear, only a sense of absolute rightness. She wanted, *needed* to feel him inside of her, *yearned* to be one with this man, her dream cowboy. She'd been waiting for this moment all her life.

When he rose above her, a blur of bronze in the deepening twilight, she smiled. He divested himself of the boxers, returned to her with a quaver of breath, and gathered her back into his arms, the swift tattoo of his heart vibrating against her breast, bare skin against bare skin, his muscular body slick with water and sweat. Breathless, they looked into each other's eyes, once again communicating without words. His gaze clouded with tenderness. Gently he nudged at her passage with the head of his shaft. She opened herself to him, her hands clenched over his shoulders.

"I'm not afraid," she assured him.

"I *am*," he confessed, his body trembling. "I don't want to hurt you."

Her gaze locked on his, Loni lifted her hips to impale herself. The pain was sharp, a tearing sensation deep within her. She clenched her teeth against it, straining upward, until he finally cursed under his breath, drew her close, and broke through the barrier with one smooth thrust. She gasped and dug her nails into his skin, her body arching against the brief flare of discomfort. But then, as quickly as it came, it began to abate to a slight burning sensation.

Clint held perfectly still, watching her face, his breath coming in sharp, uneven rasps. Knowing that he held himself in check out of concern for her, Loni dredged up a tremulous smile, encouraging him to move slightly. The molten friction set off explosions of delight within her.

"Oh, *yes*," she whispered. "Oh, *yes*."

The words seemed to release him. White teeth clenched in a grimace of restrained passion, he withdrew and then plunged deep, magnifying the feelings within her. A glorious, white-hot tingling spread through her.

"Oh, yes . . ."

With jarring force he set the pace, and she rocked her hips to his rhythm, sobbing as renewed need mounted inside her. Higher. Higher. He pushed her ever upward toward a zenith of pleasure. *Clint.* His name resounded in her mind like a song. *Clint.* And then she reached the crest, spinning off into a dizzying darkness sparkling with fragments of brightness. It was like plunging off a cliff, only she wasn't afraid because his arms were around her. On the descent, she felt his body snap taut, his thrusts quickening to a jarring intensity, and then he jerked and froze, his body shuddering with release. A tingling heat pulsed into her.

As he went limp on top of her, Loni enfolded him in her arms, too exhausted to move, too satiated to care. Vaguely she registered the soft twittering of birds in the trees around them, their voices heralding the darkness soon to come. Somewhere near them water trickled, the sound almost musical as rivulets spattered onto the rocks. As a backdrop, the evening breeze whispered in the pines, creating a ghostlike moan that reminded her just how vast the wilderness around them was. In that moment, as she absorbed the sounds, she believed with all her heart that it *was* a song—a composition of nature, a celebratory symphony, perhaps sent from on high.

Clint stirred slightly, his damp hair feathering against her cheek. "Why don't I feel guilty?"

Loni grinned and trailed her fingers through the waves that fell over his forehead. "Because nothing so beautiful could possibly be wrong."

Bracing on an elbow, he shifted his weight onto the rocks to lie on his side, his broad chest still canopying hers. His eyes misty with tenderness, he traced the shape of her lips with a fingertip. "I feel it, too. The rightness. I feel complete for the first time in my life— like part of me has always been missing until now."

In a fluid display of masculine grace he moved off the rocks and back into the pool, beckoning for her to join him. There in the deep, with the steam rising white against the gathering darkness, they floated in the embrace of the hot water, their hands joined, their gazes locked, no further words necessary between them.

It was almost full dark when Loni got a strange crawling sensation at the nape of her neck—as if someone were watching them. Trailing her gaze around the pool she saw why. Above them on the rocks, the dark, silvery shape of a wolf was delineated in the gloaming. Her heart caught with sheer terror.

"Clint," she whispered.

As if he sensed the presence, too, he jerked his head around. "Oh, shit," he said softly. "My rifle. *Shit.*"

Looming above them, the huge animal had the advantage. If he leaped the very impact of his weight would cause at least one of them injury, his feral teeth compounding the damage in short order. They were helpless, their only defense—the rifle—lying several feet away, well beyond quick reach. It also occurred to Loni that the female wolf might be behind them. She felt chilled, even with the hot water sluicing over her skin.

But the wolf didn't leap. Instead he lowered his noble head and appeared to drop something—a dark, shapeless something—on the rocks at his feet. Then he retreated a step and whined softly, almost as if he were inviting them to come see what he'd left. Loni was too terrified to move, and her heart lurched into her throat when Clint cut through the water, climbed onto the ledge, and braced his hands at the edge of the pool to lean in close.

After a taut silence, during which Loni's pulse went *whoosh whoosh-whoosh* in her ears, Clint said, "Thanks, buddy."

The wolf whirled and vanished into the shadows, becoming a part of the darkness so quickly that he might never have been there at all.

"Wh-what is it?" she asked thinly.

"Meat."

"What?"

"*Meat.*" Clint turned. His white teeth glimmered in a grin. "Deer, from the looks of it. He must have had some luck hunting today."

Scarcely able to believe her ears, Loni paddled across the pool to scramble up onto the ledge beside him. Peering through the gloom, she laughed shakily. "It *is* meat. Why on earth would he bring it here?"

Clint slipped an arm around her waist and drew her close against him. Pressing his face against her wet hair, he said, "We gave them food, possibly saved their pups. I think it's his way of saying thank-you." With a muffled laugh, he added, "We can't very well eat the meat. God knows how filthy it may be. But we can take it back to camp with us and toss it on the fire. That way he'll smell it cooking and know we've accepted his offering."

He'd no sooner finished speaking than a high-pitched, mournful howl came to them from the darkness. This time Loni had no doubt that the animal truly was saying good-bye. It made her feel sad and happy, both at once. Her encounter with the huge creatures had taught her an invaluable lesson: that as dangerous and feral as they could be, they also had undeniably beautiful and noble spirits, making them a species worth protecting. As Clint had said, if men could travel to the moon, they could surely find a way to live in harmony with one of God's most beautiful creations, the gray wolf.

Chapter Twelve

Once back at camp, Loni lay with Clint on their sleeping bags by the fire, content simply to be in his arms. There were things she wanted to say to him, mainly that she'd never dreamed it possible for anything between a man and a woman to be so wonderful. She felt happy in the strangest places. Even the tips of her toes felt as if they were glowing.

But once they started talking, reality would push its way between them, and though it was selfish, she wanted to protect this moment and savor it—just for a little while.

In the end, though, she was the first to break the silence. "Are you feeling guilty? About what we did, I mean."

He smiled against her hair and tightened his arms around her. "I'm a *Catholic*, and you ask if I feel guilty?"

Loni giggled. It was good to be with someone who would always understand her religious quirks. "We had good intentions."

"I'll stress that to Father Mike when I go to confession. 'I had good intentions, Father. I don't know how the hell it happened when we both had our clothes on.'"

"I'm sure he'll understand."

"Oh, yeah. He's a good man, down-to-earth, and knows I'm only human. I'm just afraid he'll make me say five hundred rosaries as my penance."

"Five *hundred*?"

"A gross exaggeration, but the man *does* believe in the power of prayer."

Loni giggled again. "You'll live through it. We'll say our rosaries together. How's that?"

"Just so long as you don't wear a wet T-shirt. I'm afraid I might jump you between decades."

She succumbed to helpless laughter again. "Just *saying* that is sacrilegious. I'd *never* leave off saying Hail Marys to have sex."

"I'm glad to hear one of us has some fortitude. I sure as hell can't count on mine." He grew quiet for a moment. "All joking aside, I don't regret what happened between us, Loni. It was the most beautiful and perfect experience of my whole life."

"Mine, too." She pressed her nose to the V of bare skin at the open collar of his shirt. She loved the smell of him, a wondrous combination of male musk, leather, pine, and horses. "I know we should have waited, and I wish I'd had more willpower, and I *definitely* think we should try to be good from here on out. But I love you too much to have any serious regrets."

"There is one thing I'm a trifle worried about," he said softly.

"What's that?"

"I didn't use any protection. It never even entered my mind. You could be pregnant with my child."

Loni's stomach lurched. She was new to sexual intimacy and hadn't thought about using any kind of protection either. "Oh, Clint."

"What?" He stiffened. "You're not unhappy about the possibility, are you?"

"No, *no*, never that. The thought of having your baby fills me with joy. It's just that everything has happened so fast. I'd hoped to give you some time to really think about things when we go home. If I'm pregnant, I'm afraid you may feel obligated to marry me regardless of any misgivings."

"Misgivings? I'll never have any. If you're pregnant we'll go through the fastest marriage preparation course in history and get married lickety-split. Unless, of course, you're having second thoughts."

"I'm not having second thoughts. I *love* you. I think I have all my life. It's just . . ."

"Just what?"

"My gift. After the Cheryl Blain incident I decided marriage to anyone was totally out of the question for me."

"That's crazy, sweetheart. You're young and beautiful and sweet. Any man on earth would count himself lucky to have you in his life."

"But what if it starts all over again? Reporters and frantic parents hounding me, and by extension also hounding you?"

"That won't happen. Trust me, Loni. We're meant to be together. We'll find a way to make it work." His voice went thick and tight. "I don't know what I'd do if I lost you. I don't think I could live through it."

Loni closed her eyes against a rush of tears, for she felt exactly the same way.

Before settling in for the night Clint watched Loni go to her saddlebags and draw Boo from a pouch. Sitting well away from him at the opposite side of the fire, she crossed herself and prayed for a while. Then she took the stuffed bear into her hands, held it over her heart, and closed her eyes. Soon she was smiling tenderly, and Clint knew she was no longer with him, but with Trevor and Nana instead.

After a few minutes passed she looked across the leaping flames at him. "That Nana has to be the most wonderful dog in the world."

Clint wondered how he'd come to love another person so much that her happiness had become his happiness, but that was exactly how he felt. Loni's smile made him feel as if everything was right in his world. "More wonderful than Hannah?"

She rolled her eyes and laughed. "Hannah excluded, of course."

"So what is the fabulous Nana doing now?"

"She's curled around Trevor, keeping him as warm as a little bug in a fur rug. The remains of a squirrel and rabbit are lying by the fire, so they clearly enjoyed supper." She arched a fine brow. "I wonder how on earth a big, lumbering dog like her catches all those animals. And she's essentially a city dog, to boot."

"Size and agility have little to do with a dog's hunting prowess. Ranch dogs are usually pretty agile, and

I've seldom seen one outrun a rabbit or squirrel. They catch them with intelligence and cunning more times than not, by running them to ground, feinting to instill terror in the prey, and watching all the escape routes. As for city dog versus country dog, all dogs can hunt. It's instinctive."

"Hmm." She shrugged. "Well, I'm definitely glad of Nana's hunting skills." Her smile faded. "I'm not certain, but I think the snack foods are all gone. All along I've seen him eating things Nana caught but also occasional goodies, like a candy bar or corn chips. Tonight I saw nothing like that."

"We knew from the first that the packaged stuff wouldn't last for more than a few days. And no worries, right? Nana's proven herself to be an accomplished huntress."

Loni nodded, returned Boo to the saddlebag, and rejoined Clint on their sleeping bags. "Time is running out, though," she said softly. "I feel it in my bones."

Clint gathered her close. They had unzipped their sleeping bags to create flat quilts, one for under them, the other for on top. He drew the thick folds of the upper layer over them to keep her warm. "I'm hoping we'll catch up to him tomorrow."

"What if we have no phone reception when we find him? We've ridden so far getting here. If I'm right and Trevor is going to get hurt, how on earth will we get him to help?"

"Let's hope we can call out when we find him, and then get him to an open area where a helicopter can land to pick him up."

"And if we have no phone reception?"

"Then we'll ride like hell."

"But it's so far."

"Going back the way we came, yeah, but we'll go the way a crow flies. The highway we took to the main trailhead continues north and then northeast, weaving through the mountains. We'll ride due west to tie into it. It'll be steep and very hard on the horses, but I can't let myself worry about that. There's a small community called Wagon Wheel that isn't all that far from where we are tonight. Ten miles, maybe. It's an outdoor-recreation hub, both winter and summer, so they've set up a small emergency clinic there with a helicopter pad."

"You've been thinking about this."

"Ever since you told me about seeing blood in your visions. One good thing is that I have training. Working with horses is potentially dangerous, especially when someone makes stupid mistakes, the big problem being that you never know for certain how inept someone may be until he messes up and gets hurt. With my ranch being so far from town, I wanted to know what to do in case someone needed emergency medical care, so I took classes and became a certified first responder. Then, with my dad growing older, I decided that wasn't enough, so I took courses out at the college to become an EMT. It's a pain in the butt to remain certified, but worth it in the long run. I brought my first-aid satchel. I've also got heaps of stuff for the horses. Hopefully I'll have everything I need to care for Trevor until we can get him help."

"I'm feeling better already."

"Good. You need to get some sleep. Tomorrow may be one hell of a day."

He left her for a few minutes to check on the horses. When he returned he added wood to the fire and then rejoined her in bed. As he gathered her into his arms, Loni sighed with contentment. She fell asleep with a smile, knowing deep in her heart that she was exactly where God meant for her to be, in Clint Harrigan's arms.

After a final cup of coffee the next morning, Loni once again took Boo from her saddlebag and held the bear close to her heart. When the white light flashed, obscuring her vision for a moment, she was prepared for it. The next instant she was with Trevor and Nana. The Saint Bernard sat beside the child, her muzzle smeared with blood, while Trevor skinned a rabbit that the dog had apparently just caught.

"I don't really like rabbit without my mom here to cook it," Trevor told her. "I wish we had some salt to make it taste better."

Nana whined and then went, "Woof!" Her jowls dripped reddish pink drool as she watched Trevor prepare their breakfast.

"I guess dogs like rabbit without salt better than boys do." He sighed and made a face. "It's better than being hungry, though. I'm glad Daddy taught me how to skin one." His small mouth quivered, and he blinked away tears. "He'd be really proud of us, huh, Nana? We're doing everything just like he said."

The dog barked again, as if in agreement. When the small animal was cleaned Trevor spitted it on a branch that he'd shaved clean with his knife. Then he rested the spit on two Y-shaped sticks that he'd driven into the ground at either side of the fire pit.

"We need wood," he informed Nana as he dug through one of the packs. When he found a small double-edged ax, he took off through the trees with Nana at his heels until he came upon a large limb that lay on the forest floor. "This is dry. It'll make a good fire."

With surprising skill the little boy began chopping the wood, striking the cut again and again at the same angle until he separated a foot-long piece of wood from the limb. Then he began the process all over again. Only the second time he swung the hatchet, it hit the wood and bounced back, striking his left shoulder. He cried out and grabbed his arm. Loni saw blood oozing through his jacket to collect in crimson lines between his fingers.

"Uh-oh, Nana." He made a shrill, whimpering sound. "Uh-oh."

The dog began to bark and run in circles around the child. Trevor staggered to his feet, still holding his shoulder. Nana continued to bark and circle him all the way back to their small camp.

Ready to ride, Clint went to put out their fire. He'd already kicked some dirt on the feeble flames when he glanced up and saw the stricken look on Loni's face. She held Boo clutched to her breasts. Her eyes sparkled with tears. Her mouth twisted and quivered.

"Loni? Sweetheart, what's wrong?"

No answer. Clint realized she wasn't with him, and

his gut clenched. Her expression clearly told him that she was seeing something terrible. He circled the fire to crouch down in front of her. It was eerie to watch the light come back into her eyes as she left the vision and returned to him. He saw her hands slowly relax around the stuffed bear.

"It's happened," she told him with a sob. "The ax. It bounced back off a limb and laid his shoulder open." Dropping the bear, she grabbed the front of his shirt. "Oh, *God*, Clint. He's bleeding. He's bleeding bad! He tried using pressure, but he can't make it stop."

Clint clutched her wrists. "Okay, okay, sweetheart. Panicking won't help him. Can you describe the area he's in?"

"There are rocks. A tall wall of rocks, kind of like here. He's still by the creek."

Clint shoved to his feet. "Let's ride." He began kicking dirt onto the fire. "Don't forget Boo. We may need him."

Loni ran to her horse, put the bear into a saddlebag, then mounted up with amazing speed for a woman who'd been riding for only a few days.

When Clint had finished smothering the fire, he hurried to Malachi and mounted up himself. "Let's go!" he shouted.

He whistled to the horses as he nudged Malachi into a trot. With a child bleeding to death somewhere up ahead, he didn't allow himself to worry about one of the horses having a wreck in the deadfall. A piece of him would die if he had to shoot one of his animals. Just the thought made his blood run cold. But Trevor's life was far more important.

They rode hard and fast. At times, when the terrain became treacherous, Clint was forced to slow the pace, fearing that Loni's inexperience in the saddle might cause her to fall. He could put his horses at risk, but he couldn't endanger the woman he'd come to love more than life itself.

Clint wasn't sure how long they'd been plunging forward down the slope. Minutes, hours? Time had become an indiscernible blur when he suddenly heard the frantic barking of a dog somewhere up ahead. He kicked Malachi's flanks to press the gelding to greater speed, praying that Loni could safely keep up with him and the pack animals.

They came around a bend in the creek, and finally Clint got to see Nana, the wonderful Saint Bernard, for the very first time. She was a huge animal. When she barked with eager delight at the sight of humans and came running toward them, Malachi spooked, tossing up his head and rearing to strike the air with his front hooves. Throwing his weight forward over Malachi's neck, Clint rode the horse down, soothed him with reassurances and pats on the neck, and then swung from the saddle to pet Nana. The dog's fur was matted with blood. The warm stickiness made Clint's heart twist with fear.

"Where is he, Nana? Take me to Trevor."

The Saint Bernard whirled and ran, setting a pace that Clint feared he couldn't match. Fortunately the boy wasn't far away. Clint found him lying beside a burned-out fire, the left side of his lightweight jacket and the earth beneath him soaked with blood, his small face as pale as death. Clint was taken back through the years to the day his mother died. He knew firsthand what pallor like that might mean. Nana circled Clint and the child, whining incessantly.

"It's okay, Nana. Lie down, girl. You did good. He'll be okay."

Trevor's black eyelashes fluttered. His coffee brown eyes focused blearily on Clint's face. "Who're you?" he asked faintly.

"A friend. We've been looking for you for days." Clint performed a quick triage. Weak, rapid pulse. Cold, clammy skin. He whipped his pocketknife from his jeans, opened the blade, and carefully cut away the child's jacket and shirt to expose the wound. A dozen curses zigzagged through his mind. The cut was deep, almost to the bone, and blood pulsed weakly from the gash.

"Am I gonna die?" the boy whispered.

"No way, little man. You're gonna be fine. You hear?"

"Are you a doctor?" His voice had grown more faint, and even as he spoke, his eyes went unfocused.

"No, but I'm the next best thing."

As Clint ripped his shirt off he heard Loni approaching, her boots scrabbling on the loose rocks behind him. "Get me one of our sleeping bags," he ordered. "He's in shock. We have to keep him warm. Then I'll need some water and soap to wash my hands, and some alcohol swabs to sterilize them."

As Loni ran to do his bidding, Clint used his knife to slash his shirt into strips, made a pad, and tightly wrapped the boy's shoulder in hopes of slowing the blood flow until he could fetch his first-aid satchel.

"How bad is it?" Loni dropped a canteen, soap, and swab packets on the ground. Then she bent to cover the child with the sleeping bag, careful to avoid the injured shoulder. "He's so pale."

Nana started whining again. Loni hugged the huge dog's neck. "It'll be all right now, sweetheart. You've done such a fine job of taking care of him. Yes, you have. It'll be all right now."

"He's about done for," Clint said softly, just in case Trevor might hear.

"We've got no cell phone reception here. Should I ride back to last night's camp to see if I can call out from there?"

"No time," Clint murmured.

Loni's face drained of color. "No time? He's dying right *now*, you mean?"

"That's why the dog's so frantic. Somehow she senses it." Clint leaped to his feet, veering around Loni to retrace his steps to the horses. Then, like a madman, he began slashing the bindings on all the packs to get them off the animals' backs. When Loni reached him he gave her the knife.

"Packs off. All of them. Leave them where they land."

He ran to the pack that held all his first-aid equipment for both humans and equines. His hands shook as he opened the horse satchel and rifled through the contents to find the syringes, catheters, and saline solution, thankful as he tossed things into his first-aid satchel that he'd been so meticulous about planning ahead for every possible catastrophe.

"What are those for?" Loni's blue eyes looked huge

in her pale face as she regarded the oversize syringes and needles.

Clint met her gaze. His heart was thundering in his chest like a jackhammer. "I'm going to give him blood. If I don't we're going to lose him."

"Blood? A transfusion, you mean? Isn't that dangerous?"

"Very dangerous. If I do it wrong or my blood's a bad match, it'll kill him. But I've got no alternative, honey. He's almost dead. There's no time to ride for help, no time for anything, not until I get some blood into him."

Clint ran back to the child, praying with every step. He'd never given a transfusion, never even contemplated the possibility. For a host of medical reasons it was not a recommended emergency treatment in the field. As he knelt beside Trevor again, he had to go still for a moment and take deep breaths. He couldn't operate efficiently in a panic. As he washed and sterilized his hands, he lectured himself to find his center and remember everything he'd ever been taught. Even then he was going to need a lot of luck and a miracle.

Otherwise this little boy was going to die. He was already in shock, his pulse rapid and faint. *Please, God. This is insane. I know it's insane. You've got to help me. Reach down. Help me do this right. Please let it work.*

He grabbed the child-size blood pressure cuff, secured it around Trevor's uninjured arm, and got a reading that terrified him. The boy had lost a dangerous amount of blood.

Most of Clint's adult life he'd been interested in articles about emergency blood transfusions because he'd always believed his mother might have lived if she'd gotten one in time. On an Internet medical site he had read about two direct, whole-blood transfusions administered in emergency settings with intravenous catheters, eighteen-gauge needles, and large syringes, one to a woman hemorrhaging after childbirth during a terrible storm, the other to an old man, also stranded by inclement weather, who had been bleeding internally. In both instances the caregivers had had charts on the patients and donors, eliminating most dangers of administering mismatched blood to the recipients.

Clint didn't have Trevor's medical charts and wasn't sure, in his present state of mind, if he'd understand the medical jargon if he did. He had only one thought to console him: that his type O-negative blood made a transfusion from him safer than from ninety-three percent of the world's population. That was the only hope he had, that by some miracle nothing in his blood would cause Trevor to have a reaction.

Please, God, please, God. The words ricocheted through his mind. Some of his horse syringes held a hundred cc's, large enough for him to use. Saline. He needed to inject Trevor with that before each blood transfer to help prevent clotting. He had no idea how much blood he should give the boy. He could only hope frequent blood pressure readings would give him an indication. He decided to start with a half pint. He would discard and replace syringes in between infusions to minimize the risk of contamination.

Vaguely aware of Loni washing her hands nearby, he laid out several gauze pads to create a sterile work surface before sorting and organizing the syringes, catheters, and needles. Calm. He'd finally found his center. The boy was surely going to die without the blood. He had to stay focused on that. The risk of death for Trevor was far greater without a transfusion than from any post-transfusion reactions he might have. Clint told himself he could do this. He *would* do this. It was a gamble. He knew it. But it was the child's only chance.

Loni knelt beside him. "How can I help?"

Clint handed her a rubber tourniquet. "Put this around my upper arm and sterilize the bend of my elbow with one of those alcohol pads."

To his surprise Loni seemed absolutely calm. As she dabbed his arm she glanced up. "It's going to work, Clint. Stop torturing yourself."

"You've seen something?" he asked hopefully.

"No, but from the very start I've always known you would save his life."

"Even though I'm a universal donor, complications may arise through alloimmunity to my red or white blood cells and various other minor antigens that play a role in compatibility."

"You're his father. I'm betting your blood is an almost perfect match."

Clint jerked his gaze to Trevor's face. Now that he was seeing the boy in person, he noted a resemblance that couldn't be denied. Trevor Stiles's small countenance bore the Harrigan stamp. There was no mistaking it. He looked so much like Clint at that age, it was uncanny. The implications pushed the breath from his lungs as effectively as if he'd been punched in the solar plexus by a brutal fist. His son. Sandra had *lied*.

Not allowing himself to dwell on it, Clint put a rubber tourniquet around the child's good arm, tapped for a vein, and inserted a catheter. After releasing the tourniquet and taping the catheter in place, he injected the boy with some sterile saline. "I don't have enough of this. I should be pumping him full, and I can't. Isn't that a hell of a note?"

"What's it do?"

"Aids in prevention of clotting. Also builds volume and keeps the patient hydrated. All I can do is hope that the amount I have will help."

Her voice calm and soothing, Loni said, "He won't get a clot."

After administering some saline he waited a few seconds, allowing it to work its magic before tapping for a vein on his own arm. When he got a catheter inserted, Loni removed the rubber band and anchored the IV device to his skin with tape. Slowly Clint drew blood into a syringe. Then, even more slowly, he began injecting it into Trevor's arm through the other catheter.

"Why are you doing it so slowly?"

"Trust me, I'm not going slow enough. In a hospital infusion room they take anywhere from one hour to four to transfuse a patient with one pint. There's no way I can set up a slow drip, and we can't spare the time. We have to get him transported to a trauma center as fast as we can."

"I could go looking for a flat area. Maybe I'll find a place where my phone will work."

Clint shook his head. "No, I need you here. I don't have enough hands to do this without help."

When the transfusion process had been repeated a second time, he sat back on his boot heels to rest.

"His color is better," she whispered. "Or am I only imagining it?"

"I haven't given him nearly enough to make a real difference yet, less than half a pint." To be certain, Clint took the child's blood pressure again. "It's come up a hair, but not nearly enough. I'm guessing he weighs about fifty pounds. On the seven-percent-of-body-weight scale, his total normal blood volume probably ranges from two and a half to three and a half pints. Judging by his pallor, the clamminess of his skin, his blood pressure, and his pulse, I think he's damned near bled out."

"Do you know how many cc's are in one pint?"

"Five hundred. I'll wait a few minutes before giving him more blood. I don't want to shock his heart. Jesus help me. I don't know what the hell I'm doing."

"You know just enough, Clint. God will do the rest."

During the lull Clint removed the shirt strips from the child's shoulder, enlisting Loni's help in applying pressure with sterile gauze while he cleaned the wound. "Thank God he's out of it. If he were awake this'd hurt like hell."

When the wound was dressed, Loni continued to apply pressure in between helping Clint administer more blood. It was a painstaking and lengthy process, making her want to scream. But as Clint worked, she saw a faint pinkness returning to Trevor's lips.

"His color *is* a bit better," she noted aloud. Nana whined and licked the child's limp hand. "There, you see? Even Nana agrees with me."

"Just pray he doesn't have a reaction. The signs will be hard to detect in an unconscious child. If his pulse accelerates, if you notice him starting to wheeze, if he feels feverish, or if his skin suddenly grows cooler and clammier, be sure to tell me. Adverse reactions usually come on in thirty to sixty minutes. I have nothing on hand to help him through something like that. No liquid hydrocortisone, no oxygen, no bronchodilator for wheezing, *nothing*. All I'll be able to do is stop the transfusions until the symptoms abate."

"Aren't you supposed to donate only one pint of blood at a time?"

Clint fixed his gaze on the boy's face. "If he needs two pints, that's what he'll get. I may become light-headed, but that's no big deal. You could fetch me some water so I can keep myself hydrated, though."

Loni ran to the horses to find the other canteens. She also fished through the discarded packs to get Clint a fresh shirt. When she returned to him he was praying out loud. "Please, God, don't let me muck this up. Don't let me kill him."

"You're going to save his life," Loni insisted as she passed him an uncapped canteen. "God didn't give me the visions and bring us all this way only to let him die. You have to have faith, Clint."

"Until now I thought I did. Funny how when it's put to the test, it goes flying out the window."

"That's not true. You're just scared, and you have every right to be. Has anyone ever done something like this in the wilderness before?"

"Probably not. It's totally nuts. My EMT certification may be revoked."

While Clint worked to transfuse the child with another syringeful of blood, Loni stroked Trevor's forehead, smiling sadly. "He's so darling, Clint. He's going to live. I just know it."

Clint began pumping up the blood pressure cuff again. "I pray to God you're right."

Chapter Thirteen

The ride that followed was more grueling than Loni had ever imagined the horses could withstand. True to his word, Clint headed due west with Trevor and the sleeping bag cradled in one arm, the unburdened packhorses scrambling up the steep, rocky inclines behind him. He set such a fast pace that Uriah, Loni's mount, was soon blowing with exhaustion, his huge body foamy with sweat. Even Nana's energy seemed to flag on the steepest parts of the slopes.

At the crest of the second mountain Clint threw up a hand to halt the horses, slid from Malachi's back, and gently deposited the bundled child on the ground. To Loni he yelled, "Unsaddle Uriah. We'll go bareback from here."

Bareback? Loni was only just now growing accustomed to the saddle. But she obeyed Clint's orders without hesitation, her heart breaking for Uriah, who stood on trembling legs, his great head hanging. Clint removed Malachi's bridle and put it on Jemima. Then he came to remove Uriah's head tack and put it on Ezekiel.

Patting the fresh gelding's shoulder, he said, "Ezekiel is sure-footed. Hold tight with your knees and make a fist in his mane to keep your seat. It won't hurt him if you pull on his hair a little. They don't feel it the same way humans do." He interlaced his fingers to give her a leg up onto the animal. "You doing okay?"

Loni nodded as she got seated on the horse. "How's Trevor?"

Clint swiped at his crimson-stained shirt. "Still bleeding. My guess is he'll need more blood when we reach Wagon Wheel. I'm trying not to jostle him, but it's damned near impossible not to on horseback. I think all the movement is reopening the wound." He swept off his hat to wipe his brow with his sleeve. "Pray that he doesn't bleed out before we reach help."

"I will. With every step, Clint, I'll be praying." Loni glanced at the spent geldings. "What about Uriah and Malachi? They're too exhausted to keep up now."

"We're leaving them."

"Oh, Clint, *no.*"

"We have no choice." His jaw muscle rippled in his lean cheek. With his dark complexion it was difficult to tell for sure, but Loni thought he looked a little pale. "Hopefully they'll stay put or return to the main trailhead. I'll come back for them. Just say a few extra prayers that I can find them when I do."

Loni nodded and then watched as he gathered Trevor and the sleeping bag back into his arms. He led the mare to a log to assist him in mounting, a feat that he executed with amazing strength and agility with a child in his arms. When Jemima headed out with the shorter string of packhorses behind her, Loni fell in at the end of the line. She twisted at the waist to gaze sadly back at Uriah and Malachi, neither of whom had the strength to lift their heads, let alone follow.

After only a few days in the company of horses, Loni knew the overheated geldings should have been rubbed down and then walked. Even after a less strenuous ride Clint never failed to do that, and she knew it was breaking his heart to ride off and leave them like this now, especially after they'd run their hearts out for him.

But Clint didn't look back. Shoulders hunched around the child in his arms, he pressed forward, once again pushing the horses to the limit of their endurance. Nana bounded to the front of the line to trot abreast of Jemima at Clint's right side, where she could be closest to Trevor. Loni found the dog's steadfast devotion nothing short of amazing.

Fear and outrage warred for supremacy in Clint's mind as he urged Jemima up the next incline. His son. He held the child in the bend of one arm, acutely aware of his precious little face peeking out from the cocoon of warmth supplied by the sleeping bag. His baby. On the one hand, Clint had never felt so terrified in his life. To learn that he had a boy, only to lose him like this— the very thought hurt beyond bearing. But equally prominent in Clint's thoughts was his sense of helpless anger. The child was eight years old. *Eight years*, and Clint had missed out on all of them, never attending a birthday party, never sending a Christmas gift, never telephoning to hear his son's voice. *Who're you?* Trevor had asked. And Clint had replied, *A friend.*

He felt robbed. If Sandra had still been alive Clint would have looked her up and given her a piece of his mind. It wasn't *right* to deprive a man of knowing his child. And how had that been fair to Trevor? The boy was the spitting image of Frank Harrigan, just as Clint and all his brothers were. Trevor had a family, an entire *family*, that he didn't know existed, a grandfather who would have worshiped the ground he walked on, an aunt and three uncles who would have spoiled him rotten, and a *father*, damn it. Clint wanted to throw his head back and howl in anguish, not only over all the memories that he and Trevor had never made, but also over the future they might never be able to share.

Death. It came for the young as well as the old, and it might come for Trevor.

For Loni, the remainder of the journey passed in a blur of worry, exhaustion, and heartbreak as they left four more horses behind. When they were down to the last two mounts, Bathsheba and Delilah, Loni rode directly behind Clint.

"Still no phone reception!" she called ahead to him.

"Might not get any," he yelled back. "We're much deeper into the mountains than last night, farther from any towers."

Delilah didn't seem as sure on her feet as Loni's other mounts, so Loni was grateful when the terrain leveled out. "How much farther?"

"We're almost there."

It seemed to Loni that they were in the wilderness one second and at the edge of a two-lane highway the next. Keeping to the shoulder of the road, Clint turned right, which she concluded must be north. It took all the strength she had to stay seated on Delilah during the race for town that followed. Once again Clint pushed the horses to the point of exhaustion, the weary Nana falling behind to catch her breath and then racing to catch up.

Just when Loni feared that Delilah might collapse beneath her, they reached the edge of Wagon Wheel. Clint didn't slow the pace even then. He rode Bathsheba at the same brutal speed, cutting through traffic at one point and bringing cars to a screeching halt. He didn't slow down until they came to a small log structure with a gravel parking lot out front.

"This is *it*?" Loni couldn't believe her eyes. The building looked like no emergency clinic she'd ever seen. "Is it even open?"

Trevor clutched in his arms, Clint slid off Bathsheba and ran up rickety steps onto a covered front veranda. "Tie off the horses!"

Calling to Nana, Loni tied the mares' reins to the porch posts before following Clint into the building. Her jeans were hot and wet with horse sweat, and coated with coarse hair. When she plucked the sticky denim from her skin, her fingers came away furry and smeared with grime.

"I hope they don't have a rule against dogs," she told Nana. "No way am I leaving you out here and risking your getting hit by a car."

Nana barked, clearly impatient to go inside with the child. They entered the clinic just in time for Loni to hear a man, somewhere at the back of the building, shouting at the top of his lungs. "You crazy son of a bitch! Are you out of your mind? A transfusion with blood that wasn't cross-matched could kill him. That isn't to mention possible death from shock or agglutination. If any clots hit his lungs he's a goner. Do you realize that?"

With no inflection in his voice, Clint replied, "I injected saline before each infusion to help prevent clotting. I used all I had. Without the blood he would have died where we found him."

Upon hearing Clint's voice Nana took off like a bullet from the barrel of a gun. A second later the doctor was yelling again.

"Get that goddamned dog out of here! Where the hell did it come from?"

"That's Nana," Clint explained. "She was in the raft when it capsized and pulled Trevor to shore so he didn't drown with the adults. Since then she's protected him from wolves, prevented him from getting hypothermia, and hunted for rabbits and squirrels to keep him from starving. She's *earned* the right to be here."

"Not in my treatment room, she hasn't. Get that flea-bitten mongrel out of here."

Clint led the dog by her collar back to the front. "Keep her here," he said. "The good doctor has the personality of a rattlesnake."

When Clint turned away, Loni curled her hand over Nana's collar. The dog whined pathetically. "I'm sorry, sweetie. Dogs can't be in sterile environments."

As Loni's eyes adjusted to the dim light she took in the waiting room, a square area lined with cheap metal chairs. She glimpsed a nurse in blue scrub pants and a flowered smock rushing about in the treatment room, located behind an unimpressive check-in counter and office area. There came quick verbal exchanges between the doctor and nurse, followed by a spurt of frenetic activity. Loni couldn't see Trevor or Clint and could only imagine what was happening in there.

The nurse hurried out to the counter, grabbed the phone, and punched in some numbers. She barely glanced at Loni. "Lorna at Wagon Wheel. Trevor Stiles was just brought in. Trauma to the left shoulder, shock, near exsanguination. We need his blood stats, ASAP, and we need a helicopter lift to Saint Matthew's as fast as you can get someone here."

The nurse hung up the phone and raced back to the treatment room. "They'll call with his stats as soon as they can. The grandparents are in Crystal Falls, so hopefully they'll know who to contact."

"He needs more blood *now*, not in ten minutes."

"Use mine," Clint said. "It hasn't killed him yet."

"*Jesus!*" the doctor cried. "Do you think I'm *nuts*? Do you have your donor card with you?"

"No."

"Then I'm not touching it with a ten-foot pole. I can't verify your blood type. I can't be sure you don't check positive for hepatitis or HIV. No way, Jack."

"I donate all the time. I'm certain I don't check positive for anything bad."

Loni collapsed onto a chair, suddenly so weak in the legs she could no longer stand. Would Clint be endangering himself by giving the child more blood? She nearly jumped out of her skin when the phone rang. Lorna reached the desk before the second ring, grabbed the receiver, and barked, "Yes?" She furiously jotted down notes, hung up with a clipped, "Thanks!" and darted back to the treatment room. "He's an O-neg. That's all they could give me."

"Do we have any on hand?"

"No."

"Well, that's just *great*. Are you sure? Check the fridge."

"I don't need to check the fridge. I know our inventory. We used the last of the O-neg this morning on the motorcycle vic."

"So why didn't you call for more to be delivered? It's the most important blood type to have on hand."

"I *forgot!*" Lorna cried. "It's been a circus in here all day. I'm only human. It's not my fault that Beth called in sick and we've been shorthanded!"

"Use *mine*," Clint said again. "I'm an EMT, damn it. I guess I know what my blood type is. And I'll remind you again, it hasn't killed him yet!"

The doctor cursed under his breath. "Lorna, get the man on a table. Set me up with a direct line."

Loni heard another rush of activity.

"How much have you already given him?" the doctor asked.

"Only a little," Clint replied. "A half pint, maybe. Take what he needs and don't worry about me. I'm fine."

"Let's give this boy some blood, then. He runs a higher risk of dying without it than he will from possible reactions."

"My thought exactly," Clint said dryly. "Maybe I am

a crazy son of a bitch, but if anything goes wrong I won't hold you responsible."

"It'll be the good senator's parents who'll sue my ass off, cowboy, not you."

"The good senator wasn't his father. I am."

"What? This is the Stiles boy. Correct?"

"I'm his biological father," Clint insisted. "You have my word, and even though you're a prickly bastard with the rottenest bedside manner I've ever seen, I won't allow any lawsuits to be filed against you if the transfusion kills him."

"A prickly bastard, am I?" The doctor laughed humorlessly. "That's fair, I guess. It's not every day I get a kid who's almost bled dry and been transfused out in the woods by an unqualified goat roper. That *isn't* to mention having a stinky dog the size of a horse enter my treatment room."

"Yeah, well, count your blessings. We left the actual horses outside."

Trevor got the blood he needed. When Clint joined Loni in the waiting room over thirty minutes later, the doctor and nurse were still working over the child. Loni clasped Clint's hand, noting that he shook like a leaf and looked a little gray under his dark tan.

"Feeling weak?"

"Yeah. I'll be all right, though. I'll just drink tons of water and dose up with iron."

Loni went to the treatment room and asked the nurse if they had any juice or bottled water. The woman got some orange juice from the fridge. When Loni returned to the waiting room, she unscrewed the cap and thrust the container at Clint. "Bottoms up."

Complying, he gulped down the fluid. Then he leaned back in the chair and closed his eyes, the brim of his hat shadowing his face. "My son, my very own son, and I only find out about him when he may be dying."

Loni patted Nana on the head and sat down again. "He won't die."

His lashes fluttered up. His dark eyes sought and held her gaze. "You sure?"

Loni nodded. "I've been certain of it from the first. You believed me, Clint. Don't you see? This time my visions will save a life, and it's all because you took that calculated leap of faith."

He smiled wearily. "Damn, I was a pompous jackass that night. How did you put up with me?"

"I don't know. Maybe it'll come clear to me over the next fifty years or so."

He hooked an arm around her shoulders and drew her close. Although his embrace was limp with weakness, and the chair arms were digging into her stomach, and his hat was bumping her forehead, Loni knew she would never receive another hug quite so wonderful as that one.

"You're the one who saved his life, not me," he whispered huskily. "You put everything on the line—your new life here, your new business. You're a very brave lady, Loni MacEwen. If you hadn't sought me out and told me a story I refused to believe, I never would have known I had a son, and Trevor would be dead right now."

A few minutes later, when the helicopter landed behind the clinic and Trevor had been taken outside, Clint wasn't allowed to accompany Trevor to the hospital.

"I'm his *father*!" Clint cried. "I want to go with him."

"Sorry, sir. You have no proof that you're his father."

"What if he needs more blood?" Clint demanded.

"Then he'll get more. Saint Matthew's is fully equipped to handle that."

"What about cross-matching? I'm his donor. If he has any reactions won't you need my blood stats?"

The paramedic held up a vial. "Got that covered. The doc gave us a sample."

Standing off to one side, Loni could have wept. To the paramedics Clint was only the man who'd found Trevor Stiles, and that afforded him no special treatment.

When the helicopter door closed Loni touched Clint's sleeve. "I'm so sorry, Clint. So *very* sorry."

He rested a heavy arm across her shoulders. "*Damn* them. He's been kept away from me all his life, and now, when he might die en route to the hospital, they won't let me be with him."

The blades of the helicopter began to rotate just then, forcing Loni and Clint to bend forward at the waist and shield their eyes from the flying dust and debris. When the stir of air finally abated, the helicopter was gone, and so was Clint's son. Nana plopped her broad rump on the gravel and howled forlornly.

"Once we get to your truck, we can rush to the hospital and get there an hour or so after he does," Loni said.

Tears slipped down Clint's dusty cheeks. His larynx bobbed as he swallowed. "He doesn't know me from Adam. What good would I be to him?"

Loni consoled the heartbroken Saint Bernard with

pats on the head and then locked arms with Clint. "If nothing else, we can pace the halls and pray for his swift recovery."

Clint nodded, flashing her a shaky smile. "Sandra's folks will be waiting for him. He'll be in good hands until I can get there."

"Do you know them? Sandra's parents, I mean."

"Nope. But I knew Sandra. They're fine people to have raised a woman like that." A shadow crossed his face. "I'll never understand how she could keep my child from me. It goes against everything I thought I knew about her."

"I'm sure there was a reason, Clint. A compelling one, in her opinion."

Arrangements had to be made for the care of Delilah and Bathsheba. A sheriff's deputy offered to trailer the horses out to his farm and keep them there until Clint could pick them up. Another deputy gave Clint, Loni, and Nana a ride to Clint's truck at the north trailhead.

Once there, Clint unhooked the horse trailer from the rig so they could make better time. Then he leaned against a bumper, his booted feet set wide apart, his shoulders limp with weariness. He looked as if he'd just left a battle zone, the loose tails and the front of his shirt stained with blood.

Concerned, Loni hurried to his side. "Are you all right?"

He nodded. "Just exhausted. Might've let him take a little more blood than I should've." He lifted his head to search her gaze. "You think you can drive Big Gulp? Maybe I'll feel better with some shut-eye."

Loni had never driven so large a vehicle. The long

wheelbase would make it difficult to corner. But over the last few days she'd come to realize she could do almost anything she set her mind to.

"Sure, I can drive." She flashed him a grin. "Maybe I'll even get my first speeding ticket."

He smiled wanly. "You're one hell of a lady, Loni mine."

Climbing into the truck from the driver's side was a snap. Loni grabbed hold of the steering wheel, braced a boot on the door runner, and hoisted herself up on the first try. It was Clint who had trouble getting in. He made two false starts before finally reaching the seat.

"Are you sure you're all right? Maybe you need some blood yourself. I could take you back to Wagon Wheel."

"All their O-neg is gone. Remember? I can't be transfused with any other type. It'd kill me."

He rested his head against the window, his face ashen. "Just get us to Saint Matthew's in one piece. I'm okay for now."

Seconds later they were en route to Crystal Falls and Saint Matthew's Hospital. Nana lay on the backseat with her massive head resting on the center console. On the way, though Clint didn't sleep, neither he nor Loni talked very much. Loni imagined that his thoughts were centered on his son. Hers were focused on a dozen different concerns, first and foremost Clint's physical well-being. She was also worried about the horses they'd left behind in the wilderness, especially Uriah. Loni had developed a deep fondness for the big old love. She could only hope the animals met with no mishaps and that Clint could find them once Trevor's life was out of danger.

Saint Matthew's was a state-of-the-art medical facility, more in keeping with Loni's idea of what a hospital should be. She and Clint went directly to the ER waiting room, where the front receptionist refused to give Clint any information. Their patient-privacy policies forbade them to tell Clint even whether Trevor had been admitted to the facility.

Clint's temper snapped. He brought his fist down on the startled blonde's desk with such force that its surface shook. Leaning forward to get nose-to-nose with her, he said, "Trevor Stiles is my *son*! Do you read me loud and clear? I don't give a flying leap about patients' rights or the kid's celebrity status because you think he's the senator's boy. All I want is to know how my child's doing."

"Do you have any documentation to prove you're the child's father?"

"Of course not. Do you think I walk around with documentation in my pocket? Just take my word for it."

"I can't do that. I've heard nothing on the news to indicate that anyone other than Senator Stiles is the child's biological father."

"It hasn't hit any newscasts yet, but trust me, it will, and I'll make sure everyone knows how I've been treated at this facility when it does."

"Calm down, sir. I don't make the rules. I just have to follow them."

"I will *not* calm down. If you don't find out how he's

doing right now, I'll raise so much sand they'll hear me yelling clear up on the third floor."

The blonde angled him an arch look. "You're under security-camera surveillance, sir. I suggest you calm down."

"And I suggest you do what I ask, or I'll slap this hospital with a lawsuit so fast it'll make your head spin."

The receptionist sat back on her chair to put space between them just as two armed security guards appeared. They flanked Clint, each of them grabbing one of his arms.

"All I want is to know how my little boy is," Clint protested, his words sounding oddly slurred.

"Let's step outside, sir."

Clint jerked his cell phone from his belt and tossed it to Loni. "Call my dad. He's in my contact list. Tell him to get here as fast as he can."

Loni had met only Clint's sister, so she felt nervous as she called Frank Harrigan. When the man answered, his voice reminded her so much of Clint's that tears came to her eyes.

"Mr. Harrigan, this is Loni MacEwen."

"The psychic?"

Since knowing Clint, Loni no longer started to sweat when she confessed to being a clairvoyant. "Yes, the psychic. We found Trevor Stiles this morning." She quickly related the events that had taken place since. "Anyway, you need to come." She could hear Clint yelling through the revolving doors. "Clint's totally lost it. Trevor is his son, and the hospital employees won't even tell him if the child is here, let alone if he's alive or dead. I also think Clint allowed the doctor in Wagon Wheel to take too much blood. He doesn't look good, but he's refusing to see a doctor until he finds out how Trevor's doing."

"Sweet Mother Mary. You tell that boy to hold his temper. If they push him too far, he's liable to start knockin' heads together."

Loni swallowed hard. "I don't think he has the strength for any head knocking right now. In fact, I think it's all he can do to stay on his feet."

"I'll be there as fast as I can."

Loni was already rushing out through the revolving doors as she closed the phone and shoved it in her jacket pocket. To her horror one of the security guards was bent forward at the waist, holding his bloody nose, and the other one had gotten Clint in a half-nelson wrestling hold while they both were still standing partially erect. Clint was reeling like a drunk.

Loni leaped to Clint's defense. "Stop it!" she cried. "Can't you see that he's sick?" She grabbed the front of Clint's shirt. "You have to calm down, sweetie. I know how you feel, but this will accomplish nothing. What good to Trevor will you be if they throw you in jail?"

He froze in midmotion to glare at her. His hat had been knocked from his head, and his black hair looked as if it had been stirred with a wire whisk. The security guard still rode his back, now attempting without much success to get a full-nelson hold on his prisoner.

"Your father is coming," Loni said. "How's about we just wait for him. Maybe he can get something done."

Clint closed his eyes, his face twisted in a grimace of sheer anguish. "He's my boy, Loni. I don't even know if he's *alive*."

"I know, sweetheart. I know." Loni gestured at the security guard to release his hold. "Please," she urged. "Don't you have children?"

The guard nodded.

"How would *you* feel if no one would tell you if *your* child was alive or dead?"

Cautiously, and with obvious trepidation, the guard let go of his prisoner. Clint grabbed Loni to his chest, buried his face against her hair, and let loose with a sob that nearly broke her heart. She hugged him back with all her strength.

"He's okay, Clint. He's okay. If you've never believed a single thing I've ever told you, please believe that. He's okay, and everything's going to work out. I promise."

Just then a police car screeched up to the unloading area, its lights flashing red and blue. Two Crystal Falls policemen in tan uniforms spilled from the vehicle. When they saw the security guard with the bloody nose, Loni thought for sure Clint would be arrested. But to her surprise the injured guard shook his head and held up a staying hand.

"He didn't punch me. I just got in the way of his elbow. It was an accident."

Loni kept a firm hold on Clint, splayed hands pressed hard over his back. He remained in the same hunched posture, his face hidden in her hair, every inch of his muscular body shaking.

"It's a misunderstanding," she informed the officers.

"This man is Trevor Stiles's biological father. He hasn't any documentation with him to verify that, and the people inside won't even tell him if his child survived the helicopter flight from Wagon Wheel."

"That true?" the shorter, brown-haired policeman asked of a guard.

"It's their damned privacy policies," the guard replied. "They're only supposed to give out information to the immediate family, and they're being worse sticklers than usual because it's Senator Stiles's child."

"Seems to me they should make an exception for the boy's biological father, whether he's got documentation or not."

The security guard with the bloody nose said, "I'll go in and see what I can do."

While the guard went off to rattle cages, Loni led Clint to a nearby rest area and sat with him on a bench. Elbows propped on his knees, head in his hands, Clint said nothing. Loni communicated her concern to him by gently rubbing his back. After conferring with the remaining security guard, the two policemen finally left. The guard nodded to Loni as he reentered the ER waiting area.

"Clint, I really think maybe you should see a doctor," Loni said.

"Not *yet*," he said hoarsely. "I'll worry about myself once I find out how Trevor is."

Minutes dragged by as slowly as a fly walking across tacky paper. Every once in a while Nana howled, the sound drifting faintly on the afternoon breeze. Loni had parked under a tree to keep the truck in the shade, and all four windows had been rolled halfway down. She knew the dog's distress was due more to separation from Trevor than to any physical discomfort.

She had just glanced at her watch for what seemed like the umpteenth time when five dusty, four-wheel-drive trucks zoomed into the parking area just beyond the grass median. Loni knew instantly that the Harrigan family had arrived in force. Four men and one woman swung from the vehicles. Even at a distance Loni recognized Clint's pretty, petite sister, Samantha Coulter.

The eldest of the four men reached Loni and Clint first. He was dressed in what Loni was quickly coming to think of as ranch-issue clothing, a Stetson, a blue chambray work shirt, faded Wranglers, and dusty riding boots. Her first thought was that Clint had come by his compact, muscular body and dark good looks naturally. Frank Harrigan appeared to be in his early sixties, but he was still incredibly handsome, his burnished face traced with lines from years of harsh exposure to the central Oregon sun. He crouched in front of his eldest offspring. Though shaded by his Stetson, his dark brown eyes reflected an undiminished glimmer of concern when he glanced at Loni.

"He punch anybody's lights out yet?"

Loni nearly smiled. "No, but I'm sure he felt like it. They still haven't told him how Trevor is."

"That so?" Clint's father pushed erect. "Well, I guess I'll just mosey on in and see what the hell the holdup is."

"Dad!" Another Clint look-alike fell in at Frank's heels. "Don't go losing your temper."

"I haven't lost my temper for damned near a year, Quincy," the patriarch retorted. "A man's gotta get riled every once in a while to keep the plaque flushed out of his arteries."

Quincy threw up his hands and turned to yet another man who resembled Clint, except that he looked a bit younger. "Parker, he listens to you. Go settle him down."

"He doesn't listen to me." Parker glanced at Samantha. "You'd best go. At least he won't turn the air blue if you're in there."

Samantha set out after her father, her slender, denim-sheathed legs scissoring in her haste to reach the revolving doors before Frank disappeared inside. The youngest of the brothers grinned at Loni, his dark eyes dancing with laughter. "You the psychic lady?"

Loni nodded.

"I'm Zachary, Clint's baby brother. You certain sure that boy in there is my nephew?"

"Yes," Loni replied.

Zachary removed his Stetson, combed his fingers through his jet-black hair, and then resettled the hat on his head. As he turned toward the doors he said, "In that case, I reckon I'll go in as backup. Dad might need me to put a boot up somebody's ass."

Parker hurried after his younger brother. "No way are you going in without me. I know you and your temper. We'll end up with practically the whole family locked up in the hoosegow with only me to post bail."

Quincy groaned and came to join Clint and Loni on the bench, sitting at his brother's opposite side. He leaned forward to flash Loni a winsome grin. "Aren't we entertaining? A whole family of hotheads."

"I'm not a hothead," Clint protested thickly. "And neither is Dad. He only gets pissed when he's got good reason, and this is one of those times. That's my *son* in there."

"How can you know for certain without a paternity test?" Quincy asked.

Clint lifted his head to glare at his brother. "He's got your nose."

Quincy rubbed beside the offending appendage. "I've got *Dad's* nose."

"All right, Dad's nose, then. There's no mistake, Quincy. Trevor Stiles is my son."

"So why are you sitting here with your thumb up your ass? If he's your kid, go in there and help Dad raise hell until they revise their hospital policies."

"Can't." Clint rested his head in his hands again. "I'm low on oil. Down four, maybe five pints. Got the shakes, feel sick, and my heart's racing like a stock market ticker."

Quincy's grin faded. "Holy shit, bro. You need a transfusion yourself. When you lose two liters, it's dangerous."

"Maybe so," Clint replied. "Fact is, Quincy, I think you need to go get someone."

And just like that Clint toppled forward off the bench, passed out cold. Quincy jumped up. "Ah, shit. Watch after him for me," he told Loni, and then took off at a dead run.

"Oh, my God." Loni dropped to her knees beside the man she loved. He had hit the cement face-first.

Heart slamming, she pushed with all her might to roll him onto his side. Relief flooded through her when she saw that he had only a scrape at his temple. "Clint?" She gave him a shake. Nothing. "Oh, my God, Clint, what have you done to yourself? I *knew* you needed to see a doctor."

Within seconds two male nurses in blue scrubs rushed from the building, carrying a stretcher. Loni was promptly pushed out of the way as they lifted Clint's inert body onto the stretcher, hefted his weight between them, and raced back toward the ER.

Loni was right at their heels. When she made it through the revolving doors, she met with a mass of Harrigans, all standing in a clump with their backs to her, their gazes fixed on the male nurses who were carrying Clint down a hall. Elbowing men aside, Loni found a place in their ranks.

"Damn fool boy," Frank said. "He knows better than to let them drain him that low."

"He had to," Loni said with a catch in her voice that was very close to a sob. "Trevor would have died without the blood. Clint didn't care about himself. All that mattered to him was saving the child."

Frank turned to regard her for a long, silent moment. Then he came to her side and curled a hard arm around her shoulders. "He'll be all right, honey. No point in you gettin' so upset. We don't want you endin' up in the ER, too. You're lookin' a little pale."

Loni *did* feel a little light-headed. "What if he isn't all right? If you lose too much blood it can be fatal."

"One thing you'll learn over time is that Clint always bounces back." Frank gave her a comforting jostle. "He's in good hands."

Parker snorted. "Too damned ornery to die over a little blood loss, that's for sure."

"Clint isn't ornery," Samantha protested. "He's just a little opinionated."

"And obstinate," Zachary tossed in.

"Stubborn as a mule with its hooves set in concrete," Quincy added. "He knew damned well he was in trouble out there, but he took his own sweet time before telling me."

Frank chuckled. "That's my boy. Got himself a fine set of character traits." He smiled down at Loni. "And now he's got a pretty little gal to parade on his arm, too, I'm thinkin'."

Pretty? Loni had never felt so grungy. Her face hadn't seen makeup in nearly a week, she couldn't remember the last time she'd brushed her hair, and her jeans had sprouted a fur coat from the inner knees up to her rump.

Keeping an arm around Loni's shoulders, Frank Harrigan put Quincy in charge of garnering information about his brother's condition and trying to find out what he could about Trevor. Then the family patriarch led Loni to an adjoining sitting area where the family could wait in privacy and helped her to a chair. "Take a load off, sweetheart, and tell the old man what that boy's been up to out in that wilderness."

"Dad," Samantha said in a hushed, scolding tone. "It's none of your business what Clint was up to. Can't you see you're embarrassing her?" She sighed as she sat down beside Loni. "Don't pay him any mind. He just fell off the turnip truck."

Frank kept his arm around Loni's shoulders. "Don't listen to her. I've never farmed turnips. Carrots were my specialty. Gave me damned good vision, so I can't help but notice when a pretty young gal looks at my son with her heart in her eyes." He arched a grizzled eyebrow at Loni. "Am I readin' you right, darlin'? You got a soft spot for our Clint?"

"Yes." Loni could think of nothing else to say. He'd asked a direct question, and she gave him a direct answer.

"I like a woman who doesn't prevaricate," Frank said with a grin. "Seems to me our Clint found himself a pot of gold out there in the back of beyond."

"You're impossible," Samantha said with a huff. "Just ignore him, Loni. He's an incurable tease and too thick between the ears to know when he's stepping over the line." Leaning forward, she fixed her father with a glare. "That's enough, Dad. Leave her alone."

"I'm fine." The moment Loni spoke, she realized it was true. She was feeling better. It was hard to think grim thoughts with so much foolishness going on around her, much of which, she suspected, had been staged for her benefit. She smiled at Frank Harrigan. "Clint's very lucky to have such a wonderful family."

All Clint's brothers, save Quincy, had taken seats across from them. "Wonderful?" Zachary echoed. "Interesting, maybe."

"And a little dysfunctional," Samantha interjected.

"We're not dysfunctional," Parker protested.

Just then Quincy rejoined his family.

"What did you find out?" Frank asked.

"Jack shit." Quincy hooked his thumbs over his belt. "A doctor is seeing Clint right now. He'll be out in a few minutes to update us. As for Trevor, he's a senator's son, higher security required, yada, yada, yada. You'd think we were assassins and they were guarding the president or something."

"And you just walked away with your tail between your legs?" Parker demanded.

"Yeah, Quincy. If it were me, I'd still be out there arguing," Zachary put in.

"That's about all you're good at, arguing," Samantha said. "What we need here is a little diplomacy."

"You're elected then," Zachary shot back. "I don't have a diplomatic bone in my whole body, and I'm damn glad of it."

Quincy held up a hand. "Does anyone want to hear the rest?"

"The rest of what?"

"If you all would shut up for a second, I might just tell you." When a sudden silence fell, he went on to say, "They've agreed to ask Trevor's grandparents to come down and talk to us." He slanted his brothers a glare. "That's more than either of you could have accomplished. If you don't like the way I handled it, feel free. At least I got them to make a concession."

"Some concession. He's our own flesh and blood, and they won't tell us anything."

And so it went, with the Harrigans firing verbal shots across the waiting area, keeping Loni so distracted that she forgot to worry about Clint.

Finally a doctor came out to see them. When Frank's

name was called, he surged to his feet. "You the man takin' care of my boy?"

The doctor nodded and shook Frank's hand. "He'll be fine. We're hitting him hard with fluids and packed red blood cells. That'll take several hours. Then, barring any complications, he should be able to go home."

"Is he awake?" Samantha asked.

"He is. The immediate family can go back in pairs to see him if you'd like."

Samantha grasped Loni's elbow. "My sister and I will go back first."

Loni blinked in confusion until she understood Samantha's ploy and went along with the lie. Immediate family. Clint's sisters qualified. An exhausted clairvoyant with blood all over her clothes did not.

Hooked up to IVs, Clint was in a hospital recliner, siphoning orange juice from a carton with a bendable straw, when Loni and Samantha entered his cubicle. He smiled wanly and held out a hand to Loni. She noticed that his fingers felt cold and clammy when they intertwined with hers. "My two favorite girls. How lucky can a guy be?"

Samantha stepped to the opposite side of his chair and bent to kiss his forehead. "Where's your hat? You look naked without a Stetson clapped on that lump you call a head."

"Don't know where it went. Might've got knocked off when I was scuffling with the security guards."

Samantha lifted the bag of blood suspended from an IV tree beside him. "Yuck. I wonder whose blood you're getting."

"Could be my own. I donate enough of it." He let his

head fall back against the chair cushion and closed his eyes. "Sorry. I feel like I've been rode hard and put away wet." His lashes fluttered back up. "Which reminds me. I left six of my horses out in the wilderness area. You s'pose Dad and the boys might go get 'em for me?"

Samantha smiled and took the empty carton from his limp hand. "You know they will, Clint."

"We fell out at milepost four-eighty-six. If they head due east from there, they can maybe pick up their tracks."

"I'll tell them." Samantha set the drink aside, smoothed a lock of black hair from her brother's brow, and smiled tenderly. "I love you. You know that, I hope."

"You got any news about my son yet?"

Samantha grinned. "Quincy's working on it. The moment we hear something, one of us will come in to let you know."

Clint's sister looked at Loni. "I'll go back to the waiting room now so Dad and one of my brothers can come in. Don't stay too long. All right? If they're as strict about their ER visitation rules as they are about patient-privacy policies, two more people won't be allowed to come back until you leave."

Loni nodded. When Samantha had exited the cubicle, she crouched by Clint's chair. "You scared me half to death."

"I'm sorry."

"There you go again, saying those words that can never fix anything."

"Yeah, well, since meeting you the habit's starting to grow on me. I really am sorry for scaring you. I knew I felt really funny, but I was so upset about Trevor I kept thinking I could wait."

"That doctor in Wagon Wheel should be shot for taking more blood than it was safe for you to give."

"Not his fault," Clint said drowsily. "I knew if I told him how much I gave Trevor to start with, he wouldn't take any more." His eyes fell closed again. "Sorry, honey. I want to stay awake, but I can't."

Loni pushed erect and followed Samantha's example, leaning down to kiss his forehead. "I love you, Clint." Oh, how she loved him. "Whenever you wake up, imagine that I'm here hugging you."

He didn't answer. She slipped quietly from the cubicle to rejoin the Harrigans in the waiting area.

Frank Harrigan was engaged in an intense conversation with a well-dressed, middle-aged couple seated across from him when Loni resumed her place at his side.

"So the child's going to be all right?"

The woman, a slender brunette with gentle green eyes, nodded and smiled tremulously. "They'll be keeping a very close eye on him for the next twenty-four hours, but the shoulder surgery went well, and the blood your son gave him was an almost perfect match. They don't anticipate any serious complications. He's running a slight fever right now, but we were told that's fairly normal after a transfusion."

Loni realized the couple must be Sandra Stiles's parents. No wonder both of them looked relieved yet forlorn. Their grandson had been saved, but they'd lost their daughter, and their grief still had to be fresh and painful.

"I appreciate you comin' down to update us on the child's condition, Mr. and Mrs. Michaels," Frank said softly. "Do they have him in a private room now?"

"Yes, up in pediatrics."

"My son Clint will be glad to hear that." He took off his hat and turned it in his hands. "I know you folks are feelin' real sad right now about your daughter and that you've been through a rough time, worryin' over the boy. I hate like hell addin' to your woes. But some things need sayin' and can't be put on hold till later."

Mr. Michaels, a brown-haired man of diminutive stature with kindly blue eyes, nodded solemnly.

Frank sighed and gave his hat another turn. "We've got reason to believe that Trevor is Clint's child. He was datin' your daughter about the time the boy was conceived. Did she ever mention the possibility that Trevor wasn't sired by Senator Stiles?"

Sandra's father ran a hand over his thinning pate. "Our daughter knew for certain that Clint was the father of her baby."

A stunned silence followed that pronouncement.

Samantha, sitting beside Loni, crossed her slender legs and began swinging her booted foot in an agitated manner. Even in dusty jeans with her curly black hair pulled through the back of a red baseball cap, Clint's sister managed to look elegant. With an edge to her voice, she asked, "If Sandra knew Clint was the father, why on earth did she never tell him?"

The woman shifted on her chair, a clutch purse held tightly in her white-knuckled hands. "Please don't think badly of Sandra. It nearly broke her heart when she told Clint she wasn't pregnant. But she honestly had no choice."

"There's always a choice," Samantha retorted softly but firmly. "My brother had a right to know his son, and Sandra deprived him of that."

Frank reached across Loni to pat his daughter's knee. "These folks have been through hell over the last week, honey. Let's not go too hard on them." To Sandra's father he said, "Can you explain the situation to me, Jacob? Why was it impossible for Sandra to tell Clint about the baby?"

Jacob Michaels sat forward on his chair. "Shortly after moving back to Sweet Home, Sandra became active on the local level as a campaign worker to secure Robert Stiles a senatorial seat in the 1998 elections. At the time she still didn't know she was pregnant, and when Robert stopped in at the campaign center one afternoon, he and Sandra hit it off."

"And once they hit it off, Mr. Stiles couldn't afford to risk any hint of scandal by marrying a woman pregnant with another man's child," Frank supplied.

"Not if he hoped to become a state senator." Jacob Michaels tugged at his shirt collar. "He and Sandra were deeply in love. The only way they could possibly be together was for Robert to claim the child as his own."

"It was the *only* way," Sandra's mother interjected. "Sandra couldn't take a chance that Robert's political career might be derailed because of her pregnancy. Can you imagine the media heyday if a story like that had surfaced? The incumbent, who'd held the seat for eighteen years, would have leaped at the opportunity to throw garbage, calling into question Robert's morals, his good judgment, and God only knows what else. Robert's reputation and credibility would have taken a very hard hit. Sandra believed in Robert and felt he would do great things for our state. She could walk away from her relationship with him and tell Clint about the child. Or she could keep silent, marry Robert, and be happy with the man she loved."

"So she chose the latter," Quincy said with undisguised disgust. "You do realize that Clint will fight tooth and nail to get his son. Nothing this side of heaven or hell will keep him away from that boy. It'll be a very simple matter for him to get a court-ordered paternity test. If he can prove the child is his, getting custody will be a shoo-in."

"A paternity test and court proceedings won't be necessary," Jacob Michaels said. "I know all of you feel bitter and deeply angry with our daughter. To be honest, my wife and I never agreed with Sandra's decision to cut Clint out of her child's life. But over time, when we saw how blissfully happy she and Robert were, and what a wonderful father Robert was to our grandson, we did come to accept it.

"We didn't argue when Sandra and Robert came to us after they drew up a will and told us that they hadn't chosen a member of the family to be Trevor's guardian in the event of their deaths." Jacob's eyes filled with tears, and his mouth started to quiver. "They both wanted Clint to raise the boy. Robert felt a great deal of guilt over the wrong they'd done to protect his political career, and so did Sandra. If anything ever happened, they wanted Trevor to be with his real father."

"So as soon as the will is read, Clint will get custody?" Parker asked.

"Yes," Mrs. Michaels said.

Jacob Michaels sobbed brokenly and buried his face in his hands. "When they told us about the will, I never dreamed . . . I just never *dreamed* that guardianship of Trevor would ever be an issue. And now my girl is dead."

Loni closed her eyes against a rush of tears. What Sandra Stiles had done to Clint, and by extension to her son, was unforgivable, but it was also understandable. Sandra had unexpectedly met and fallen in love with her dream man, just as Loni had. When Loni tried to imagine moving on with her life without Clint in it, her mind went blank and her heart hurt. Sandra must have felt much the same way when she contemplated ending her relationship with Robert.

True love came along only once in a lifetime. Loni's chance to be happy—loving a man, making babies with him, and then growing old with him—would never come again. Loni had grabbed at her chance to be with Clint. Should Sandra be reviled beyond the grave for making the same decision?

It was a hard call, but having come to know Clint the way she did, Loni knew his anger at Sandra would pass.

"It's difficult, but over time I know Clint will work it all out in his mind," she said, mildly surprised at her own audacity for speaking. But it was something she had to do. Clint wasn't there to talk for himself. "It may not have been the right choice for Sandra to make, but I know in my heart that Clint won't hold it against her.

He's spoken to me about Sandra, and he's had nothing but good to say about her. He's told me more than once that she was one of the finest people he's ever known."

Loni half expected one of the exuberant, outspoken Harrigans to ask what right she had to open her mouth. This was, after all, *their* family tragedy, and absolution to Sandra wasn't Loni's to give. But no one in Clint's family called her on it.

Frank settled a knowing gaze on Loni, smiled slightly, and said by way of introduction, "Forgive my oversight. This young lady is Loni MacEwen. She's a clairvoyant, and if it weren't for her our little Trevor would be dead right now."

At Frank's revelation, Loni's spine stiffened, and she shifted on her seat, feeling suddenly uncomfortable.

Sandra's parents stared at her for a long moment. Then Jacob said, "Come again?"

Frank settled a big, warm hand on Loni's shoulder. "This young lady had a vision of the raftin' accident. She went to Clint and told him a crazy story about a son he didn't even know he had. She claimed Trevor had survived the accident, was still alive and lost in the Shoshone Wilderness Area. If not for her Clint never would have known he had a child, let alone that he was in danger. It follows that Clint never would have gone into the wilderness to find Trevor, and the boy would be dead right now. You'd be grieving not only for your daughter, but also for your grandson."

"Oh, my. So *that's* why it was Clint who found our boy. We wondered at the coincidence. Of all the men in Crystal Falls to have rescued Trevor, how could it possibly be Clint, the child's real father?" Sandra's mother came to her feet, stepped across the carpet, and held out a hand to Loni. "So you saved our Trevor's life."

Loni stood to shake the woman's hand. "I never got your name."

"Sharon." She smiled even though tears swam in her eyes. "Thank you so much for all you've done. Our Trevor is so special. Right now having him to think about is all that's keeping me going." She tipped her head to give Loni a quizzical look. "I've never believed in clairvoyants. I can't imagine how you knew he was still alive when all the authorities believed he'd drowned. But however it came about, I'm eternally grateful."

Loni gave the older woman a quick hug. "I didn't save Trevor's life. Clint did. I only accompanied him into the wilderness to help search."

"Sandra always spoke so highly of Clint. Even after they stopped seeing each other, she always smiled when she talked about him."

As everyone resumed their seats, Jacob Michaels continued the conversation. "Sharon and I want it made clear right from the start that we're in complete agreement with Sandra's decision to reveal Clint's relationship to our grandson and name him as the child's guardian in her will. Don't get me wrong. We love the boy with our whole hearts and would like nothing more than to raise him ourselves. But we're getting on in years, with a few too many cricks in our joints to be decent parents to a rambunctious little boy. We feel very strongly that Trevor will have a more normal childhood with his father, while we do the grandparent thing whenever Clint gives us the opportunity."

"I hear a 'but' danglin' at the end of that," Frank said.

"There is a concern," Jacob admitted. "Trevor has just lost his mama and the only father he's ever known. We're afraid it will be extremely traumatic for him if Clint takes him away from Sharon and me too quickly. We're hoping that your son will go slowly, coming to Sweet Home for short visits at first, and then maybe inviting him on afternoon outings for a while. Trevor needs time to get to know Clint and come to understand that Clint's his real daddy."

Frank nodded. "My son's a fine young man. He'll do nothin' that isn't in the child's best interests. If that means a few months of visitation before he takes custody, I'm sure he'll agree to it without a quarrel."

Sharon sighed with relief. "I'm so glad to meet all of you. It soothes my heart to know Trevor will have such a wonderful new family. Now I have only one more concern."

"What's that?" Frank asked.

"Where is our precious Nana? Was she with Trevor? Did she drown? I know it sounds silly, but she's a member of our family, too. We love her very much."

"Nana is fine," Loni said with a laugh. "She deserves the Most Wonderful Dog of the Year award." She quickly related to the Michaelses how Nana had saved Trevor's life, not once but many times over the last several days. "If you'd like to see her she's out in Clint's truck."

Sharon leaped up from her chair. "I'd *love* to see her. And if you don't mind, we'll take her to our motel. They allow pets, and she'll be more comfortable there."

Chapter Fourteen

Loni stayed at the hospital until nearly midnight to be there when Clint was finally released. Because he was in the ER receiving an infusion, he was considered to be an outpatient and would be able to go as soon as his treatment was completed. Samantha's husband, Tucker, had joined her, and they stayed until almost ten, but after visiting Clint several times and peeking in on a sleeping Trevor in the pediatric wing, the handsome veterinarian and his pretty wife finally yawned good nights at Loni and went home. Clint's father and brothers had left hours before to go into the wilderness after the abandoned horses. In the end it was only Loni in the waiting area when Clint emerged from the ER.

"I've been given permission to go up and look in on Trevor," he told her after a brief embrace. "You want to come up with me?"

"Can I?"

"Now that all these idiots finally believe I'm his dad, I guess I can take his future mama up to see him. If they say anything, I'll tell them to go get stuffed."

Loni smiled. "You're feeling better."

"Of course I'm feeling better. All I needed was a lube job."

Once in the elevator he gathered her into his arms and kissed her until they were both breathless. "I love you. I don't remember if I mentioned that today."

Loni trailed her gaze over his face, glad to see a healthy glow under his dark skin. "If you told me a dozen times, it never hurts to say it again."

"I love you, lady. Thanks for looking out for me this afternoon. I wasn't thinking very clearly when that security guard was crawling up my back. Lack of oxygen to the brain, I guess. If I'd had the strength, I would have pretended he was a mud hole and stomped him dry."

"Fortunately that didn't happen. You'd be banging a tin cup on cell bars right now, asking to call your lawyer."

He chuckled. "Possibly so."

When the elevator doors opened and they stepped out on the third floor, Clint reeled to a halt. "I'm so scared I couldn't spit if you yelled, 'Fire.' I can't tell him I'm his daddy. What excuse will I give him for being there if he happens to wake up? He was pretty out of it when we found him. He may not remember my face."

Loni plucked at his stained shirt. "He'll remember." She took his hand. "Come on, old man. This won't be the last time he'll scare you spitless. Just wait until you teach him to drive."

Trevor appeared to be asleep when they entered his room. Sharon Michaels sat beside the child's bed. When she saw them, she smiled tearfully and stepped around the foot to hug Clint's neck. "Thank you," she whispered. "If it weren't for you I would be without *both* my babies."

Clint acted as if he weren't quite sure what to do with his hands. Then he enfolded the older woman in his arms. "I loved your Sandra. Only as a friend, but she was a really *good* friend. I'm sorrier than I can say for your loss."

Sharon drew back and wiped her cheeks. "I'll leave you for a bit to sit with him. I could use a break." She patted Loni's arm. "I'll be back in about thirty minutes."

Loni and Clint commandeered the two chairs in the small room. Clint sat forward on his seat, arms braced on his spread knees, gaze fixed on Trevor's small face. "Isn't he something?" he whispered.

"He's perfect," Loni agreed, her voice barely a murmur. And she meant it with all her heart. If she was fortunate enough to become Clint's wife, she would love his son as if he were her own. "I can't believe how much he looks like you."

"He does, doesn't he?"

Trevor stirred just then. Clint placed a finger over his lips, signaling Loni that they needed to stop whispering back and forth. But it was too late. Trevor's thick black lashes fluttered open, his big, liquid brown eyes focused on Clint, and his sweet mouth tipped into a replica of his father's crooked grin.

"I remember you," he said sleepily. "You're the friend who found me."

Clint nodded, his larynx riding high in his throat,

then bottoming out. "That's me, partner. You had us worried there for a while."

"You told me I'd be okay," Trevor replied. "So I wasn't scared."

The child tried to shift on his pillow and winced. Clint shot to his feet and helped him to get more comfortable. "That better?"

Trevor nodded. He gazed solemnly up at Clint. "My grandma said God sent you to me."

"She did?" A ruddy flush crept up Clint's neck.

"Yep. She says when really sad things happen, God always sends us something to make us feel happy again. My mom and dad drowned, you know. I almost did, but Nana saved me."

"I know, partner." Clint smoothed the child's black hair. "Your mother was a good friend of mine. I'm so sorry you lost her."

Trevor's eyes went bright with tears. He plucked at the hospital sheet. "Me, too. But Grandma says she's happy in heaven now with Daddy. Did you know there's angel music up there twenty-four hours a day, and the streets are paved in gold?"

"I've heard that." Clint pulled his chair closer, sat back down, and took the boy's hand in his. "It's the place where wonderful people go when they leave here. Your mommy and daddy will be really happy up there."

Tears burned Loni's eyes, for she could only guess what it cost Clint to pretend that Robert Stiles had been Trevor's father. But that was her dream cowboy. When he loved, he loved with everything he had, even if it meant setting his own feelings and needs aside.

"They'll miss you, though," Clint hurried to add. "A whole lot. But there's another neat thing about heaven besides the angel music and golden streets."

"There is?"

"Oh, yeah. Time goes by really fast up there. To them it'll seem like they are away from you only for a few minutes, and soon you'll be an old man, and then there you'll be, up in heaven with them."

Loni knew by the look in Clint's eyes that he'd been told that same comforting story when he'd been a child, mourning for his mother.

"I'm glad," Trevor said tremulously. "My mom didn't like to be away from me. She always cried when she had to go on trips, and she called me a gazillion times a day so she could talk to me and cry some more."

"Well, she's not crying now," Clint assured him. "You'll miss her a lot longer than she'll miss you, because time is different up there."

Trevor yawned. Clint pushed to his feet and drew the sheet up under the child's chin. "We need to stop talking, partner. You're getting tired."

With his good hand Trevor grabbed Clint's wrist, his tiny brown fingers barely curling over one side of his father's forearm. "My grandma says all my blood drained out, and you filled me back up again with all of yours."

Clint swallowed hard. "Not all, and they gave me some more. You don't need to worry."

"I'm not worried." Trevor fixed him with a wondering, dark gaze. "It's just that Grandma says that makes you kind of like my new daddy, 'cause now all my blood is your blood."

Clint sank back down on the chair as if a blow had been dealt to the back of his legs. "She did, did she?"

"She says maybe God sent you because he knows how sad I am right now." Trevor's bottom lip quivered. "I don't have a mom or dad anymore, and Grandma says, as much as they love me, they're getting too old to do lots of fun things with a little boy. Grandpa's back hurts, and he's got a bad knee. He can still play with me right now, but in a couple more years he might be too old to do all the things I like."

"Bummer," Clint said tautly. "What kind of things do you like?"

"I like camping. My dad taught me how to do lots. He said no man should ever go into the woods without knowing how to take care of himself."

"Your dad was absolutely right," Clint agreed. "He must have spent a lot of time teaching you camping stuff. You did a great job of taking care of yourself out there."

"Until I cut myself. Daddy always told me not to hold the ax halfway up the handle 'cause it might jump back, but I forgot."

"One little mistake. You did a grand job of surviving out there otherwise, Trevor. I'm sure your daddy was up there watching and felt very proud of you."

"Nana helped. She's got real thick fur that kept me warm, and she's a real good hunter. I tried to catch fish in the creek."

"Any luck?"

"Nope. I made a spear, just like my dad showed me,

but the fish weren't where I thought they were, and I always missed."

"It takes lots of practice to spear fish. The water acts like a magnifying glass and distorts your vision."

Trevor gave Clint a startled look. "That's what Daddy said. He was real good at spearing fish. Are you good at camping stuff, just like him?"

"Fair to middlin'. I've speared a couple of fish in my day, though."

"My dad speared *lots*." Tears filled Trevor's eyes again. "Mommy used to cook 'em in a skillet over the fire. She made them taste real good."

"I'll bet she did."

"Lots better than rabbit without salt." Trevor brushed at his cheeks. "We had lots of fun."

"It'll take a while for you to stop missing them and start feeling better, Trevor. When you lose your folks when you're only eight, it's a very hard thing."

Trevor's gaze clung to his father's. "Did you lose your mom and dad?"

"Only my mom. I was about your age. It took a long time before I started to feel better."

"How long before it stops hurting like I swallowed an ice cube?"

Clint's face reflected the pain he felt for his child. "That part goes away after a couple of weeks, but you still feel like crying sometimes. When you do, you just need to do it. That helps a lot. My dad used to tell me that God gave us tears to wash away the pain. So don't feel embarrassed. It's okay to cry, even if you're a guy. He told me that one time when he found me hiding in the closet, ashamed for anybody to see me bawling.

Afterward I still hid in the closet sometimes when I needed to cry, but I wish now that I hadn't."

"How come?"

"Because there's no shame in loving people and feeling really sad when you lose them. Every tear tells the world how much you cared. Your mom and dad were the best. Right?"

"Yep."

"Well, then, they deserve all your tears, and crying will make the ice cube feeling in your chest go away."

"It will?"

"Guaranteed."

Trevor's eyes welled up. "Do you still cry?"

Clint wiped under one eye. "Oh, yeah."

"You're crying now. How come?"

"Because." Clint shrugged. "Like I said, your mama was really special to me, and you're her little boy, so seeing you hurt makes me hurt."

"Do you like to play soccer?"

Clint chuckled. "I haven't done that for a few years, but I used to be pretty good at it."

"I'm real good at soccer and baseball. Grandpa says I've got such a great pitching arm on me I could be the next Cy Young."

"Wow. That's a high recommendation."

"Yep. The doctor says it's a good thing I cut my left shoulder, 'cause I pitch with my right arm."

"Definitely a plus. It'd be a shame for the next Cy Young to hurt his pitching arm."

"Yep." Trevor began fiddling with the sheet again. "Grandma says I'm going to need a new dad before I get much older, somebody closer to my real daddy's age, somebody who isn't too old to play ball with me."

"I can see the problem," Clint agreed. "Every boy needs to practice his soccer and pitching."

"Grandma thinks, since you gave me all new blood from out of you, maybe you'd like to be my new dad someday."

Clint said nothing for several long seconds, and before he collected himself, Trevor added, "If you think it'd be a bunch of trouble, I won't be mad at you or anything," Trevor added. "My dad used to say I was more trouble than two cats fighting in a gunnysack."

Clint chuckled. "All dads say things like that, son. They're only joking."

Trevor smiled sleepily. "Yep. My dad told lots of jokes." His lashes fluttered back up. "Do you like jokes?"

"Oh, yeah," Clint replied in a thick voice. "Especially when they're on me." He glanced at Loni. Then he looked at Trevor again. "I don't have a little boy. I've always wanted one. Now that we've got the same blood, maybe we should work out some kind of an agreement. Do you want to be my little boy?"

"I don't know."

Clint's dark face fell. "Oh. Well. That's okay. It's pretty soon after losing your dad to be thinking about getting a new one."

"Nope," Trevor replied. "My daddy talked to me once. He said if anything ever happened to him and Mommy, they'd already picked me out another dad who'd take care of me and love me just like they did. Grandma says you're the dad they picked."

"Really?" Clint's Adam's apple bobbed again. "Well. In that case." He rubbed a big hand over his burnished face and blinked. "Sounds to me like maybe I'm the man for the job."

Trevor frowned around a huge yawn. "I got a big dog. She sheds all over, and sometimes, 'cause she's so tall, she snitches food off the counter or table. You might not like her."

"Nana?" Clint smiled. "I *love* that dog. If she ever comes to visit at my house she's going to be served sirloin steak." Clint regarded his son with a bewildered frown. "I take it the deal's off if I have a problem with your dog."

Trevor nodded. "I can't ever leave Nana. She's my best friend."

Clint settled back on the chair. "Well, I've got horses, and they're my best friends. You like horses?"

"A lot. I've only seen them in movies, though."

"One of these days maybe you can come to visit at my ranch, and you can see some for real."

Trevor nodded again. "If I like horses and you like Nana, maybe we'll like each other, too. For when Grandpa can't play ball with me anymore. Maybe then, if you still want a boy, we can see how it works."

"I think that's a very good plan." Clint's eyes were sparkling with tears when he looked at Loni. "Go to sleep now, partner. I'll come visit you again tomorrow."

Trevor's lashes fluttered closed.

Loni and Clint sat in silence, watching the child sleep. Loni occasionally saw Clint wipe beneath his eyes. She kept her gaze fixed on Trevor, allowing Clint to shed his tears.

When Sharon Michaels returned to the room, Clint rose from the chair, gathered her into his arms, and gave her a fierce hug. "Thank you," he said.

"For what?"

"Paving the way for me."

Sharon cupped Clint's face between her hands. "You gave him life, and now you've saved it. It's nothing more than you deserve. I have only one request."

"What's that?"

"Let us have him for visits as often as you can. It's going to be hard when I have to let go."

"You've got it."

When Loni and Clint exited the hospital, the cold embrace of the wee-hour air felt fabulous. They both dragged in huge drafts and then laughed simultaneously.

"I miss our campfire," she said.

"Me, too."

He curled an arm around her shoulders as they walked toward his truck. "That was one of the most difficult conversations I've ever had, but one of the greatest, too. Thanks to Sandra's mom, Trevor's accepting a connection between us."

"Yes, he is. And I suspect that his grandpa's pitching arm will be wearing out in only a few months. In the ER waiting room he and Sharon both made it clear that they want you to raise Trevor. They feel that they're getting a bit too old to keep up with him." She went on to tell him all that had been said, giving him her spin on why Sandra had lied to him about being pregnant. "I know you feel angry and betrayed, but from this point forward I hope you'll be able to come to a peaceful place and be patient about getting custody of Trevor."

He glanced down at her and smiled. "For the first time in my life I can understand how devastating it would be to lose the love of my life. Doesn't mean I'll immediately come to grips with what Sandra did or forgive her for it. But she was a fine person, and I'll get there. As for being patient about custody, I know I'll have to, but, man, it's tempting to take him home with me as soon as he gets released."

"All in good time. Meanwhile you'll visit and ease your way into a solid relationship with him. That will be best for Trevor."

"I know," he said with a sigh. "If I take you home to grab a change of clothes, will you sleep over at my place tonight? I don't want to be alone, and I really need to stay at the ranch, just in case Dad and the boys roll in with my horses. They'll be needing some TLC."

Loni had been worrying about Uriah all day. She liked the thought of being present when the gelding arrived at the ranch. She also liked the thought of being with Clint for a few more hours before everyday life forced them to separate. "If I stay with you, we'll have to behave ourselves."

Clint bent to kiss her cheek. "Do I have *idiot* branded on my forehead? I definitely do *not* want to tell Father Mike that I sinned not once, but twice. He'll cut me some slack over one mistake. His patience will bottom out if I go in as a repeat offender."

"I'll sleep on the sofa."

"I've got spare bedrooms."

"Well, then." She rested her cheek against his arm, loving the flex of muscle under his shirtsleeve whenever he moved. "I'll sleep in the spare bedroom, then."

"Like hell. I need you close. We'll build a barricade or something."

"A what?"

"A barricade, kind of like those traveling-salesmen jokes, where the guy gets stranded and has to sleep with the farmer's daughter, so they pile pillows between them."

"What help would that be?"

He chuckled and bent to kiss her again. "No help at all. That's exactly the point."

Loni giggled and wrapped both arms around his waist as they walked the remaining distance to his vehicle. Now that loose-hipped swagger that she'd secretly admired so many times became a very personal thing, her thigh bumping against his hard one with every step they took. *Yum.* But she'd already played Eve, tempting Adam with the apple. She'd be strong tonight. She *would.*

"We can't go there again," she said. "Physical intimacy between a man and woman should be a sacred thing."

"I absolutely agree. We have to be strong."

"Anything worth having is worth waiting for."

"You are *so* worth waiting for."

"How many pillows do you have?"

"Not enough. Nowhere near enough."

An hour and a half later, after showering separately, Loni and Clint crawled onto his bed with a mountain of pillows between them. Clint had collected them from every bedroom in the house, and they were piled like a wall from the top of the bed to the foot. Loni was exhausted. It felt so good to be clean, with freshly brushed teeth, clean pajamas on her body, and a headful of shampooed hair that had been blown dry and had no tangles. She almost groaned at the sheer, sleepy delight of it.

Clint searched for and found her hand, enveloped it in long, hard, deliciously warm fingers, and rested their wrists atop the barricade. "This is kuh-nuts."

Loni stifled a yawn and blinked awake. "I'm sorry?"

"Kuh-nuts, as in crazy. This lends a whole new definition to the term *pillow talk*."

Loni struggled to keep her eyes open. Dimly it occurred to her that he'd probably slept through his transfusion. She, on the other hand, had been pacing the halls. When she recalled the last twenty-four hours, just the thought of all that had transpired made her weary.

"Where'd you get the Snoopy pajamas?" he asked with a faint note of disapproval. "When a guy imagines what a beautiful woman like you wears to bed, Snoopy is *not* on his list. Haven't you ever heard of Victoria's Secret?"

Loni smiled drowsily. "Of course. But what was the point? When a woman lives alone, Snoopy pajamas work just fine."

"You gonna change your habits once we get married?"

"Only if you're paying. Lingerie is expensive."

"How many thousands do you need?"

Loni came wide-awake and giggled. "How much variety do you want?"

"Five thousand dollars' worth might cover it. I want mostly strings, with no actual material unless it's see-through."

She laughed again. "I'm sorry my PJs disappoint you."

"What's under them doesn't." He released a long sigh. "You wanna go take a shower with our clothes on?"

"*What?*"

"You heard me. Father Mike might fall for another I-don't-know-how-it-happened incident."

"You don't answer to Father Mike." Loni drew her fingers from his grasp, rolled partly onto her right side, snuggled her cheek into the pillow, and tossed her left arm, limp with exhaustion, over the top the barricade to clasp his hand again. "You answer to God."

"You ever hear the term *wet blanket*?"

"Yes. I've also heard the term *wet T-shirt*. I'm pretty sure my Snoopy top will be just as bad if it gets wet."

"*Bad* isn't the word. *Irresistible* is the word. How about a bubble bath? I'll even scrounge up a candle."

"Nope. We're going to be good."

"I've got whiskey downstairs. How about if we get roaring drunk so we can't be held responsible?"

"That won't work. We'd be responsible for drinking so much whiskey that we lost control."

"You drive a really hard bargain."

"We agreed that we'd be good from here on out. It's not *my* bargain."

He sighed heavily. "You're right. I'm sorry. I'm so weak. Maybe I'll just get drunk so I can fall asleep."

Gathering all her strength, Loni pushed up on an elbow to peer over the pillows at him. "Are you in that much discomfort?"

"I knew you were over there somewhere."

She grabbed a pillow and shoved it over his face. "You are *impossible*."

"I got a rise out of you. You wanna try to get one out of me?"

Loni figured the *rise* had already occurred. She flopped back down on the mattress. "You may be able to tempt me tomorrow."

"*Tomorrow?* Do you realize how many seconds that is from now?"

"Yes. Sixty seconds in every minute, sixty minutes in every hour, and I plan to sleep through every millisecond until about noon. I'm exhausted."

"Ah, honey, I'm sorry. Of course you're exhausted. You want me to rub your back?"

Loni turned her face into her pillow to smother another laugh. "Go to sleep, cowboy. I'll see you in my dreams."

"What fun will that be? All you ever did was look at me."

When Loni awakened the next morning, Clint's side of the bed was vacant. As she sat up, squinting against the bright sunlight that slanted through the vertical blinds, she saw a note on the nightstand. Smiling sleepily, she unfolded it to read the masculine scrawl. *Horses came in. At the arena. Coffee's fresh. Bagels and cream cheese for breakfast. Love, Clint.*

"A man of few words."

Loni went into the large master bathroom to luxuriate under another hot shower. After drying her hair, getting dressed, and applying a light layer of makeup, using what she'd brought from home last night, she hurried down the stairs to the main floor, taking in one bare wall after another en route. Clint had a beautiful post-and-beam home, but it was pathetically lacking in decor. The furniture was utilitarian at best, and he truly hadn't hung a single picture. In the kitchen above the phone a calendar had been tacked on the wall, but that was it.

While sipping a cup of coffee, Loni went on a snooping expedition. Finding the promised bootjacks in every room made her smile. At least they were relatively small. If this became her home, she could work around them.

Standing at the center of the living room, she tried to come up with a plan for decorating and quickly concluded that the entire house would be a creative challenge such as she had never tackled. The style of the home would *not* lend itself well to anything very feminine. She could brighten the walls with some bold designer colors and Western art, but the furniture and all accessories would have to be in keeping with the ranch house design.

She could do this, she thought as she turned with the hot mug clutched between her palms. While she and Clint were taking marriage preparation classes, she would be searching her catalogs and all the shops for just the right items, and when she was finished this home would reflect Clint's personality as well as her own, a lovely and attractive blend of earthy and refined.

A few minutes later, as Loni walked toward the arena, she filled her lungs with the fresh morning air and enjoyed the audible delights of ranch life. Birds were singing. A light breeze whispered across the pastureland. Horses whinnied and whickered when they glimpsed her passing. So *many* horses. A week ago Loni would have been intimidated, but now she was anxious to meet them all.

She found Clint inside the arena, working in tandem with his father, brothers, and the foreman, Hooter, to check the horses for injuries and then get them groomed and fed.

"Morning!" Zachary called from a stall. His dark eyes danced with mischief. "Hope you slept well."

Until that instant it hadn't occurred to Loni how her presence at the ranch at so early an hour might look. Clearly the implications had not been lost on Zachary. She felt a blush pool in her cheeks and spread up to her hairline.

Busy in another stall caring for Ezekiel, Clint hollered, "Zach, stuff a sock in it. Nothing went on. It was all totally on the up-and-up."

Zachary shrugged, winked at Loni, and said, "You're the first, so far as I know. One thing Clint's never done is have women stay overnight."

Clint threw down the grooming brush, burst from Ezekiel's stall, and advanced on his brother. Judging by the glower on his dark face, he was ready to fight.

Loni's heart leaped into her throat. She looked wildly around for Frank, saw him in a stall, and gaped in befuddlement when he calmly continued what he was doing, apparently unperturbed by the possibility of a physical confrontation between his grown sons.

Clint stepped to the opening of Jemima's stall, where Zachary was working. "I asked you not to embarrass her, damn it! You're such a little shit, Zachary. Sometimes I wanna knock you up alongside the head."

"I didn't say anything bad. Only that she's the first gal to stay overnight."

Clint jabbed a sturdy finger at his brother's nose. "I know it'll be a challenge, but from this point forward you are not to address her, *period*, unless you can manage to show her proper respect."

A ropey-dope look came over Zach's face. "Well, excuse me for breathin'."

"Apologize," Clint demanded.

Zachary leaned sideways to look around Clint's shoulder, met Loni's appalled gaze, and said, "I'm sorry, Loni. I was just giving you a hard time. Unfortunately some individuals in this crazy family have *no* sense of humor."

"*That's* your idea of an apology?" Clint cried.

"You want it written in blood or what?"

Clint threw up his hands. He turned to Loni. "Pretend he never said anything. If he had a brain he'd play kickball with it."

Frank began whistling. When Loni passed the stall with Clint at her side, the Harrigan family patriarch winked at her, clearly more amused than alarmed by his sons' exchange.

Hooter, whom Loni had met the first time she visited the stable, worked on Uriah in the stall next to Ezekiel's. Loni stepped in to greet her equine friend. As she stroked the gentle gelding's nose, Hooter tweaked his handlebar mustache, watching her curiously. Finally he said, "You reckon you can find my truck keys?"

"I'd be happy to help," Loni replied. "Do you need them right now?"

"Hooter," Clint interrupted from the adjacent enclosure, "she doesn't do keys. She can only help find them the regular way."

"Lookin' for 'em, you mean?"

"Precisely."

"Well, what use is that?" Hooter snorted. "I already looked everywhere."

Loni was grinning when she went to Ezekiel's stall. Clint glanced up from checking the gelding's hoof. "I love those alfalfa green britches. You were wearing them the first time I saw you."

"Whoa!" Zachary hollered. "Keep it clean. Your baby brother can hear you."

Clint rolled his eyes. "You *sure* about marrying me and having to put up with that all the time?"

"I'm positive," Loni answered.

"Hallelujah! You hear that, Dad? Clint's gonna tie the knot."

From the other side of the arena, Parker yelled, "Congratulations, bro." Then, "My condolences, Loni. You sure you know what you're getting into?"

Clint grimaced. "God save me. One of these days

they'll push me too far and I'll cheerfully murder one of them."

Loni was quickly coming to realize that arguing was a form of entertainment in the Harrigan family. Though they seemed to grow angry, it was actually all in good fun. If push ever came to shove, she imagined that the four brothers would lay down their lives for one another.

"Don't worry about it," Loni whispered to Clint. "I enjoy all the foolishness."

He dipped his head under Ezekiel's neck to give her a quick kiss. "You are so damned beautiful, both inside and out."

"The slacks are patina."

He snorted with laughter. "Repeat after me. 'Thank you for the compliment, Clint.'"

She grinned and leaned forward under Ezekiel's neck to kiss him back.

That afternoon everyone went to the hospital to see Trevor. In an attempt to avoid overwhelming the child, only one person went in at once, and they limited each visit to ten minutes, spacing them an hour apart. Only Clint stayed in the child's room the entire time.

When Loni's turn came she found father and son having a grand time playing tic-tac-toe. Clint appeared to be losing continually, possibly by design. She couldn't help but laugh at Trevor's unrestrained victory yells each time he won.

"I totally rock!"

Clint chuckled. "You do. How did you get so good?"

"Practice." Trevor stifled a grin. "How'd you get so *bad*?"

"I'm not bad. I've been letting you win."

"Nuh-uh."

Observing the pair, Loni could easily imagine Trevor soon taking his place among the rough-and-tumble Harrigan males. Someday he'd be exchanging insults and ribbing his uncles as if he'd been born into the fold.

When her ten minutes were up, Loni said, "I think I'd better go now."

Clint glanced up from the game in progress. "Not home."

Loni had been thinking exactly that. She had her dog staying at her sister's, Trevor was no longer in danger, and though she and Clint were now bound together by avowals of love and plans to marry, they each had their separate enterprises, and her shop still wasn't open yet. Only, when she looked into his eyes, she saw a vulnerability and need completely at odds with the strong man she'd come to know. Discovering that Trevor was his son and then almost losing him had rocked Clint's world, and he obviously still didn't feel steady on his feet.

Loni had learned a lot about this man during their time in the wilderness and knew that if she so much as hinted at his need for her, his pride would take a hit. So instead she said, "I can't possibly go home. Not yet. I know it's silly, but after the last few days I don't feel good about being away from you."

The taut, anxious look on his face dissipated. He chucked Trevor under the chin, excused himself, and followed Loni out into the hall to take her into his arms with a ferocity that startled her. "I can't be away from you yet either. My emotions feel like they've been stirred with a whisk, and having you with me is all that keeps me from losing it."

Clint Harrigan was one of the strongest, most level-headed men she'd ever met, but she understood what he meant. In a very short time she'd become his anchor, and he'd become hers. "Still mad at Sandra?"

"Pissed is a better word." He glanced back toward Trevor, visible behind the glassed-in walls. "I look at him and I see myself, and my brothers, and my dad. When I think of the eight years she robbed us of, I feel crazy inside." His gaze came back to her face. "Until I look at you." His Adam's apple bobbed. "Then I understand. I'd lie to keep you in my life. I love you so much I think I might even be capable of violence to keep you there. Does that make any sense? Or do you think I'm totally nuts?"

Loni remembered how she had rationalized Sandra's behavior. "Love doesn't come along every day, Clint. When we find it I think we all go just a little crazy. Sandra *needed* to be with Robert. She saw no future she wanted without him, so she made a selfish choice. But can I say for sure I wouldn't also make a selfish choice if I might lose you?" She shook her head. "No. I think I'd probably be very selfish, because the thought of a future without you makes me feel desolate."

He nodded. "Exactly, and that's why seeing you keeps me sane. I can look at you and not feel quite so furious. If Sandra loved Robert the way I love you . . ." He gazed off down the hallway. Then he smiled wryly.

"Can't condemn someone else for doing what I might have done myself." His eyes held hers for a long moment. "I couldn't let you go. No way. I forget that when you're not with me, and my feelings of anger take over. I don't want to take it out on her parents—or let Trevor sense it. It's important right now for him to know that I'm on his side."

Loni looped her arms around his neck and hugged him hard. Her shop could wait for a few more days. She had plenty of money in the bank from the sale of her Lynwood home to sustain her—and she would soon be marrying a millionaire. The thought brought a smile to her lips as she nuzzled said millionaire's neck. Clint Harrigan definitely didn't fit the stereotype, and, oh, how glad she was that he didn't. She'd come to like Wranglers jeans and riding boots, and when they got married she'd be disappointed if he wasn't wearing a dress Stetson and a Western-cut tuxedo.

"I like feeling needed," she said softly.

He bent his dark head and kissed her. Not as deeply as they both might have liked, but Trevor might be watching. She felt his yearning when they drew apart and saw it etched on his dark features.

"When you go downstairs, don't let Zach give you a hard time. Tell him to stuff a sock in it."

She nodded.

"And don't let Dad give you the third degree. He's bad about that."

She laughed. "Samantha will keep him on the straight and narrow. No worries." As she spoke, Loni realized that was one of Clint's favorite sayings. *No worries*. It felt nice to be picking up his habits. She couldn't think of anyone she'd rather emulate. "How much longer do you plan to stay?"

"Until they kick my ass out."

She understood and nodded. "I'll be waiting with your family downstairs somewhere."

"Your family now."

She gave him a teasing look. "If I take on your family, you have to take on mine," she warned him, "and mine is decidedly weirder."

He kissed her again, this time just a quick touch of their lips. "It's a very nice kind of weird."

Loni spent the next two hours in the cafeteria with Clint's family, an experience that convinced her she would never feel bored as a member of the Harrigan clan. Frank drank copious amounts of coffee, which he complained about with every sip. "I could make stronger brew if I shoved a coffee bean up a duck's butt and ran downstream for a cup of water." Zach was a perfect gentleman to Loni, but she was the only person he didn't target. He tugged on Samantha's hair, clearly determined to get a rise out of her. When she didn't take the bait, he tried to engage his brothers in arguments. The young woman busing tables got so flustered when he flirted with her that she dropped a stack of trays, prompting Zach to get up and help her clear away the mess. Before the job was done, he'd asked her for a date and had her phone number, inspiring Parker and Quincy to rib him unmercifully about robbing the cradle.

Dee Dee, whom Loni hadn't yet met, had stayed home with a headache, and Frank called her every half hour to check on her. Loni found his concern touching but secretly wondered if Dee Dee was rolling her eyes when the phone rang. When Loni had a headache she liked to lie down in a dark room, and the last thing she wanted was to answer calls.

"Damn, Dad, you need to leave the poor woman alone," Parker suggested. "You afraid she'll forget you're married if you don't ring her every five minutes?"

"Just goes to show how little you know about women," Frank popped back. "They *like* being fussed over. No wonder you're still not married."

Parker snorted. "If marriage means having a phone attached to my ear, I'll pass."

"Yeah, right," Zach sniped. "You'd tie the knot in a minute if you could find anyone decent who'd have you."

And so it went. The Harrigans fascinated Loni. They argued more often than not, yet none of them ever seemed to get angry, and under it all there was no mistaking their love for one another.

Everyone had grown hungry during the wait, so when Clint finally joined them the entire clan got in the buffet line. Quincy, the health nut, slapped his father's hand when Frank reached for fried chicken.

"Damn it, son. A man's gotta eat real food sometimes. Dee Dee never lets me have fried chicken anymore."

"Good for her," Quincy retorted. "The stuff will kill you. It's not as if you peel away the skin. Hell, no, you eat every greasy morsel, clear down to the bones."

Frank grabbed for the spoon to a creamy potato

dish, and Quincy redirected his reach. "Red potatoes are better for you."

On the other side of the buffet shelf, Samantha forked some salad onto her father's plate. "There, Daddy. Fill up on that."

"What do I look like, a rabbit?"

As Loni moved down the line, she was so captivated by their antics that she almost forgot to make her own choices. When she glanced up at Clint, he winked at her, his teasing expression saying more clearly than words, *Can your family measure up to this?*

When everyone was seated at the table, a sudden solemnity overtook them. Hats came off. Heads were bowed. Hands quickly made the sign of the cross. Loni's family didn't usually pray over a meal at restaurants, but the Harrigans did so unabashedly, their combined voices as they recited the blessing creating a deep drone. As Loni said the familiar prayer with them, she realized that *this* was what she loved about Clint and enjoyed about his family. They were what they were and didn't change their colors to please the public.

Frank had just tucked into his baked chicken breast when his cell phone chirped. Excusing himself, he took the call, which was clearly from Dee Dee. "Hi, sweetheart," he said. "How you feelin'?"

He listened for a moment, then quietly said goodbye. Loni knew something was wrong when he directed a serious look at Clint.

"We got trouble," he said.

Clint pocketed a bite of steak in his cheek. "What kind of trouble?"

Frank wadded his napkin and tossed it on his plate.

"Dee Dee was lyin' on the sofa, watchin' television. Sandra's mother was just interviewed by a reporter, live. She told him all about you givin' Trevor blood and about Loni bein' a clairvoyant and leadin' you to the boy. Dee Dee says our phone has started ringin' off the hook, newshounds tryin' to get an exclusive. They want to talk to Loni, and I reckon they've figured out she must still be with you. Chances are they're callin' every Harrigan in the phone book, tryin' to find her."

Clint stiffened and dropped his fork onto the plate. For a long moment he didn't speak. Then he directed an anguished look at Loni. "How did Sharon find out about your clairvoyance? You didn't tell her, did you?"

"I told her," Frank inserted.

Clint sent his dad a fulminating glare.

"I didn't see the harm," Frank added quickly. "It never occurred to me that she'd do an interview and blab it to the world."

"Her son-in-law was a senator," Clint pointed out. "Of *course* she'd be interviewed. Robert Stiles's death is big news all over the state. Do you realize the ramifications of this?"

Loni curled her hand over Clint's knee. "It's not his fault, Clint. He didn't know. Quite honestly, as wary as I am about telling anyone, I didn't consider the possibilities either. We were all upset, and Sharon and Jacob are so nice, I honestly forgot how important their son was."

Parker leveled a curious look at Loni. "Dad didn't know what?" he asked. "I'm not following. So you're a clairvoyant. Big deal." He switched his gaze to Clint. "Why are you acting like it's such a disaster?"

Clint briefed his family on Loni's past and her reasons for having to leave the Seattle area. When he finished speaking, everyone at the table had gone quiet.

"Maybe it'll blow over," Zach finally said. "You see it happen all the time. Something's hot news, and then something else takes the limelight and people forget all about it."

"I can only hope," Loni said.

Following his father's example, Clint crumpled his napkin and threw it on top of his nearly untouched food. Pushing back in his chair he said, "We need to get out of here. It won't take them long to figure out you may be at the hospital."

Quincy pushed his food away. "As bad as it may have been before, Clint, there's nothing to say it'll be like that this time. So what if she helped you find the boy? You're automatically assuming that the reporters down here in Oregon are going to link Loni to that mess in Washington, but chances are good that they won't. Crystal Falls is a good-size town now, but our news crews aren't exactly hooked into the mainstream."

"What makes you think it's Crystal Falls reporters calling?" Clint asked. "It's far more likely that the Portland news teams have gotten wind of it." To Loni he said, "I'm sorry, honey. If we'd had some time to take a breath I would have told everybody to keep their mouths shut about your being a psychic. But for reasons beyond me, I never even thought about needing to."

Loni felt oddly calm. Maybe, she decided, it was because she'd always known this would happen. Even as she'd escaped Lynwood, hoping to build a new life, a part of her had recognized the futility of it. Like Gram had said, she couldn't run from who and what she was.

There were no reporters camped out at the gate to Clint's ranch. Yard lights around the house and outbuildings created a nimbus of gold over the ranch proper, but the entrance to the property was cloaked in darkness. As Clint drove under the log arch, Loni breathed a sigh of relief that prompted him to look over at her.

"Don't worry. All right? I won't let them hound you like before. You'll be perfectly safe here."

On the one hand Loni didn't want to overreact, but a part of her had lost hope. Her name had been broadcast all over the state, and it was entirely possible, given Robert Stiles's political status, that the story had gone national. How long would it take for people in the Seattle area to recognize her name and make the connection? Not long, she was afraid, and once that connection was made, her anonymity in Crystal Falls would be obliterated.

"Quincy had a good point, you know." Clint steered around a pothole. "Hot news today, old news tomorrow. It'll be okay."

"And if it's not?"

He reached over to rub her shoulder. "If it's not then we move to plan B."

"What's plan B?"

"I don't know yet. But stop looking like a rabbit staring into the barrel of a shotgun. I'll take care of it."

Loni knew it wouldn't be that simple, but she didn't

want to think about it right then. Instead she took comfort from the darkness and isolation, and she allowed herself to cling to the dream that had taken shape over the last few days, of her and Clint living happily ever after on this ranch, creating a magical compromise between his lifestyle and hers. Theater in Portland. Horseback rides into the wilderness. Getting married and starting a family. The images were seductive, and she didn't want to turn them loose.

Maybe Quincy was right, and interest in her would die down quickly. There was no point in panicking. She could handle anything for a while, especially when the future beckoned with such promise.

Clint's kitchen answering machine was blinking wildly when they entered the house. He glanced at her before punching the playback button. Several calls were from local reporters wanting to interview her. Apparently the media had ferreted out the fact that Loni was staying at the ranch. The first calls seemed harmless enough, but the last call was a shocker—some man from a publishing company wanting to discuss a book deal. He mentioned no specific amount of money, only that his publisher might be prepared to make a tempting offer for exclusive rights to her story.

"They know," she said hollowly when the machine clicked off. "Crystal Falls may not be in the mainstream, but somehow they've already made the connection. He even mentioned Cheryl Blain by name."

Clint leaned his hips against the counter and pinched the bridge of his nose. "Okay, so they know. We'll deal with it."

"How?" Loni shivered and rubbed her arms. "You

don't know what it's like. I'll be like a hunk of meat being fed upon by flies."

He dropped his hand and fixed her with a determined gaze. "Sweetheart, we'll deal with it. I don't know how yet. I only know I love you, and you love me. I believe with all my heart that God means for us to be together. Don't we need to trust in that? I may not have all the answers off the top of my head, but He does, and in His own good time He'll reveal them to us."

He opened his arms, and Loni walked into them. As his hard, warm embrace enfolded her against him, she knew that she was exactly where she was supposed to be. "I'm gun-shy, I guess, and overreacting."

"Very gun-shy. Listen." He buried his face in her hair. She felt the heat of his breath feathering over her scalp. "Just *listen*."

Loni did as he asked. "I don't hear anything but the refrigerator humming and the clock ticking."

"Exactly. You were in the center of urban sprawl up in Lynwood. That isn't the case here. We're thirty minutes away from Crystal Falls, the largest community in a radius of two hundred miles. It's not a spot in the road. We've got a great hospital, a college, and just about everything else most towns offer, but it isn't the big city. Maybe you couldn't insulate yourself in Lynwood, but you can down here. There are geographical barriers around this ranch, long stretches of land separating the house from the road. Even if reporters do gather at the gate, they won't bother you here."

Loni pressed closer to him, wanting with every fiber

of her being to believe he was right. "What if they cross the property line?"

"Trespassing," he murmured. "They wouldn't dare."

Because they hadn't eaten their meal at the hospital, both of them were hungry and worked together to fix ham and eggs. When Loni saw that the trash needed to be emptied, she pulled the plastic can from under the sink and lifted the full bag out. "Where are your outdoor trash receptacles?" she asked.

Clint took the bag from her hand. "You watch the ham. I'll take it out."

As Loni manned the skillet she gazed after him. When the door closed behind him, she sighed and forked a piece of meat to turn it over. He didn't want her going outside alone. That was the truth of it. He could talk himself blue about how isolated his house was, but deep down he was afraid some crazy reporter *would* cross the property line.

Cheryl Blain. She had haunted Loni's dreams for nearly two years, and now, once again, it appeared that she would haunt her daily life.

Refraining from having sex wasn't so easy for Loni that night. Despite the barrier of pillows she was acutely aware of Clint stretched out on the bed beside her. She *needed* to feel his arms around her. She *yearned* to feel him inside of her, with an almost frantic sense of urgency. Impending doom hovered over her like a dark cloud, and she couldn't shake it. *What if . . . ?* Genuine clairvoyants fascinated people. Through no fault of her own she'd come under the microscope in an extraordinary way—not once, but twice. Robert Stiles's death was big news, and she'd saved his son. What if interest in her didn't wane as Quincy predicted? What if the situation escalated, and she soon found herself in as big a mess as the one she'd only recently escaped in Lynwood? A book deal. Why couldn't people just leave her alone?

"You're thinking so hard, I can almost hear your wheels turning," Clint startled her by saying.

"I thought you were asleep."

"Nope. You're thinking so loud, you're keeping me awake."

Loni smiled against her pillow. "Sorry. I have a lot on my mind."

"Me, too," he said huskily. "The phone hasn't rung once since we got home. I think you're making too big a deal out of this. I know you're wary, and with good reason, but let's play wait-and-see. If the situation gets out of hand, we'll figure out how to handle it together. All right?"

Loni swallowed hard. "I can't shake the feeling that everything is going to be ruined. You and me, I mean. That I've foolishly allowed myself to buy into an impossible dream, and now I've gotten the wake-up call."

He shoved the pillows between them toward the foot of the bed. "Come here."

"I can't. If I do we'll have sex, and we've made a pact not to."

"To hell with sex. I just want to hold you."

Loni needed him to hold her, so she scooted across the mattress. When his arms came around her she sighed. "I feel better already."

"That's because you're right where you belong." He pressed a kiss to the crown of her head. "Relax. I'll behave myself."

She grinned against his shoulder. "Is that a threat or a promise?"

"A promise." He ran a big hand along her spine. "The Snoopy pajamas are growing on me, though. I think you'd look sexy in a gunnysack."

She rested her hand over his heart, measuring the rhythmic thumps. "I'm afraid, Clint. I've finally found everything I ever wanted, and I feel as if the rug's going to be jerked out from under me."

"Never happen. I love you, lady. We're in this together, and we'll figure out a way to get through it."

Loni wanted and needed to believe he was right, so she snuggled closer, yawned wearily, and closed her eyes. "Together," she whispered. "I like the sound of that."

Chapter Fifteen

In the morning Loni left Clint to shower and shave while she went downstairs for a cup of the coffee that he'd set last night to brew automatically. Cradling a hot mug in her hands, she leaned against the counter to enjoy her new favorite morning ritual. Nothing woke her up quite so pleasantly as sniffing the aromatic steam from a cup she held just under her nose. Normally she preferred tea, but since she'd come to know Clint, her tastes seemed to be changing. The rich, hard kick of strong coffee had its merits.

As she sipped the scalding-hot brew, Loni noticed that the answering machine light was blinking. Clint had played all the messages last night, and so far as she knew, the phone hadn't rung again after they went to bed. Feeling like Pandora approaching the infamous box, Loni leaned close to study the apparatus. It was different from hers at home, but it took her only a moment to determine which button performed what function. She was also quick to notice that Clint had turned off all the ringers on the phones so they wouldn't ring during the night.

No more calls, he'd pointed out to her. Instead of feeling miffed, Loni smiled sadly. He'd known that the constant ringing would upset her. It was difficult to feel angry with him for the deception. She *had* been upset, and his ploy to hold the world at bay for a few hours had allowed her to relax and get some rest.

She was awake now, though, and ready to face reality. With a trembling fingertip she pressed the playback button. The first message was from Zach.

"Hey, bro, I don't mean to bitch like an old lady, but I just caught two dudes going through my trash cans out back. How am I supposed to handle that? Tell them they've got the wrong brother, or declare open season and shoot the buggers? I'm leaning real strongly toward the latter. Been a while since I got in any target practice. Might be entertaining."

Smiling at Zach's nonsense, Loni noted that his call had come in at a little after ten last night. As if he'd ever really shoot somebody. Although, Loni mused, firing a few rounds off into the air might go a long way toward discouraging trespassers.

The next call was a reporter. "My name's Alex Baldini." He rushed to list his news affiliations. "I'm trying to get in touch with Loni Kendra MacEwen. Please have her call me." He went on to recite both his office and cell phone numbers. "I'll make it worth her while if she contacts me first."

Then a woman's voice, someone named Serena from a Portland chapter of a club called Witches without Brooms. She invited Loni to speak at their annual nationwide conference in September at the City of Roses. The next caller was another reporter, followed by yet another. Each person took a different tack, but the gist of each appeal was the same. Could he or she have just a few minutes of Loni's time? Then she wouldn't be bothered again.

Yeah, right. Loni had learned the hard way that tossing the media a crumb only made them hungry for the whole loaf. The last message, at shortly after three in the morning, was from the man at the publishing house again, only this time he offered her a whopping two hundred thousand dollars in advance for a book deal. The sum boggled Loni's mind.

Needing a breath of fresh air, Loni decided to take a turn around the ranch proper while she sipped her coffee. As she stepped off the veranda into the gentle lemon yellow sunlight of early day, she dragged in a deep, cleansing breath that did a lot more to clear her senses than the coffee had done so far. Off to the right were open-sided pole sheds that sheltered a number of horses. Loni walked in that direction, eager to meet a few more of Clint's furry friends.

To her delight the outdoor stalls housed mares with new foals. Lacking an experienced eye, Loni couldn't guess the babies' ages, but they all were darling, with long, gangly legs, knobby knees, little switch tails, and overlarge ears. They greeted her with rambunctious nudges through the rails, velvety nostrils chuffing as they sniffed her clothing. Loni realized they were expecting treats.

Setting her coffee atop a post, she devoted herself to doling out rubs and scratches. "I'm sorry, little one. Next time I'll bring you goodies. Silly me for forgetting.

If I'm going to live on a horse ranch I have a lot to learn, don't I?"

One little fellow was not to be put off so easily. He wanted a treat and clearly thought one might spring from her slacks pocket if he persisted. Loni gave a startled laugh. "Hey, little guy, don't get fresh."

"What the *hell* are you doing out here alone?"

At the question Loni spun to find Clint standing behind her. Booted feet set wide apart, fists knotted on his hips, he gave her a burning look.

"Enjoying the sunshine?" she offered. "I figured you'd guess that I'd stepped outside. I didn't mean to alarm you."

"*Alarm* me? Zach had two men going through his garbage last night. Quincy just called to tell me his phone rang no less than fifteen times before bed, and then, suddenly, the calls stopped. He thinks they've finally figured out which Harrigan you're hanging out with, and that means they'll be concentrating on my place now. I don't want you wandering around out here alone."

Despite his overbearing manner, Loni wanted to hug him. "I'm perfectly fine, Clint. I've only been accosted by this little guy." She petted the colt again. "I didn't bring treats, and he's letting me know that isn't okay."

"I'm serious, Loni. Until things cool down you can't be walking around out here unless I'm with you."

Folding her arms at her waist, she offered a smile, hoping it might lighten his mood. He continued to glower at her.

"You need to work on remembering to say *please*," she informed him.

"You need to work on using the brains God gave you. Coming out here was not smart. What if a half-dozen reporters or frantic parents had been lying in wait?"

She started tapping her toe. "In that event I would have handled it."

"Like you did the furious father who got physically violent?"

Loni regretted telling him about that. "He didn't hurt me, Clint. He just shook me by the shoulders and shoved me against a wall."

His jaw muscle started to tic. "*Just?* He put his hands on you. That's all I need to know. God as my witness, I'll never let it happen again."

Loni was beginning to realize that he was more upset than she'd first thought. At the start of their relationship, she might have gotten miffed at his high-handedness, but having come to know him so well, she couldn't muster any indignation. He was afraid for her, plain and simple, and his anger was only a smoke screen.

She stepped close to loop her arms around his hard middle. Beneath her splayed hands his back muscles were knotted with tension. "I'm sorry I frightened you. Until this blows over I won't come out alone again. Okay?"

He released a taut breath and returned her embrace. "See that you don't. If I catch some jerk-off putting his hands on you, I'll kill the son of a bitch."

Loni buried her nose against the front of his fresh

shirt. It smelled of sunshine, scented laundry soap, and faint male musk, a wonderful blend of scents that made her want to inhale as if it were an intoxicant. "We can't have that. You'd go to prison, and I'd be left all alone."

He tightened his arms around her and dipped his head to press his lips against her hair. "This love business is going to take some getting used to," he said gruffly. "When I think that something might happen to you, I can't breathe."

"Nothing's going to happen to me. If reporters start swarming I won't be physically harmed, Clint. The damage is only emotional."

"Yeah, well, I don't want any part of you hurt in any way. So bear with me, all right? Stick close to me for a few days until the interest in you dies down."

But what if it didn't die down? In Lynwood there'd been occasional lulls, allowing Loni to think the worst was over. But then a young woman would go missing again, and the first thing she knew her name would start popping up in the news, and the general public's interest in her would be rekindled.

She chose not to mention that to Clint, though. "Let's go get some coffee and breakfast," she suggested. "We can lay out the ground rules while we eat."

Twenty minutes later they were seated across from each other at his kitchen table. As he smeared cream cheese onto one half of a large bagel, he glared at the answering machine, which kept clicking on. With the machine turned to its lowest volume the people leaving messages could barely be heard, but their calls were still intrusive, reminding both Loni and Clint that the peace and tranquillity of the ranch provided scant protection from the media hype about Loni that was quickly escalating.

"Maybe I should go away for a while," she suggested.

"Not a chance."

"Not for long. A few days, maybe. I can come home when things calm down."

"*No.* If you leave I'm going with you, end of subject."

Tucking into her diced fruit, Loni let the idea drop. She didn't really want to leave anyway. "Are you going to be one of those husbands who worries every time I'm out of your sight?"

He arched one black brow. "Depends on the circumstances. If I have reason to worry, then yes, I'll worry."

"And be grouchy?"

"Grouchy? Have I been grouchy?"

Loni giggled. "Out in the stable yard you looked ready to rip someone apart with your bare hands."

"That's not being grouchy."

"It isn't?"

"No. It's being justifiably upset." He relented and chuckled. "I don't mean to be grouchy, darlin'. The next time I start grumping at you, remind me, and I'll be so sweet your teeth will ache."

Loni laughed again. "I'll settle for reasonable. I was only petting the babies."

"Foals. You're going to be a rancher's wife. You have to learn the lingo."

"Foals, then. To me they're babies. I don't see the big difference."

He shook his head, his dark eyes twinkling. "I can tell right now that you're going to take some work."

"I'm a fast learner. That little guy who was trying to eat my slacks—what's his name?"

"Glutton."

She almost choked on a berry. "I thought everyone had a biblical name."

"Gluttony is mentioned in the Bible. As a nickname, it'll do for now. I like to think on it for a while before coming up with official names for the quarter-horse registry. I'm sure there's a character in scripture who always worried about where his next meal would come from. I'll probably name Glutton after him."

"Hmm. I'll keep that in mind. Maybe I'll come up with something."

"See there?" He offered her a grape from his bowl. "You're already acting like a rancher's wife."

Loni accompanied Clint to the stables while he did morning chores. When she grabbed a pitchfork to help him and Hooter clean stalls, he protested.

"You don't have to do that, honey. Hooter and I've got it covered." He glanced at his watch. "Reinforcements will be rolling in soon. I keep a full crew on weekdays. My wife won't be needed or expected to do any dirty work."

Loni pitched some hay from Uriah's stall out into the paddock, where someone would soon collect it with a small tractor equipped with a forked shovel. "I want to learn," she protested. "That way if you ever do need my help, I'll know what to do."

Uriah, who'd been left to wander loose in the arena

while his stall was cleaned, snorted and bobbed his head.

"See?" Loni said with a laugh. "Uriah votes in my favor. I may never do any of this stuff on a regular basis, but being familiar with all the chores surely can't hurt."

Clint leaned across the gate to give her a quick kiss. "I love you. Have I mentioned that yet this morning?"

He'd told her in a dozen different ways. "No," she lied with a grin.

"I love you, lady. More than you'll ever know."

"Back to work!" Hooter hollered from across the arena, looking like the very epitome of an Old West movie character in his battered Stetson, red suspenders, shortened jeans, and scuffed boots. The improbable protrusions of his handlebar mustache at each side of his craggy face only added to the effect. "You young pups are makin' my ears burn."

Clint winked at Loni. "As soon as we're married I'll make love to you in the hayloft," he whispered. "After-hours, of course, so we'll have some privacy. Once Hooter goes up to his apartment, nothing but horse noises wakes him."

She wrinkled her nose. "Isn't hay prickly?"

He grinned devilishly. "If you notice the prickles, darlin', I won't be doing my job."

Loni resumed forking soiled clumps of hay from Uriah's stall. In what seemed like no time at all her palms started to sting, and when she looked down she saw that the soft flesh at the base of her fingers was turning red. Blisters. Or what soon would be blisters. She set the fork aside to exit the stall.

"Clint? Do you have any spare gloves?" she called.

"There she is!" a man shouted.

For a moment Loni blinked in stunned amazement as cameras began flashing all around her. *What?* That was the only thought her startled mind could formulate as reporters scurried forth from hiding places like ants from under mopboards. She threw up her arm to shield her eyes from the flare of bright lights, only dimly aware of Uriah whinnying behind her, then of Hooter dashing across the arena toward her.

A microphone was shoved in her face. "Ms. MacEwen, how did it feel to save Senator Stiles's son's life?"

"How does your clairvoyance work?" someone else shouted. "Did you need an article of the boy's clothing to home in on his whereabouts?"

Loni couldn't see, couldn't think. The lights. Her vision was obliterated by white spots. But the questions kept coming like bullets fired from guns and hitting her from all directions. She heard Clint shout something. The next instant something struck Loni full-length and sent her tumbling to the ground. She hit the dirt with such force, all the breath was knocked from her lungs. In the dizzying swirl of dust and voices raised in anger, she heard a high-pitched scream, followed by Clint crying, "Sweet Jesus, *no!*"

Rolling onto her side, Loni fought as frantically for breath as she did to clear her vision. Uriah. As the spots before her eyes faded, she saw the horse rearing high above her, his front hooves slashing the air in a panicked assault. Clint had hold of the horse's halter and with the swing of his weight was trying to gain control, but the suddenness of the reporters' ambush had frightened the gelding beyond reason.

For an instant Loni thought Clint was trying to protect her from Uriah's hooves. Only then did she see Hooter lying a few feet away, and remembered seeing him run toward her. It hit her then, like a cruel fist to her heart, that Hooter had thrown her out of harm's way and taken the brunt of the frantic horse's hooves in her stead.

"No!" she screamed. Crawling toward Hooter's still form, she sobbed and cried again, "No, no, *no!*"

Hooter's old hat had been knocked from his head, and blood pooled crimson over a deep gash on his scalp. Even in her panic Loni tried to feel for a pulse, but her hand was shaking so badly she couldn't tell whether the foreman was dead or merely unconscious. Clint was still struggling to control Uriah.

Rage mushroomed within Loni. She pushed to her feet, fury glazing her vision with red. "You *bastards!*" she yelled. "Just *look* what you've done. You've got your damned story now! *This* is how it feels to be a clairvoyant. Get out! You're all *idiots!* Any fool knows not to flash lights and start shouting around horses. *Get out!* You've killed my *friend.* Put that in your story, damn you!"

The reporters, male and female alike, retreated as if a sudden force field were shoving them back. Loni stared at the blur of white faces. The cameras had stopped flashing now. Except for Uriah's shrill screams and the frightened whinnying of other horses, the arena had gone deathly quiet. Loni swallowed, knotted her hands, and advanced a step on her tormentors.

"I said get out. I mean *now*."

The reporters ran as if all the hounds of hell were nipping at their heels. Loni raced for one of the phones stationed around the arena. With trembling hands she dialed 911 and asked for an ambulance to be sent out ASAP.

Uriah was still trembling when Loni ended the call, but the gelding was no longer kicking up a fuss. Clint was bent over Hooter, feeling for a pulse. Loni dropped to her knees beside him.

"I'm so sorry. I'm so sorry." Tears, hot and burning, filled her eyes and seared her throat. "Oh, Clint, this is my fault. My fault."

"I need some towels." He jabbed a thumb toward the rear of the arena. "The supply room. Hurry."

He began stripping off his shirt as Loni raced to do his bidding. *Hooter*. A half-dozen memories of the funny, older man spun through Loni's mind. Clint loved Hooter. What if the foreman died?

Loni would never forgive herself if that happened. Not for as long as she lived.

Chapter Sixteen

Once again Loni found herself in the ER waiting room, surrounded by members of Clint's family. Clint was with Hooter, wherever that might be. The old foreman had still been alive when the ambulance brought him in, but the head injury was serious, and so far Loni and the others had received no updates.

Frank rested a comforting hand on Loni's knee. "He's a tough old fart, honey. He's goin' to be okay."

"Hell, yes," Quincy seconded. "Hooter's survived worse than this. Remember the time he forgot to shift the tractor out of gear, climbed off to do something, and got run over?"

The family spent a moment reminiscing about that event. Then Samantha said, "Quit blaming yourself, Loni. It's not your fault that a bunch of idiotic reporters sneaked into the stable and spooked Uriah."

Loni's throat felt as if a steel band were tightening around it. "Hooter pushed me out of the way. He saved me and took the punishment himself."

Frank patted her knee. "Damn straight. He wouldn't

be worth the powder it'd take to blow him to hell if he'd done otherwise."

"You had your back to the horse," Parker inserted.

"You didn't know you were in danger," Zach added. "Folks watch out for one another on a ranch. Hooter did what any of us—including you—would have done. He probably meant to get out of the way himself and tripped or something."

Loni appreciated their attempts to make her feel better, she truly did, but the truth of the matter was inescapable: Hooter would never have been hurt if not for her. The reporters wouldn't have sneaked into the stable. They wouldn't have flashed cameras and shouted questions. Uriah was a wonderful, gentle horse that would never hurt Hooter or anyone else under normal circumstances.

Loni had been the fly in the ointment. The knowledge ached in her chest like a huge boil that was about to erupt.

When Clint finally emerged from the ER, his dark face still looked ashen. He had his shirt back on, the front smeared with Hooter's blood. At their questions he just shook his head. "They're working on him. That's all I know. It got so busy, with so many people in there, they booted me out. Now all we can do is wait."

And wait they did, talking little, each lost in his own thoughts. Occasionally one of the Harrigan males rose to pace. Samantha crossed and uncrossed her legs and swung her foot. Loni just huddled on the chair, feeling numb on the outside but hurting on the inside.

What if Trevor had been in the stable when Uriah went nuts? Someday soon the child would visit his father at the ranch. What if it were Clint's son who was in the ER right now, possibly dying? One by one, other horrible possibilities circled through Loni's mind. She loved Clint so very much, and the last thing she wanted was to leave him. But she couldn't bear the thought of this ever happening again.

When the waiting became unbearable, Frank suggested that they all go up to the pediatric wing to visit Trevor. "It'll take our mind off our worries," he said. "We can tell the gal at the desk where we'll be so they can get word to us of Hooter's condition."

Everyone welcomed the idea, and Loni soon found herself hunched, arm-to-arm between Zach Harrigan and Tucker Coulter as the entire family jostled to fit inside the elevator. Moments later they were in the waiting area just down the hall from Trevor's room. The head ward nurse once again requested that only one person go in at a time, limiting each visit to ten minutes, spaced a quarter hour apart this time. Again, only Clint was allowed to stay in the child's room.

Loni excused herself and went to the ladies' room. Once in a stall with the door locked, she called her sister.

Deirdre answered on the second ring. "You all right?"

Loni couldn't think what to say. Finally she managed a muffled, "Mm." Then she took a deep breath and whispered, "I need you to come get me. I'm at the hospital. Meet me in the main lobby in, say, thirty minutes?"

"You're leaving," Deirdre said. It wasn't a question.

"I'll explain when I see you," Loni said tightly. But

then, giving way to tears, she blurted out the whole, terrible story. "Hooter may die, Deirdre." She held a knotted hand to her heart. "It never would have happened if not for me. I feel so . . . *awful*. I'm poison. Don't you see? All the interest in me may die down for a while, but then another kid will go missing and it'll happen all over again. I don't have a choice. I have to leave."

"Oh, sweetie. Have you told Clint how you feel?"

"No, and I won't. He'll be gallant. He won't let me go. Just meet me in the lobby. All right? I need you, Deirdre. Don't let me down."

After ending the call, Loni bathed her face in cold water. She tried to do something with her hair. Impossible. She finally decided she probably looked no worse than she had fifteen minutes ago. Maybe no one would notice her red eyes and nose.

To her relief Frank was on the phone when she returned to the waiting room, Samantha was in seeing Trevor, and all the younger men were gathered around the television, watching a rodeo competition. No one bothered to look at her, let alone study her face.

When it came Loni's turn to go see Trevor, she found father and son once again playing tic-tac-toe. She could only marvel at Clint's acting ability, for she knew how worried he was about Hooter. But he seemed to be having a good time. He also appeared to be losing again.

Loni played one game with the child. That was all her ten minutes allowed for. She kept a bright smile on her face and avoided Clint's gaze as much as possible, afraid he might see the anguish in her eyes. Nothing, absolutely nothing, should be allowed to interfere with

Clint's happy future with his son. The pair had already lost eight years. When Trevor finally came to live with his dad, the ranch should be a peaceful, safe place for him to grow up, not a three-ring circus with crazy newspeople flashing cameras and frightening the horses.

A hard knot of regret lodged at the base of Loni's throat, but she struggled not to let the turmoil of her feelings show on her face. It helped that Clint knew she was concerned about Hooter. If he noticed that she seemed sad, he evidently laid it off on that.

When her time was up, Loni said, "I think I'd better go now."

Clint glanced up from the game in progress. "Wait for me downstairs?"

She couldn't bring herself to lie to this man, so she settled for smiling and kissing his lean cheek. "Later, alligator."

Deirdre was waiting for Loni in the main lobby. When she saw Loni walking toward her, she jumped up from the overstuffed chair she'd been sitting in and hurried across the carpeted lounge area. Her face was pinched, and her short dark hair looked as if she'd been caught in a high wind.

Deirdre slapped a newspaper into Loni's hands. "This is a disaster. It's even worse than I thought. You're front-page news!"

Loni unfolded the newspaper. The bold front-page headline read: PSYCHIC HELPS FIND SENATOR'S MISSING CHILD. She wasn't really surprised, but her legs went a little watery all the same. She stared at the grainy photo of her face, then at the small print wrapped around the frame.

"Sharon Michaels did quite a number on you. Mom says you're on the front page in Lynwood, too. Evidently the Portland media somehow got wind of the Cheryl Blain case, and they've unearthed all of that again to spice up a story that's already huge."

"I know." Loni told her sister about the man who'd been offering her a book deal. "But we mustn't blame Sharon Michaels. She had no idea her being open with the press might cause me harm."

Deirdre clasped her arm. "It gets worse. I don't know how to tell you."

"Tell me what?"

"They're camped outside your house. Reporters everywhere. You can't go home to get any clothes or anything else. Michael thinks we need to get you the hell out of town."

Loni had already reached that conclusion herself, and though the thought broke her heart, she knew she would never be coming back.

"Michael drove over to your place in a friend's car to get some of your clothes and personal stuff. That way they can't trace the license plate number to us, and it'll hold them off from our house for at least a little while. But they'll make the connection soon. The media are experts at rooting people out of their hidey-holes. They've got your full name. It's only a matter of time before they'll have all the details on your family history."

Loni thought of Clint upstairs with his sweet little boy, and her heart squeezed with such pain it was almost unbearable. Though she knew that Clint loved her and wanted to be with her, she also understood that he had no idea how disruptive a connection to her would continue to be. He was only just now establishing a relationship with his child. She couldn't bring something like this into his life on an ongoing basis when he needed to be focusing on his relationship with his son.

"It sounds as if you and Michael are already making decisions," she mused aloud to her sister.

"Yes. First we'll go to my place. Then . . ." Deirdre shrugged and shook her head. "We'll have a conference call with Mom and Dad, I guess. Maybe if we put our heads together we can come up with a plan."

Four hours later Loni sat at Deirdre's kitchen table with a red wig on her head, a cup of tea between her hands, and a lavender candle burning near her elbow, the scent of which, according to her sister, was guaranteed to settle her nerves.

"I *hate* red hair."

Deirdre fussed with the curls, arranging them around Loni's face. "As soon as you cross the Idaho border, you can take it off. Besides, it's more of a strawberry blond."

"Where on earth did you get it, and *why*?"

"I got it at a garage sale for a Halloween party last year. I was Endora. Remember her, Samantha's mother in *Bewitched*?"

Michael came in from the garage. "I've got the rental car loaded up." He glanced at his watch. "You and

Hannah need to be heading out pretty soon if you want to meet Gram at Haley's Junction by midnight."

Without a word Loni went to the guest bathroom to use the toilet. It was a shock seeing herself in the mirror. A cloud of red Bozo curls surrounded her head and spilled in all their radiant glory to her shoulders. Tears filled her eyes. She would never forget how Clint had liked touching her hair. He would hate how she looked now. *Only temporary.* Deirdre insisted the disguise was necessary, and Loni wasn't about to test the theory. All she wanted was to reach the Idaho border and put this insanity behind her.

Determined not to think about Clint, she straightened her shoulders and exited the bathroom. She was doing the right thing. If she went back to Clint reporters would soon be huddling in clutches around his front porch. His phone would continue to ring off the hook. Grief-crazed parents would be invading his outbuildings, offering him money or the titles to their vehicles in exchange for an opportunity to meet with his wife. Even his outings in Sweet Home with his son might become media events. Real, bona fide psychics fascinated the general public. Even after all the interest died down Loni would find little peace, and by extension neither would Clint or his child.

She couldn't do that to him. So she was going to take a page out of her dream cowboy's book and love him more than she loved herself. Idaho wouldn't be so bad. Her parents were floating her a loan to tide her over until she could transfer funds from the bank here to one in Boise. Gram's house would be rented out. In a few weeks, as soon as Loni and her grandmother got settled somewhere outside the city, life would return to some semblance of normalcy again, and she'd be able to concentrate on rebuilding her business. Over time the hurt would dim, and she would be able to remember Clint with a smile.

"You okay?" Deirdre asked from the dining area.

Loni nodded as she walked toward her. "Aside from feeling as if my heart has been shoved through a meat grinder, I'm fine."

Deirdre gathered her close in a hug. "Ah, sweetie, this breaks my heart, too. I tried to warn you."

Loni thought of Trevor as he'd looked last night lying on the hospital bed. The little boy would have died if she had listened to Deirdre. Loni had done what had to be done. The cost to herself couldn't be factored into the equation. "The minute I had the vision about the rafting accident, the die was cast."

"Next time take my advice and ignore the vision. You have a right to a life, Loni."

"The only one I'll ever want is right here."

"Maybe after all the hoopla is over you can come back and take up with Clint again."

Drawing away from her sister, Loni forced a bright smile. "Maybe."

Moments later, when Loni crouched down to tell her nephews good-bye, Kinnon, the younger, stared in wide-eyed wonder at her hair. "Did you eat too many carrots?"

Loni laughed and hugged him close. "No, it's only a wig. I just wanted a new look for the day. Tomorrow I'll be normal again." She kissed the child's plump cheek. "You be a good boy for your mom."

She turned to repeat the process with Kirk. Then she pushed to her feet, hugged Michael and her sister good-bye, and exited with Hannah into the adjoining garage. The huge yellow dog took up the entire backseat of the rented Ford Explorer.

"Thank goodness you didn't get me a Beetle."

Michael grinned from the kitchen doorway. "Hannah would have had to carry it on her back."

Deirdre punched the garage door opener. As the double panels rattled upward, Loni gazed over the cab for a long moment, then waved and said, "Wish me luck."

Moments later Loni was driving down the block, possibly for the last time. Unable to stop herself she headed for Oak Street, needing to see for herself that a clutch of reporters was camped outside her house. As she turned the corner her heart leaped with momentary gladness, for she saw no reporters milling in front of her residence. Maybe she could sneak in and get a few of her keepsakes, after all. But as she drove closer, her burgeoning hope withered and died. Two strange sedans and a news van were parked along the street. Through the windows she saw reporters watching her vehicle with predatory alertness.

The vultures were gathering. From this point forward they wouldn't let up until they'd picked her bones clean.

Chapter Seventeen

Clint dialed Loni's cell number yet again, left another voice message, and then slapped his phone closed. His entire family sat around his kitchen table, their expressions glum.

"This is like attending a wake without a corpse," Parker observed. "I don't know about everyone else, but I need a drink."

Tucker Coulter, Samantha's husband, rested his elbows on the table, his forehead pleated in a thoughtful frown. "Why would she refuse to answer her phone? Was she pissed at you when she left the hospital?"

Clint tossed the cell phone onto the table. "No. It's about the media and what happened to Hooter, I'm telling you. She's gotten it into her damned fool head that she needs to protect me, and count on it—she won't have any contact with me until she feels sure I won't suffer for it."

"I'm so sorry," Frank said gruffly. "When I told Sharon Michaels about Loni's being a psychic, I never dreamed this might happen."

Clint passed a hand over his eyes. "I should have

told you about the Cheryl Blain thing. Then you could have warned Sharon and Jacob to keep their mouths shut."

"You were receiving a transfusion," Samantha reminded him. "It's not as if there was much time for talking."

Clint met his father's gaze. "I love her, Dad."

Frank rubbed his jaw. "I kind of figured."

"What'll I do if she's left town or some damned thing? It'd be just like her." Searing heat washed over Clint's eyes. "She'll be thinking how bad this mess would be for me and Trevor. I suspect she's at her sister's house, but I don't know Deirdre's last name."

"You could try to contact her folks," Quincy suggested. "You know their last name. Right?"

Clint shot to his feet and started toward his portable kitchen phone. "Hold up!" Frank ordered. "Don't go off half-cocked. Before you call them, you need to have some solutions worked out."

"Solutions?"

Frank motioned his eldest son back to his seat. Dee Dee patted Clint's shoulder as he dropped back down on the chair.

"What solutions are there?" Clint asked hopelessly. "The media and crazy parents ran her out of Lynwood."

"Lynwood. That's near Seattle, right?" Tucker asked.

"It used to be a separate little town," Parker inserted, "but now, with all the sprawl, each community bleeds into the next, or damn close to it. Without heavy traffic it's probably about twenty or thirty minutes from the city. I can't remember exactly."

"Can we stay focused?" Clint requested. "They drove her out of Lynwood, and now they'll do the same thing here. What's the solution?"

Frank sat back. "It's called security."

Tucker sent his father-in-law a sharp look. "Like you set up around Samantha's ranch last year when her horses were being poisoned?"

"Nothing quite that extensive. I don't think it'd be necessary. But it's sure as hell possible for Clint to secure his property. As valuable as our horses are, we should all probably think about doing it. But that's a topic for another day." He looked at Clint. "You can secure your ranch until this blows over, just like we did Samantha's. If it doesn't blow over then you can make the arrangements permanent. Hawkeye Security did a damned fine job for me. That little gal Nona Redcliff was a sharp little cookie." Frank sat back and raked a hand through his graying hair. "They've got electronic devices that are so high-tech, a flea couldn't get on this property without an engraved invite. Nona would know how to set things up to minimize the need for on-site personnel. Chances are, with the property perimeters under surveillance, you'd only need a full-time guard at the front gate to send reporters packing."

Clint sat forward on the chair. "Dad, you're a genius. With secure perimeters nobody could bother Loni and me. We could use the answering machine to screen our calls. I could hire a bodyguard to go with her to the shop and when she's working at a site."

"Won't that be terribly expensive?" Dee Dee asked.

Frank grinned. "Clint's not exactly a pauper, darlin'.

It all depends on how much he's willin' to spend in order to be happy with his lady."

"Any amount," Clint replied. "I'd spend my last dollar."

Frank rubbed his jaw again. "I kind of figured that too."

Annabel MacEwen did not sound pleased when she answered the phone and found her daughter's seducer on the other end of the line. Clint talked fast, determined to pry information out of the woman.

"So you want me to tell you where she is?" Annabel said with a hint of sarcasm. "After you've destroyed her life in one fell blow, you actually think I might trust you to fix the mess you've caused?"

"I promise you, Mrs. MacEwen, I *will* fix the mess." A tension-packed silence followed. "I love her," Clint added. "Her happiness is very important to me. I'll make sure she can have a normal life here in Crystal Falls. If I fail, what has she got to lose? Nothing more than she's already lost. *Please.* Think about what her life will be like if she isn't here with me. Do you think her visions are suddenly going to stop? Do you think she'll suddenly develop a hard heart and pretend she doesn't know about the next child who may die if she does nothing? If you think that, you're dreaming, Mrs. MacEwen. Loni will step forward again, and she'll put everything on the line again. Only next time she won't have me around to protect her."

"I *knew* this would happen. Before she left Lynwood I begged her never to tell anyone of her gift again. It was her only hope of having a good life."

"No," Clint corrected. "Going that route, there was no hope at all of Loni's ever being happy. You were asking her to deny who she was. That isn't the answer. It's *never* been the answer. She can't pretend she doesn't possess her gift. She can only learn how to control it and then hopefully put it to good use, like God intended."

Annabel huffed with humorless laughter. "You are telling *me* how my daughter can best handle being a clairvoyant? When did you become such an expert?"

Clint could see this wasn't going well, and Annabel MacEwen was his only link to Loni. He gripped the phone more tightly. "I'm sorry." The moment he spoke, he thought of Loni, smiling impishly at him and saying, *There are those words that never fix anything again.* God, how he missed her. He honestly couldn't imagine living the rest of his life without her. "I'm not an expert on clairvoyance. But I do love your daughter, Mrs. MacEwen. I can't force you to tell me where she is. But I'll beg, if that's what it takes. Please give me a chance."

She sighed. "Stop calling me Mrs. MacEwen. You're making me feel older than dirt. The name is Annabel."

"Annabel," Clint repeated. "Please give me a chance."

"The plan you've told me about doesn't sound very practical," she pointed out. "Have you any idea how much security like that might cost?"

"Yes, and it'll be worth every cent. If you're thinking I can't afford it, you're wrong. I can. I give you my word, Loni will not be hounded by reporters or frantic parents if she's with me."

"She's on her way to Idaho," Annabel finally confessed.

"Idaho?" Clint echoed. "What the hell is in Idaho?"

"A chance to start over again, and it's closer to home
than California. She's meeting her grandmother at
midnight at a place called Haley's Junction. I have no
idea where they plan to stay the night. I can only call
and ask."

"No, don't do that. Loni's not going to believe I have
a failure-proof plan to stop all this craziness unless I
can explain it to her myself. I'll be at Haley's Junction
before she gets there."

"That's impossible. She's two, maybe three hours
ahead of you."

"I'll find a way."

"I hope your security plan works," Annabel said
softly.

"I'll make it work. All you have to worry about is
picking out a dress for the wedding."

She laughed. "Once I get over being mad at you, I
think I might just like you."

"Once I get you broken of the habit of spying on
your daughter at inopportune moments, I might just
like you, too."

After ending the call, Clint turned to look at Tucker.
"Do I remember you saying that your sister Bethany's
brother-in-law has a private plane?"

"Rafe Kendrick? Yeah, he has a couple, I think."

"You think I could hire him to fly me to Haley's
Junction just this side of the Idaho border and get me
there before midnight?"

"Rafe's richer than Croesus and probably won't

charge you. In fact, he's raising quarter horses now as well as beef, and he'd probably love the opportunity to pick your brain during the flight." He glanced at his watch. "But that's not allowing him a whole lot of time. He'll have to preflight the plane, do a flight plan, and call to get air clearance. You'll be pushing it."

Clint held out the phone. "Would you mind breaking the ice for me? I've met him at a couple of horse shows, but he's not what I'd call a friend."

Loni hadn't stopped crying since she'd left Deirdre's house. Now her eyes were so swollen she could barely see the highway lines, a problem at the best of times because she couldn't drive that well in the dark. *A nightblind psychic.* Remembering the night Clint had flung that accusation at her brought fresh tears to her eyes, and she nearly choked on a sob. How would she live without him? Already she felt as if her heart had been sliced to ribbons with a razor.

And he'd stopped calling, she thought miserably. At least then she'd been able to hear his voice in his messages. Now . . . nothing. Her mother had called a couple of times within the last hour, concerned because she knew it was hard for Loni to see at night, and Gram had phoned about fifteen minutes ago to let Loni know she was running about twenty minutes late. Loni would have to wait for her at Haley's Junction.

Hannah was whining to go potty by the time Loni pulled off onto a packed-dirt parking area at the junction where she'd arranged to meet her grandmother. There was another vehicle parked across the road, which made Loni a little nervous. Haley's Junction was deserted, a place in the eastern Oregon desert where two highways intersected. No businesses, no streetlights, no houses. What if the occupant of the other car was a monster, like Cheryl Blain's killer? Loni briefly yearned for her cozy little bungalow with its solid doors, triple dead bolts, and security system. Then she forced herself to get out of the car.

Clint's heart sank when a woman with reddish-blond hair crawled out of the Ford Explorer parked across the highway. *Damn.* It was ten after twelve. What if Loni and her grandmother had gotten here early, and he'd just missed them? Rafe Kendrick had broken all the records, flying Clint to a podunk airport only twenty minutes away, but Clint had still made it to his destination only by the skin of his teeth, parking and cutting the engine of the Chevy SUV at precisely eleven fifty-nine. How would he find Loni if she'd already hooked up with her grandmother and was heading east over the Idaho border? He couldn't check out the roadside motels. He had no idea what model car she was driving.

Whoa. The redhead was letting a huge yellow dog out the back door of the Explorer. *Hannah.* Clint would have recognized the animal anywhere. Clumsy, gigantic mastiffs with whiplike tails didn't grow on trees in Oregon. It had to be Loni. Only what in Sam Hill had she done to her beautiful dark hair? He pushed open the door of the Blazer and stepped out into the cool night air. His runaway bride jumped at the sound of the door closing. Pulling hard on Hannah's leash, she took the dog around the opposite side of the Ford.

Eating up the asphalt with long strides, Clint crossed the highway.

Loni heard the man walking across the road. She tried frantically to pull Hannah back to the vehicle, but the two-hundred-pound pup had a full bladder, and her muscular bulk was such that she seemed barely to notice the urgent jerks on her leash. *Oh, God.* Pictures of Cheryl Blain's killer flashed through Loni's mind. His insane eyes. His leering grin. The pleased gleam that brightened his gaze as he inflicted pain. The memories would haunt Loni for the rest of her life.

Hannah suddenly registered the approach of a stranger and straightened from a squat to let loose with a rumbling growl.

"Stay back!" Loni called to the man. "My mastiff isn't obedience trained, and I won't be able to hold her if she decides to attack you."

The footsteps just kept coming, and to Loni's dismay her stupid dog began wagging her tail. Loni wanted to bean her. Right when she needed protection most, Hannah crapped out on her.

The man finally drew to a stop a few feet shy of where Loni stood. In the darkness all she could make out was a shadow. "I sure as hell hope that's only a wig. If you ruined your beautiful hair by dyeing it, I'm gonna be royally pissed."

"Clint?" Loni could scarcely believe her ears. "How on earth? What're you *doing* here?"

He moved closer so she could finally make out his shape. "What the hell do you think I'm doing here? I've come to collect my lady. And don't start arguing with me about how marrying you will ruin my life. *Losing* you will *destroy* my life, so our only option is to come up with solutions."

Fresh tears welled in Loni's eyes. "There *are* no solutions. Do you think I would have left if there were any possible way for me to stay? You already may lose Hooter because of me. No more. I'm done. We're finished. That's how it has to be."

"Hooter's going to pull through, so I won't lose him. But that's beside the point. I thought you loved me."

"I *do* love you, Clint. But *that's* beside the point. I can't turn your life upside down, especially not right now, when you're establishing a relationship with Trevor. Can you imagine how frightened he'd be of a swarm of reporters shouting questions and flashing lights in his eyes? What if he'd been in the arena this morning? It might have been him who got hurt."

"First of all, Trevor is a senator's son. He's used to reporters and lights. Second, there'll be no more arena ambushes. I have a plan already in execution that will put a stop to that. But, as you said, that's beside the point. You and I are a *team*. You have no right to make life-altering decisions without talking them over with me first. What did you think, that I'd just say, 'Oh, well, she's gone'?" He stepped even closer and planted his hands on his hips. "I'm going to start this conversation with a disclaimer. Until recently my dad had been a widower since I was seven years old. None of my brothers is married, either. So the only husband I've seen in action is Tucker, Sammy's husband, and he's new on the job. I don't have much point of reference, so I'm not real sure if I should yell, turn you over my knee, or kiss you senseless. I may make some mistakes as we muddle our way toward a solution. I may offend your dignity. I may even piss you off. But we're gonna get this ironed out, and if you *ever* hare off again with some misguided notion that you're doing me a favor, you won't be able to sit down for a week. Do I make myself perfectly clear?"

Loni had been around the Harrigans just enough to know they were mostly all bark and no bite. She wasn't afraid of Clint, no matter how mad he might be. "I did what I felt I had to do to protect you and Trevor."

He moved a bit closer and held a rigid finger in front of her nose. "One, when the day comes that my lady has to protect me—from *anything*—I'll have one boot in the grave and the other on a banana peel." Another finger shot up. "Two, as much as I appreciate your thinking of our boy, parenting is a team operation, and any decision made on behalf of Trevor needs to be discussed with *me*. I *am* his father, after all." He inched even nearer, and this time, when the third finger shot up, Loni blinked and drew back to avoid getting a digit up her nostril. "Third, when we lost it up at that hot spring and had sex, you became *mine*." His face moved within six inches of hers. "*Mine*. It's a done deal. No second-guessing. No deciding you'll be bad for me. No being a martyr. If you ever leave me again, let me know so I can leave with you."

Loni could barely see now through her tears. It was equally difficult for her to speak. "You *can't* leave." She gulped and stifled a sob. "You have your ranch, and you have Trevor. You can't just up and *leave*."

"The hell I can't. With one snap of my fingers my

family would take care of my ranch. We could vanish and be sipping drinks in the tropics under a palm tree in less than twenty-four hours. I also have custody of Trevor, so I could take him with me. I told you once and I'll tell you again, *nothing* will ever be more important to me than being with you. And I mean no slight to my son. I love him, and we'll always put him first, just as we will our other kids when they come along. Putting him first right now, we can't deprive him of his mom. Every child needs a mother. How in the hell can you think that Trevor would be better off without his?"

"I'm not his mother."

"The hell you aren't. You love me, right? I'm a package deal. And I saw how you looked at him. You love him as much as I do."

Loni couldn't deny it. "That's why I left. Don't you see? There *is* no escape, Clint. Once they get on your trail they're like dogs after a scent. They'll never leave me alone. It'll be one mess after another. Your ranch will be overrun by reporters. Do you think they'll care if they disrupt your life? All they'll care about is the story. They have kids to feed, just like everyone else. It'll be their income on the line."

In the moonlight Clint could see tears slipping like silver threads down her cheeks. He could also see how swollen her eyelids were from crying. And no matter how he tried, he couldn't stay upset with her. She was so damned precious to him. Even with the sniffles, a red nose, and that cloud of reddish-blond hair, she was still the most beautiful thing he'd ever clapped eyes on, and he knew firsthand that her loveliness ran bone-deep. She cared about Trevor, she cared about Nana, and she cared about Clint's horses almost as much as he did. How could any man stay pissed off at someone who was so wonderful?

"Will you listen to me?" Clint said.

"It depends on what you say. I'm not staying in Crystal Falls and turning your life into a media circus."

"I have a plan."

He slowly outlined his dad's idea to beef up security at his ranch, telling her how Nona Redcliff could put all the perimeters under camera surveillance and how anything bigger than a small dog crossing the line would set off the alarms.

"Dad's getting it set up right now," he assured her. "We'll have to build a gatehouse to shelter round-the-clock guards at the front entrance, but until that's built, they can sit in their cars, or we'll erect an awning to provide shade. We can screen phone calls with a professional answering service. I'll hire a bodyguard to go with you to your decorating shop and protect you from idiots when you're working in the field." Borrowing his father's phraseology, Clint finished with, "Not even a *flea* will be able to step foot on that property without an engraved invite."

She hugged her waist, her slender shoulders jerking on a sob. "You can't live like that. It'd be like living in prison."

"The perimeter surveillance is practically invisible. It won't be like a prison. And I've been thinking about doing something along these lines someday soon, anyway. My horses are very valuable animals. Some of Samantha's got poisoned last year. It only makes good sense to keep interlopers off the property. This situation is just forcing me to do something sooner than I planned, that's all."

"I don't know if I'd like having a bodyguard."

"We'll hire someone you do like. All I care about is making sure no crazy father ever puts his hands on you again. Every time I think about it I could chew nails and spit out screws. The next time you get approached by someone who steps over the line, he'll get his lights punched out."

"But the money, Clint. It'll cost a fortune. You're talking about hiring gate guards, twenty-four/seven, and a bodyguard probably forty hours a week. Say what you want, but you wouldn't have to do all that simply to protect your horses."

Clint wanted so badly to snatch her up into his arms. But they had to finish this, and then they had to bury it once and for all. "Loni, I have over four million stashed away in the bank, and every year I add to it. Do you think I *care* about a few measly bucks spent on security so I can have a wonderful life with the woman I love? As for Trevor and any kids we have together, I have two hundred acres. That isn't to mention the adjoining thousand belonging to my family. Trevor can run, play, ride horses, take off on an ATV, and he'll never see anyone outside the fences. Our children won't be the targets of the media. You will be. But only for a time. This interest is going to die down eventually, and I've got an uncle in law enforcement. You've proven yourself to be a genuine prophetess, not some flash-in-the-pan shyster out to make a name or big bucks for herself. Do you think the cops are nuts? If they come to understand your abilities, they'll jump at the chance to bring you

Boo bears so you can help them find missing kids, and we can let them, with the understanding that they keep you out of the public eye."

Swimming with tears, her big blue eyes shimmered like silver in the moonlight. "What if it doesn't work?"

"Then, Costa Rica, here we come. It'll work. I've *seen* it work. When Sammy's horses were in danger, Hawk-eye Security had the place protected in only a few hours. When we go home tomorrow, I'll have to show ID to get in my own gate."

Her chin started to quiver. Clint gathered her into his arms, buried his face in her horrible-looking hair, and thanked God that he'd managed something close to eloquence for once in his misbegotten life. "Please," he whispered. "At least come home and see if we can make it work. You're a fighter, Loni mine. I know you are. Fight for our life together."

He knew he'd won when she hooked her slender arms around his neck, pressed her body close to his, and began sobbing. He tightened his hold on her, closed his eyes, and vowed with everything within him that no one—*no one*—would ever make her suffer for being a clairvoyant again.

Clint was about to lay a tongue lock on her that would have totally obliterated any further concerns she might have had when headlights pooled over them. An invisible cloud of dust soon rushed from the darkness to envelop them, and when the sound of a car door opening and closing came through the night air, Hannah gave a happy bark, lunged against the leash, the handle of which was still looped over Loni's arm, and nearly jerked both Clint and Loni off their feet.

Gram had arrived. Clint needed no formal introduction. He knew the moment she spoke from the gloom that she was Annabel MacEwen's mother. "If you don't want saltpeter in your morning porridge for the rest of your natural life, young man, kindly remove your hands from my granddaughter's butt until you've got a ring on her finger."

Until that instant Clint hadn't consciously registered that he had a hold on Loni's butt. He dropped his arms.

"That's better," she said. "Call me old-fashioned, but there'll be no more hanky-panky going on in this family without benefit of holy matrimony."

Gram was slightly built, just like her granddaughter, and in the dimness Clint could see that she had the same delicate facial features. There all resemblance ended. She was puffing on a cigarette, for starters, and judging by the brace of her body, she was fully prepared to kick him in the balls and ask questions later.

Clint had no desire to tangle with a wiry old lady. He promptly stepped away from her granddaughter. His daddy hadn't raised no fool. "We were only talking."

She bent over to hug Hannah's thick neck. "Hello, dolly. I know you're going to rip out someone's throat someday, but I love you all the same. Yes, I do. Just make sure you kill someone who deserves it." She gave Clint an assessing look. "Eat his boots, too."

Hannah shivered with delight and wiggled all the way from her loose jowls to her thick tail, which never stopped wagging.

Straightening from petting the dog, Loni's grandmother thrust out her hand to Clint. "I'm Aislinn

MacDuff, a Scot to the marrow of my bones. I'm not sure how I feel about mixing our pure blood with an Irishman's, so don't trifle with my granddaughter and further prejudice me against you."

Clint decided that was a fair enough warning. "I'll try not to."

"Well, forget that damned foolishness about the pillows, then. Put her in a spare bedroom with a lock on the door."

Clint felt the blood run from his head. *Damn.* He had another voyeur on his hands. "Excuse me?"

"You heard me. And she's pregnant, by the way. I got a vision when I stopped to rest for a few minutes while driving here. That little hot-spring episode did you in. You'll not be waltzing home to Crystal Falls without taking her with you. And if you treat her bad, I'll hunt you down with Angus's shotgun. Don't think I don't know how to use it. I sure as sand do, and I'll be aiming for body parts that'll make you wish you'd kept your trousers zipped."

"Gram!" Loni cried, scandalized. "I'm not a sixteen-year-old girl. I don't need you threatening the man I love. I'll take care of this myself."

Aislinn chuckled and thrust out a hand to Clint. "Stop fretting, sweetkins. Clint and I are just getting acquainted." She met Clint's gaze. "The child will have the mark, by the way. If you think Loni's mother and I are a pain in the ass, you've not seen anything yet, young man. Your daughter will be extraordinarily blessed with second sight."

Clint didn't care how blessed his daughter might be. He and Loni would teach her how to deal with it, one way or another. He also totally understood where the old lady was coming from. He'd never realized before just how much the Scots and the Irish had in common. He liked Aislinn MacDuff. She said it the way it was, didn't pull her punches, and tossed in a threat now and again to get her point across. In short, she talked Clint's language.

"From this moment forward you don't need to worry about her. She's mine to take care of now."

Aislinn nodded. "I know it. Just be sure you do a proper job of it." She grabbed Loni to give her a hug. "Drove all this way. Now I'm guessing I need to turn around and go back home to Lynwood. I'm happy for you, sweetness."

When the hugging had ended, Clint couldn't resist asking, "So what do you use to spy on her?"

"Her baby rattle. All I have to do is touch it and I'm right there."

Clint assimilated that information much the same way that he imagined men of old had once tried to comprehend that the world was round. "I want it as a wedding present."

"You what?"

"You heard me," Clint replied. "I want that baby rattle, all wrapped up with a bow. And in the card we'll have your promise that you'll never again spy on us while we're making love."

Aislinn folded her arms over her chest. "And in return what do I get?"

"A standing invitation to visit your granddaughter whenever the mood strikes you, and we'll also drive up to visit you at least twice a year."

"And you'll put up at Annabel's? That won't be a visit to see *me*. I want you staying at my place, and each visit has to include at least two overnights. Otherwise, no bargain."

Clint wondered if she had crystal balls stashed all over her house, and decided it didn't matter. Her eyes reminded him of Loni's, and that was all the recommend he needed. "All right, two visits a year, two nights each, and we'll stay at your place." He thrust out a hand. "Do we have a deal?"

Aislinn appeared to consider the offer. Then she reached out to grasp his hand. "It's a deal."

After Aislinn had driven toward the next town to find a motel room for the night, Clint gathered his lady into his arms. She let her head fall back, exposing her slender throat to him, and Clint honestly considered having a taste. But Hannah had wandered off into the darkness somewhere, necessitating that he go find her. He also wasn't fond of the thought that an elderly grandmother might come searching for him tomorrow with a shotgun.

So instead he simply drew Loni close—so close that a sheet of onionskin couldn't have slipped between them. "Have I told you lately that I love you?"

She turned her cheek against his shirt. "It doesn't last me from one time to the next. I think you'll have to tell me all the time."

That was a request Clint could deliver on. He would never tire of saying he loved her, for that was the truth that had taken root in his heart and now resounded through his soul. He loved her. He felt as if he'd always loved her.

And perhaps he had. When she'd dreamed of him all those many times, some part of him must have been there, and for the remainder of his life, he'd always believe that he'd been subconsciously in love with her long before he'd ever met her. That was why he'd never met someone else and been able to settle for second-best.

Second-best was never quite good enough when you knew deep down that your true heart's desire was waiting for you somewhere, possibly just around the corner.

Epilogue

Loni stood on the front porch beside her husband, watching Sharon and Jacob Michaels's car bump along the road leading up to the ranch house. When the cream-colored sedan rolled to a stop the back door flew open. Trevor and Nana, both scrambling to go first, tumbled out onto the dirt, the dog barking with excitement, the child yelling, "Hi, Daddy!"

It was early October, nearly four months since the rafting accident, and Loni and Clint had driven north countless times to see the child, but this was Trevor's first weekend visit at the ranch. Clint was so excited that he'd been pacing the floors all morning. What if Trevor hated his room? What if he disliked the horses? Loni had talked herself almost blue in the face trying to reassure him, but he'd persisted in worrying. Now, despite Trevor's obvious delight at being there, Clint still looked apprehensive.

"Go," Loni whispered. "It'll be fine. Have faith."

With the loose-hipped grace that Loni had always so admired, Clint finally descended the steps two at a time to grab the child up in his arms. "Hi, yourself!" He turned a full circle, his gaze never leaving Trevor's face. "I thought you'd never get here. What did you do, sleep in until noon?"

"No, we hurried real fast!" The boy looked expectantly at his father. "Where's my boots?"

Clint had purchased Trevor his first pair of riding boots the previous week and had told the child about them over the phone. "*Boots?* I've been waiting for five days to get a hug, and all you can think about is boots?"

Trevor giggled with unbridled delight when his father lifted him high into the air to gobble his stomach while growling like a bear. Sharon Michaels met Loni's laughing gaze and waved hello. Jacob, climbing out on the driver's side of the vehicle, grinned broadly as he watched Clint play with his son. Trevor's happiness at being there was the result of much hard work on everyone's part, so this was a very rewarding moment for all four adults.

"How come do you have a policeman at your gate?" Trevor asked his father when their rambunctious hellos were finally concluded.

Clint's dark eyes twinkled up at Loni. "He's not a policeman. He's a security guard," he told the child. "He makes sure no reporters come onto the property."

"Oh." Trevor seemed to take that explanation in stride. "Is the guard going to put them in handcuffs if they won't go away? My other dad hated reporters. He said they were royal pains in the butt."

Clint laughed and swung the boy around to ride on his opposite hip. "They *can* be royal pains sometimes, but handcuffing people can be hard to do, even for a security guard, so he just keeps the gate closed and calls the police instead." Clint locked gazes with Loni again. "Isn't that right, sweetheart?"

Loni couldn't help but smile. "Yes, that's right. Your daddy makes sure no reporters bother us here."

"Cool!" Trevor cried. "I like it better when nobody takes my picture."

Loni shared the sentiment. Clint's plan to secure the ranch and hire a bodyguard had changed her life. She never worried about being hounded by the press nowadays, and any frantic parents who needed help were directed by the ranch house answering service to contact her through proper law-enforcement channels.

"Where are the horses?" Trevor asked his dad.

Clint did a half turn and gestured with his hand. "They're all over the place."

The child saw a group of mares in one of the pastures and whooped with excitement. "Can I pet one, Daddy?"

"Pet one?" Clint chuckled. "Is petting one all you want to do? How about *riding* one?"

In the recent past Trevor would have looked to his grandparents for permission, but now he looked only to his father. "Can I, Daddy? *Really?*"

"I think we can arrange it. Your boots are over at the arena. We'll need to get those on you first. A proper horseman always wears a Stetson and riding boots."

Trevor's eyes went round. "You got me a Stetson, too?"

"You're my boy now, aren't you?" Clint replied with a chuckle. "I can't have you looking like a city slicker."

At precisely that moment Hannah lumbered out

from behind the house. When she saw her canine friend Nana whom she'd met the previous weekend in Sweet Home, she gave a happy bark. Within seconds the two huge dogs were tumbling over the grass, a gigantic blur of yellow, white, and brown fur.

"I think Nana has finally met her match," Sharon observed as she approached the porch. "She's never been around another dog big enough to play with her until now."

"Hannah definitely isn't lacking in size," Loni said, laughing at their antics.

"Can I ride a horse now, Daddy?" Trevor cried. "Please, please, *please*?"

Loni was delighted by the child's enthusiasm. "And you were worried?" she called to Clint. "I told you horses are in his blood."

Clint beamed a proud smile. "Maybe so."

Loni gestured to the child's grandfather. "Please do come in, Jacob. I'm sure you're weary after the long drive. I just pulled a coffee cake from the oven."

"Oh, that sounds lovely," Sharon replied. "But first let us get a look at the ranch." She ascended the steps to stand with Loni on the veranda. "My goodness, it's big. And so beautiful." She smiled happily. "Trevor will be so happy here. You just can't know how glad that makes me feel."

If all went well during this visit—and Loni felt certain it would—future visitations would take place at the ranch throughout the winter, preparing Trevor to come live with Clint and Loni on a permanent basis when school was out in June.

"I think I'll go with Clint and Trevor to see the

horses," Jacob told them. "I'll only be gone for a few minutes."

"No hurry!" Sharon called. "Just be really careful so you don't get hurt."

"He'll be fine," Loni assured the older woman. "Clint's horses are big loves. Neither of your fellows will be in any danger."

"That's good to know," Sharon said with a laugh. "It'll be a wonderful place to raise children then. Surely you and Clint plan to have more."

"Oh, yes. Clint wants a whole baseball team."

"Good heavens. I hope you've gotten that notion out of his head."

"We're still negotiating."

Gazing after Clint as he walked with Jacob and Trevor toward the arena, Loni smiled dreamily. Life had been so busy since Trevor's rescue in June, with Loni and Clint rushing through marriage preparation classes with Father Mike, having their wedding in August, and also traveling so often to visit Trevor, that she hadn't made an official announcement about her pregnancy yet. She and Clint wanted to hold the joyful secret close to their hearts for a while, with only Father Mike and her and Clint's family sharing the knowledge.

In a precognitive vision, Loni had seen Trevor leading his baby sister by the hand across the stable yard next winter. Aliza Candrima, whose first and middle names meant "joyful light of the moon," would have her father's dark skin and jet-black hair, but she would take after her mother as well. In the vision Loni had seen a deep crimson birthmark on the nape of her daughter's neck.

"Look at that child run!" Sharon cried.

Loni nodded. "He's so excited he can barely contain himself."

"Clint is good for him," Sharon observed. "When Clint is with him the sadness goes out of Trevor's eyes."

Clint was good for everyone, Loni thought. Being with him was her lifelong dream come true.

"Can I help with your suitcases before we go in?" Loni offered. Sharon and Jacob planned to spend the night so Trevor would experience no separation anxiety. "Then we'll sit down at the table with fresh coffee and some of that cake."

After helping Trevor's grandmother get settled in the guest room, Loni hurried to the kitchen, still smiling secretly over her vision of Trevor and his baby sister. A few months ago Loni would not have been happy to know that her daughter would inherit "the sight," but now she was absolutely thrilled. Annabel MacEwen had been right all along: Having the sight was a very special blessing. It had just taken Loni a while to come to that realization. Her gift had not only enabled her to help save Trevor's life but had led her straight into the arms of her dream cowboy.

"My goodness! That cake does smell good."

Loni gestured at the table. "Have a seat. Which do you prefer, coffee or tea?"

"Coffee, please. I missed my second cup this morning."

Loni had just served her guest when the phone rang.

After drying her hands on a towel, she hurried across the kitchen. "Excuse me for a moment, Sharon," she said after glimpsing the caller ID. "This may be important. I need to take it."

"Don't worry about me," Sharon said. "If I want seconds I'll just help myself."

"Hello, Jim," Loni said when she answered the phone. "You have something for me again today?"

The Crystal Falls police detective wasted no time on pleasantries. "A baby just went missing in Denver, Colorado. Six months old, female, Caucasian."

Loni's hand tightened over the receiver. Thanks to Clint's family connections with law enforcement and his exhaustive efforts to create channels of communication, she now worked frequently with the FBI, enabling her to take cases across state lines. "Do you have a photo for me?"

"I do. I'm e-mailing it to you in an attachment as I speak. Can you take a look ASAP and get right back to me?"

Loni understood that the survival rate of missing children greatly increased if they were found within twenty-four hours. "You got it." She ended the call. "Sharon, I'm sorry, but I've got an important e-mail that I need to go open."

"Stop apologizing. I'm happy as a clam."

Loni rushed to Clint's downstairs office. Now that the FBI often called upon her for help, she was using her gift more than she'd ever dreamed possible. Over the last week she'd helped pinpoint the whereabouts of six small children before their abductors could harm them. One little boy had been as far away as Portland,

Maine, a distance that would have been a major stumbling block for Loni only a few months ago. But with a lot of prayer, practice, and unfailing support from Clint, she had strengthened her abilities. Regardless of distance, she was now able to home in on a child's location simply by gazing at a photograph.

When cases went badly, which they sometimes did, and Loni felt devastated because she'd failed to save a life, her husband was always there to hold her in his arms and remind her of her successes and of the victories that still lay ahead. *You can't save the whole world, only one tiny corner,* he would say, and then he would point out that most people went to the grave without ever saving anyone.

Slowly but surely Loni was learning to put the failures behind her and focus on the joyous successes. The nightmares still came to haunt her sometimes. Loni couldn't honestly say that her gift had suddenly become a walk in the park. But with Clint beside her and his strong arms around her, she no longer felt quite so devastated when things went wrong. She was becoming adept at blocking signals now, picking and choosing the times when a vision would come. That had helped immensely, because she was able to brace herself, step back emotionally, and control the vision instead of allowing the vision to control her.

Do your best, Clint always said. *Give it all you've got, trust in God, and then don't dwell on it.* Loni was getting there.

Within seconds she was printing out a picture of an adorable baby girl with big blue eyes, chubby cheeks, and a ribbon around a shock of black hair that poked straight up from her head. Loni couldn't help but smile as she took the picture into her hands. After making the sign of the cross, she prayed fervently for God's help before allowing herself to focus on the baby's face.

White light flashed, obscuring her vision. The next instant Loni was there with the child. A thin woman with brown hair sat in a rocker with the baby in her arms. As she pushed with her feet, she hummed a lullaby. Loni was learning how to glean as much information as quickly as possible during a vision, so she fastened her gaze on the window. Through the glass she saw shrubbery, a maple tree that had lost almost all its leaves, and also a hedge that divided the woman's yard off from the one next door. Beyond the hedge Loni saw police cars and a television news van parked in front of a home across the street.

Tossing the picture aside, Loni called the detective back. "Hi, Jim. A neighbor woman has the child. Brown hair, green eyes, very thin. She lives across the street and about three houses down from the parents. The yard is surrounded by a privacy hedge, and the window trim I saw looked dark blue."

"That's amazing, absolutely amazing. Thanks, Loni."

"When you connect with whoever's in charge at that end, tell them to be careful. I think the woman may be delusional. She's totally oblivious to what's going on outside her house. They don't want to startle her. She might panic and accidentally hurt the baby."

"I'll pass it on," Jim said. "Thanks, doll."

When Loni returned to the kitchen, Sharon had helped herself to a second piece of cake. "This is delicious." She tipped her head to study Loni's face. "You look happy. Things must have gone well."

Loni grinned. "Exceedingly well. A baby in Denver this time. A crazy neighbor woman took her."

"It must be so rewarding to have such a wonderful gift and be able to save innocent children."

"Yes, it is rewarding," Loni replied, meaning it with all her heart.

Stepping over to the window, she gazed across the pastureland that stretched endlessly in all directions. *Home.* She had such a fulfilling life to look forward to now with her wonderful dream cowboy, their son, and their little girl. Loni felt as if her cup were brimming over.

At peace with whatever might come, she turned to join her guest at the table and enjoy a piece of that coffee cake.

Turn the page for an excerpt from
one of Catherine Anderson's
early historical romances,
first published in 1991,

COMANCHE MOON

Available from Signet

The Prophecy

From the place where the sun rises, there will come to the People a great warrior who will stand tall above his brothers and see far into the great beyond with eyes like the midnight sky. This Comanche shall carry the sign of the wolf upon his shield, yet none shall call him chief. To his people shall come much sadness, and the rivers will run red with the blood of his nation. Mountains of white bones will mark where the mighty buffalo once grazed. In the sky, black smoke will carry away the death cries of helpless women and children. He will make big talk against the White-Eyes and fierce war, but the battles shall stretch before him with no horizon.

When his hatred for the White-Eyes is hot like the summer sun and cold like the winter snow, there will come to him a gentle maiden from *tosi tivo* land. Though her voice will have been silenced by great sorrow, her eyes shall speak into his of a morning with new beginnings. She will be golden like the new day, with skin as white as the night moon, hair like rippling honey, and eyes like the summer sky. The People will call her the Little Wise One.

The Comanche will raise his blade to slay her, but honor will stay his hand. She will divide his Comanche heart, so his hate that burns hot like the sun will make war with his hate that is cold like the winter snow, and the hate shall melt and flow out of him to some far-away place he cannot find. Just as the dawn streaks the night sky, he will chase the shadows from her heart and return her voice to her.

When this is done, the warrior and his maiden shall walk together to a high place on the night of the Co-manche moon. He will stand on the land of the Co-manche, she on the land of the *tosi tivo*. Between them will be a great canyon that runs high with blood. The warrior will reach across the canyon to his maiden, and she will take his hand. Together they will travel a great distance into the west lands, where they will give birth to a new tomorrow and a new nation where the Co-manche and the *tosi tivo* will live as one forever.

Texas, August 1859

As pale as fresh cream, a full moon shone against the midnight sky, casting a silver aura across the star-studded blackness. A killing moon, some called it, and tonight that seemed fitting. The screams of dying women and children rang no more, as if, like the wind, they had come to this place only briefly and now were gone.

In the distance a coyote howled, the sound rising in a mournful crescendo, then trailing off into a wail that made Hunter of the Wolf shiver. He knelt alone on the bluff, his indigo eyes fastened on the trampled ground below the promontory. Judging by the swath of hoof marks, the Blue Coats had fled southeast after their attack on his village earlier that day.

He clenched his hands into fists. His wife's name rang like a litany inside his head, calling out to him for vengeance. Willow by the Stream had been heavy with his child. He wished he could gather his war gear and set out immediately after her killers, but he and the other young men were needed here to tend the injured and bury the dead. Soon, though, he would make war as he never had before. He would hunt down the Blue Coats like the animals they were and return the pain they had wrought a hundredfold.

Hunter was no stranger to grief, but never had he experienced this terrible feeling of emptiness. Even as children he and Willow had been a pair, their laughter ringing across windswept grasslands. No other's hand had ever felt right in his. No other's smile had made a glad song within him. He had thought to have her always at his side. And now she was gone, leaving behind a canyon within him as vast as the plains that stretched forever into the horizon. Despite everything he had done to save her, she had lost their child and slowly bled to death in his arms. Her injuries, the result of vicious and repeated rape, had been inside of her where they couldn't be seen. Up to the last, he had kept hoping she would recover.

He could almost feel her spirit leaving him, see her running gracefully across the stepping-stones made of stars into the land of the dead. His gut tightened as he contemplated the path she might take. She had never been good at finding her way, depending always upon him to guide her. He prayed the Great Ones held her hand to show her which direction to go. If she was all alone, she would surely get lost. The thought made unwanted tears well in his eyes.

The night wind had dried her blood on his hands and buckskin breeches. Hunching his broad shoulders, he emitted a keening cry of sorrow that echoed in the air around him. Drawing his knife, he hacked off his mahogany hair close to the scalp. Then he lifted his razor-sharp blade and slashed himself from the outside tip of his right eyebrow to his chin, his sign to all the People that Willow by the Stream would live forever within his heart. His blood stained the blade crimson. He wished it were the blood of a *tabeboh*, any *tabeboh*.

A movement to his left caught his attention, and he turned to see his mother approaching, her moccasins touching softly upon the ground as if she trod upon his grief. He made a quick swipe at his cheek, ashamed for her to see his tears.

An apologetic look crossed her face. "My *tua*, I know I should not approach you now," whispered Woman with Many Robes, "but I must talk with you."

She came to kneel with him. A tight, suffocating ache centered itself in his throat. Her smell was familiar and dear, reminiscent of his childhood when her gentle hands had soothed all his hurts. He yearned to bury his face in her ample breasts, to cry as only a child could. "She trusted me to protect her," he whispered raggedly. "It was my promise to her in the song we sang together. I should never have left her."

Woman with Many Robes clucked her tongue, much as she had done years ago when he had come to her as a boy spouting foolish stories. "You wish to walk backward, *tua*, and it cannot be. I know it is hard to accept, but your wife has been taken because the song you sang with her was meant to be sung with another. "

"The blood of my woman is still warm on my leggings, yet you mention the prophecy? You have sung the words to me all my life, and I have listened like a dutiful son. I won't tonight."

She stared into the distance. A cloud drifted across the moon, shadowing her face. "In a few hours, you will ride out. I must tell you something first, that you are the Comanche of the prophecy. You came to me from the place where the sun rises—from the loins of a Blue Coat twenty-six winters ago."

The air gushed from his chest as if she had struck him. "No! I have asked my father many times. Always he said I was his son! You will not speak such a lie."

He made as if to rise, but she grabbed his arm. "It is no lie. You have indigo eyes, not black, and you stand a head taller than your brothers." With her other hand, she caught hold of his medallion, turning the stone so he could see the image carved there. "You bear the sign of the wolf, yet none call you chief."

For a moment he could only stare at her in frozen silence. "You, the mother that I love, and a Blue Coat?"

"I did nothing wrong. It happened during an attack, much like the one today. The men were gone hunting. I tried to run, and the Blue Coat saw me." Her voice went reed thin. "He raped me and left me for dead. When I found I was with child, your *ap* claimed the babe was his and sang with me at the central fire."

"Why are you telling me this? So I won't avenge my wife?" His voice grew thick with rage, and he jerked his medallion from her grasp. "I will reclaim her honor. I must."

"Find her killers, yes, but don't take part in the bloodbath I've heard the others planning." Her tear-filled eyes implored him. "Your life is not your own. The fate of your people rests on your shoulders. You must find the honey-haired woman with no voice,

bring her to us, and honor her as you never will another."

"I'll honor her with a quick death."

"Do not speak such a thing, for then it must be." She
sighed and pushed to her feet. Placing her hands on her
hips, she made much of the horizon for a long while.
Then she touched his bowed head. "I will not ask you
to strike the hate from your heart, for that too is fore-
told in the prophecy. As for love, it wells up like a
spring from a hidden place, and you cannot command
that of anyone. But, *tua*, for the sake of your people,
you must find the honey-haired woman and bring her
to us."

His answer was taut silence.

"I know it is a hard thing. That is why you were chosen, because you are strong. The People will go the way
of the wind one day soon. The Great Ones have chosen
you to sing our song and keep our ways alive."

He threw her an incredulous glance. "Do I look
weak like a woman? I am a warrior, not a storyteller."

Her smile was filled with sadness. "There are many
ways to fight the great fight. The bravest warrior of all
is the one with no shield. Your people need you to fight
the *last* fight, the most bitter battle of all. And you must
do it alone. When the time comes, you will see the path
the Great Ones have chosen for you and walk it with
courage."

"The Comanche of the prophecy must leave the People. I would never do that, especially not with a white
woman. I'm afraid you underestimate my hatred, *pia*."

"Remember one thing. I have cause to hate the *tosi
tivo*, too. The dreams about the Blue Coat will haunt me

always. But I took a *tosi tivo* into my buffalo robes. I held him to my breast and called him son. And my love for him burns like the brightest star in the heavens. You are that *tosi tivo*. Strike it from your heart, deny it as you will, there is a place within you that is not Comanche."

The *New York Times* bestseller
from
Catherine Anderson

Star Bright

Faking her own death to escape her murderous
husband, Rainie Hall takes refuge in the rural
community of Crystal Falls, where she finds work
as a bookkeeper on a horse ranch run by
good-looking Parker Harrigan. But as their
initial attraction blossoms, Rainie fears she can
never escape retribution from the man who has
sworn to kill her—and that her mere presence
could jeopardize everything the Harrigan family
holds dear.

**Available wherever books are sold or at
penguin.com**

New York Times bestselling author

Catherine Anderson

Sun Kissed

When Samantha Harrigan attends the local
rodeo, she doesn't expect to wind up in jail.
But that's what happens when she tries to
stop a drunkard from abusing his horse.
Tucker Coulter, a handsome local
veterinarian, comes to her defense, and
both of them are arrested. The charges
are dropped, but Sam's troubles have
only started...

**Available wherever books are sold or at
penguin.com**